Cutting edge science is the foundation for the powerful weapons at the core of the American military might. It's a lesson learned in World War II: top scientists are recruited from wherever available for advancing the necessary science. The Atomic Bomb was developed by European immigrant scientists. The Moon was reached using rockets designed by German scientists captured at the end of the war. That's why modern America employs weapon scientists born elsewhere, even if some of them arrive in the USA with complex loyalties hidden in their consciences. But modern America is also broke. Weapon research labs and Pentagon contractors struggle for funds as they dump some of their best talent on the streets.

One such talent is Mathew Salagen: late night on a Los Angeles beach, the cold steel of a 9 mm Beretta seems his last and only answer for his shattered life. An immigrant missile scientist with shady and unfinished business left in his past, he is unemployed, at the end of a bitter divorce, and broke. Nothing seems left for him but a pull of the trigger. But that's not how fate plays it. Salagen is forced into a hard reassessment of his deadly science and his loyalties. Searching for answers, he finds a strange love, and gets caught into webs of espionage networks and political interests. Now, his quest for life and survival depends on his ability to unravel the secrets of the shadow circle around him. And none of his friends, lovers, or foes are who they say they are.

PROJECT MORPHEM

Bogdan Marcu

A Quiet Sierra Book

The manuscript has been originally published under the title "Hard Thrust". This is a revised edition.

Published by Quiet Sierra Incorporated
2207 Perkins Lane, Suite A
Redondo Beach, CA 90278
www.quietsierra.com

Book cover by Zoe Olaru, www.zoeolaru.com, London

Printed in the United States of America

To the memory of Professor Dr. Victor Pimsner.

To the memory of Harold F. Graifer.

To my fellow graduates of the Polytechnic Institute of Bucharest, Aeronave section.

The 747 seemed to be floating over the 110-South. An aluminum whale full of tired people on final approach at the Los Angeles International Airport.

In the congested freeway traffic below, Julia leaned forward from the back seat and rested her chin on my shoulder. Her eyes followed the plane through the windshield.

"How come it's flying so slowly?" she asked.

I told her about wings, flaps and air angle of attack, all the while thinking of the Beretta in my briefcase. I had made the decision days before their departure, with a strange relief coming over me ever since. That relief forced a certain detachment from reality, as I drove towards the airport.

Julia asked something else, and I listened to my voice answering. It was somebody else's voice, talking to his thirteen year old daughter.

Christine sat with her usual cold quietness in the front seat. Everything in her composure suggested distance, a long distance from everybody else. One of those flying whales was going to take her and Julia away.

Inside the terminal, things started getting blurry. Depression was taking over the relief again. It felt like a bundle of heavy hooks hanging on my chest. Julia started crying, slowly, bowing her head.

We waited for a while before the last security check point.

"Dad," Julia pulled my arm gently. "When will you come visit? Can you come for my birthday?"

"We'll see," I said, and held her

On my left, I glanced at Christine, standing straight and quiet. Listening. She touched my arm, lightly.

"Matt, please use the bank account," she said. "There should be enough in there to keep you covered for a while. Please promise you're going to take care, OK?"

I nodded, with a knife-stab feeling in my stomach. That would be the last thing, use her money. I was broke and she knew it. She'd left some dollars in an old common account, for her peace of mind. We'd been separated for more than three years, but I knew her too well.

A metallic intercom voice announced their flight was boarding. They had to rush to their plane. Julia glanced back again, from the far side of the check-point.

"I'll e-mail you pictures soon," she shouted, and vanished behind the crowd lined up for screening.

There had been no glance from Christine. Only a cold embrace before checking through.

I walked back to the car. No thought was taking shape in my mind, only a gray fuzziness. There was only one thing left to do. End it.

I took Lincoln Boulevard north, and as I drove through the Playa del Rey wetlands the view opened up towards the ocean. The sunset sky over the ocean had filled with those intense shades of purple the LA beaches are spoiled with.

After cruising through Playa and Marina, I passed the pier and merged onto the Pacific Coast Highway, picking up speed with the traffic. By the time I made it to Point Dume it had gotten dark. I was tempted to drive further north and return later but I swerved left and drove along the water towards the state beach. I parked the car before the entrance check booth, closed and deserted for the day. Several other cars were parked on the side of the road. There was motion on the sand and a red spot of a cigarette.

From the trunk, I grabbed the briefcase. Inside it, the Beretta was cold, a strange touch to my hands. I picked a loaded clip and a fresh pack of Camels. Before stepping on the sand, I opened the driver's door and threw the keys on the seat.

Through the soles of my shoes, I felt the sand still warm from the day's sun, but daylight was all gone. Electric lights up on the tall cliff diffused faint glares in the thin mist coming from the ocean.

I found a spot and sat on the sand, leaning against a mound. I didn't smoke. I wanted to be a non-presence, remain there unknown and wait for those late people to leave one by one and let me have the whole beach for myself. Time was no longer of essence. I waited.

Warm sand against my back, I let my mind wander. Thought fragments came and vanished before taking shape. Music erupted from one of the houses up on the cliff. Some grooves I didn't know, with a touch of Wayne Shorter sax.

I browsed old memories, images from younger years, reminiscences of dreams and hopes long gone. I remembered myself in the old Pan Am liner crossing the Atlantic for the first time, watching the Canadian coast line from thirty thousand feet. There was hope then, the strong feeling of incredible, of escape.

The memory made me hold my breath for a moment. Then, the present came back and the knife stab feeling crept again in my stomach.

I hardened and looked around. I was alone on the beach. It was time.

I felt for the gun in my pocket, and extracted it out, slowly. My hand was shaking. I loaded the clip and armed. Incredibly easy, it was all ready to go. Nothing to stop me. How does it feel, I thought, how quick? No more than a tenth of a second, with a good bullet. Does one get punished with a dilation to infinity of that tenth of a second?

I thought it over again. I was afraid. I was mad. Furious at the unfairness, at the thought that nothing was resolved by this, no injustice was being reversed. Squeeze the trigger and the only tangible result would be just one less guy on this crowded part of the world.

The world. I didn't like what the world had become. I didn't like and didn't accept what my life had become. What I had become. Fuck. Let's just finish it.

I raised the steel.

Then, the chirping sound came from my pocket. A thin thread, a fragile connection to the world. A cell phone.

The sound came again. Once... Twice... Three times... Enough times.

I lowered the gun, and grabbed the phone. The moment I opened connection I recognized the heavy breath, the short moment of effort before talking.

"Matthew?" the voice asked, fighting lack of oxygen and lack of strength, as an ill body was betraying a good mind.

"Yes, Hal," I said. I pictured the old man on his chair at home, next to the oxygen tank, in front of his computer, his desk crowded with files, handwritten notes and data printouts.

"Where the hell are you?" he asked.

I forced my mind on words, enabling myself to speak.

"I'm on the beach," I said. "Point Dume."

"So late?" he asked. "It's dark out there."

"I thought of finishing it, Hal."

He fought his breath again, and then asked: "Where is Julia?"

"Christine took her away. They're in a 747 enjoying airline dinner. They're gone."

There was silence. The old man was thinking, a quick, good mind trapped by illness within his own body.

"Listen, Matt, hold on a second," he said, more vigorously now, his mind focused. "I know what you've been through. I understand and I'm not going to tell you it makes no sense."

I heard noises. He was fixing his oxygen, a rich dose, as he usually did when he wanted no interruption from his weakness.

"Let me tell you this, Matt, and listen carefully. You're not done. I got a couple of calls today. Lockwell men. Government people also. All looking for you. It's important. There are new developments. You hear me?"

I heard him. I let the information sink. Images from the past were coming alive. Lawyers, trials, alienating years lived with my fists clenched. Wasn't it the reason I was on that deserted beach with a 9mm in my hand?

"What do those people want?" I asked, ready to say the hell with them, who the fuck cares now, let me get back to the trigger. But there was one thing stopping me, one little whisper in the back of my head. The essence of what every guy thinking he's ready to jump from the top of a building wants. A voice, a person, a sign to tell him he's left some value in him, that the world still needs him, the chaos of the universe is missing the flap of his little butterfly wings.

"They're turning over every rock on your former project at Lockwell," Hal said, with anxiety. In spite of the oxygen boost, his lungs were not keeping up with the demand of his effort. His words got broken by a gurgling cough.

I heard a car approaching on the sand. Its headlights beamed parallel to the shore while a manually operated light was circling methodically around the beach. As soon as it found me, it centered steadily on my presence while the car turned and came straight towards me.

I hid the gun. On the phone, Hal overcame the coughing.

"Why did those people call you, Hal?" I asked again. "Who exactly called you?"

"You left my number with Lockwell. It's still in your file. Several people called, each independently."

He paused, breathing hard. Then, he said, "Do you understand, Matt? You have a big chance to re-evaluate everything."

A state trooper stepped off the patrol car. Besides the light beaming from the vehicle, he was holding a Maglite with a mile long handle.

"Are you OK, sir?" he boomed as if we were on different ships at sea, in rough weather. "Sir, are you OK, sir?" he shouted again, his right hand resting on the butt of his gun.

I kept my voice calm and flat. "Yes, officer," I said. "I am all right."

"What's happening?" Hal's voice came on the phone, intrigued.

"It's a beach patrol, Hal. I'll have to call you back," I said and cut the connection off.

The trooper came closer. He was one of those tall guys with the kind of natural built-in robustness developed from something like farm work in their younger years. His face had a rough skin, showing prominent pores in the strong light coming from the headlights of his patrol jeep. The car engine was purring behind him, the driver's door left wide open. His right hand was now resting steadily on his belt, but not too far from the butt of his gun. He wasn't shouting anymore.

"Are you the owner of a 1968 Ford Mustang, sir?" he asked with a sound in his voice that was not quite official. His Maglite beam was hitting me straight in the face.

I closed my eyes for a second and opened them again into the blinding lights. I needed to catch up with events. Minutes ago I had been ready for a definitive departure. I had perceived Hal's call as one last second delay, the last cigarette before the firing squad, and I thought I was ready to continue, go back to the trigger and finalize it. But Hal's news had twisted my determination. My mind was crunching the information as I was staring blind at the beam of light in my face. What did Hal say? People looking for me, evaluating my work? Did they understand it was my work? The information was stirring deep layers of barely forgotten and settled pain. And now, that beam of light in my face was bringing a sense of bifurcation in my fate. There was no going back to the moment of final departure, not possible anymore. Fate was stronger that my will. I made and effort and cleared my mind. I kept my hands steady and visible.

"Yeah," I said. "I own a Mustang, what's the problem?"

He looked at me as if working a decision. He frowned.

"We're just trying to make sure nobody had gone surfing and had some accident," he said, and paused choosing his words. "Make sure nobody had run into any sort of trouble. Just making sure, sir. Do you need any assistance, sir?"

I watched his face again, best I could against the annoying flashlight.

"No, I'm fine," I said. "I'm all right," I repeated while standing up.

He offered a ride back to my car and I took it. My legs were shaky and weak; cold sweat was all over my body. The man drove tensely, the jeep unsteady on the soft beach sand, his hands firm on the wheel. He stopped the jeep next to my car, and remained seated. I got out, and walked to the Mustang, with the odd feeling of seeing again an object from which I seemed to have had departed for ever. I grabbed the handle to open the door, but it was locked. I pulled again, but the door was indeed locked, and the odd feeling deepened. Then the trooper made a quick gesture and threw me the keys.

"A 68 Mustang, very cool rod, sir," he said. "Woulda been a pity to have it stolen by some beach bum, those keys left on the seat like that."

He finished the speech and drove off, didn't even glance back at me. The motherfucker had probably guessed it all along, I thought, the smart son of a bitch. He had searched for me deliberately.

I started the engine, and remembered Hal's call. There was a strange feeling throughout my whole body. Tiredness as if I'd ran a marathon, but also a quantum of heat, filling my bones and my blood. And the hooks, the hooks hanging on my chest were gone.

I was alive. That strange feeling was life. Life again.

0 2

The voice woke me up with news about the Iranians and the Chinese. It was a perfect, soft voice, coming out with metallic inflections from the alarm radio.

I rolled over and faced the ceiling illuminated by the morning light and stared at the plastered white surface, not really understanding what's wrong in the Middle East, or the Far East, just trying to remember who and where I was.

I had slept fully dressed. Night sweat was all over my body, the leather jacket still on me, my shoes tangled in the bed sheets. I rolled and sat on the edge of the bed, rubbing my face with my hands. Then, I felt the Beretta, still in my pocket. Everything came back in a quick roll of the day before. I pulled out the weapon. It had sand on it and it smelled of oil and steel. I carefully removed the cartridge from the barrel, reloaded it on the clip and threw the weapon in a drawer by the bed.

I replayed the events of the day before in my mind again, slower, thinking. I undressed and got in the shower. Hot water flowed down my chest and I felt the touch of every drop. I looked in the mirror while shaving. Forty seven. Muscles still good. Tired eyes. Sandy gray hair. The man looked familiar. I was willing to learn to live with myself again.

I fixed a large cup of espresso and drank it outside on the terrace, watching the San Gabriel Mountains in the morning sun. I thought things over again. Hal's call. Lockwell, my former employer. My work there. People turning every stone on my former project with them. Why?

I finished the coffee, walked into the office room and sat down at my computer. I went through the firewall and accessed bank accounts, keying in passwords and numbers. A couple of thousand dollars were left in Christine's account. Christine's money. I no longer cared whose money it was. Wounded pride was gone too. It was enough money to live on for a short while, pay back some mortgage and avoid foreclosure.

I got dressed and left for the door. From the coffee table I picked up a half size padded manila envelope. Several words were written on it: *For Mr. Harold G. Mason. To be handed to him personally.* It was my handwriting. I watched the written words again, thinking. The man who'd written those words the day before had become a stranger.

I grabbed the keys and walked out.

***

110 South from Pasadena towards down-town is one of the oldest stretches of freeway in LA. There are moments when no new Toyota or Honda is in sight, only an old Chevy pick-up one turn ahead, and it looks like the old times when a man by the name of Hendrix used to play his own music and nobody tried to wrap him in plastic for better marketing. Several miles down the road interstate 5 joins in from the north and always brings a flow of Japanese and Korean cars which kill the good illusion.

I switched lanes through the interchange and headed west on the 10, exited at Crenshaw, and cut through Venice Boulevard towards La Brea. I parked under the sycamore trees on Citrus street, in front of a two story mansion built with expensive and discrete good taste.

The street was quiet. I extracted a key from the manila envelope and headed for the front gate. After introducing the key in the special lock, I punched four fives on a numerical pad next to the door. It was a complicated security system. The key had the security transmitter. The code punched had to match a sequence transmitted by the chip in the key. The code on the pad was also identifying who I was to the unseen watchers guarding Hal.

I walked across a narrow yard and entered the house. A black statue stared at me impassively as I walked on a thick beige carpet along the corridor, and then up a gracious staircase. The stairs led to a small hallway illuminated by a ceiling window worked in stained glass. The door of a large office room was wide open.

The old man was asleep in front of a computer terminal, thin plastic oxygen tubes fixed to his nostrils. At the sound of my steps, he raised his head and stared at me.

I smiled and he smiled back and pointed to the dark brown leather couch stretched on the side of the office. I sat down while he turned his mechanical chair towards me.

The old man was ill, cancer eating his insides. He had gotten used to speaking less since his illness hit. Over the last two years, with his condition deteriorating and his speech more and more difficult, he had started saving energy and speaking only the essential. His sharp brain was trapped in a dying body whose life he was trying to extend and control by means of the best medical technology money could buy.

Now, his eyes examined mine, reading into me.

"Risen from the dead," he said. "What happened?"

I remembered the end of our phone conversation, when the beach cop came, and realized Hal had waited patiently for me to call or show up. He didn't use to be that patient.

"Not much to say," I said. "You know what my life has been these last three, four years. Down, down... Christine decided to leave to France, for good. She took Julia with her. I gave them a ride to the airport, and I was ready for departure myself."

He kept his gaze on me with impartial friendliness.

"What was to accomplish?" he asked.

I leaned back on the comfort of the leather couch.

"Nothing," I admitted.

Suddenly, he burst into a severe cough. Phlegm came out, choking him. With great effort, he suppressed the coughing and cleared his mouth and his throat into a medical dispenser.

I watched him, helpless, as he moaned, forcing himself to relax and breathe.

"How is it going Hal?" I asked, and tried to make it sound flat, unimportant.

He heard the tenderness in my voice and didn't accept it.

"I'm all right," he growled. He pointed to his left, "Drinks."

I went to the small bar he kept in the office and fixed him a drink: a few drops of scotch wetting two ice cubes. I handed him the glass and fixed me a much stiffer one and returned to the couch.

"What's the story with Lockwell?" I asked.

He moved his chair again. It was a complex machine with a small control panel on the side. Hal had become an expert at those controls to the extent of forming a sort of a body language of the chair's movements. That language was telling me he was organizing his thoughts and sorting what to say.

"Someone named Garland called," he said.

"He's the chief engineer. What did he want?"

"Nothing specific. He mentioned an investigation."

"That's strange," I said. "They kicked me out five years ago. They'd filed claims for all the patents on the project through their chief scientist, a guy by the name of Varese. I sued them and lost. You know the story."

"I know it and I repeat the same question: why didn't you come to me? Why did you fight on your own?"

His question bore deep in me. I had no answer. I was going way back with the old man in a strange sort of a friendship. We had met in Romania, sixteen years back. Life and death ties were between us. Strangely, throughout our years of friendship I had avoided asking him about his business. I felt it from the beginning that this was the way it should be, no questions. I never asked him why was he there, in Romania, when we met during such troubled times. On his side, Hal had carefully adopted me. Although he never asked, I often spoke to him about my work. He was fascinated by it, having a passion for engineering. I had explained to him all the details of the conventional rocket engines and then initiated him on the details of my special project as it took shape. Engineering was only a part of Hal's passions. Above everything else, Hal's mind was an encyclopedia of how the world works. He intimately understood that reality of the world related to the human implementation of any concept, any system, and how and to what extent it could be screwed up by stupidity, incompetence, and greed. And how one can do business based on that. He would assimilate scientific information by stripping out the details beyond his theoretical grasp, and retain that essential substance of the information that was directly related to how and if a particular piece of science would impact society. Therefore he had followed my work in most of the details. However, in dealing with my personal life and my family, I had drawn boundaries. Hal loved my daughter Julia, and had known Christine closely, consulting with her on the medical issues of his concern, yet, I had instinctively set out limits for him. I'd felt there were things I had to deal with completely on my own.

"I don't know," I said. "My mistake. I fought them, and lost, and then tried to fight again. I hung on to the fight for too long and lost the rest of what I had. What the hell they want now?"

Hal had watched me carefully while I spoke.

"Would you start with a clean sheet, if you had the chance?" he asked unexpectedly. "Rethink the whole thing?"

His question took me by surprise. I didn't answer. Only felt a jolt of hope in my chest. Life again. My project, code named MORPHEM by my own inspiration and born from my own ideas, had been taken away from me, years back, by the corporation I was working for, Lockwell Aerospace. I had lost all rights to the concept. Would it be possible to start my research again with a clean sheet?

Hal read the reluctant hope on my face.

"Listen carefully Matt," he said. "I made some phone calls myself. There are serious reasons for which high-ranking people want to look closely into how your project ended. Not only industry people. People from the FBI, and other agencies. Whatever happens, keep your balance. The true knowledge belongs to you, just play it right"

"Did you say FBI? The feds?"

"Yes. And possibly other agencies."

"Why? What the hell happened there?"

"My guess is you'll learn soon enough. And I repeat, my advice is to keep your balance. I will be here to help. This time, Matt, please use my help."

I leaned back on the soft leather and closed my eyes. I examined my newly found feeling of life, now wrapped in layers of tension brought up by his words. I thought again, in a new nuance, just how close I had been the night before. Now, only several hours later, the thought of suicide seemed so strange. Life and its worries were taking over.

"I must repeat this," Hal said, "I want you to use my help."

I nodded, thinking, rolling thoughts in my mind.

"Thanks Hal," I said. "Don't know what else to say."

He laughed, slowly. "Please stay for lunch," he asked, warmly. "Do you have time?"

I nodded. He manipulated the chair closer to the terminal and typed a few lines. None of his people were in the house. Ever since he'd gotten ill, he had been giving orders by typing rather than speaking. Someone was always receiving his instructions, somewhere, and execution was very prompt.

Hal didn't want to leave the house on Citrus street. He knew it's topography by heart, his security and communication links were installed there, but above all, he loved the place. He also loved to be alone, as a proof to himself of the independence he in fact no longer had. He was a prisoner, pretending otherwise, knowing that his body was the real prison, no matter where he would establish headquarters.

We sat together in the quiet noon light filtered by the wooden blinds, waiting for lunch to be served. I thought about everything he'd just told me. I felt there was something amiss, something I didn't understand. And I also felt tension; the tension I used to get when I served with the paratroopers, when I had my gear on, and the dive training plane was revving up its engines for take off.

0 3

Santa Monica Boulevard looks better when seen through the windshield, while driving through. On the posh stretches of the boulevard, each restaurant is the one you want to be in, each girl should be your love mate. But I was on the sidewalk, walking towards a coffee shop I knew, and I could see the tiredness in the women's eyes and the wear in the men's walk. The City of Los Angeles is a soul-crunching machine. For some, the fact is depressing when they move in, but, in time, it fades into the background.

I got myself a coffee, and then grabbed a table in a remote corner of the outside terrace, where I could blow smoke from a Dominican cigar without irritating too many health-conscious people.

Then, I went back inside the shop and bought the Times and grabbed some of the LA free press from the heaps by the door. The headlines on the prints talked about a world that had gone ahead of me and my little troubles.

The woman was thin and blonde. I found her sitting at my table, lighting up a cigarette. She raised her face at me, smiled with her lips, and mimicked a faint intention to leave, as if she had mistaken the table for being unoccupied. I glanced quickly at my cigar, carefully balanced on the edge of the ashtray, and the barely touched coffee cup. I studied her face. Somehow, her presence didn't feel bad and it dissolved my annoyance. I had been away from people for too long. I shrugged and motioned to her to stay.

The newspapers smelled of warm and fresh ink. It had been a long time during which I'd been oblivious to the outside world. I needed an update. I began reading. Among several tons of nonsense there were a few good articles about old, new and future possible threats against the USA, energy, defense, and who bribes who, and how legal, in the United States Congress.

I was folding the calendar section when I noticed the blonde woman's eyes. She was watching me openly, in a reserved fashion, with no attitude. I watched her back, studying her closer. She was thin, without fragility, just fiber. Young age was giving that fiber sex appeal and freshness. She was wearing a pale blue shirt, with a net type of a texture. Her face was smooth, without any visible signs of vice on the slightly pigmented skin, eyes deep black, with a trace of a hidden wound in their gaze.

I offered her the pile of paper, but she made a quick negative gesture with the cigarette. She asked something I couldn't hear. I made a vague sign.

"How much money you have?" she asked again.

I raised my eyebrows. She didn't look like a hustler, but who can tell, in this city.

"Not much," I said. "I'm traveling light."

"You're a tourist?"

I raised my arms. "We all are. The planet is four billion years old. We live a couple a decades. We're all just visiting."

"Bullshit is cheap," she snapped. "What I meant is how much cash do you have on you?"

I looked at her again. She leaned towards me.

"I'm desperate," she said. "You might've been through this drill before, I don't care. I'm in trouble and I need to raise cash, anyway I can. So, I'm asking you, how much cash you got on you, and how much of it you don't really need?"

I thought of smiling but didn't. Slowly, I emptied my pockets. A couple of twenties, tens, change, all on the table.

"Here it is," I said.

She looked at it.

"I need it," she said.

I checked her out again. The people in LA who play cheap money tricks have more or less dirt on them. If it's no dirt at all, it's still an acrid smell of sweat and cheap toxins. The smell of fallen people. This woman didn't have it. She had a good, clean scent.

"Then take it," I said.

No greed, no spark, she bent forward and took it. Then, she leaned back and kept smoking, her eyes blank.

This fucking city, I thought, and drank from my coffee, puffed the cigar.

"I guess you really need it," I told her.

"You'll get it back," she replied, flatly. "Gimme an address and I'll send it back."

I bet you will, I thought. I didn't care. Some of Uncle Sam's paper had changed hands. What was she going to do with it, get some crack or whatever was in fashion those days, buy some oblivion? Or, maybe with that bit of cash, one could get enough stuff to get overdosed, take a hike on the other side. Was she looking for her departure with some dope instead of a 9 mm?

"What do you need it for, may I ask?"

She didn't answer. Kept smoking, blank faced. I looked at her insistently, knowing she sees me through her apparent freeze.

"Look, I just bought you a ticket to wherever you want to go, talk to me a bit, will you? For example, what do you do for a living?"

I left the question hanging in the air by body language, leaning forward, watching her closely, and not moving. I let it hang and took my time, using the kind of patience one should have with a lunatic, if one cares for wasting time on lunatics, or makes money on them by profession. Nothing happened, she didn't answer, she didn't move except to work the cigarette. I kept my posture, nevertheless. She reminded me of someone else, an old story from when I was younger and able to love deeply. And she was also reminding me of the night before, on the beach. Those reminiscences were holding me there with her; otherwise I should've been gone, away from that terrace, minding my own trouble. I could see the brown nipples of her breasts pointing delicately against the blue net of her blouse. I could also smell some faint scent. Scent as in perfume, a discrete scent of good quality.

"I'm an actress," she said, fixing me. She quickly read my face and blanked. I was thinking, of course, what else a desperate girl could be in this damned city but one sort of an actress or another. What the hell am I doing? Why don't I just get up and take the hell off. It's a big city, I've just wasted a couple of bucks on it, move on.

"Listen," I said, "will you be okay for today? I gotta go."

I stood up and offered my hand. She took it reluctantly as if the gesture was not part of any routine she used.

"Take care," I said and turned around to leave.

"My name is Jane," she said, stopping me. "And I'll be fine. If you want your money back, leave me an address."

I watched her face again. Prudence made me hesitate. On the other hand, the night before I was putting a gun to my head, so what was it that would make sense anymore? I wrote down my address and phone number on the edge of the newspaper page. "Take care, Jane," I said, and left.

0 4

I kept thinking of her while crawling north on 110. The downtown interchange was packed with wheels. Not even a clown on a one wheel bike would have had room to squeeze in a lane. The 101 ramp into the 110 proved the assessment wrong and pushed more cars into the old three lanes loading the road with more nerves and engine heat.

I owned a house in the northern side of Pasadena, on a small street branching off Mountain Avenue. It was a quiet, yuppie neighborhood, all familiar faces, all unknown people.

The dark blue sedan was parked at the curb, twenty feet away from my house. It didn't belong there. I ignored it and parked in my driveway. While I unlocked my front door, the sedan's doors slammed behind me.

There were two men. The older one was the one in charge. About sixty, decently fit, somber, with a bit of a gumshoe walk and a very exact haircut. As he walked towards me, he calmly reached his pocket and got out a badge.

"Dr. Salagen," he asked, not really asking, rather stating my name. "Special agent Roger Bronson from the FBI, can we have a minute with you please."

His questions lacked the question mark, they were statements. There was a low key but unmistakable determination in his body language. One shouldn't oppose agent Bronson, unless for a strong reason.

I showed them in. The younger chap introduced himself as Steve somebody, then followed my invitation and sat down, mouth shut. The old one did the talking.

"Dr. Salagen, the objective of this visit is to deliver an invitation. A special meeting is scheduled for Monday, March 21 at the Lockwell corporate headquarters here in town. Your presence at this meeting will be appreciated. I apologize for the short notice. A context of events demands some urgency. As a former employee, you are familiar with the location, I presume. I would also emphasize to you that your presence on Monday is of utmost importance, however, you are not legally obliged to attend."

I watched them, thinking and guessing, rolling in mind the earlier discussion with Hal. Bronson waited, his tired eyes locked on my face. Steve somebody sat uncomfortably, as if ready to get up and leave, or twist my arm behind my back.

"Can I offer you guys anything," I stalled. "A drink? Water? Coffee?"

"No thank you, you are very kind," Bronson rejected. "We'll be on our way as soon as we have your response, Dr. Salagen."

"Slam your breaks a bit," I said. "I have some bad history with Lockwell. It's rather surprising to see someone coming out of the blue with an invitation for a meeting there. Someone from the FBI. What is this? Do I need my lawyer? Am I under some sort of an investigation? You people have to tell more before asking me to be there for a meeting."

Bronson scanned me quickly. He'd seen many folks of many kinds while doing his job, I could tell by the routine motion of his pupils, the immobility of his face. He was probably good at his evaluations.

"What I can tell you, Dr. Salagen, is that there is indeed a Bureau investigation, as a part of a larger investigation. There are new developments regarding a project in which you were directly involved, and of which project you hold a very direct expertise. It is with this respect that your presence is considered necessary."

All calmly said, routinely smooth. The "*Dr*" in front of my name was a deliberate hint: it delivered some respect, meaning the Bureau people were talking to the scientist, not to the humble citizen under the law.

"My expertise?" I asked.

"Dr. Salagen, you are a specialist in rocket propulsion, with special expertise in plasma physics, are you not?"

"Yes."

"And you were, initially, the principal investigator for the MORPHEM project, were you not?"

"Yes."

"We need that expertise on Monday."

"At Lockwell?"

"Yes."

I weighed the implications of his request. It was the moment before the bell, my instinct said, the beginning of a very tough game.

"All right," I said. "I will be there. You'll need to make some arrangements to get me past security."

"The arrangements have already been made. Thank you, Dr. Salagen, here is the formal invitation," he handed me an envelope and a business card. "Please show the invitation at the front gate on Monday. Should you have any problems, do not hesitate to call me at the numbers on the card. I wish you a good night."

They turned to leave. I read the business card.

"Agent Bronson," I called.

They stopped. Bronson turned towards me.

"Was the other option available?" I asked.

"You mean, refusing the invitation?"

"Yes."

Bronson's lips tightened in a crooked smile.

"I believe it would've been an unwise decision, Dr. Salagen," he said.

Both agents turned towards the door and stepped out as calmly as they had stepped in, walked to their car and slammed the sedan's doors with moderate but appropriate strength, and then took off.

I opened a beer, and sat down. I read the invitation. Formally stating what Bronson had said. The son of a bitch had handed me the invitation only after I'd said yes. I finished the beer and turned on the TV. I had thrown my dice. I was going to read my luck on Monday.

0 5

Lockwell's Gate A lobby had been the latest fashion of interior design in late sixties. It still was. It'd been left largely unchanged ever since.

I gave my invitation letter to the security guard. He read the name, stiffened, grabbed the phone and made a mumbled call. He pushed a stack of papers on the counter, towards me.

"Please fill this forms, sir," he requested. "Somebody will come shortly to escort you."

I filled the forms with a version of my life's story in bureaucratic format, leaving out some little crazy things I did in kindergarten. The guard grabbed the forms and gave me a bright yellow badge with "visitor" marked on it. I was to wear the thing throughout my visit there.

Through the inner yard access doors a man entered the lobby and walked towards me.

"Good morning, Matt," the man said. He offered his hand. "It's been a while."

"How're you doing, Meinhardt?" I said and accepted his hand. "Since when do physicists carry security escort jobs at Lockwell?"

He laughed and led me into the Lockwell grounds.

"What brings you back?" he asked directly. "I was surprised when they asked me to come escort you. I got instructions to take you to some big meeting over at the HQ. What did you do to get in, bring money?"

"Don't know anything about any money," I said. "Why, business that bad?"

We walked towards the old A-21 building I remembered from my time there. Gray pipes and air ducts were riding the concrete windowless walls. Electrical fans filled the air with machine noise.

"As bad as I ever remember," Meinhardt said. "We laid-off people. A few others quit. We lost expertise, loosing these people. We've seen better times."

He led me along an alley paved with rough concrete. I still remembered each crack on it.

"What business is left"? I asked.

"No much. We hang by a thread on contracts for the Air Force."

"What about MORPHEM? I hear the program was shut down."

Meinhardt didn't answer immediately.

"Yes," he said, after a while.

"When?"

"Last year. It's all classified, Matt. Sorry."

I had lost my security clearance when I had left Lockwell, five years back. Meinhardt knew it. He wasn't comfortable with the restriction, but he played by the rules. Meinhardt was a conscientious professional.

We entered the A-21 and walked through dimly lit hallways on floors covered with gray carpets.

The building's second floor was filled with a maze of cubicles. There was no window anywhere, all light coming from fluorescent lamps on the ceilings. Bulletin boards were scattered on the walls, filled mostly with corporate metrics indicating how well the people there were squeezed to produce more with less money, and how happy they were about it.

"Coffee?" Meinhardt asked. "There's time."

I accepted. Meinhardt led me towards a room designated as the coffee area. We poured coffee in Styrofoam cups.

The smell of the old A-21 building brought back old memories. For more than ten years I'd been buried in those offices and cubicles. I looked around and tried to guess for what reason I had been asked to come back. Would they restart the MORPHEM project? I dismissed the idea. First, I was *persona non grata* for Lockwell. Secondly, Lockwell wouldn't have needed the FBI to invite me for that. It was something else.

"Ah, an interesting surprise," someone said behind me.

I turned and faced a tall Chinese man.

"Xiao," I answered as we shook hands. "You still around? I thought you've left this dump a long time ago."

"Yes, please give advice to your humble servant: where should I go after twenty two years of very specialized high temperature analysis?"

"Still doing thermal analysis?"

"If there's work."

"Dr. Xiao Lin, you're underestimating yourself. With your expertise, any smart corporation will grab you."

The man smiled.

"I thought you were to be shot on sight," he said.

"Just got in here. They still have time."

"What brings you back, Matt?"

His smile vanished at the end of his question. He seemed anxious. I shrugged.

"Don't know exactly. Some meeting I was strongly suggested to attend. Whatever the reason, it's good to see you people."

Meinhardt went out to make a phone call, and I was left with Xiao in the coffee room. I could sense strong interest towards my visit in Xiao, yet, his self discipline prevented him from any further inquiry. He was a native of mainland China, the PRC, but he never spoke about his past. Xiao had never opened completely to anyone for as long as I'd known him. From behind his black thoughtful eyes, he would always carefully screen the world for glitches and threats.

A few more people came for coffee. I shook hands, slapped a few shoulders. The invariable issue came over and over: was there any new money coming. Like most aerospace companies with roots in the cold war era, Lockwell was an organization created on a research and development structure fueled by government contracts. Budgets had been generous from its creation in the sixties and all the way through the early nineties. After the end of the Cold War, government money dried up. For a while, the trend in the industry had been towards going commercial. It could have worked, given a few conditions: a large launch market, with many commercial satellites consuming one big rocket per launch, and in need of many small chemical and electric thrusters for orbital maneuvering and station-keeping propulsion. With the big financial disaster of Iridium, the first network of low orbit satellites meant to provide mobile access to communication worldwide, the launch market shrank instead of growing. Launch providers started fighting for a limited number of launches per year, competing on the tightest market ever. Commercial launches went abroad, on cheap Russian and Chinese launchers. The Europeans were pragmatically launching every payload they had on their own Ariane family of rockets. The government had been left as the only large customer on the US market. And it was a tight customer, given the burden of terrorism and the Middle East.

"Isn't there a bounty on this guy's head?" another voice asked.

It belonged to a tall and heavy man, wearing his long white hair held in a pony tail. Robert Cruiff was Lockwell's top specialist in 3-D Computer Aided Design modeling, a technology known as CAD. He didn't show his age, which was over sixty to my count. I knew him well: a strong personality and a shrewd player: he knew well when to push and when to bail out of a difficult project. Or bail out of anything he smelled foul. He always made me think of someone who grew up alone on the streets. Rumors had it that Cruiff did two tours of duty in Vietnam at age nineteen, then spent some time in Laos and Cambodia on his own. He never spoke directly about it, but admitted it to me once, when he explained to me how to shoot an M-16. He'd been smart enough to use the GI bill to get an education and had worked his way into becoming a top aerospace design specialist, but he never became the typical engineer. He was a lone rider. I'd worked with him as close as I had with Xiao Lin. The relationship had been good at the time: he was the super-competent and innovative senior professional, and I was the outsider, doing OK. Judging by the way he eyed me now, nothing had changed.

"Good to see you stranger," he spoke softly and gave me a wink. "I heard you're around."

"What's an old devil like you doing these days, Cruiff?"

He didn't dislike the old devil part.

"Doing all right," he said, and tasted his coffee. "Just designed some fixtures on our excellent propulsion products so they can go either on Delta IV or Atlas V rockets, whoever has the green bucks."

"Got a closed deal on those?"

He shook his head.

"You never know with those motherfuckers. This ramshackle of an industry is going down, God bless the mighty dollar. Atlas uses a Russian engine for the main booster. Why not use some fucking Chinese solids instead of ours? Save a buck or two for the beloved shareholder."

His blue eyes laughed at me with an edge on their light.

I sipped some coffee and gave him the grin he expected.

"It's called capitalism," I said.

Cruiff became suddenly serious.

"Greed is good, kid," he said slowly. "But it can also kill you. This country, son, is loosing it."

I let the topic die. Cruiff relaxed. "What's the story with you here?" he asked.

"Invited to a meeting."

"That big powwow later this morning? It's all under wraps, I hear. Who asked you to come?"

"It's complicated," I said.

He watched me closely, sensing my reserve.

"Is it about your old project? Any money?"

"I don't know. Don't raise your hopes."

He nodded.

"Listen, Bob," I said and pulled him on the side of the room and he lowered his ear, expecting some inside info. Instead, I asked: "Is Stefan Mora still around?"

"Your Romanian pal, the hot shot physicist?"

"Yes."

"No, he's gone. About a year now. We laid-off a few folks. Consultants, like your friend Mora, were the first to go."

He eyed me, waiting to see if I had anything else to ask. I didn't. We shook hands and he left. Lin threw me a smile, sipping his tea. He had impassively witnessed the whole conversation. We both knew Cruiff very well.

Meinhardt came back and gestured that we should go. We left the building and crossed the concrete yard towards the main A-1 building also known as the HQ or the Main. All glass and steel, it contrasted with the old stenciled look of the rest of the buildings. We entered the building and crossed several halls sprinkled with mahogany desks and well dressed secretaries, and reached a large hall adjacent to a conference room.

Meinhardt indicated a group of security guards with a move of his chin.

"Go have fun," he said. We shook hands and he left.

The guards were Lockwell security and other men dressed in dark suits. One of the dark suits checked my name and ID against a short list. He then looked me in the eye and let me in.

Refreshments and coffee were served on a table along the wall opposite to the conference room. I stopped by the table and poured myself coffee in a porcelain cup. The coffee was good. Like the cups, it was better stuff than what my former colleagues sipped while working.

A group of people came in through an inside door. A bunch of suits, looking important. I recognized Jim Garland the chief engineer, and Craig McNutt, Lockwell's President and CEO. Garland eyed me shortly and nodded a silent greeting. McNutt didn't greet anyone. Then, from behind them, Paul Varese walked directly towards the coffee table. He saw me only when he was close. He kept his eyes on me for a second, and then went past me without a word.

I placed my cup and saucer back on the table and walked towards the rest of the group. I shook hands with Garland. He was a tough manager, with good ability to recognize and use talent, able to play corporate politics when needed, but usually playing straight. His voice had a low and firm resonance, which imposed in any discussion. With over thirty years of industry experience behind him, he was one of the most capable men in Lockwell.

A second group came through the same door. A group of suits of different polish than the Lockwell men. Amidst the new group there was a red haired woman in a dark blue dress. In front of the group I recognized the FBI man, Bronson. He appeared to be leading the group without really doing so, knowing his way around. He spotted me.

"Dr. Salagen, glad you could come," he said. "Please come in."

He invited everybody in his group to the conference room, helped by Garland, who issued instructions to his people.

I turned and walked towards the conference room door, watching the faces of the people around and exhaling slowly, controlling my nerves. The air was filled with tension, like electric charges before a storm. I remembered Hal's words: *"Keep your balance."*

What balance? I asked myself, and entered the room.

0 6

The conference room was long and narrow, split in half by a mahogany table. At one end of the room, a large wall screen brightened in the blue light of an LCD ceiling projector. A computer was booting up. The men in suits moved quickly in taking seats. Bronson sat at the screen end of the table with a computer terminal in front of him. Apparently, he was going to lead the meeting.

I took the empty seat closest to the door. Across from me were the Lockwell men: McNutt, Garland and Varese. Besides them and Bronson I didn't know anybody around.

"Let's get started," Bronson called with a strong voice and waited for the noises and whispered voices to die out. "I'm special agent Roger Bronson, with the National Security Division of the FBI. We've asked Lockwell to make arrangements for this meeting and we do appreciate the cooperation. Each person present in this room is here by special invitation. Each of you should be aware that everything we will discuss is highly confidential. With the exception of Dr. Salagen, everyone present carries an active top secret level security clearance."

He stopped and swept the room with his eyes.

"What about Salagen?" Varese asked, icily. "I was asked to present confidential and proprietary information and I definitely object to his presence."

Bronson gave him a detailed scrutiny; his facial expression changed subtly into a nuance of patience one needs when taking many pills of needed medicine.

"Dr. Salagen is here at the Bureau's invitation," he spoke dryly. He eyed McNutt in a short glance. "An invitation endorsed by Lockwell's management."

Varese turned towards McNutt. Lockwell's CEO gave him a faint smile and placed his hand on Varese's forearm, nodding. McNutt also had the face of a man who had swallowed bitter pills. His gesture quieted Varese.

Bronson removed his severe gaze from Varese and surveyed the room again.

"Some of you have already been briefed on the situation to be discussed," he continued. "However, I ask you to allow the scheduled presentations to follow course. We'll discuss all the implications afterwards. Some decisions will have to be made. Dr. Varese, please begin."

As Varese stood up and walked to the screens, Bronson brought up a chart: one word, in the middle: MORPHEM. Bellow the project title, the logos of Lockwell and several government agencies involved in the project, and the marking of confidential and proprietary material.

"The MORPHEM project emerged as a need to introduce new concepts into rocket propulsion," Varese said and tested the spot of his laser pointer. He looked sharp, distinguished and competent. Bronson produced another chart, showing a simplified schematic of a rocket engine.

"Ever since Goddard's inventions[1] and the V-2's built by the Germans[2], rocket propulsion has been based on the same principles," Varese said, moving the pointer's red dot on the screen.

"Pressurize oxidizer and fuel, inject and mix them into a high pressure combustion chamber, generate combustion and expel the resulting hot gas at as high a velocity the device can achieve. The net result is thrust force. The engine ensemble is complicated and designed at the edge of material resistance. However, it basically consists of pumps, valves, plumbing, and a big oven with carefully cooled walls."

A new chart followed. Pictures of various rockets, operational or defunct: Saturn V of the 1960's Apollo missions, Atlas V, the Space Shuttle, Delta II, and Delta IV. Varese moved the red dot over each picture: "Over the years, the design of these engines has become better controlled, with the help of computer modeling and analysis. Several versions of rocket thermodynamic cycles have

---

[1] Robert Goddard is the father of rocketry in the US. His rocket experiments began in the early 1920's. Later, during 1930's, the German rocket scientists have consulted him. Before WWII the US Army had ignored Goddard's ideas, dismissing them as impractical. At the end of WWII, when Goddard inspected a captured German V-2 rocket, he realized the device design had been inspired by his own patents.

[2] V-2 rockets were developed during WW II by Nazi Germany and launched against allied cities like London and Amsterdam. Although very innovative and impossible to intercept with allied technology at the time, the V-2's did not have a significant material impact on the war. Nevertheless, the V-2 technology lies at the core of the modern nuclear Intercontinental Ballistic Missiles (ICBM's).

been defined. But no fundamental change in the physics of these engines has been made since Wernher von Braun's time[3]."

Bronson leaned back, focusing his eyes at the screen. He'd concentrated on the topic, watching Varese with expressionless eyes. The suits on my side of the table were quiet and motionless. The red-haired woman crossed her legs showing an unexpected, discretely flowered edge of her stockings, through a side cut of her blue dress.

"A significant addition to the typical rocket engine cycle has been introduced by the MORPHEM project," Varese continued. "We have developed a special technology based on plasma physics. It is an original Lockwell idea, patented to us."

He said that in a casual but definite manner. In multiple ways, it was a false statement.

The idea of accelerating charged gas particles, such as ions and electrons, in order to produce thrust was not new. Goddard himself had obtained a patent on such a device. Soviet satellites have been using electric thrusters based on ionized gas for orbit positioning and orbital maneuvering ever since 1960's. The thrust levels obtained by those devices were very small however, less than a pound force of thrust usually. Although small, such thrusts could be sustained continuously for hours, days or weeks as necessary, accelerating a satellite or a space vehicle continuously and very efficiently.

The MORPHEM engine was entirely different. Similar in size with the classic design engines pictured on the screen, it could produce enormous thrust force: under certain conditions of operation, the thrust produced by a full scale MORPHEM engine exceeded the thrust of a conventional chemical rocket by several orders of magnitude.

There was a problem nevertheless: the operation of MORPHEM engines could not be explained by the plasma physics. I had discovered the MORPHEM effect by accident, on experiments I did before coming to the States. I had learned - by

---

[3] Wernher von Braun was the leading German rocket scientist developing the famous V-2 rockets for the Nazi regime. Brought in the US after WWII he became the leading scientist for the US rocket development programs his career culminating with the development of the Saturn V rocket for the Apollo missions which placed the first man on the Moon on July 20th 1969.

empirical research - that the effect is produced only for very specific geometric configurations. For the MORPHEM design, geometry was the key.

After three ears of employment with Lockwell I decided to propose the project to them. I had designed a small scale MORPHEM engine core, a proof of concept. After two years of various attempts, my team captured the MORPHEM effect on several tests. It was clear to me, at the time, that we know nothing about the physics of the phenomena at work in that engine. And it was also clear to me that we can produce something very dangerous. I proposed a joint investigation of the fundamental physics using collaborations with academia and the national labs. We needed guidance in fundamental physics if we wanted to understand what we were doing.

Lockwell management had refused. They wanted to build a full scale engine and cash in. I had strongly opposed the idea. On one hand, I deeply wanted to understand the science behind the effect; it was a mystery that was eating at my mind. On the other hand, Lockwell's plan was just plainly dangerous: it could generate a dud or an uncontrolled nuclear bomb.

But Varese had taken over the lead. He was brilliant in his own way: a smooth brilliancy that was not scientific in nature, but rather a mix of advanced engineering knowledge, excellent sense of direction in corporate politics, and a fierce selfishness. He had pushed the full engine idea and demanded from me the scaling criteria. I refused and entered the long conflict with Lockwell which destroyed my life.

Carried by thoughts, I had missed some of Varese's words. I focused back on his presentation.

"The basic idea for our new technology," he explained, "is to go beyond the limitations of simple combustion chemistry and enter the realm of plasma physics. The objective is to significantly enhance the amount of thrust obtained per every pound of exhaust material."

He showed a few charts explaining the MORPHEM potential benefits and showing pictures of futuristic space vehicles.

Garland stood up and walked to a coffee pot placed in a corner of the room. He was relaxed. Lockwell's CEO, Craig McNutt, stood anxious, with his face crippled by a grimace.

McNutt was a slick dealmaker and an able corporate politician, but he was scientifically incompetent. Keeping his jaw tensed and eyebrows low may have fooled any of the people in the room, except his own.

Varese waited for Garland to return to his seat before going on. The following chart showed the picture of a steel structure extending into a large conical nozzle. A maze of cables, steel ducts and valves surrounded the head of the structure. The conical nozzle was wrapped in metallic sheaths hosting power coils, looking as if some strange metallic creature was embracing it.

I absorbed the details in the image: it was the picture of the large size MORPHEM prototype as Lockwell had built it.

"The full scale MORPHEM project was finalized with the prototype shown here," Varese explained. "This image shows the prototype before the test. It took two years to build this prototype due to high precision machining of the engine cores. Budget limitations precluded the assembly of more than one test item. Core engine parts have been manufactured for two other prototypes but haven't been used and are currently in storage. We tested the prototype about a year ago. Unfortunately, the test ended in a tragic accident."

A new chart appeared on the screen. The image showed a jet of hot gas: the test had been made in vertical position at almost one hundred feet elevation above the ground, with the engine exhaust deflected by an angled massive concrete structure at the bottom. For those unfamiliar with rocket engines, the image wasn't very different from other images of rocket engines firing. For the specialist, the jet appeared completely non-typical. After exiting the nozzle, the gas formed a long cylindrical plume without any expansion looking like a rod of red-hot steel radiating a blue glow. After the cylindrical stretch, the jet opened up in the typical diamond structure of shock waves, the image being cut at the bottom edge of the chart. A timer had imprinted the elapsed time of the test at the moment the image was recorded, indicating 44 seconds.

"The team of the AFRL's test engineers lost their lives in the accident," Varese explained. He indicated the chart. "This is the last image frame recorded by the test cameras. The engine exploded at 44 seconds after start, and destroyed a large part of the test facility. We believe that a stress-induced failure in the engine core housing wall was the cause of the accident."

A new chart appeared on the screens, showing one diagram plot.

"This chart shows the temperatures at the engine core," Varese pointed to the diagram lines on the images. "At 44 seconds, marked here in the plot, the explosion occurred."

My eyes locked on the plots. A red line depicting the temperature showed a noisy signal of about 15 electron-volts in the confinement section going steady until the 44 seconds time instance indicated by Varese. Beyond that point, the signal line raised sharply - a fast temperature rise, and then dropped to flat zero.

I watched the graph line on the screen and I could hear my heart beats, and it seemed to me that everyone in the room could hear them too. According to Varese, the explosion time was before the sharp rise in the signal values.

He was dead wrong. Lockwell ignored the very objective they should have pursued. The sharp rise in temperature showed that something mysterious had happened within the core of the engine. Out of nowhere, a large amount of unexplained energy was created. A phenomenon I have been hunting for years. I felt, desperately, the need to obtain that set of measurements from Lockwell and analyze them on my own.

Varese had finished. I didn't hear his last words, something about the termination of the program.

"Thank you Dr. Varese," Bronson said. "This background information is absolutely necessary for understanding the implications of Miss Nahman's analysis. Miss Nahman, if you please."

The woman in the blue dress stood up and walked to the screens. She was a strange appearance in the austere environment at Lockwell. Her dress had a simple and elegant cut, which, in spite of its sobriety, emphasized the discrete sensual features of her body. The woman's red hair seemed her natural color. Her skin was milky white, impeccably smooth.

"Thank you Roger," she said in a steely voice. "Gentlemen, my name is Yvette Nahman. I do decrypting work for the Information Systems Security division of the National Security

Agency. Before getting into my analysis, I need to give you some background of a different nature."

Bronson produced a surprising image on the screen: a blond child laughing and cuddling a cat.

Yvette Nahman remained serious and silent, letting the image work its soothing effect. She explained in dry professional tone:

"Terrorist organizations and espionage networks around the world have learned to communicate securely through the internet, rather than using cell phones or calling cards vulnerable to interception and tracking. A particular type of encryption technology uses the information needed for a computer to code images. Look at this one, isn't she sweet?"

People in the room had involuntarily relaxed. Some smiled.

Bronson brought a new chart on the screen. It contained lines of meaningless text, a mixture of letters, numbers and various symbols.

The woman named Nahman continued:

"This is the coded information the computer uses to compose and project the image of the child and the kitten on the screen. Hidden within this coding, there is another image. It could be an image, or a virus code, or some other type of information. The technique is called *steganography*. An ordinary computer will ignore the additional information, and will display only the child image. But a computer instructed with a decryption key will also display this."

Bronson brought a new image on the screens. It showed an M-16 rifle. A wave of rumor went through the room. Yvette Nahman let the effect of the second image mark the audience. Her eyes brushed by me for a short fraction of a second. Her presence had a note of surreal, like a set-up. She made a sign towards Bronson, and continued.

"Recently, our internet surveillance section intercepted a picture posted on a pornographic website in the Netherlands. This is the picture."

Bronson brought the picture on the screen. The image was a slightly censored pornographic picture. Yvette Nahman let it sink, standing silent, next to the screen.

In the image, an Asian male, standing, was thrusting himself against the face of a dark haired girl, probably Asian as well. A dark square on the image censored her explicit oral performance and covered most of her face. The man was pulling her hair, in a gesture denoting cruelty. I studied his face on the screen. His features showed a genuine cruelty, something the man had been born with.

"The Dutch website vanished after posting for ten days a set of pictures including this one. We analyzed all of them: they're all clean, except this one. Embedded in this image is another one. This is the second image."

Bronson brought it up. A second wave of murmurs propagated through the room.

Suddenly, I felt my back cold. The picture showed a jet of gas exiting an engine nozzle from a test facility. The structure of the jet was strikingly similar to the MORPHEM's jet shown moments before by Varese. The difference was in the cylindrical section, which, in this case was longer and brighter. I swept the image on the screen in all directions, looking for clues. Who? Where?

Bronson's eyes had locked on me. A strong and steady lock, with no room for avoidance.

Suddenly, two hands grabbed the lapels of my coat and pulled at me with a vicious jerk. Varese's face was one inch from mine, yelling.

"You motherfucker! Who did you sell it to? Who? Answer me, you son of a bitch!"

I hit him in the chest. He let go of me and fell back. Bronson's men jumped and held me down on my chair. Another man pulled Varese back from his attempt to grab at me again.

I lost track of reality. It was the surreal again, with the room starting to spin around and my heart beats the only thing I could hear.

0 7

I had the acuity of perception that is given sometimes by certain drugs. However, the time sequence had ruptures. Across the table, Varese was standing and I didn't remember him standing up. His face was blue green with patches of red. McNutt and Garland sat, poker faced, with their eyes fixed on me.

The two men holding me down on my chair released their grip. I didn't move. The men went away and sat down on their chairs.

"Sit down, Dr. Varese!" Bronson said, and his calm voice sounded with a tone of disdain. His eyes circled the audience.

"We need to keep calm, gentlemen!" he said, loudly. "We will continue this meeting without any disorder."

He turned towards a thin man with short black hair and pale white skin sitting across the table from him.

"Mr. Balder, your turn."

The thin man got up and pushed his chair away. There was a peculiar toughness in his moves as he walked towards the screen. His voice came as a surprise, balanced and professional.

"You've all been asked to understand the sensitivity of what is being discussed here," he said, severely. "I believe now you get the picture."

The silence in the room was absolute. The only sound was made by the cooling fans of the LCD projectors.

"My name is Benjamin Balder," the man continued. "I work for the Directorate of Science and Technology of the Central Intelligence Agency. Before I begin my briefing, I need to make one point crystal clear. Given the MORPHEM performance parameters as explained to us by Lockwell, a missile equipped with this type of engine can deliver a nuclear warhead anywhere in the US from anywhere in the world with a single stage rocket deployed on mobile platforms hard to detect. This is a clear, significant, and unprecedented threat to the United States security."

He let the information sink in. He continued in aggressive speech as if holding the audience responsible for the evils of the world.

"At present, there is a vast effort directed at rocket propulsion development by countries that are emerging military powers.

They're scrambling to acquire advanced launch capabilities and become an increasing challenge to the US, and a possible military threat."

Bronson produced a new chart on the screen. The chart contained an art-like image: a navy blue background and, in the middle, a concentric set of irregular patches of red, orange, yellow and green.

Balder pointed to the image, "The Los Alamos National Laboratory has developed and deployed a space surveillance system, known as FORTE. The system detects electromagnetic pulses and analyzes their source. The result is a unique electromagnetic fingerprint associated with any event detected."

"This is an image recorded by FORTE on July 7th, last year. What you see in this image is the Air Force Research Laboratory 2-S testing facility, viewed from an altitude of 800 kilometers in VHM electromagnetic spectrum. The time frame of this image corresponds to the failed MORPHEM test. The bright pattern of colors you see in the middle of this image is the very unique electromagnetic fingerprint of the MORPHEM engine exploding. It has the characteristics of a small nuclear detonation."

He surveyed the attendance again, making sure he had enforced in everyone's mind a clear understanding of what he was showing.

"Next chart, please," he requested.

A new image appeared displayed on the screens. It seemed a slightly modified copy of the one before. The same dark blue background, the same pattern of red, orange, yellow and green in the middle. The contours were somewhat different, but essentially it was the same picture.

"This second image was recorded two months ago, on January 20th," Balder continued. "The view is from the same altitude and in the same VHF spectrum. The image shows the testing facilities of the Aerospace Base 067, located in the city of Xi'an, Shaanxi Province, People's Republic of China"

A wave of rumor traversed the room again. Balder ignored it.

"The electromagnetic pattern is similar, if not identical to the pattern observed during MORPHEM explosion," he said.

He gave everyone time to examine the image.

"Next chart please," he requested.

Bronson put the requested new chart on the screens. It was a high resolution spy satellite picture, shot in normal, visual spectrum. It showed a complex of buildings which appeared as rectangular patches on a dry land crossed by roads. On the upper left of the image, one of the rectangles was broken into a dark, irregular stain, as if some careless artist had dropped ink on the spot.

"This is a picture of the same facility the very next day, taken in visible spectrum," Balder said. "Here, in this picture, test stand number 9 appears to have been destroyed by an explosion. From the limited HUMINT we've obtained, the accident appears to have been similar to the one Dr. Varese described earlier. Taken together with the similarity of the electromagnetic signatures of the explosions, this is strong evidence the Chinese are developing a propulsion system similar or identical to the MORPHEM system."

Balder stopped pacing the floor and stood in the path of the projector beam. The image of the Chinese facility wrapped around him with a chameleonic effect.

"It is uncertain if the Chinese have pursued an original idea of their own," Balder said. "Their efforts so far have been focused on conventional propulsion. This possible MORPHEM experiment is a sudden development in their research. The implications for US national security are extremely important. If the Chinese achieved success in this, it would give them access to weaponry with unprecedented ability to hit our territory. It would also give them unprecedented access to space. And presently we are in a race for space with the Chinese."

His mouth discharged the words against the light of the projector. The light beam didn't appear to bother him. His teeth and tongue appeared strangely emphasized by the strong illumination.

"What are the odds for similar failures and similar explosions in independent parallel developments? Or did the Chinese obtain information on Lockwell design? If yes, then, how?"

I felt Varese's gaze on me, filled with hate. I kept my eyes on the screen, carefully resting my hands on the table and kept listening to Balder.

"The picture decrypted by the NSA shown here poses another hugely disturbing question. The date of the image is uncertain. Does this picture show a Chinese experiment, or it is an entirely different project? Who is working on it? Where?"

His last set of questions rang a strange note. The NSA picture showed a *working* MORPHEM engine. The Chinese MORHEM *didn't work*: they had an explosion just as Lockwell did. And the CIA didn't know who it was that got the engine running.

Balder made a sign towards Bronson indicating he's done. Bronson acknowledged and swung his chair so he can face the rest of the conference table. The room lights came on.

"I believe we have a better understanding of the whole situation now," Bronson said. "Before we discuss any plan of action, I'd like to ask for analysis from the expert people in the room."

He turned his eyes on me.

"Dr. Salagen, we would appreciate your interpretation of this image."

He brought the NSA image back on the screen. The room went completely silent again. I tried to mentally dismiss the sense of personal danger and I studied again the image.

I cleared my throat.

"I must clarify one thing first," I said. "The physics of the phenomena generating the large thrust in MORPHEM engines is not understood. It cannot be explained with what we know. I challenge anyone at Lockwell to contradict my statement."

The room remained silent. The government men turned their heads towards Varese and McNutt. Varese made a dismissive gesture with his hand.

"I won't discuss any of this man's speculations," he said.

"I wasn't expecting you would," I said. "Furthermore, geometry is crucial in MORPHEM engines. Extremely crucial. Do not ask me why, it has been empirically determined. My conflict with this corporation has stemmed from their inability to accept these facts."

Varese placed his hands on the table and opened his mouth, but McNutt stopped him. I waited for more reaction from the Lockwell people. There wasn't any.

"MORPHEM engines need an empirical electromagnetic tuning," I explained further, over their silence. "When this tuning is right, we get an enormous thrust force. Hard thrust. If the engine is mistuned, two things can happen: either it does not work, or it deflagrates with the same unusual energy observed in the hard thrust operation."

I waited again for a reaction from Lockwell. The men stood silent.

"The experiments I did with small scale engines here at Lockwell worked. Those small scale engines were my design. I would like to examine the design of the large scale engine shown here."

"That is not an option," Varese said.

"Why not?"

Varese exchanged a look with McNutt.

"The CAD files containing the design are no longer available. A computer system failure corrupted the files."

"Don't you people have a back-up system?"

"We do. The backed up files are corrupted as well. Unreadable."

"You're telling me you have no CAD files for the engine design you've tested?"

"That seems to be the case."

I looked at Bronson and the rest of the suits. They sat, poker faced. The issue was serious. It couldn't have been just an accident. But those were the cards of the game.

"About this image," I said, indicating the screen. "The jet structure indicates a very similar concept."

"Similar to MORPHEM you mean?" Balder asked.

"Yes. Unfortunately, I cannot establish a dimensional scale. Scale is crucial for MORPHEM engines. As I said, the small scale experiment I conducted at Lockwell has been successful. However, scaling up the design for a large size engine is not trivial. Any dimensional information about this picture would be very valuable."

"Can you speculate on the possible origin of this picture?" Bronson asked.

I swallowed with a dry mouth, and closed my eyes. Images from the past came to mind. Ghosts of old friends.

"No," I said. "I can't think of anything."

Bronson turned towards the Lockwell men.

"Dr. Varese," he invited. "What is your assessment?"

Varese turned his eyes to the screen deliberately slow. He knew he had to thread carefully.

"The picture seems to show the same type of an engine," he said. "The long jet indicates a stable core, at full hard thrust. I can only speculate here, based on visual inspection of this image. The absence of any distinguishable shock-waves in the initial sector of the exhaust shows the gas is highly ionized. I cannot estimate this engine's performance or its size."

"Why is it difficult to make a larger engine?" Balder asked.

He was looking at Varese. I let Varese answer.

"The physics of this engine is very complicated," Varese said. "We don't have calibrated models for all the phenomena we're dealing with."

"Can two independent teams make the same mistake, and blow an engine up?"

Varese frowned. "Rocket engines blow up for various reasons, but they blow up just the same".

"The FORTE analysis indicates a very peculiar electric discharge. That was not a regular explosion, Dr. Varese."

Varese hesitated.

"I'll have to look at the FORTE data before making any judgment."

"What was the cause for the MORPHEM accident?"

"As I said in my briefing, we believe it was a mechanical failure at the engine core."

"Can you be more specific?"

"The engine core is cooled by liquid hydrogen passing through many small channels. These channels can crack and leak. The leaked hydrogen can light up and cause further damage. In very short time, this cascade of damages can generate an explosion."

"A conventional explosion?" Balder pressed. "Or something along Dr. Salagen's explanations?"

"I refuse to discuss Salagen's speculations. The explosion was conventional, but don't forget, there is high temperature plasma gas at the engine core."

Balder watched Varese without asking any more questions. He suddenly turned his eyes on me.

"What's your take on this, Dr. Salagen?"

"My take on what?"

"Why is it such a big deal to make this engine larger? Why did it blow up?"

The ghosts in my mind told me it's none of their business to know. Not everything.

"I don't know."

"Maybe the engine gets mistuned when enlarged?"

"Maybe."

"Does it blow up?"

"Maybe."

"What do you think generated the explosion during testing?"

"I wasn't there, Mr. Balder. I wasn't working for this corporation anymore."

His gaze stayed on me, steady, threatening. I matched it with a blank stare.

"Thank you Dr. Varese, Dr. Salagen," Bronson intervened. He flashed a glance at Balder who slowly leaned back in his chair.

The room quieted again. The Lockwell men's eyes gleamed with confusion. Tension was gripping my back muscles. What next?

Bronson turned towards a thin man with freckled skin, wearing impeccable gold rimmed glasses and looking extremely clean, even aristocratic, his scalp shining though perfectly cut, rarefied blond hair.

"Stan," Bronson said, "all yours."

"Thank you, Roger," the thin man said, and swept the room with a pair of steely gray-blue eyes.

"Gentlemen, my name is Stan Jackobs and I represent a consortium of government agencies involved in defense. You all understand we have quite a situation in our hands: an extremely promising technology development was failed by Lockwell, while strong evidence suggests we're in competition for it with the Chinese. On top of this, some unknown party seem to have made better progress. This situation is unacceptable and must be resolved. At both the government and military high levels we consider MORPHEM a critical and extremely sensitive technology which needs be fully reevaluated. This effort will be Lockwell's top priority starting now. I will serve as the interface between the several government agencies with direct interest in the MORPHEM technology and Lockwell. I'll outline here a few details to help get this started."

He opened a leather-bound notebook and eyed the Lockwell men, McNutt, Garland and Varese.

"Number one: I need a full review of all MORPHEM related research and development activities: history, detailed experiments, tests, conclusions. I want this documentation put together ASAP," he said.

"Number two: Lockwell needs to write a proposal and a single source no-bid contract will be awarded based on it. I will handle the proposal, once it's done, on the government end. This is not a competitive bid. However, we retain the right to fund any other firm of our choosing if we feel there is lack of progress, even if it may infringe on Lockwell's patents. Any questions?"

Jackobs spoke with the voice of power and money. Amiable but impenetrable face. His words had thrown the Lockwell men out of balance. They hadn't expected an offer. Among them, Garland weighed the government man with caution.

"What should we propose, Mr. Jackobs?" he asked in his firm style. "Years ago we started this program with the intent of three prototypes and a more comprehensive test program. We could have characterized better the engine operation and perhaps avoid the catastrophe, but our budget got cut. That forced us into directly building the one prototype that exploded. How, in your view, may we proceed now, what sorts of funds are now available?"

"I have a discretionary fund of five million to get this investigation started," Jackobs said. "Based on what you guys find, you can structure a development program, and we'll talk about money again."

"Development means a hundred million plus, Mr. Jackobs."

"Let's see what went wrong first, Mr. Garland. Then we can talk about as large a budget as needed."

The game was on. McNutt's grimace had changed. He was in. That was the kind of a game and language he played and spoke well.

"I view this as a great opportunity," he said, moving his shoulders and laying his elbows on the table. "Lockwell can and will do what it does best, act as the integrator of the complex activities related to this development."

"Paul," he continued addressing Varese. "Get your people working and put the investigation proposal together. Jim," he addressed Garland, "you will provide all technical support. We will get this done, gentlemen."

I stopped paying attention to the negotiation. I was out of the game. My personal litigation with Lockwell was in the way. My presence there had been only relevant for examining the intelligence presented. At best, I'll be asked to sign a confidentiality agreement and shown the door. At worst, handcuffed and taken away.

Somebody had mentioned my name. The room had gone silent; everybody was watching me, hostility suddenly reignited on Varese and McNutt faces.

"Excuse me?" I said.

Jackobs studied me through his impeccable glasses.

"Under the circumstances, Dr. Salagen, we appreciate it is the best use of your expertise," he said.

"I beg your pardon Mr. Jackobs, I had a lapse of attention, could you repeat please?"

"The government agencies I represent for this project require a contract monitor, Dr. Salagen. I suggested you should perform this monitoring, given your expertise."

"Are you people insane?!" Varese snapped. "This man should be arrested!"

Jackobs glanced at Bronson. Bronson said nothing and watched Varese's furious face with tired eyes.

"Let me speak straight and off the record," Jackobs said, addressing mostly McNutt. "Time is pressing. You have a court order giving you rights to the engine, but it seems to me you can wipe your asses with it. I need expertise here, not legal papers."

The Lockwell men answered the statement with silence and tightened jaws. It felt strange. Jackobs had just stated a truth I had almost ceased believing in.

"I agree to provide consulting on a contract basis," I said. "I will provide analysis on the condition that I have full access to the past and future test results."

"That's unacceptable!" Varese said, coldly and in full control of his hostility. "I object again to Salagen's presence here. His interests are at conflict with the interests of this corporation. There is a court decision regarding this conflict. Any access Salagen may be permitted to past or future test results and design data would be detrimental to us as a corporation and detrimental to this country."

Jackobs' eyes toughened. He exhaled through his nostrils.

"Gentlemen, the US is at war. It's a curious state of war; nevertheless it is recognized as such. The government is legally entitled to act in many ways in the face of a threat such as this. We're talking about a very capable launcher with a nuclear warhead on top of it. There is no room for petty games. We will choose our contractors with the objective of maximum expertise and capability. You have the choice of rejecting the business, in which case we start over at other national lab with necessary capabilities. It will only create a time delay in what needs to be done, a delay to be credited to your refusal."

"Gentlemen, gentlemen, let's not get into this sort of completely unproductive rhetoric," intervened McNutt. "I completely agree with Stan, the stakes are higher than the level of conflict Paul Varese mentioned here. Paul is right in his comments, but we can construct rather that destruct here, I believe this country needs all the good brains and all the good work it can get."

Varese threw a hard look at his CEO and tightened his lips. Jackobs waited to make sure there were no more issues raised. He turned towards me.

"I need some information from you, Dr. Salagen. Someone will call you."

His steely eyes toured the table one more time from behind the elegant glasses. Nobody spoke.

"Dr. Salagen," Bronson called. "Please do not leave town without letting us know beforehand."

Everyone's eyes trained on my face. I said nothing.

Jackobs stood up.

"OK, gentlemen, let's get to work. Roger, thanks for organizing this, it's been a good meeting."

He pushed his chair away and stepped towards the door. The other men slowly followed. I remained in my chair for one more moment. Slowly, I exhaled. I even enjoyed watching Yvette Nahman's dress, as she walked towards the door. I grinned, remembering the glimpse I had at the flowered stockings she was wearing.

08

A strong evil spirit had locked on me from the outer side of the gate. It was the Devil himself. The gate was of an old castle, the kind made of thick wood slabs held together with long iron spikes. Not strong enough for the Devil, not thick enough, the gate could not stop that raw evil pressure. I was frightened. *"I am going to get you!"* the Devil growled through the door. His voice penetrated the wood and the walls around with reverberation. I shivered. Two red eyes opened in the stone above the gate, their evil gaze fixed upon me. Then, the Devil started coming through the gate, its heavy presence penetrating the wood in a viscous, poisonous flow. *"No! no!"* I cried and I stepped back. My feet tangled in something like oily ropes. I was weak, and I was loosing, but I didn't give up. I took my little sword and began stabbing the wood and the viscous presence in it. The little weapon did nothing. The spirit's evil presence was overwhelming. I heard his laugh, and the telephone ringing.

I was all sweat. The telephone kept ringing. The display of the clock blinked two thirty. I picked up.

"Who are you?" a woman's voice asked. It sounded coarse, unfriendly.

"Who is this?"

"Is your name Salagen?"

"Yes, I'm Salagen."

"Are you a friend of Jane's?"

I dug in my brain, still waking up, still scared of the Devil.

"Friend of who? Who is this?"

"I'm Jane's roommate, pal. If you are a friend of hers, you'd better come over and do something. She really did it this time."

"Who the hell is Jane?"

"Who the hell is Jane?! Fuck you. Funny how you son's of bitches forget. Jane is a blond girl, you fucked her, gave her money to buy drugs, whatever. Your name is here on a piece of paper, and she's half-dead. I figured I'd try this number before calling the cops. They'll throw her in the dump and she won't last in there."

Oh God. The girl from the coffee shop.

"What's your name?" I asked

"None of your business."

"What do you want me to do?"

Her breath came heavy into phone, as if she was lifting something.

"Nothing," she said. "Go fuck yourself!"

"Hey, wait!"

She waited, still breathing in the mike, annoyingly.

"Listen," I said, "I do remember Jane, please tell me, what is happening, what did she do?"

"Dunno exactly. She's usually clean. She's getting stuff, every now and then, passes out. No big deal. But this time she must've gotten something nasty, she's been out all night, lookin' half dead. You friend of hers?"

"No, not really. Listen, if you think it's serious, please call emergency, I'll drive over there, but it'll take me some time. What's the address?"

She gave me the address, somewhere in West Hollywood.

I crossed Pasadena and took 110 south. In a normal world, at three in the morning, roads should be empty. Los Angeles has nothing to do with normality. I reached 10 West and it was like a party had just finished and everybody was rushing to another.

I made it to West Hollywood in less than thirty minutes pushing the muscle on my old Mustang's V8. The address was two blocks west of La Brea, a street off Sunset Boulevard. I vaguely knew the area. Rental apartment buildings with large turn-over rates.

I parked at the curb, and got in the building past a faulty security gate. The apartment was on the second floor. I rang the bell, catching my breath.

The door was opened by a very tall girl. She was over six feet. Her intense upper body sex appeal was dramatically reduced by the flat conic shape of her very long legs. She was no special breed, no arches, no curved ankles, just plain conic flesh and muscle. Her voice sounded fifty, although she was about twenty-five or so.

"You Salagen?" she asked flatly.

"Yes. Where is she?"

She turned and walked past a living room furnished with worn-out couches. She led me into a bedroom. The girl from the coffee shop was lying on the bed, face up, eyes closed. The skin on her face was void of color. She was dressed in the same clothes I remembered from when I met her. She looked like a wax model.

"What happened?" I asked the tall girl. "What did she take?"

"The fuck I know," the tall woman said. "You friend of hers?" she asked again.

"No. I just met her and lend her some bucks."

She threw a careless look at the girl on the bed, and shook her head towards me.

"So what do we do here?" she asked. "Watch her die or do something?"

I felt Jane's pulse. Barely anything. Why was I there and not in my bed, away from that? I pulled my cell phone, and dialed emergency. How long was it going to take for an ambulance to come? I changed my mind. I lifted the girl in my arms and walked towards the apartment door. Her body felt strange in my arms, she was neither light nor too heavy. She felt just right.

"Open the doors for me," I asked the tall girl. "What's the phone number here?"

She gave it to me and I memorized it, carrying Jane down the stairs. I placed her onto the lowered front seat of the Mustang, helped by the other girl. I knew a hospital on Sunset, not too far. I ran a couple of red lights and slammed the breaks a few times, avoiding some drunks crossing the boulevard and a stretch limo stuck across the lanes.

The ER section at the small medical center was full of people waiting. I rushed through the crowd carrying Jane and shouted for assistance. The ER people acted with reluctance as if I cut in front of a line. I had. Some of the people waiting there didn't appear to be in a better condition than Jane. Somebody asked me if I knew what drug she was on. I told them I didn't. A male nurse helped me place Jane on a stretcher and he pushed her into the treatment section.

I found a free spot on a corner couch in the crowded room and I sat down. I wanted to smoke, but that could wait. A Latino clerk woman came and handed me a clipboard filled with paper forms. I handed it back to her.

She protested, "We need you to fill out this information, sir. Are you the husband of the lady?"

"No. I'm just a friend."

"Who is the responsible party?"

"Responsible party?"

"Financial responsible party, sir. Does the patient have insurance?"

"I don't know. I just brought her here so she doesn't die."

"What's her social?"

I shrugged. "I don't know. I only know her name. Wait a second."

I called the number the tall girl gave me. No answer. It kept ringing, not even an answering machine or service.

"Sorry," I said, "I don't know."

She left, glancing suspiciously at me, and entered the treatment section. I waited. On the wall there was an AIDS awareness poster, explaining in English and Spanish what AIDS is. The need for clean needles seemed to be the most important point there. It didn't say one could get AIDS as a bonus on top of sixty dollars blow-jobs offered on the street less than a block away. A man on my right was pressing his abdomen with his hands. He seemed meek, accepting the shit happening to him as his life default.

The Latino clerk came back with a doctor. She pointed towards me.

"Good evening sir. I am doctor Rishab. How are you doing?" the doctor said, politely.

"I'm fine. What is it with the girl?"

He spoke in same blankly polite style, "Your wife is in a condition that was probably induced by a strong substance, sir. We don't know the nature of the substance your wife used. It is nothing she ate or swallowed, neither is it inhaled. From our examination, it is very likely something that has been injected. Does your wife have a history of heroin use?"

"She's not my wife. I'm a friend of this woman. I don't know what she's been using, if anything."

He shuffled the papers clipped on the pad he was holding. He quickly glanced at me.

"OK, sir, thank you," he said and left.

I waited some more. I read the AIDS poster again. It did say about the sex transmission of the virus, in dry medical language nobody reads. In bad neighborhoods people don't copulate, they just fuck.

Thirty more minutes passed. The double door from the outside burst open. Two paramedics rushed in, pushing a stretcher, and entered the treatment section. The stretcher was empty. A woman sitting on a bench opposite to me started crying. Then, she moaned in pain.

The paramedics rushed back through the double white doors. Jane was on the stretcher. I looked again, making sure.

"Hey!" I shouted, and stood up, "hey, what are you doing!?"

Someone pulled on my elbow. It was doctor Rishab.

"Sir, we can't handle your friend's condition here, we don't have the proper equipment. She's going to be better taken care of at the county."

"What the fuck you're talking about?" I yelled, "Where are they taking her? You guys just called the paramedics? Why don't you treat her here?"

"Sir, please calm down, there is equipment we don't have." His English became heavily accented. "Our emergency personal is all tied up with the cases here," he made a vague gesture towards a man with a blood-soaked shirt. "Your friend will be under better emergency care at the LA County."

"It's there where they're taking her? You're telling me you don't have a lab here? Or you don't mess with people without insurance, is that the deal?"

Some heads raised and some faces glanced at me with the interest people have for others with troubles stronger than theirs.

"Sir, please calm down, there is nothing we can do, if you want you can follow the ambulance, they're on their way now."

It was an efficient way of getting rid of me. There was no point in arguing with one Rishab or another. I saved my breath and left after the ambulance. I followed it through Sunset, then the 101 free-way and the Downtown interchange towards East LA. I kept driving, following the sound of the siren.

The faces of the people at the Lockwell meeting surfaced in my memory. At that moment, they seemed elements of another life. I was driving in the night, following an ambulance carrying a stranger whose life or death seemed suddenly linked to my own. As if two or more different lives were sheltered in my chest, immiscible, unrelated.

The ER people at the LA County Hospital acted with tired efficiency. The paramedics rushed Jane in. The whole place was a zoo of patients, nurses, paramedics, and some cops. A black female clerk pushed some paperwork towards me. I left most of it blank, except for the address, telephone number and the first name where I wrote "Jane," and then handed the forms back to the woman. She looked at the sheet, glanced at me without a word and mentally dismissed my existence.

I walked outside and lit up a Marlboro, waiting. It was still dark but the traffic was already heavy on the I-5. It was packed with gray rectangular shapes of trucks lit by each other's head lights.

I went back inside. The black clerk woman was talking to a young man, dressed in green surgeon outfit. The man was blond, with long sideburns. An unlit cigarette was dangling from his upper lip. The woman pointed towards me. The doctor wrote something on her wad of papers and came straight towards me, offering his hand.

"Got a match?" he asked, and smiled. "Let's go outside, I need a smoke."

Outside, on the concrete platform, I lit his cigarette and one more for me.

"Doctor De Fuentes," he introduced himself, after drawing a long smoke and blowing it out through his nostrils. "You're a friend of the patient, family?"

"I'm a friend. Her roommate called. She seemed in a serious condition. How is she doing?"

"Looks like a heroin overdose. A small overdose I'd say, otherwise she would've been dead by now. She had all the symptoms, except muscle spasticity, which is rather strange, because she seems to have taken some strong variety of a drug. I gave her the standard stuff, Naxalone, IV fluids and so on. Good response, she seems to be out of it."

"So she's OK."

"For now, yes. Do you know what stuff she took? Where she got it from?"

"No idea. Didn't you say heroin?"

"Yes and no. I don't feel this case is typical, more exactly she injected herself with some opiate derivative I haven't seen before. It may be some new shit on the street, I don't know."

He inhaled smoke, watching me. I thought about what he said, about the lousy fistful of cash I gave the girl.

"Anyway," he said, "my bet is she's going to be fine from this one, but you don't know with the next one."

"Is she addicted?"

"They all are. Although, in her case, it's kinda funny, no needle marks on her arms, nowhere. Yet, she takes an overdose. I don't know. Gotta go, anyway," he said throwing the cigarette but. "Nice meeting you."

I went to the desk where the clerk woman was working her papers. I took out a business card and placed it on the counter.

"Could someone call me when she's to be released?" I asked, and left without waiting for, or getting an answer.

09

By the time I made it back home, the dawning sun was shedding purple light on the upper slopes of the San Gabriel Mountains. I contemplated a weak temptation to sleep, and gave it up. I fixed the water steaming hot, and stood in the shower thinking about what the hell I was doing, not doing, or should be doing. The hot water didn't help. Neither did cold water. It was all a blur. I wrapped myself in a thick old bathrobe, prepared an espresso, and went to the computer. There was a message from Julia, waiting.

"*Hello Dad,*" she wrote, "*We arrived yesterday, after several days in Paris. I am still on California time, sleeping during the day, and I watching TV or reading at night. Mom is busy at work. She started setting up her lab right away. I don't have much stuff to read, I finished all the books from home in the plane and in Paris, and so there is only TV. French sounds funny here, distinguished but funny not like the stuff I studied with Miss Demortier in LA or the way mom talks at home. It's like guys pretending to be high class all the time. Something funny: I saw The Sting on TV. Can you imagine Redford speaking French? I was so surprised I watched the whole movie again. There are French actors speaking over the real voices. It's called dubbing. Anyway, this is my life here. Oh, I forgot, they have here these really cool trains. They are fast and smooth, I only read a magazine, (it's called Paris Match and it had an old picture of Madonna with her boobies showing!), and we were already in Grenoble. Well, again, this is the news. I miss you. Love, Julia.*"

My chest was hurting. I missed Julia. I missed people being close, people from whom I didn't need to hide. Suddenly, I remembered Jane's body in my arms, the good feel of her weight. She had been warm, as if in fever, despite the apparent coma. The memory of another time came, another body in my arms, twenty years before. Someone looking like Jane. But different hair, different eyes, different soul. An old story with no more relevance, no more meaning. A scar.

And if so, why hadn't I just slept nicely, the whole night, in my bed?

The phone rang. I grabbed it at the half of the first ring. I heard a click, and a young man's voice.

"Mr. Salagen? Good morning, this is Ernesto, please hold for Mr. Mason."

Ernesto. One of the very few men Hal allowed around him. Discrete, efficient, trustworthy.

"Matt," Hal came on line, "is this too early to call?"

I glanced at the wall clock. A bit after seven. The old man couldn't sleep.

"I was having coffee," I said.

"The Lockwell meeting you told me about," Hal said. "How was it?"

I searched for a word. "Complicated," I said. "It's a long story."

He laughed. "I'd like to hear it. Are you free this evening?"

"Yes."

"Good. Dorothy Chandler Pavilion, the little plaza in front. Be there at seven. Get a drink."

"What's on the program?"

"Bach. And an exceptional German soprano."

"I'll be there. Don't know about the soprano, but Bach is always okay."

Hal laughed and then coughed and then closed connection. I read Julia's message again. And I thought again about Jane's good weight in my arms.

***

In the evening, I parked on Temple Street at the curb, a block away. Parking deep underground at the LA Music Center feels funny in a place not so far from the San Adreas Fault. I walked the block to the small plaza between the Dorothy Chandler Pavilion and Mark Taper building. People were having their little pre-concert fun. A bar was open in the middle of the place, with small tall tables scattered around. The trees around were decorated with hundreds of tiny electric lights, making the place a fairy scene. I ordered a Manhattan at the bar and settled at a narrow tall table, watching people. The Music Center crowd is one of the few decent crowds in LA. Folks would not come there as much to schmooze or to see and be seen, but mostly for the pleasure of listening. I saw again faces of women over fifty looking young and fresh as if they were twenty, men in club jackets with smart eyes and slow, well-mannered moves. Here and there an eye popping and out of fashion dress of a vain woman who had lost track of time and herself.

I felt a light touch on my elbow. Ernesto, wearing tuxedo and a discrete ear-piece made of translucent skin-color plastic, a tiny translucent wire thin as hair extending a microphone shaped like a grain of rice to the corner of his lips. He smiled and greeted me with a nod. I liked Ernesto. He was always efficient and genuinely courteous.

"Mr. Mason is waiting for you inside," Ernesto said. He slipped a piece of paper on the table. It was an admission ticket.

"Thanks," I nodded, "I'll be there in a minute." I raised my drink while he silently vanished into the crowd.

The bartender had used some good bourbon for the mix. I was set to enjoy two more minutes of the good drink, the fairy lights and the come and go of the well-dressed people.

Suddenly, an acute feeling of tension gripped the nerves on my back. The feeling of being watched by a predator. I looked around. The usual crowd, the discrete laughs and conversation. Nothing threatening. I searched the street beyond the plaza, focusing my sight on the shadowed corners, searching. Nothing. Reluctantly, I shook off the feeling.

I found Hal on a side platform extending from the thirteenth row in the lower left side of the concert hall. He was installed on a mobile version of his home chair, a sophisticated device with motion gear and batteries, fitted with a small pressurized oxygen tank and a supply control system. Thin tubes of the same color as Ernesto's mouth piece were fixed to Hal's nostrils, pumping oxygen into his tired lungs. He was reading the program.

My seat was next to Hal's chair. I touched his shoulder and sat down, unfolding the program brochure myself. Hal acknowledged my presence with a smile, and pointed to the program's page. It was a picture of the German soprano, blond and attractive, with an out-of-fashion hairstyle.

"That's a high school picture?" I asked.

"She's an excellent singer," he answered.

Bach went fine. His music has a rhythm to which one can tune one's mind and spirit. Just let the music do the good tuning job, and let your mind wander freely. I watched the musicians in the orchestra. Well shampooed men, with nails well groomed. Women's hands with long, beautiful, sensitive fingers. So many lives, personal destinies, hopes, divorces and mortgages geared together for the one hour of the Brandenburg Concerto No. 6. It was over after a long and yet very short breath of mind.

People rose, for the break, leaving the hall for refreshments. We remained in our seats, Hal a prisoner of his wheelchair. He coughed in a handkerchief. He had controlled his cough all throughout the first part of the concert, helping it with richer dozes of oxygen. The effort he had to make was tremendous.

I read the life story of the German soprano, relaxing in the comfort of the seat.

"I can't go out to dinner anymore," Hal said. "Let's have a drink in the car after this. I have everything ready."

"All right," I said.

We used to go for dinner at a nearby café after concerts. We would sit at the bar and have a salad, a cocktail, or just a few beers, and Hal would tell me some of his stories or opinions of which he had plenty. I was always curious. He always had good and exact information about everything. When Richard Nixon died, he told me a few stories about the Nixon days in California. A crooked son of a bitch, in summary.

It was time for the second part. The hall had filled again with people, the air buzzing with conversation. The Finnish conductor came, accepted the applause and introduced the famous German singer. She showed up, walking from the left side of the stage. It was a sudden and strong silent reaction from the crowd. A general suppression of breath, *oh-my-God*'s swallowed and air sucked suddenly in short intakes. The woman was enormous. She was tall and huge, her dress made from a vaporous gray-blue material, a floating iceberg. I liked her from the very first second. She knew how huge she is, and she knew her weight, in both physical and artistic dimensions. She walked up there full of confidence, without arrogance, without defiance. She was far above all of that. She was generously embracing the world at that huge chest of hers.

The director tapped on his music stand, the orchestra froze for a second in concentration, then, the enchantment commenced. After a few introductory bars, she started singing, spelling magic. A smooth, perfect voice, a human instrument of many tones. She sang for what seemed to be only a few minutes. It had been, in fact, more than an hour. The time had been shrunk by her magic. When she finished the last piece, there was a moment of silence, then the good folks in the audience stood up applauding frenetically and asking for encores. Hal had listened with his eyes closed, as if asleep. As the applause started, he looked at me and raised his eyebrows. I raised my hands, admitting. Damn good.

***

Hal Mason's car was a special order Deville. As American as a Cadillac can be. Hal was a patriot. The car wasn't one of those kitsch limousines, long and ridiculous. Strongly built, with custom reinforcements and suspensions and with a sophisticated finish, it had just the right room to comfortably fit two large leather guest seats across the empty space in the back fitted to accommodate his mobile mechanical chair.

Once in the car, Hal coughed extensively. I waited, helpless in my impossibility to help him. When finished, he rested his head back on the cushion of his chair, exhausted. I pretended to ignore the cough, like always, and fixed drinks, the usual.

Hal caught his breath.

"Okay," he sighed, exhausted, "Please, do tell."

I explained the whole mess, in order. Bronson's invitation, the Lockwell meeting, the NSA picture of the alien MORPHEM engine, the intel on the Chinese, and the surprising offer made by the government man, Jackobs. I didn't worry about secrecy. The information was safer with Hal than with anybody else. He kept his eyes closed while I spoke, only nodding once in a while. After I finished, we rode in silence for several minutes.

"What do you think about the intel on the Chinese?" he asked.

I shrugged. "It looks bad."

"Could they have done it on their own?"

"The Chinese? Designing the engine? Maybe."

I'd been twisting that question in my mind ever since the meeting.

"It's not impossible," I said. "But unlikely."

He tightened his lips in a severe line. His face had become hard, as if cut in stone.

"Unlikely," he repeated. "What sort of information did they need to fabricate a prototype, assuming it's not their idea?"

I sipped some scotch, thinking.

"Blue prints," I said. "CAD computer files."

Hal's eyes searched my face, sharply focused. He smiled and leaned back on his chair again.

"That's what I thought," he said, his smile still broad on his face, "CAD files."

We rode in silence again.

"What about the NSA picture?" he asked. "What do you think about it?"

Slowly, I moved my eyes away from his. There was a shadow of a thought, born as I kept recalling that picture in mind again and again. I didn't want to touch that thought.

"I don't know," I said.

"But is it the same kind of system?"

"Yes."

His face hardened again. He looked out through the windows, thinking. I watched the empty sidewalks as well. The car was riding west along the 3rd Street.

"That picture is a big problem," he said. "Even bigger than the Chinese problem."

"Why?"

He grinned. "Because that device is working. Because nobody knows who made it work. And because whoever made it work can sell it to anybody holding enough cash."

I didn't agree. The device in the picture was probably a crude prototype. The feel of the image suggested some amount of tinkering, some rudimentary set-up.

"What's gonna happen next?" I asked.

"They'll use you as leverage," Hal said. "You're at the center of many circles. Lockwell knows they're in some deep shit. They also understand they don't have the expertise, with all their patent rights."

"I'm nobody, Hal. I'm at the center of nothing. They threw me out."

"You just got back in."

"And who's gonna try use me?"

"Everyone. The government, the feds, Lockwell."

"Use me for what?"

"For their different agendas," Hal said, and leaned towards me. "I want you to understand one thing very well: you can't fight this alone. You'll call me any time you need help. You'll call me even if you don't need help. This is too big of a game, Matt. You're allowed no mistakes. Do you understand?"

I looked in my glass. It was empty. I didn't say anything.

Hal loosened his scrutiny on me, and leaned back on his chair. His face relaxed. The car was swinging comfortably, passing the slow cars on the city street, the driver ignoring the speed limit. After a while, the car slowed down, turned sharply and rode up the familiar driveway on Citrus street. The trip was over. Hal began coughing. I waited, while Ernesto opened the Deville's side door. He waited too.

Hal's coughing finally stopped. The outburst had exhausted him. I got out of the car, and Hal maneuvered the chair with its electric power to exit as well.

"Ernesto," he called in a whisper, "please take Matt back to his car. I'll be all right with Sam and the nurse."

Another man came from the house and held the car door open without a word. From the driveway, a ramp paved with pieces of dark red marble led towards a set of French doors in the back of the house. Through the doors I could see a nurse waiting. This was unusual for Hal. In the past, he wouldn't have allowed so many people around him. They would have irritated him beyond belief. If he allowed all that help, the state of his health was worse than I thought.

"Good night Hal," I said, "I'll keep you updated."

"Good night," he answered, his voice exhausted. "Remember, you can't play this alone. We'll talk."

I watched him driving his mobile chair up the ramp.

I loved Hal. It hurt tremendously to know he was dying, to watch him going down. Besides the emotion, I felt an acute feeling of waste. His brilliant mind, his wisdom, it was all going to be wasted soon. Perhaps that's why humanity always screws up and never learns, age after age. Because wisdom always goes down the drain.

"We can leave any time you're ready, Mr. Salagen," Ernesto said. "Where did you park?"

He was anxious to come back. He had become attached to the old man, just as I did, and considered Hal's security a personal responsibility. I got back into the DeVille, in the front seat.

We drove back taking the freeway, the heavy Deville, with its powerful V8 seeming to have a life of its own in Ernesto's hands. We made it back to Temple street without a word. I was ready to get out and say good night, when Ernesto raised a finger to draw my attention, then pressed it against his ear piece. He listened, squinting, then turned towards me.

"Mr. Salagen, it seems that a car had tailed us after the concert all the way. It's now parked two blocks down on Temple as well. We will see if it will tail us back or will follow you. Please be aware. I'll inform Mr. Mason."

I remembered the sense of being watched while having my drink before the concert. They could be Bronson's people, I thought.

"Thanks Ernesto," I said. "I'll watch for it. Don't bring more worries to the old man. Let's see first who it is."

He nodded with reluctance, and said good night. I watched the Deville take the turn on Hope Street and vanish in the night.

10

I remained standing next to the cold Mustang, keys in my hand. Down along Temple Street a long row of cars were parked in the dark. There was no motion, no trace of any presence. The cool night was full of distant sounds of traffic from the 101 and 110 freeways intersecting not too far away. Some Mexican music tunes blended with the noise of traffic. Distant headlights towards Grand and Broadway, and aircraft blinking lights were the only visible signs of life. The sidewalks were empty, just as my mind was empty of thoughts. Only random images and impressions came to life and vanished. The German soprano's voice, smoothing the insides of my chest. Harold's coughing. Jane's warm weight. Jane.

Jane.

I got in the car and brought life to the old V8. I drove east on Temple and swerved left on Main. East LA streets were empty, showing their graffiti to a starless dark sky. I kept driving on Main until I saw the buildings of the LA County Hospital. I guessed my way towards the buildings not very familiar with the area. One street took me to what appeared to be the entrance. I was confused. The previous night I had followed the ambulance without paying much attention to the itinerary, and then I had left, tired and absentminded. There was no recollection of the place.

I drove around and passed several gates, including one marked "EMERGENCY." Next to it there was another gate marked "Doctor's entrance." I entered that one and passed a security booth containing an apathetic Latino woman. I drove up an access ramp full of parked cars. Judging from those cars, most of the doctors were interns fresh out of college with heavy student loans not yet paid. The ramp ended in a parking structure, which appeared to be empty. I found a spot outside of the parking building for my Mustang as well.

I looked around, lost. Where could Jane be in this strange place?

I walked through the parking structure looking for an elevator. There was nobody around. Only an old Mercedes parked alone in the middle of the empty concrete space. The sound of electric ventilation reverberated on the concrete walls. A woman emerged from a hallway walking nervously on high heels. She saw me and seemed extremely uncomfortable.

"Do you know where the elevators are?" I asked her, and she tightened her lips fussing with the coat she was carrying.

"I'm looking for it myself," she said and then felt sorry for divulging this little truth.

She was afraid I was going to grab her, put my hand on her mouth and rape her right there in that ugly concrete building, behind the old and lonely Mercedes.

I left her alone with her little nightmare and walked through the parking rows. Through a large niche in the concrete, I saw a small hall opening and the elevator. I walked there and pushed the call button. The cage came down in a crawl. As I got in, I saw the thin woman approaching, walking fast behind me, and rushing up a flight of stairs.

I shrugged and went up a floor. When the door opened, the woman was there, waiting to get in. She hesitated, then seeing that I'm getting out, she sneaked in the elevator. When the elevator door was about to close, I stuck my foot in, and stopped it.

"Do you know, by any chance, where the information desk is?" I asked while propping the door back open.

"Leave me alone!" she cried, then pointed nervously to a door with a dark stained glass window in it. "Take that door!" she urged, "See that door? It takes you to the main lobby, please, leave me alone!" She was both scared and irritated.

"Thanks. You're very kind," I said, and withdrew my foot.

I went through the door she had pointed to. It led to the main entrance, indeed. It was a dark and very spacious hall. The LA County Hospital had been built before the last world war. Its style, the hallway volumes and space were typical for those times.

Two security guards were watching me. They were dressed in the typical navy blue coat and gray slacks, made of synthetic fabric. The younger man was black, while the older one seemed a dark skinned Latino, the darkness of his skin accentuated by the carefully combed white hair.

"How do I get to Emergency?" I asked them straight, already tired of the search.

"Are you looking for a patient, sir?"

"Yes, a friend."

"OK, sir, first please leave all metal objects on this box here and go through the detector, all right sir?"

I did it. Nothing beeped. I grabbed my keys, change, lighter and a pen.

"OK sir, now please go through this door and follow the red lines on the floor, and look for room 3850. All right sir?"

I thanked them and left. The hallways were wide and tall, the floors mopped clean. People were scattered around, walking slowly from an unknown direction to another. They were all Latinos. Mexicans, Ecuadorians, people from El Salvador. Tired people, young men, old women, a few younger women with children. I found a large board, up on the ceiling, pointing me to the room 3850. The board was mounted above long rows of mail-boxes. Further down the hall a sign read "Police Station." Maybe they even had a Mayor's office. Room 3850 was not a room, but a section of the hospital. The large hallways crossed in wide intersections, with corners guarded by bored security guards, dressed in oversized blue coats, gray nylon slacks and worn out shoes. I found the way to Emergency. As I tried to enter the hallway towards it, one of the security guys barred my way.

"Excuse me, sir?" he said, politely.

He was a middle aged man, speaking with a strong Spanish accent.

"I am trying to get to Emergency," I said, patiently, "I'm looking for a friend."

"Ok, sir, you need to wait until eleven, then access is open. You can wait in the cafeteria, if you want, please."

"Why can't I go right now?"

"Sir, I'm sorry, you need to wait until eleven."

He was just doing his job. Perhaps there was the evening doctor's visit going on. I slowly took out my wallet, casually, as if looking for a name. I slipped out a twenty dollars bill.

"Listen," I said, "I just need to find out where my friend is, a room number or something."

He eyed the twenty and quickly looked around. No matter how discreet I was, the bill must have made some typical sound on a frequency to which the people around were highly sensitive. Faces had turned towards us, shiny eyes following our moves.

"Sir," the guard said, a bit louder than before, "you need to wait until eleven, it's not too long, please. The cafeteria is right over there."

I watched him with calm. I folded the twenty in a thin roll, and talked softly to him.

"Her name is Jane. She was brought in this morning, an overdose, probably China white, you know, heroine. I need to speak to her and I would appreciate your help. I'll go in the cafeteria and wait, okay?"

The cafeteria was half full with the same people of mixed Latino origin. Their faces had features reminding me of the Navajo men in the Havasu reservation. Very little real Spanish blood in the poor searching for a better life in LA. It was only the language they had inherited from the conquistadors.

I waited. At one table, a group seemed to be in better spirits. Laughter could be heard several times. Two of the women wore short skirts showing voluptuous thighs. On a wall, a picture from 1930's showed a group of nurses. They were all white women, dressed in starched white uniforms, with clean, unattractive faces. I smiled at the irony. None of the people around the place was white, except for me.

Somebody coughed behind me. It was the security guard.

"Sir," he said, "it's hard to go ask, but I did go sir. I asked about the woman, sir."

He stopped. I made the rolled twenty appear from between my fingers. He didn't trust me, didn't say anything, didn't move. I thrust my hand forward.

"It is good to meet you again, my friend," I said, freeing the rolled bill into his hand. "Please tell me what you found."

He fought the impulse to pocket the bill immediately. He brought his hands together and smiled uneasily.

"The woman Jane, sir, she left this afternoon."

"She was discharged?"

"No sir, she left."

"Left? How do you know, did you ask the office?"

"No sir, I know."

"What do you mean you know? What do you know?"

"She left sir, she just left. She had some treatment to do, and she had no clothes. A friend mine, security here and another security guy here, they got called to look for her, but she just left. The doctor was very upset."

I tried recalling the name, "Doctor Fuentes?"

"Yes, sir. Doctor De Fuentes, it was his patient. Also people from some office downtown came to talk to her. That is all sir, they looked for her and didn't find her, she left."

He nodded a few more times, and turned to leave.

"Did she go home?" I asked absurdly.

He looked at me, uneasily. He had spent too much time off his corner of duty.

"She left, sir. Just gone. How would I know where the woman go?"

I let him leave. It was all stupid of my part, time wasted. I walked back the long hallways out through the guarded doors, and found out that the door with the tinted window was locked. I couldn't go back to the elevator. A card reader with a red light on was next to the door. The doctors probably had some access cards to go back to their cars. I went back to the security guards, asking them to open the door for me. I was growing tired, impatient.

"Sir, you came through that door sir? That's the doctor's door sir, you must have a card key. Do you have a card key?"

"No, I have no fucking card! All I want is get back to my car, OK?"

"We cannot give you access, sir, under no circumstance, sir, all right sir?"

I tried to calm down. I didn't want any complication, I had no more stomach for anything.

"Okay," I said, "please explain to me how can I get to that part of the building," and I pointed to the approximate direction I came from.

"All right sir, you must go out through the main door, right there sir, and go left all around sir, all right sir?"

I just left. I wandered around the building, walking along ramps that looked unfamiliar, until I found myself out on an empty street full of graffiti. I walked back, trying to think. Then, through an open wrought iron gate, I just saw my old Mustang. I had no idea it could be there. And then, I realized the concrete parking structure where I had met the nervous woman was just cutting though the lower floor across the main entrance above, from one side of the building to the other.

I got in the car and drove home.

***

The house was quiet, dark. I filled a glass with ice cubes and poured Jack Daniels over them. The night asked for some Coltrane music. I searched for a CD and played and old Blue Note recording and I sat down, listening, drinking. I remembered the Devil in my dream. Funny, I thought, it had the voice of an old friend.

11

The big trucks clogging the 5 freeway north made me arrive at Lockwell thirty minutes late.

"I'll take you straight to McNutt," Meinhardt said while escorting me again through the Lockwell grounds. "From there you're on your own, I gotta go back and make sure I get enough space for the damn computers. We're all being moved to A-25."

On the fifth floor of the HQ building he led me along a short hallway towards a large mahogany desk. The desk was decorated with a blond woman dressed in an exquisite beige business suit. Aged around thirty five, her body was fit and slender, the low cut of her coat falling in a well shaped cleavage which revealed the exact amount of body detail allowed by political correctness in corporate America. She was McNutt's secretary.

"Hi Jennie," Meinhardt greeted the woman. "This is Matt Salagen. He's all yours." He patted me on the shoulder. "Here you go pal," he said. "Good luck on whatever it is you're here for. Keep it up, we'll be making animal sacrifices and burn incents for you in the A-25 temple back there. Keep the damn money coming. Also tell McNutt how fucking marvelous we think the new cubicles are."

The blond woman stood up while Meinhardt said his good bye. She looked at him as if he was some sort of a pest infesting her environment. As Meinhardt walked away, she turned towards me and her face changed dramatically. An elaborate smile got composed by her delicate face muscles. Her eyes were on my eyes. I had her full attention.

"Dr. Salagen, as I understand?" she said with feeling. My presence was giving a new meaning to her life.

"I do apologize for being late," I said. "Bad traffic."

"Oh, isn't it awful?" she chirped. "Just this morning, on my way here I saw an accident! Mr. McNutt and Mr. Jackobs are waiting for you, Dr. Salagen." She delivered the statements with equal emphasis on each. She was a perfect mechanical doll. I wandered if she had a secret button, and I imagined it being pushed, as I walked inside McNutt's office.

McNutt sat at his large shiny desk, laid back on his leather chair. A meeting table extended from McNutt's desk towards the door. Seated on one of the side leather chairs, was Stan Jackobs.

In spite of McNutt's relaxed attitude the atmosphere in the room seemed tense. Jackobs rose from his chair.

"Dr. Salagen," he said, offering his hand, "I am glad you made it."

McNutt only nodded. He motioned towards the chairs around the table and played it friendly.

"Take a seat, Matt," he said. "We were wandering if you'd received Stan's invitation."

"Yes I did. I do apologize for the delay. Very bad traffic."

"Can't you rocket scientists do something about this traffic?" Jackobs joked. "It can't be as complicated as one of these engines, can it?"

"Please help yourself with some coffee, Matt," McNutt invited and pointed to a coffee-maker in a corner.

I walked to the coffeemaker and poured me a cup. A porcelain cup just like the ones I remembered from the previous meeting.

Jackobs shuffled a stack of papers in front of him.

"Dr. Salagen," he said, "let me get straight to the point. I believe we are initiating a valuable R&D program here, and, as I already proposed at the meeting last week, I also believe we can use, and we should use, all the best talent available."

He paused, shortly, as if waiting for a reply. I said nothing. McNutt had returned to his regular frowning grimace.

"We would like to make you an offer," Jackobs continued. "And we'd like to discuss it here, all cards on the table."

I used my hands on the coffee cup; lifted it to my lips, made sure I didn't spill. I made myself enjoy the taste. McNutt's secretary was brewing some good stuff.

"Looks like things are moving fast, Mr. Jackobs" I said. "I hear the MORPHEM people are being moved from A-21 to A-25."

"Yes," he confirmed. "Like I said, the program has been initiated."

"What is your proposition, Mr. Jackobs?"

He locked his fingers, elbows on the table.

"Dr. Salagen," he started, "the reassessment of the MORPHEM technology is a very unconventional project. We need good monitoring of the new project, and a competent survey of the progress being made, essentially a good understanding of what is being done."

"One thing, Mr. Jackobs," I interrupted. "If I may ask, who is 'we'? Who is it that you are representing?"

"Fair question," he said. "I represent here a consortium of government agencies which are financing this new research. I can give you a list with details if you wish. Does this answer your question?"

"I believe it does."

"Good, we're clear here. In short, Dr. Salagen, we offer to employ your services in monitoring this program. The offer is this: you will monitor the progress on the MORPHEM contract and provide the periodic progress reports, and in general you will be responsible for the full reporting activity during the MORPHEM reassessment work."

He stood up, and walked to the window wall, pacing back and forth.

"I have discussed this with Craig," he continued, pointing to McNutt. "We believe this would be a good use of your expertise, to the mutual benefit of all parties involved."

"Is Lockwell OK with this?" I asked.

McNutt leaned forward in his chair, hands on the desk.

"I must clarify a certain position we have, Matt," he said, directly. "I've discussed the context of your litigation with us with Stan, and we agreed that it is of the best interest of all parties to put everything behind us. The point is that you have a certain expertise, and in the present situation, which has a certain level of emergency, we can use all the good people we can get."

I watched him as he spoke. He had practiced the short speech.

"How are we going to do this, formally?" I asked.

Jackobs leaned back on his chair, masking a certain relaxation. He knew I can't afford to refuse the offer.

"We will have a draft of a contract for you," he said.

"Who am I contracting with?"

Jackobs cleared his throat.

"There is a special arrangement. Given the sensitivity of the entire project, and the necessity of special financial mechanisms, the several government agencies which I am representing have set-up a special corporate entity referred to as the Joint Consortium Agency. This corporation operates under the leadership of a board of directors. I am a member of this board. The MORPHEM contract with the Lockwell Corporation is written with us. Your contract will be written with us as well."

"Who is the MORPHEM project team leader?" I asked.

"Dr. Varese has been appointed to the position."

It was to be expected.

"This arrangement will create conflicts," I said. "Varese will continuously try to block my access to data."

"You will have a word to say, as an expert consultant," Jackobs said.

"That doesn't mean anything, Mr. Jackobs. I need access to all the information."

Jackobs cut it. "There will be no room for local politics, Dr. Salagen," he said. "We're here to make things work. If things don't work, and you have something to say about it, there will be plenty of people listening. Perhaps that doesn't give you a direct power of decision, but it gives you enough leverage"

I didn't like the arrangement. I also knew I had to keep something separate, away from them, out of their reach.

"I have one request, Mr. Jackobs," I said.

Jackobs smiled, broadly.

"Well," he replied, in good mood, "let's hear it."

"I want a separate contract, with funding for the theoretical analysis of the physics underlying the MORPHEM concept. With this contract, I would like access to the NASA Advanced Supercomputing Division facilities at Moffet Field."

Jackobs smile froze in a grin. McNutt only raised his eyebrows. NAS was a very powerful computational center, ranked third in the world.

"Dr. Salagen, Jackobs said, why would you separate…" He stopped in the middle of the question, thinking. His smile became genuine. "That's not a bad idea," he said. He thought more about it and continued. "When can you get me a proposal?"

McNutt kept his eyebrows raised with a cold smile. He had already estimated that my request didn't cost Lockwell any money.

"I need about a week." I said.

"A week is OK," Jackobs said.

He was pleased. He grabbed again the stack of papers in front of him and meticulously chose a page. He spoke while examining it.

"I've browsed the reports from your previous work at Lockwell, Dr. Salagen," he said. "Excellent work. And an excellent team, I'd say. Would you consider collaborating again with the same people?"

"Lockwell people?"

"Yes."

"Who is it you have on that list, Mr. Jackobs?"

He caressed the surface of the page with his fine hands.

"Robert Cruiff for example" he said. "Is he available?" he asked turning his head towards McNutt.

McNutt approved with a deep nod of his head.

"Yes, Bob's with us. Our top CAD modeling and design expert."

"Good," Jackobs said, and raised his eyebrows towards me.

"No problem," I said.

Jackobs examined the sheet again.

"Xiao Lin?"

McNutt nodded again.

"No problem," I said.

"John Meinhardt?"

"Sure."

"Stefan Mora?"

I stood silent. Jackobs turned his head again towards McNutt.

"Mr. Mora worked here as a consultant," McNutt said. "We let him go a while back."

"What was his expertise?" Jackobs asked.

"Physics of dense plasmas." I said.

"Was he good?"

"Very good."

Jackobs reached for his briefcase laid on a chair next to him. He extracted several files, chose one, and opened it.

"You had a special relationship with Mr. Mora, besides work, is that correct?"

"Yes," I said.

"How did you meet Mr. Mora?"

"We worked together back in Europe, many years back."

"You were working for the Soviet Block, at the time. Mr. Mora defected to Turkey in 1987, I see here," Jackobs said.

"Yes," I said. "At the time, we were working together at a national research institute in Bucharest."

"And you arrived in the US in 1990?"

"Yes."

"How did you meet Mr. Mora here in the US?"

"I met him at a physics seminar, here in town. In fact, it was Stefan Mora who suggested I should apply for a position with Lockwell."

"Did he facilitate it?"

"No, he just indicated there were openings."

"When was this?"

"In 92."

"Indeed a long way back"

"That's correct."

"Are you in touch with Mr. Mora now?"

"No."

"My understanding is that you two were friends?"

"We drifted apart, I would say."

"But would you collaborate on the reassessment project should Mr. Mora be available?"

"Yes."

"Well, let's try getting him back. From what I read here in these resumes, Mr. Mora seems the essential guy you may want. I strongly suggest we should get him back."

"I could try," I said. "Either here at Lockwell, or for the computations I am planning."

"Very well," Jackobs glanced at McNutt, "Lockwell OK with that?"

McNutt shrugged.

"If you think it's essential, Stan, I have no problem."

They both looked at me.

"I'll see if I can locate Stefan Mora," I said.

"Excellent," Jackobs said.

He was ready to close the meeting. He stood up and we shook hands. I shook McNutt's hand as well. He pushed the intercom button.

"Jenny, could you please call Meinhardt or somebody from MORPHEM to escort Salagen. I meant Dr. Salagen. Thanks."

"Well, Matt," he addressed me again, "soon you won't need an escort through Lockwell. Welcome back."

I offered him my rubber smile.

1 2

"I need to see Cruiff," I told Meinhardt once outside the building.

"All right, follow me. What's the news, you back for good?"

"In a week or so," I said.

He made an appreciative grimace and led me to the A-25 building at a fast pace.

Inside, boxes with documentation, computers and books were all over the place, in the corridors, within the maze of cubicles. IT people were busy pulling wires, drilling holes, connecting the network links and powering up machines.

Meinhardt pointed to Cruiff, who was carrying a big box.

"Here's the man. Call me when you're ready to leave."

"Thanks," I said, and walked towards Cruiff's office. It was a real office, not a cubicle, given his seniority.

"You on board?" he asked as he carefully placed the big box on the floor.

"In a week."

He looked at me and rubbed his ear.

"I heard some things," he said and unwrapped a piece of chewing gum, placing it in his mouth. He watched me carefully. I shook my head.

"You may hear even more things. That's all I can say. There is money, and there is work."

Cruiff raised his eyebrows and shook his head. He removed the piles of boxes from two chairs and sat down on one pointing to the other one in a muted invitation. I sat down, and dragged the chair closer to him.

"I heard Varese saying there are two more engine cores left."

"That's correct," Cruiff said.

"Where are the parts?"

"We have them in storage."

"They're important, Bob. I need forensics on those parts, both of them. Geometry."

"We can arrange that," Cruiff said.

"One other thing. I also heard you guys lost the CAD files for the entire project."

Cruiff blew air through his tightened lips in a long exhale.

"We used to store the model files on a share server, as you may remember," he explained. "Secure access, encryption, all that. Somehow, a large part of the files got corrupted. They're there in their folders, but they cannot be read into the CAD system."

"How did they get corrupted?"

"IT can't figure that out. The files contain garbage."

"Can't you restore them from the back-up?"

"We tried. The back-up files are corrupted as well, up to three layers back."

"I need the geometry of the test engine," I said. "I will require the back-up core parts measured by the Coordinate Measurement Machine lab. Those parts must be secured, Bob. It's crucial."

He understood. His face expression didn't change but he understood.

"I'll take care of it," he said.

"And I have one more thing to ask you"

He grinned. "Yes, sonny?"

I picked a pencil from his desk and played with it.

"I need a CAD model for a new engine design," I said. "Concept level. I don't care for nuts and bolts. Just volumes and walls."

"Which design are we talking about?"

"Only a concept. My concept."

He frowned. "Awright," he said, "Tell me what you need, in detail, and then I'll tell you what I need to make it happen."

I started sketching, using the pencil. He followed the sketch and asked questions. We worked more on it and established a work plan. He needed geometry, curves, coordinates. We agreed on a format.

"How long is this going to take?" I asked, at the end.

"If you give me everything I need when I need it, no more than a week."

I nodded. "We need special handling on this, Bob."

He leaned back on his tall leather chair and fixed me with his blue eyes. "Like?" he said.

"Like keeping this model under the radar."

He raised his eyebrows. "How low under the radar, stranger?"

"As low as it is right now. Just you and me."

He grinned again. "That figures. I'll see what I can do."

I thanked him and left. Meinhardt escorted me back to the Gate A where he threw a quick good-bye and ran back. A woman guard showed me her beautiful white teeth, and I was out in the sun.

1 3

I leaned against my old Mustang, hands stuck in my pockets. I was trying to think, but my mind was stuck on some elusive thought running in the back of my head. I raised my face in the sun, and remembered calmly, almost with curiosity, my evening at Point Dume. Then, I knew where I had to go.

I drove across the Valley, and took the 405 South. The traffic was a crawl and my mind empty of thoughts. I filled it with radio news. An airplane had crashed. No bomb, just crashed, back East. The news men talked about strong air vorticity and then switched to child abuse and education. Not enough money was allocated for computers and materials. A girl's parents had sued a school in LA because she wasn't allowed to walk at graduation due to a failed math class. I switched to a talk radio show. The talk show host from New York was introducing the latest CD with fart and belching sounds. Finally, a great product made in the USA.

Traffic eased up by the Getty center. I exited on Sunset, and cut it through the city towards West Hollywood.

The street was quiet. Sounds from an Oprah TV show came from a window. At the corner, two men were talking, leaning against the cars parked at the curb. They watched me carefully, figuring me out.

The faulty security gate let me in, with its lock stuck open. On the second floor I opened the door, without giving a thought to the idea of ringing the bell. The living room looked deserted. Magazines were thrown on the floor. But the apartment was not empty, I felt it. I remembered the way to Jane's room and walked across the empty living room towards it.

The room had been cleaned out, no bed sheets, closets doors open, showing empty shelves, as if ready for rent. Jane was lying in bed, her back against the wall, eyes closed, white wires running from a small white music player to the plugs on her ears. I touched her hair and she opened her eyes. Their black fixed on me without any smile.

I sat down on the edge of the bed.

"How are you doing?" I asked, feeling silly.

She took off the ear plugs, and arranged her long blonde hair.

"I was waiting for you," she said.

14

I brought her home. I showed her my old makeshift bedroom. The room had a bed and a small bathroom with a shower.

"This is good," she said. "Thank you."

"There are some other rooms," I said. "Not much furniture, I had to sell stuff."

"No, this is one is good. Thank you."

"Let me know if you need anything."

"I need sleep," she said.

"Then go ahead and sleep," I said.

She did. I heard the shower for a few minutes, and then nothing. Nothing for hours.

The night came. I checked on her; she was curled in bed, embracing the pillow, deep asleep.

I walked back into the living room and poured an inch of scotch and sat down, drinking it slowly. Sometimes, scotch helps you listen to the time flying by.

***

I checked again in the morning, the following day. She was in the same state, deeply asleep. I waited for a few moments by the bed, making sure I hear her breath. She was breathing all right, almost without noise, long regular breaths of a good sleep.

I let her sleep.

I went into the office room and sat down, collecting my thoughts. It was time to start working again. The deep dig at the mystery. I unlocked a large safe box made of steel. There, in a drawer, lay an old notebook. There was a hand written name on the cover, Matei Salajan. My old name, the way it was spelled in Romanian. Under the title, there was scribbled a year. 1989.

At the end of the notebook, there were several pages of tabulated numbers. I started reading the handwritten notes from the note book, consulting the results from the table. It was slow. I hadn't touched that work in more than two years. The brain, the mind and intelligence of a scientist are similar to the body of an athlete. The performance degrades proportional to the lack of practice. I had difficulties following my own notes, my own thoughts and ideas of several years back.

Yet, I persevered. Giving up would have meant a trip back to Point Dume. I made new notes in pencil. Slowly, the information was being absorbed and reactivated in my mind. I kept working without breaks for the rest of the day, making photocopies of specific pages in the old notebook, and annotating them. I got hungry, but I kept working until everything became fuzzy and blurry, until the pain in my back grew into numbness.

Only then I stopped. It was early evening, red sunset light still lingering on the top slopes of the San Gabriels. I hit the scotch again, relaxing on the old worn-out leather couch in the study. It felt good, to have stopped thinking, let the alcohol take over and relax both neurons and muscles.

I thought I closed my eyes for only a second. But when I opened them back, the house was dark and quiet, the day's sun gone. The only light was coming from a lamp in a different room. A vague shape was contoured next to the desk. I focused my eyes on it. The shape was Jane's back. She was looking at my papers, without moving. Her naked back was beautifully contoured in the faint light. She was wearing a towel around her waist, her arms folded on her breasts.

I moved on the couch and her shoulders jerked at the noise. She turned towards me, slowly, dropping her hands along the sides of her body, watching me with an impenetrable expression on her face. I watched her body with unexpected hunger, beautiful round breasts with firm and small nipples, a flat and smooth belly, wet hair falling on her shoulders and touching the very fine line of the collarbone. She stepped towards me while her hands slowly removed the towel and let it fall on the floor. She stopped by the edge of the couch looking down at me, pushing the image of her body in my eyes, without thrust, but without shyness.

I didn't move. Her body language was as impenetrable as her face. Before I could decide or think what to do, she mounted me in a slow but definite move. I touched her knees, feeling the warmth of her flesh though my jeans. She pushed my shirt up and caressed my chest in long and well-felt strokes, her face not loosing the impenetrable look. I pulled her towards me, and she came almost as close as to kiss me, then she avoided my lips and kissed my temple, and then felt my neck with her lips, tracking the line of my collar bone. She kissed my nipples and I gently pushed her up. I wanted my nipples left alone. She cambered up, not liking the rejection, her hands in my hands, intertwined fingers, holding herself against me. She watched me again, as if in a duel, then she started to move her hips slowly, feeling me as I was getting hard, still holding her weight up against my hands. I tensed my abdominal muscles.

"I haven't touched a woman in three years," I said.

The expression of her face changed slightly. I couldn't read what the change meant. Slowly, she eased the tension of her body camber, released my hands from the grip of her fingers, turned my palms around, and pressed them against her breasts. She kept watching me, while very slowly driving my hands up and down.

"Then, it's about time to touch one again," she said.

***

The cool Monday morning air came through the open terrace doors and crept under the thin blanket. Jane's body was warm, but my back felt the light grip of the cold and I woke up. I didn't move, however. Holding Jane's body was a forgotten joy suddenly brought back to my male instinct. I extended the moment, ignoring the cold morning air and breathing in sync with her, feeling her arms holding mine wrapped around her.

I slid out from under the blanket, found another, thicker one and covered Jane who moaned softly. I fixed breakfast and drank coffee, thinking of Stefan Mora, and the insistence of the government man, Jackobs, to find him. It made sense, assembling the old team together. But with Mora, it was going to be difficult.

Jane walked in, naked. Her face was rested and fresh. She'd brushed her teeth and combed her hair. She leaned on my shoulder kissing me lightly and then took a sip from my coffee cup.

"Can I have some of this?" she asked, in a natural way, as if she'd been coming naked every morning in my life, in my house, for years. I watched her, trying to grasp the reality of her presence.

"Sure," I said. "Aren't you cold?"

She smiled, and sat down.

"Not really," she answered. "I feel good."

I fixed more espresso, threw some croissants in the electric toaster, and cut strawberries in small chunks. When everything was ready, I brought it all in front of her, coffee, croissants, butter, jelly, fruit, orange juice.

She was hungry. She ate like a wild animal, fast, vigorously. That wild animal hidden in her was not defenseless. Something in her body language suggested she was no prey.

I watched her, trying to understand how much I liked the change brought by her very presence. I recalled rolling her on the narrow coach the night before and the image mixed with the memory of her body lying inert, warm and with that good weight in my arms when I found her dying.

"Any plans for today?" I asked.

She sipped some coffee and shrugged, "I have no plans."

I sipped some of my coffee. It was bitter and cold.

"Let's go out for dinner when I come back from work," I said.

She raised her face and watched me.

"Do you want to have dinner or make love to me?" she asked, leaning forward, getting as close as having me feel her breath. It smelled of coffee, butter, and a strange good scent of her own.

"I want to feel alive," I said.

15

"It's there, in the second building, if you remember," Cruiff said, walking ahead. "We've got the core already on the machine."

We entered a hall lit by strong fluorescent lights. The floor was covered with sticky sheets of plastic to remove the dirt from the soles of our shoes. An electric brush and vacuum machine cleaned the rest of the footwear. From behind a counter, a tiny Chinese woman came and handed us clean white covers for our clothes, white caps and gloves. The precision measurement machines were located in a large CCCR - climate controlled clean room. We both looked ridiculous in the protective gear.

The CCCR hosted two large Coordinate Measurement Machines, known as CMM's. Each machine consisted of a large, massive and carefully polished granite platform, and a complicated frame of robotic mechanisms moving and pointing a sensor around the edges and contours of the object to be measured. On one of the platforms there was a large and complicated metal part, the MORPHEM engine core. An operator was controlling the robotic motion of the sensor with what appeared to be a sophisticated relative of a video game controller. Standing behind the operator was a tall man, completely bald. His face had no trace of any hair, no eyebrows, no eyelashes. He had an extremely clean look, wearing spotless rimless eyeglasses. His name was Henry Hoover. We knew him, he was the master of the place.

Cruiff shook his hand. "How're you doin' H.H.?"

"Gentlemen," Hoover nodded a greeting and inspected me with a pair of cold eyes. "Matt Salagen, the prodigal son" he said. "Welcome back."

His shake was firm though the clean glove. I smiled and said nothing. It was a bad idea to answer Hoover's caustic comments.

"You're on it already?" Cruiff asked, jerking his thumb towards the shiny steel piece fixed on the platform.

"Not yet. We're just making calibrations. Besides, you boys haven't told me what you want."

"That's his call," Cruiff pointed at me.

I leaned forward and looked at the engine core. The inner volume was an annulus, extended several inches, then opening up into an oval plenum and ending with a thick flange. Opposite to the flanged end was an injector plate, and about half way in between the two, five fixtures extending in both axial and radial directions.

"I'm interested in two things H.H.," I said. "First the symmetries. I want the inner and the outer cylindrical surfaces within the core, their concentricity, the alignment of the injector plate with the rest of the volume. I need the walls picked up with as good resolution as you can for volume identification. Secondly, the alignment of the branch ducts, I need the angles and displacement of each confinement volume, and the location where the five axes intersect in the main volume."

I indicated the locations as I spoke, touching the part lightly with my gloved hand. Hoover had listened carefully. He shook his head, and eyed Cruiff.

"It's gonna take weeks," he said.

The electric mechanism of the main door buzzed on and the door opened. Three more men came in. Varese led the group followed by two side-kicks. His eyes searched our faces, identifying each one. Without any greeting he studied the engine part fixed on the platform.

"What's the status?" he asked Hoover, as he leaned forward and placed his hands on the platform, further studying the engine part.

"I'd appreciate if you didn't lean on the platform," Hoover said, coldly. "We're doing calibrations for the reference coordinates, that's the status. And as massive as this stone looks like, it can still pick up some effect of your weight."

Varese straightened up, reluctantly.

"Did you set up a schedule for the measurements?" he asked extracting his PDA.

"Are you giving me the requirements?"

"You don't need requirements!" Varese replied sharlpy. "Get interface dimensions, and confirm datum points at concept level."

"No detail?" Hoover asked.

"No need." Varese said. "We'll have new CAD models when we redesign this thing."

"If that's what you want," Hoover said, glancing at me with his cold eyes. "Salagen wants more detail."

Varese narrowed his eyes on Hoover. "What detail?" he asked.

"I want thorough measurement of all volumes" I said. "Especially the core confinement volume."

The room went quiet. Varese straightened and faced me, coldly.

"It's not up to you to set up requirements," he said. "What you're asking is a waste of money and time."

"Geometry is crucial." I said.

"Keep your theories for yourself," Varese sneered. "They're garbage."

The air in the room had become charged. Hoover was enjoying it.

"Funny," Cruiff said, "if I think about what you two are requesting is not that much different." He turned towards Hoover. "Watch this H.H." he asked. "If you have the sensor doing travels towards the diameters you can have the machine pick up points along the wall. I can help you write vectoring scripts for guidance."

Hoover played it along. He didn't even glance at the part.

"Yes, that's possible. I believe there is no more than ten to fifteen percent extra time required for that, and in fact it would improve the measurements per specification with better reference."

He delivered the bullshit without blinking. He had understood the necessity of detailed measurements from the beginning and it was clear to everyone in the room that he was going to make those measurements no matter what Varese said.

Varese understood. "I expect a schedule," he said. "And Henry, one more thing. The measurement data is confidential. It will be reported to me, and to me only."

He turned and walked towards the door, with the two sidekicks following him, without greeting, without any other word. By the door, he turned towards Hoover one more time.

"Don't fuck with me on this, Henry. That data will stay locked until I say otherwise."

He stepped through the automatic door and left, followed by his men.

There was silence in the room, broken only by the sound of the fans cooling the CMM machines' electronics.

"Well, send me those vectoring scripts" Hoover said, addressing Cruiff. "We'll just see how fast this goes."

"You bet," Cruiff accepted.

We shook hands and left. I let Cruiff walk back to his building alone. I had to get some answers in the investigation before Varese would screw it up one way or another. But I needed extra brain power.

16

I turned left on Bali Way in Marina del Rey and made my way to the north dock's parking lot. Low clouds gave the ocean a gray shade which made the boats in the marinas appear tired of all that water.

The gate towards the boat slips was locked. I looked around for someone to help. A minivan drove up Bali until it reached the dead end and turned back. From the water side of the fence an old man showed up and walked towards the gate, carrying two rolls of rope. I waited until he unlocked the gate, held the gate open for him, and then entered the dock area. He hesitated at my intrusion, but swallowed his question and kept going. I let the gate slam shut behind me and walked towards the water.

Suddenly, the feeling of being watched hit me again. I turned. The old man was still walking slowly towards the parking lot. There was no one else in sight. I swept the surroundings carefully again. Several cars were scattered around the parking spaces, cold and empty.

I resumed my walk towards the boats.

I reached the fourth row. The long sailboat I was searching for was docked at the third slip. Her upper deck was made of dark wood, old but shiny and well maintained. The reels and the supports for the ropes and sails were well kept and spotless, functional, yet with a flavor of a museum piece. Memories flashed in front of my eyes. There had been some good times on that boat.

Tobacco smoke rose from the aft. A blonde woman was smoking a cigarette, leaning on the boat's rail, facing the water. There was a wonderful grace in the line of her neck, in the beautiful blonde-white hair cut at the shoulder level. She was wearing a thick, comfortable brown sweater, and loose fit white cotton jeans. At the sound of my steps she turned towards me. The surprise on her face mixed quickly with a faint shade of joy.

"Matei!" she exclaimed, and then the joy vanished and her face darkened. Then, she recomposed her face.

"I wouldn't have thought..." she started, and then stopped, watching me and subduing her initial impulse. "What is it that could bring you here?"

I climbed on the boat.

"Hello Cam," I said. "Good to see you."

Her face had aged slightly, from what I remembered. "How long it's been?" I asked, "two years?"

"Three years, Matei" she said, searching my face while drawing smoke and blowing it out in the wind. "You're looking for Stefan, I can see," she continued. "He's in there. Drank himself to death last night." She drew smoke again. "I don't care to stop him anymore" she added, turning away from me, towards the water, as she was when I arrived.

"How are things, Cam?" I asked her, gently.

There was pain and resentment in her body language, on her features. She kept smoking as if she hadn't heard my question. I waited.

"Not good," she answered after a long delay. "We lost the house. We're living on the boat now. It's cheaper than renting, thank God for the boat slip. Stefan drinks every day. We can't even think of a relationship, it's mostly survival. I'm teaching, part time." She looked at me again, this time searching my face with unhidden curiosity. "What about you?" she asked.

I sat down on one of the seats around the steering column.

"Christine finally left," I spoke softly. "She moved back to France and took Julia with her. I tried to blow my brains off on a beach after they left, but someone has gotten me out of it."

She pushed the pack of Marlboro towards me and I lit one for myself.

"I'm involved again in my old project with Lockwell," I went on. "I have a contract in the works. I'd like to work with Stefan on this one. I expect it to be good, although the situation is a bit complex. I need to know if he'd be willing to work with me on this."

She threw her cigarette in a small metal container and sat down. She held her thighs with her hands, and tightened her legs, shivering.

"I don't know," she answered. She raised her head and looked at me, a quiet desperation settling on her eyes. "I don't know him anymore. He's become a strange man. A stranger, sharing the same bed with me. We never mention you, or Christine. Our old life is all but a shadow of the past." She lowered her head again. "I don't know him anymore, Matei," she repeated.

Noise came from the cabin and a man came out. He was tall and thin, his strong bones in contrast with his apparent lack of mass. His gray hair was long, clean but uncombed, giving him, along with the thick beard, a savage look. Stefan Mora's gray blue eyes brushed past me and found his wife where she sat with her head lowered, shivering. I noticed the many fine lines around the eyes, the wear on the skin, the deep lines on his cheeks. He walked to the very aft of the boat and lit a pipe he produced from his pocket. Cam didn't appear to notice him.

"What the fuck are you doing here?" he asked, as if addressing the water.

I weighed Mora's stance and understood there was only one way to deal with him, straight.

"I'm back in the MORPHEM project with Lockwell," I said. "I also have a contract in the works to do computer simulations on the MORHEM physics. I'm promised access to the supercomputers at the NAS center. I can use your brain on a task like this, and that's what I'm doing here. Think of it and let me know if you're interested or not."

I finished speaking uncertain of the result. Stefan Mora had worked his pipe while listening. Cam had raised her face watching him too.

He drew smoke from the pipe and blew it through his teeth, his jaw tight on the pipe. Then he took the pipe off his mouth and leaned forward on the rail.

"I'm not interested," he spoke, facing the water. "Do me a favor, get out and leave."

He meant it. There was no point in trying to argue, convince him. I stood up, climbed the rail and stepped on the dock.

"It was good seeing you two," I said, turning to leave.

"Matei," Cam called. She watched me, hesitating. "Is it true? Did you really try ending it?"

"Ending it?"

"On a beach, you said? Was it Point Dume?"

I thought about it, the image of the beach in the night, the trooper's flashlight in my eyes, Hal's voice.

"I'll never really know, Cam. I was as close as one can get without really doing it." I sensed her thoughts. "I'm really glad I was stopped," I added. "It would've been pointless."

My words hung in the air, then went away with the wind. I turned around and left.

I drove back to Pasadena without paying attention to the traffic. I let my instincts and my reflexes take care of that. I was thinking of the Mora's.

***

Cam hadn't changed. Her full name was Camelia, but friends called her Cam. She liked it that way. She was the same woman I remembered. The night spent with her appeared strange in my memory, a genuine surreal moment.

I'd always liked her. Nothing sexual, I just liked who she was. She was making a good couple with Stefan, her humor generous, his very caustic, dry and incisive. Stefan was a skilled yachtsman and used to organize sea trips to Catalina, south to San Diego or just day sails. Their boat was a good place to relax, feel among friends.

Then, something had happened with them. I never understood what. Stefan's humor became aggressive. He had become strange, erratic and very confrontational. Our work relationship at Lockwell became difficult. He declared several times he hated weapons research.

Then, I entered the conflict with Lockwell about the MORPHEM intellectual property rights. After a year, I had been fired. I started to fight Lockwell in courts. My wife, Christine distanced herself from the whole story. When my troubles were at their peak, Christine had left me.

I had felt hurt, discarded as a human being, and haunted by ghosts from the past. I had lost track of the Mora's. I was on a path leading me to the Point Dume attempt.

And suddenly, one night, Cam called. She said she had just left Stefan, with no place to go. She asked me for a week, several days of quiet solitude until she could clear her mind, try finding her way. She didn't explain to me what happened between her and Stefan. It had been a strange week. We shared the space of my house with almost no words, our minds and souls anesthetized by pain and disappointment, different for each of us, but common in the outcome. Stefan had kept calling, leaving angry messages, or yelling at me and hanging up. And then, on one last night, it just happened. I had touched Cam's shoulder in one strange moment, she had turned around and grabbed me, crying, on my shirt. We ended up making love the whole night, again, and again, with no words, no explanation, no excuse. The next morning the house was empty, Cam had gone back to him. I was left with only one stupid and surreal mistake.

***

My mind came back. The Mustang's engine was idling. I was in front of my house. The sun was setting, somewhere back, over the Pacific, where I had left the Mora's feeding on their unhappiness. I felt the old guilt on my shoulders, impossible to shed.

1 7

Lockwell had put me into a windowless office, furnished with a large L-shaped desk, several shelves and a small table with four chairs. The only decorations on the white walls were a calendar with a picture of the old Space Shuttle blasting off, and a large electric wall clock.

Sitting at my desk was an IT man wearing a pair of worn-out corduroy jeans and a thick brown sweater.

"Dr. Salagen," he pointed to the computer screen, "this is the internal website where you are to log all your invoice hours. You can only log invoice hours associated with a charge number corresponding to an approved Contract Work Request, referred to as a CWR. Please note and remember the access password for the invoice log web-site."

I frowned at the screen.

"Now, in order to get the approval for a specific CWR and the associated charge number from Lockwell management, you must submit the CWR request on a different website, note the link here in the bookmarks if you please. In here, if you follow the screen please, you will see a table of approved CWR's, pending CWR's submitted for approval, and eventually obsolete CWR's which I suggest you should delete as soon as you will assess their inutility. The approved or submitted CWR's must comply with the terms of your contract. Any questions please?"

Bureaucracy never dies. It only morphs.

"Just how many passwords do I need?" I asked.

"I'd say about six or seven to keep handy."

"Fine. Can you connect me to the test information databases?"

"Right away, sir. Which project?"

"MORPHEM."

"OK, just a moment, I can map the share drives as soon as I verify you have clearance for the information. OK, it seems that you do. It will take only a moment."

He established the connections and finally left. I browsed the databases. The power of concentrated information was fascinating. I had obtained access to several gigabytes of raw signal databases organized per each test ever made during the MORPHEM project.

I started working, completely focused. I read the signal descriptors and sorted the engine core pressures, temperatures, current intensities, voltage measurements. Hour after hour I opened files, sorted numbers, extracted data and downloaded it on my own machine.

After five straight hours, my fingers started disobeying my brain, striking the wrong keyboard keys. My back muscles hurt and my vision became blurry. I closed my eyes, and rubbed my face. Images flashed in my memory. The Asian man thrusting himself against the face of that woman. The secret picture of the long jet of hot ionized gas. What did those people really achieve?

The thought made me focus again. I went back to work. I needed the time sequences for the engine core parameters just before the explosion. I wrote computer code and ran it, filtering, re-arranging and smoothing the signal data, numbers, millions of numbers holding the secret of the mysterious failure of MORPHEM.

But not by themselves alone.

From my briefcase, I extracted several sheets of paper carefully folded. They were photocopies of pages from my old handwritten notes, filled with tabulated numbers. The numbers had to be keyed into the computer manually. It took more than an hour. After the numbers were in the computer, I extracted another piece of paper from the briefcase. It was another photocopy, a collage of handwritten numbers arranged in a certain order. The only way to produce the numbers was to assemble fragments from a particular set of pages from my old notes in a very specific sequence. That sequence was in my memory. I hadn't written it anywhere. It was the decryption key for the data I had keyed in manually. One essential piece of knowledge to have been lost, had I pulled the trigger at Point Dume.

The result of my calculation was a complicated calibration curve. I had constructed it over years, from various experiments. The MORPHEM effect was a strange phenomenon eluding my understanding. Eluding the understanding of anyone who had worked on it. The effect was triggered only by very specific engine core geometry. Small deviations from that geometry would kill the effect and the engine would not work. Or, it would explode. I had seen it happen only once before. A powerful cascade of vicious energies, raising fast and blasting through walls of reinforced concrete several feet thick.

Once the calibration curve calculated, I shredded the photocopied pages. The shreds fell nicely into the wastebasket. It wasn't good enough, I collected them, and slowly ripped them further apart making a pile on my desk.

I watched the pile. The surreal. Always, the feeling of surreal. Was I crazy? Can crazy people get a lucid moment sometimes, long enough to contemplate their own madness? The blank walls stared at me with the subtle question of why not let go of the whole damn thing, move away, do something else. Maybe a bullet at Point Dume was not the only other solution. Go teach high school science. Write computer math codes for a bank.

A wave of nausea hit me and I felt like vomiting.

I stood up. I needed a break.

I carefully locked the computer screen and left the office searching for the coffee machine. It was hidden in a small room, a former office converted to utility room. It had a sink, a fridge and a restaurant type coffee machine, all metal surfaces and rugged buttons.

Xiao Lin was in there, preparing tea. His face was focused, dark, watching his own hands as if they were strange foreign entities.

I greeted him in soft voice, as I entered the room. His shoulders jerked at the sound of my voice. A smile appeared on his face, but the darkness in his eyes stayed.

"I'm sleepy," he said. "I need some strong stuff, but tea is all I can handle."

He cleaned the strain, then folded a napkin and placed it on the porcelain saucer underneath the tea cup. The saucer and the cup were made of fine porcelain, with thin contours, a gracious cup handle, and golden decorative motifs. He didn't look at me.

I poured a cup of coffee for myself. The taste was bad, too weak.

"Who the hell brews this stuff?" I asked.

Nobody answered. I turned around. I was alone with the blank walls. Xiao had quietly left.

I poured the rest of the coffee in the sink, packed a new filter with enough ground coffee to get a strong brew and restarted the machine. While the coffee was dripping, I thought of Stefan Mora. I wished there was a way to straighten the things with him and Cam. I weighed in my mind the chances to make him change his mind.

The coffee was ready. I poured a full cup, and left the room.

The MORPHEM people had quickly adjusted to the new building. They were working hidden within the plastic velvet walls of their cubicles. As I walked through the area, there was mostly silence broken only by telephone conversations.

The sound of two young and stronger voices came over the velvet silence from a computer room adjacent to the coffee machine. I listened, curious, but I couldn't understand a word. I peeked through the cracked open door. Two young Chinese men were speaking fast, pointing to a computer screen. They were speaking a Chinese dialect sprinkled with English words, computer jargon.

"Our simulation experts," said a voice behind me. "UCLA graduates, got them three years ago."

I turned. Cruiff was eyeing me, sipping coffee from a black mug.

"Don't they teach English at the UCLA?" I asked.

He laughed, and scratched the crotch of his jeans.

"They're working together, always. The short guy is from mainland, the taller one is Taiwanese. Good kids. They find the mother tongue easier among them two, whatever the fuck dialect that is. They're good. You can use them for your simulations."

I watched the young men. They'd heard us and were conversing in English now, with some apparent difficulty.

"Are they cleared for MORPHEM?" I asked.

"Nobody gets in this building without an authorization."

"That's right," I said. "What's the news from Hoover?"

"They're working on it. It's gonna take time. Hoover said weeks, then it's weeks indeed."

I nodded. "OK. By late tonight I'll have the geometry for our little new engine design. I'll transfer the coordinates to you before I leave."

"Your little under-the-radar project?"

"Yes."

"No problem," he said. "I'll get to work as soon as I get the stuff from you."

"Thanks, Bob. Gotta go back to work. Let's have a beer sometime. We used to do that."

"You bet," he said, ready to leave.

"Just saw Xiao in the coffee room," I stopped him. "Is he OK?"

He turned towards me and shrugged.

"Lin? Hell I know. He's busy reviewing old reports. Why do you ask?"

I shrugged back.

"He seemed upset. Or preoccupied. I don't know, thought of asking. Gotta go, anyway."

He waved good bye and left. I went back into my office and dropped on the tall chair. I was tired and coffee wasn't helping. I leaned forward and pressed the keys and password to unlock the computer screen.

I sipped some more coffee. It was strong but still tasting bad. Anxiety helped me focus back. I started plotting the data I had extracted from the test databases. The engine parameters during the seconds just before the explosion. The signals showed an abrupt raise. Varese and his men had interpreted the values as transducer line anomalies. I knew they were wrong from the very first moment I saw Varese's charts.

I fitted math functions to the data points. Exponential variation. A graphic displayed two curves: the reality, expressed by the data points, and the curve fit, the mathematical model. The reality and the model lines overlapped. I was right. The temperature at the engine core had risen exponentially just before the explosion. Something had happened at the MORPHEM core. Something generated heat and pressure at an exponential growth rate. It had taken that energy only a fraction of a second to pulverize the engine, destroy half of the test stand and take several lives. Given the satellite image of the Chinese test facility, the Chinese must've had the taste of that unleashed strange energy as well.

I thought about it and felt the anxiety grew stronger. Just as only a specific MORPHEM geometry would work well, it was only a specific geometry, a very precise erroneous engine geometry that could generate that powerful destroying sequence. Since the Lockwell and Chinese tests were so identical, the Chinese must have obtained the plans for the Lockwell design. It was as important to understand the geometry of that design. And that geometry was in Henry Hoover's hands.

The phone on my desk rang.

I picked up the receiver. "Salagen."

"Stan Jackobs here," a voice said. "Just wanted to check how you've settled over there. Did they take good care of you?"

I looked around at the blank walls and Space Shuttle poster.

"Yes they did, Mr. Jackobs, thanks for asking."

"Good. Got your people settled too?"

"Yes."

"Does that include Dr. Stefan Mora?"

"No sir. I believe Dr. Mora is unavailable."

"Did you contact him?"

"Yes, I did. He is not interested in this collaboration"

"I see. Well, too bad. Can you find a replacement?"

"I will certainly try."

"Okay. Please let me know if I can help"

"I will, thank you."

He closed connection. I placed the telephone receiver on its support.

I stared at the telephone for a minute, my eyes blank, my mind wandering. Then, I proceeded to erase everything I did on my computer. Everything, except the secret calibration curve and the exponential growth model for the explosion. With the data on it, I began sizing a new MORPHEM engine.

18

"I can't sleep," I said.

I had merely guessed the noises of her motion rather than hearing her steps. She had walked out of her room barefooted, slowly approaching behind me.

"I can't sleep either," she said.

She leaned forward, watching the computer screen, her chin resting lightly on my shoulder.

A picture of my daughter Julia was on the screen. In only several weeks she had changed visibly. Something in the fashion of her clothes, her haircut, and somehow, also in the expression on her face. In a corner of the image there was Christine, smiling to someone on her side. She had changed as well. Her hair was cut short in a style reminding me of the young Christine of many years back, when she'd started her research, freshly arrived from France. Many years back, when she was my Christine.

"Who is the girl?" Jane asked.

I was surprised she didn't know. And then I understood. There was no picture of Julia displayed anywhere in the house.

"My daughter," I said.

Her chin left my shoulder. She kept watching the pictures without a word.

Then, she asked, "Where is your daughter now?"

"France."

"And the woman in the corner? Is she your wife?"

"We're divorced."

"Why?"

I turned around on the swiveling chair, facing her.

"I'd like a drink" I said.

"I'll get you one."

She walked noiselessly away. I moved on the leather couch. She brought two glasses of scotch, handed me one and sat next to me, crossing her legs underneath her.

"Do you always host strangers?" she asked, playing with the ice cubes in her drink, studying her toes.

"No," I said. "Why do you ask?"

"I don't know. You're not asking for anything."

"What should I ask for?"

Her eyes glanced at me. "Did that fuck the other day do you any good?"

The question hurt.

"It felt wonderful," I said.

I felt her withdrawing. I didn't understand.

"Maybe that wasn't such a good idea," she said.

We sat and drank slowly, without talking. The clinking of ice cubes in the glasses and distant sirens of police cars or fire trucks far away in the city were the only noises in the room. We were, inches away from each other, yet the distance was larger than that.

I drank the scotch and stopped analyzing. I was tired. Maybe I could sleep an hour or two. I rested my head on the smooth leather and placed the glass on the floor.

***

The following evening, I returned from Lockwell and found two large black travel bags placed next to the coffee table in the living room. I hadn't seen them before. They were neatly packed, with no bulging, no labels or tags.

I dropped my keys on the coffee table, and mixed a drink. Jane came out from her room. She was dressed in jeans and a dark blue wind jacket. Her eyes were black and deep and impenetrable as always. She came close and touched my face gently without a word.

I glanced at the two black bags. "Those yours?"

"Yes. I must leave."

I sat down. She came close to me, her knees touching my legs as she was standing, looking at me, arms hanging limp. As if somehow activated by my stare, she stuck her hands in the jeans pockets.

"It's only for several days" she said. "It's just work."

I touched her hips, feeling the jeans fabric warm from her body. I pulled her towards me. She opened, landing on my lap, riding my thighs, her hands propped against my hips.

"I don't even know your last name," I said.

She smiled. "Brayton."

"I don't want you to leave."

She got off my lap, moved next to me, wrapping her hands around my right arm, and leaning her head against my shoulder. She softened so suddenly and so clearly, I was reluctant to move.

"I'll be back in a week," she said.

"You leave tonight?"

"Yes."

I smelled her hair again and slid my hand underneath her jacket, underneath the black t-shirt, feeling the smooth skin on her back, the thin fine muscles. I wasn't ready to let go of her presence. Not that moment.

"Please stay for the night," I said.

She stood up. The black eyes watched me, her face taking that impenetrable expression again. Her hands caressed my hair. She laughed, suddenly.

"OK, I'll stay the night," she said and her laugh became a smile and then the smile died.

I rose. She didn't move, her eyes just following my movement. She let herself lifted up and carried. In my arms, she sat still, just holding my shoulders.

She remained still once laid in bed, eyes closed. I lay down next to her and closed my eyes as well, as if in a ritual. I felt her warmth, coming from inches away. I had asked her to stay one more night, and she was there. We had spent only one other night together. I hadn't known her full name until tonight, and I knew nothing about her.

I opened my eyes. The walls were waving. It was either the alcohol, or my brain giving up, dizzy of thoughts. I rose to my knees and watched Jane as she lay motionless, eyes closed, her hand resting on my thigh. I kissed her and she responded, running her fingers through my hair.

I removed her black shirt and revealed her nipples, small, pink-brown, just a shade different than the tanned skin, quickly hardening under my tongue. A scent of pheromones came from her skin and focused my instinct. I remove the rest of her clothes, awkwardly, as she tacitly helped me.

For a moment, I just watched her naked body. I began caressing her skin, researching the feel of her, the soft spots, and the fiber of her muscles. Her feet were pieces of jewelry, with fine, small, perfectly shaped toes, nails with no polish, beautifully arched ankles, the thighs narrow, with delicately shaped but well defined, strong muscles. The natural tan of the whole skin was smoothing the sharp feel of her muscle fiber, deceiving the eye.

She responded to my touch like an instrument. My hands explored she responded with her breath and half suppressed moans. My arousal changed from restrained esthetics into male hunger. Under my tongue she oozed her nectar and a new scent mixed with the scent of her skin. That mix of scents diffused away my thoughts and my frustration, leaving only the instinct.

Suddenly, with surprising and unexpected strength, she rolled me on my back and came on top. Just like the first time, she took my hands and slowly pressed them against her breasts, with a strange smile, as if in masked pain. Then, she spoke in a whisper.

"That night, when you took me to the emergency. Why did you come to help?"

"Your roommate called," I said.

"Gina, I know. But why did you come? You could've told her to fuck off."

I let the feel or her breasts fill my palms, thinking about that night. I had gone to help her because I was an old fashion hero who had just returned from a strange place on the beach.

"I'm glad I came, that night," I said. "I'm glad you're alive. It's as simple as that. What sort of stuff did you take anyway?"

She removed my hands from her body and brought them together, playing with my palms, caressing my fingers.

"Some stuff I take once in a while."

"You almost took yourself out."

"I take my stuff when I want to, exactly the way I want to."

She threw those words out like a toxic load poisoning her body.

"Did you use it here?"

"No. I haven't used it ever since"

I thought of believing her. My fingers traced the line of her collarbone, feeling the soft skin.

"Why did you wait for me in that empty apartment?" I asked. "What if I gave up? What if I didn't care to come look for you?"

She took my hands again, moving my palms slowly around her hips, her belly, on the sides of the waistline.

"I knew you were coming" she whispered, as if to herself. "Somehow, I knew."

"But who am I to you? Who was I then? Who am I now?"

Without realizing it, I had grabbed her by the shoulders, with a strong grip. She reacted fast, as if by trained instinct, blocking my arms with her elbows, the muscles on her arms and legs becoming, for a short moment, strong and tensed steel fibers.

She controlled herself and softened, letting my hands grasp her, subduing herself into my arms. But she didn't answer, she just pushed me down, quietly, lifting my shirt and caressing my chest with long motions. Her touch felt good and I relaxed under her hands.

"Sometimes, too early in your life, fate forces you to make some choices," she spoke, unexpectedly. "You can't figure out if those choices are good, because you're too young. Then, somewhere along the road, you realize you may want something else, but there is no turning back. You hope, and you hide your hope from yourself, but just keep hoping, blindly, stubbornly."

I grabbed her hands, pressing them against my chest. "Hope for what?"

She didn't like the question. With a sudden move she ripped off my shirt. She arched her body, lowering herself, rubbing her breasts on my chest, throwing her hair on my face. I embraced her and we both lost ourselves in a slow struggle, shedding away my clothes, rolling around, flexing and stretching muscles, laying motionless under each other's touch, and then struggling again. The bed sheets got tangled and wet with our perspiration. She had a beautiful sense of timing herself, feeling everything that happened in me. She rushed and waited and rushed again, and timed her climaxes with mine, long and deep.

Later into the night, the shower water smelled of desert sand, a warm but alien touch, with no cleansing power. My mind had been emptied, as my body was. I toweled, looking at my image in the mirror, trying to recognize the man trapped in the glass. The muscles had survived the late years of neglect but the face was changed. Only weeks before I had the sparkle of new life in my eyes. Now, there was a deeper and darker gleam, fired by too many unanswered questions.

Fucking answers, I thought, nobody has them.

I went back into the room, walking quietly, expecting she may be asleep. Instead, I felt the house empty. The bags in the living room were gone. I went back to bed, feeling her scent on the empty sheets, waiting to fall asleep.

19

It rained for the entire whole week. The days passed, and the house remained empty. By Saturday, the skies cleared, and I knew she's not coming back. I celebrated the realization with a jog in the morning and the decision to get back to fitness work.

I spotted the car on my way back from the jog. An older Toyota Camry, parked on Mountain Street. A man sat in the driver's seat, and there was motion from the back seat. There was something bad about that car.

Back in the house, the phone was ringing. The answering kicked in before I got to it, and whoever was calling hung up. I checked the display. Unavailable, it said.

I took a shower, shaved and got dressed

The phone rang again. I picked up at the second ring.

"Stefan Mora," the voice said flatly, and then hesitated. "Did I wake you up?"

"I wake up early," I said. "I'm surprised to hear you."

"I changed my mind regarding your offer. Sorry about last time. Too much shit lately, too many strings attached to the past. If you still need a hand, I'm in."

I paused again, trying to shake away the thought about the distressing Camry outside, trying to think.

"What made you change your mind, Stefan?"

"I have my reasons. You want a hand in that project of yours, I'm in, if you don't need it, that's fine as well, best wishes, see you around."

He remained silent after he said that. I thought of his profile against the gray sky when I saw him two weeks before.

"All right" I said, "I want you in."

"Good. What do you need me for?"

"I need to get a proposal done, before anything else."

"What project?"

"MORPHEM."

"MORPHEM? They decided to resurrect it?"

"Did you know it had been cancelled?"

"Yes. The thing blew up in their faces."

"Were you still with Lockwell when it happened?"

"Yes."

"Did you look at the data? How did they investigate?"
I had asked it too eagerly. There was silence in the receivers.
"I don't remember all the details," he said.
"Cruiff told me they laid you off."
"Yeah, couple of months after the big screw-up. They lost the contract. That genius, Varese, concluded the cause is a mechanical failure. He said the engine core walls didn't take the thermal stress and ruptured. He blamed it on you and the thermal guy, the Chinese, what's his name, Lin. Then, Lockwell ran out of money and laid a bunch of us off."
It matched what I knew.
"We'll take new shot at this," I said. "There are people who're interested in MORPHEM, and funds are available. There is a full re-evaluation of the technology underway"
"Who's interested? The project was dead."
"Uncle Sam. Various agencies."
"What changed their minds? What's the new element in this?"
I heard Cam's voice in the background. Her voice relaxed me. She was not a stranger. All of a sudden I wanted to see people that weren't strangers.
"Listen Stefan, how about you and Cam come over here for lunch," I said. "We can order in, or we can go someplace around here. I'll organize the materials you need for reading, and get you started."
He covered the receiver and said something I didn't understand.
"Matei," Cam's voice came on the phone, "why don't you come over here? The sun just came out, everything is clean and shiny. Come see the ocean."
I imagined the sky over the Pacific. Jane came to mind again, but I the pushed the thought aside.
"All right," I said. "I'll prepare some material for Stefan and come over. You guys OK?"
She took a moment to answer.
"Yes Matei, we're OK. We're waiting for you. It is..." she paused again. "It is a really beautiful day."
"All right, then. I'll be there by lunch time."

20

As I drove around the corner, the Camry turned its engine on. I kept an eye on the rearview mirror and saw it trailing me for several blocks. Then, I lost sight of it.

I sped through the tight turns of the 110 watching the rearview mirrors. There were too many silver gray sedans in the flow of cars. I gave up and drove the freeways west.

The ocean was indeed splendid. The water reflected a thousand shades of blue under a pure sky flooded by hard sunlight.

The Mora's were waiting for me in the parking lot on Bali.

"Park here," Cam shouted, pointing to a spot. "I'll give you a permit."

Stefan was leaning against the fence, by the water, smoking his pipe. Cam slipped a red piece of paper on my dashboard as I got out of the Mustang. She gave me a hug and a peek on the cheek. From the trunk I extracted out a backpack with the documentation I prepared for Stefan.

"We're going to sea," Cam said. "Can you stomach lunch at sea? You used to."

I smiled, glad to be among familiar faces, in spite of the dark light in Mora's eyes. Without a word, he held the gate leading to the docks open for me. Their boat was waiting, ready.

Mora started the Diesel and maneuvered the boat around the slips, towards the channel. Cam went inside the cabin to prepare lunch, while Stefan steered the boat. He kept his eyes on the channel water, in silence.

Just before entering the channel, a Bayliner passed us, steered by a muscular blond man, bare-chested, wearing dark sunglasses. Another, older man was on the deck, also muscular, shades of gray mixed in the gold of his hair. Three women in swimming suits, showing perfectly oiled bodies to the hard sunlight were lingering on deck chairs. In LA, reality imitates movies. The boat's engine gurgled calmly, yet, the Bayliner easily picked up moderate speed.

Once we reached open sea, I helped Mora raise the sails. Sailing was his passion and he was very good at it. Back in 1987 he had defected from communist Romania on a small boat, betting on a few days of good weather on the Black Sea. He had forged a yachting permit for a club in Contantza, a harbor city on the Black

Sea coast, while Cam was on a trip to Belgrade, Yugoslavia. Because the Romanian communist authorities had not allowed them to travel together abroad, they had coordinated each other's separate defection. Cam had slipped through the Yugoslavian border into Italy, while Stefan had left Constantza by sea. The boat he had used was only believed to be good for very short trips along the harbor: it was small, unstable, and with many defective parts. Black Sea storms are unforgiving, but Stefan Mora had been lucky. He had made it to Istanbul in five days, not only escaping storms, but also escaping the Romanian, Soviet and Bulgarian patrol boats. The Mora's had spent several months apart, Stefan in a refugee camp in Istanbul, Cam in Austria, where she had traveled from Italy, avoiding the refugee camp in Trieste, for the camp at Treiskirchen, close to Vienna. Stefan had managed to get transferred from Istanbul to Treiskirchen after six months, and then they had found sponsorship for coming into the US. Cam had told me the whole story.

"Want a beer?" Stefan asked.

He had steered the boat heading north along the coast, towards Malibu. The wind kept us at four knots speed on rare, long waves. A powerful boat roared its engines less than a hundred feet away. Muscular men and well oiled bodies of women again, all shaken by the waves and the pull of the strong engines.

"What's the choice?" I asked him.

"Gordon Biersch, lager or dark, take your pick."

"Lager."

He opened a cooler next to the steering wheel, picked up a bottle and gave it to me. I removed the cap with an opener tied with a string by the boat's steering column.

"How come you're back with Lockwell?" Stefan asked.

"They need money," I said. "They're running out of business. Besides, there is a government man forcing their hand."

He nodded and then focused on the steering. The wind picked up, pushing us at five and a half knots. One mile away from the shore the air had become cooler and the boat rocked harder.

As if the issue had been left ashore, the worry about the silver gray Camry following me had diminished. I thought of Jane again, yet her face came to my mind in a different light, as if the reality of Jane's existence itself had been left ashore as well.

Cam came out of the cabin carrying a pink cardboard box like the ones used for doughnuts.

"Sandwiches" she announced, cheerfully. "Choose by the wrap paper color: red - ham, yellow - eggplant, white - chicken salad."

Her sandwiches were always made in small triangular shapes, delicately put together, delicious. We all sat, munched on them, and sipped beer. Two miles away, the beaches were mostly deserted, shining their sands in the sun.

"Hold the wheel," Mora told me. "Just keep heading parallel to the shore, we'll go past Malibu, perhaps reach Point Dume and turn around. Where's the stuff you brought for me?"

The name of the geographical location sounded strange. As if not the place I had returned from less than two months before.

"I brought you enough to get you up to date," I told him and unzipped the back pack filled with papers. "Let me explain what you see here, what these numbers are."

I unfolded the engine schematics and explained the sort of calculations I was targeting, the modeling of the ionized fluid flow, the electromagnetic and electrostatic field lines, and the thermodynamic parameters. Mora listened carefully without speaking. Cam was leaning on his shoulder, lightly, looking at the sketches and diagrams. She got a few clip binders to secure the papers against the wind, while Mora kept reading

"What do you want from these simulations?" he asked, after a while.

"I want to understand what generates some much energy in the fluid."

He kept his head down, thinking.

"I'm not so sure you can find what you want," he said. "The results of any of these simulations will be only as good as the mathematical model we use. Let me read this more thoroughly, and we'll talk."

"You want to read now?"

"Yes," he said, "Go ahead and relax, we'll sail several hours and be back while there is still light."

Cam smiled and gave me another beer.

Mora packed the papers and went in the cabin. I kept steering the boat, while Cam cleaned up the lunch leftovers and lit up a cigarette.

Far into the ocean, the power boats were crisscrossing the waves, roaring their engines. Small jet-skis shot from one of the beaches and rushed into the ocean.

We kept sailing north. After a while, only a few lonely and silent sailboats were left around. The ride became monotonous.

I suddenly felt tired. Cam noticed it and pushed me away from the steering. "You're falling asleep," she said.

"Do you have a blanket?"

She gave me a thick sleeping bag with gray and red squares. I found a place above the cabin towards the bow and I lay down, wrapping myself in the bag. Rare and long waves swayed the boat in a motion I enjoyed. Every once in a while the bow would bite deeper into a wave crest and the deck would wobble and vibrate, but that was pleasant as well. I have never been sea sick. I watched the sky and my mind emptied not only of worries, but of thoughts as well. It all had been left ashore.

I fell asleep.

I woke up when the boat shook under a stronger wave. I rolled into the bag and propped into an elbow checking the stern. Cam was steering, watching the water, absentminded.

I searched the coastline. The houses on the tall cliffs, and the tall shoulder of land were familiar. Point Dume. I contemplated the beach, fascinated. Had I finished my departure on that night, my body would have been lying there the next morning, to be found by some early beach jogger or a beach patrol. I hadn't done it, and I was enjoying life. Yet, the potential of returning at the same spot and the same moment was not removed. I knew it. It was a part of me.

"Coffee!" Cam shouted, pointing towards her left. She'd seen me moving, awake. Stefan was still in the cabin.

I got up, refreshed by the sleep, grabbed the sleeping bag and went next to Cam. She handed me a cup of coffee and pushed a pack of cigarettes towards me on the seat. I thanked her with a smile, lit up the cigarette and sipped from the coffee.

"We must turn around," she said, pointing towards the mast, "Can you handle the sail?"

I nodded and drank more coffee before placing the cup on a special support and securing it. She steered the boat left, and, as the boat swayed tightly, I swung the main sail towards right pulling at the ropes. I fixed the sail in position and went back to Cam, pushing her gently away from the steering wheel, taking shift.

"I need to ask you something, Cam," I said as she sat down with her coffee cup.

She lit another cigarette and glanced at me, waiting.

"I'd like to know what made him change his mind," I said.

She let the question linger around us, between us, before answering.

"I may have made him do it," she said, hesitating, as if not quite convinced. "Although, I don't know if anybody can make him change his mind about anything. We've talked a couple of times after you came. We decided we need to move on somehow."

She took a sip of her coffee.

"We want to return home, Matei."

"Home?"

"Yes, home. Romania"

"Romania? Is there any particular opportunity? Why would you go back?"

"Things are changing over there, Matei. The country has been given some green light finally. They're in the NATO alliance now, soon in the European Community. Multinationals are moving in, there is opportunity. Besides, Matei, don't you miss home?"

I examined her face, the hope on it.

"My home is here, Cam," I said, pointing towards the shore. "I've left the old country for good."

She nodded.

"Perhaps I understand," she said. "For us, it's different. We lived in a rush here. We did well, then we lost it, perhaps we could do well again, so many people do. But we ran out of a spiritual fuel that cannot be replenished. We don't know how, we cannot find a way to replenish it here. We've discussed this, many times. There are issues affecting him deeply."

"What issues?"

"I can't explain."

"You can try."

"No, I can't."

She seemed on the verge of crying.

"I don't know why he changed his mind. I don't want to know. I asked him for an effort, one last tug at life, and then go back. I believe he fought himself to make him change his mind and work with you."

I didn't understand. It was important to understand. She loved her husband deeply, with no reserve, I felt it. Our old story, the old mistake was no longer relevant. It had never been relevant. Not for her.

"Something has changed deeply in this country," she continued. "It used to be fun to live here. Not anymore. We just grew tired of every complication, taxes, contracts... all of it. We've been living without health insurance. It has become a world of predators, Matei. You don't pay attention for one minute and someone, something has taken a bite from you. It's like fish life at the bottom of the ocean. We're just tired."

I watched her, trying to figure out what her hope was for.

"What makes you think things are different back in the old country?"

She didn't answer.

The sun had gone low and the waves stronger. I worked the steering to steady the direction.

Mora finally came out of the cabin. His eyes were congested. He sat down, poured himself some coffee and lit his pipe.

"Are we safe in this guy's shift?" he asked Cam. "Is this still California?" he added, searching the shore.

I let the joke go. He smiled, leaning back on his seat.

"I read everything you brought," he spoke, seriously. "If you get access to those big computers, we must improve the model equations. The formulation you use will not get you the answer you're after."

"Why not? I'm tracking the essential physics."

"You're not. The plasma models are incomplete. There are strongly coupled non-linear interactions between different regions of the fluid at the MORPHEM's core. Those I can add, not a problem."

"What is the problem, then?"

He didn't answer immediately. His eyes followed something on the horizon, unfocused.

"There is something else," he said. "Something we don't know, but essential. Let me think some more about it."

The way he spoke, I suspected he had already something in mind. I chose not to push him and focused back on the steering. We had passed the Malibu beaches, now sailing along the Santa Monica shore. As we entered the channel towards Marina, we dropped the sails and switched the Diesel on. I wrapped the sails in their special covers helped by Cam while Mora steered the boat through the channel.

All worries I'd left ashore were waiting for me intact. The moment we docked, it all came back crushing on my shoulders. Thoughts of Jane, the Camry watching my house, the numbers from MORPHEM measurements, it all mixed with the memory of Julia and Christine at the airport.

"Stay some more," Cam invited me. "We can take a walk and have dinner somewhere."

I refused. "I must go, Cam. Thank you."

I embraced her and shook Mora's hand as the sun was diving in the ocean, flooding the horizon in shades of purple.

2 1

The Camry pulled behind me on Bali Way right after I left the parking lot. It trailed me as I drove past two large boat trailers parked at the curb just before the intersection. Suddenly, a pick-up backed away from a space between the trailers and blocked my way.

I slammed the brakes and gave the steering a fast half turn. The rear of my Mustang fishtailed towards right. The Camry broke into a controlled skid and blocked my back.

The doors of both cars burst open. From the Camry, a silhouette came straight towards my right door, while a stocky man ran from the pickup and reached for the left door.

I reacted by instinct: I locked the doors and floored the gas pedal. My rear tires burned rubber. Something hit my side window, but the glass held. I swerved around the pick-up and ran over the curb without releasing the pressure on the gas. The Mustang swung madly towards the intersection ahead. The traffic light at Bali and Lincoln turned red. I ran it blind, veering left. Horns blew around, angry. I shot through the traffic, working hard at the steering to correct the side dances of the car's rear. The entrance to 90 came too fast and I broke hard, skidded in a plume of thick smoke, and turned right onto the freeway.

Panic invaded my guts. I pushed the Mustang past 100, steadily passing everyone else on the rarefied traffic. Far behind, two pairs of headlights seemed to be keeping pace.

I forced my brain to work. I reached for the cell phone and couldn't find it. I searched for it, taking my eyes from the traffic few seconds at a time, without slowing down. It was nowhere within my reach.

I engaged on the 405 southbound ramp. The lanes were packed with a creeping flow of tail lights. I used the right shoulder to gain space, a few more car lengths ahead before joining the crawl. I forced my way into the wheeled slurry pushing lane changes and squeezing the Mustang ahead. Horns blew behind, headlights flashed angrily. A voice yelled through a window, cursing.

Through the slow rush, I tried to analyze.

Who?

Why?

Why an ambush?

They know where I live.

Bronson's men? No, why would the feds try an ambush?

The questions kept rolling, while the sweat on my back was getting colder. I searched again for the cell phone reaching blindly on the floor, under the seats, on the back seats. No luck.

I worried about the Mora's. I felt that the unknown danger was extended upon them as well.

The junction to 105 north came on the right side. The moment I had the way clear I floored the gas on the Mustang again. I checked the rearview mirror: nothing but usual traffic. The junction with 110 came and I switched north and plunged into packed but fast traffic, changing lanes pushing my way. I passed a few Toyotas, a massive SUV, and then fought a silver Lexus with shiny wide rims for a spot ahead on the right lane.

I checked the rearview mirrors again. A sea of headlights, behind, speeding, the crazed LA crowd. I couldn't distinguish the attackers, if there were still behind me.

A realization swirled deep within my guts: the men in the two cars were no law. The ambush was not an attempt to arrest me. Then what? A rendition?

There was only one place I could go in full trust. Hal Mason's house.

I floored the gas again. And then I noticed it in the rearview mirror: a big and old Chevy Impala, partially restored, the old paint showing rust everywhere except in the places where the body had been altered to accommodate some extra wide and shiny rims. It had approached from the flow of traffic and became glued on my back, inches away. I kept watching it in the mirror, when it suddenly roared its engine, pushed its way on the lane on my left, and came parallel. The front side window rolled down and showed a black man smoking a cigarette and looking at me with a dead face. The car kept exactly at my speed.

I floored the gas and shot the Mustang away from them. The Chevy Impala came back again on my left. I couldn't shake it.

I changed tactic and broke hard. Tires screeched behind me. There were collisions. I made a sudden right turn through the void created in the traffic and engaged on the Slauson exit ramp. The

Chevy maneuvered around a Mercedes, then caught up with me on the ramp.

The silver gray Camry emerged from the flow of cars forcing its way out of the havoc left behind and engaged the ramp. It came in at high a speed and was forced to break hard throwing smoke from the tires. But it couldn't slow down hard enough: it hit the Chevy's rear end.

The Chevy suddenly swerved left, its driver taken by surprise.

I entered Slauson street and accelerated west, with the Camry close behind. The Chevy caught up and this time locked onto the Camry. The traffic light ahead went red. I slowed down. The Camry slowed down as well. The Chevy came parallel.

The man in the Chevy's front seat raised his hand out the window. A flash of light came from it and a bang reverberated over the street. The shot hit the Camry somewhere in the hood. I looked around trying to find a way to turn around the get away from them. The Chevy man shot another round at the Camry.

Suddenly, two long cracking sounds erupted from the Camry, light flashing from its back seat window. A fast cadence submachine gun. The volley of slugs pulverized the Chevy's glass, chipping away thousands of fragments from its body.

People in South Central LA are well trained for street shootings. Men ducked and ran away from the spot, while cars scattered and drove away, running over curbs, searching their way out as far away as possible on every side street.

Simultaneously, the Camry sped away around me and vanished on a side street. The old Chevy jerked forwardly, rolled diagonally across the street, jolted when its wheels bumped over the curb, and then crashed into a wall.

I remained motionless on the now empty road, engine idling, watching the wounded Chevy from across the street. I couldn't see the people inside. It looked as if the car was empty, its windows shattered, its engine still running, propped against the wall.

I watched and tried to think. For reasons unknown, the men in the Chevy had bought me time and paid dearly for it.

Something moved inside the old car. The back door opened, and a man rolled out, holding his hip tightly with his hand. His clothes were soaked in blood. He looked at me, confused, angry, and then limped away.

I put the Mustang in gear and drove the car straight to a row of three pay phones on the side of a 76 gas station, close enough to be able to pick up the receiver from the driver seat. The first phone wasn't working. The next one had a weak dial tone, full of crackling sounds.

I dialed Hal's number. After three rings, Ernesto's voice came on the line.

"Ernesto, it's Matt Salagen," I said into the dirty receiver, fighting to control my voice. "I'm in a serious jam. I need help."

"Where are calling from, Mr. Salagen?"

"It's a fucked up pay phone. South Central, somewhere on Slauson street. I can't find my cell phone. Two cars tried to ambush me, somewhere by the ocean, but I ran away, and one of them chased me here. There was a shootout with some gang bangers, they got chopped. Like a machine gun. It went away now. But there is one more car, and they know where I live."

"Mr. Salagen," Ernesto's voice came calmly, with a steel inflexion, "I want you to calm down. One more time, tell me where you are, one piece of information at the time. Where exactly are you?"

I found it easy to hang on to the steel in his voice, and use more brain. I looked around in the darkness poorly lit by fluorescent lights, and read the street signs.

"I'm on Slauson, corner with South Central," I said. "I'm sitting in my car, engine idling, right by the pay phone."

"Good. Is there any car, or person around you that seems a threat to you?"

"No. Not at the moment"

"Can you concentrate into driving?"

"Fucking yes!" I answered irritated. His clinical style was exasperating beyond my shock.

"Then please drive home, Mr. Salagen. I'll wait for you there. I'll inform Mr. Mason. Please use the most circulated streets on your route."

Red and blue lights shone down the street. A police cruiser stopped by the crashed Impala and flashlight beams swept the car and the sidewalk around it.

"Just drive home?," I asked.

"Yes," Ernesto said. "I'll wait for you there."

"OK," I said and he cut off connection.
I left the receiver hanging and drove off.

2 2

I leaned back on the worn out leather of my living room couch with a glass of scotch in my hand. The icy touch felt good in my hand: an anchor point to a reality beginning to slip away from my understanding.

"How do you feel, Mr. Salagen?" Ernesto asked.

"I'm fine."

"I'll be outside, taking a look at your car. It'll take me only a few minutes."

"That's OK."

I finished my drink and poured another and he returned. He was holding my cell phone in his hand.

"Stuck in between seats," he said, and handed it to me. He pulled his own mobile phone, dialed a number and waited. "He's here, Mr. Mason," he said, and handed me the phone.

Hal's voice came tensed and tired.

"Tell me what happened," he said without any introduction.

I told him what happened.

"This is very serious," he said, after a long silence. "I'd like to ask you to pull out of this project."

"Pull out of MORPHEM you mean?"

"Yes."

"Why?"

He didn't speak. His breath was heavy, but he didn't cough.

"Why should I drop it?" I asked again.

"I told you you're at the center of many things, Matt. It all converges towards you because you hold the expertise."

Again, I didn't understand the old man's words.

"I'm not going to give up," I said.

"Life doesn't stop here, Matt. The hell with this MORPHEM thing."

"I have nothing else, Hal."

"Any man with a few years of life ahead of him has plenty of directions to go, Matt."

"I want to stick to this one," I said.

"Is it worth your life?"

"I was ready to blow it away, not to long ago. It's worth the fight, the search."

He paused and I heard him shuffling some papers.

"OK," he said. "Write this down. It's a secure office building, the type you asked me about."

He gave me an address in Eagle Rock.

"There is a man there by the name of Herb Wayne," Hal said, "You can trust him."

I wrote the name next to the address.

"Matt," Hal said, "Please understand: you must be very careful. Very careful."

"I understand," I said. "Good night Hal."

He started coughing. The connection closed.

I threw myself on the bed, with my clothes on. I was tired, but incapable of sleep. I reached on the drawer by the bed, and found the Beretta. It still had grains of sand on it from the Point Dume beach. I hold it in my hand, smelling its metal and oil odor, staring blindly at the dark shades on the ceiling, letting the night flow away.

   ***

A voice outside the house said something. It had been almost a whisper. I woke up. I moved my arm, and touched the Beretta, lost in the sheets, grabbed it and stood up, listening. I left the bed, barefooted, and walked into the living room.

The two black duffel bags were on the floor. She was standing against the bar, watching the gun in my hand. She had tiredness on her shoulders and something like sadness on her face.

"Welcome back, Jane," I told her, the weapon weighing heavy my hand.

"What's happening?" she asked. Her voice was tired. "Can you put that away, please?"

I put the gun away. I walked slowly to her, and embraced her. I recognized her scent with quiet joy. She returned the embrace, leaning her head on my shoulder, as if heavy with other thoughts.

"I could use a shower," she said, removing herself from the embrace.

She touched the collar of my shirt, soaked with sweat from the earlier sleep.

"You could use one too."

We didn't make love, just leaned against each other under the jets of hot water. We washed each other, slowly, as if thinking of something else, with no reason to rush.

2 3

"I'm Herb Wayne," the man said.

A short man, old and hard, he shook my hand with a steely grip. I liked his eyes. Cold gray-blue and very much awake.

"I'm in charge of the security for this building and office facilities," he said. "Let's take a tour."

The building was on Colorado close to Figueroa. Glass and steel, no more than twenty floors.

"All security issues, incidents, etcetera are reported to my office," Herb Wayne continued. "We take it very seriously. We host businesses with very sensitive activity. Faults are not tolerated".

He showed me the security lock on the main entrance door. "You need your badge to open this," he said. "We'll issue badges for the people on the list you've provided to us. That makes two badges, one for you and one for Dr. Stefan Mora."

He produced the badges from his folder as we took the elevator up. I signed a form he had placed on a clipboard and received the two badges. He shuffled several sheets of paper on a stack he was holding, and placed one more sheet on the clipboard.

"You're also leasing two broadband computer network lines on these premises, Dr. Salagen. These are open lines. Any computer security issue related to your business is your responsibility. Are you aware of that?"

"Yes."

"Then please also sign this form releasing us from this particular responsibility".

I signed the form.

"Welcome to Diamond Business Incorporated, Dr. Salagen", he said officially as he retrieved the clip-board. "I wish you good luck in your enterprise."

I entered the office and looked around. Mahogany office furniture, bookshelves, beige carpet of decent quality. There was enough room to bring in and install the computers. The windows were facing west and north. Noise from the 134 freeway was distinguishable even through the thick glass.

I dialed Mora's number.

"We're on," I said, when Stefan Mora picked up. "Beautiful office space."

"How many access lines?"

"Two."

"That should do."

I took Herb Wayne's business card and read him the information.

"Call this guy and arrange to move in the computers and the equipment. We're responsible for our own network security. How soon can we be up and running?"

"Twenty four hours after everything is installed on our end. I talked to the NAS people already."

"Is the access open?"

"We got the accounts. First class machines."

Mora was excited.

"We're talking terabytes of active memory, world's third fastest system", he said.

I let him speak more about the computer details. I had to be careful with Mora. There were resentments in him, perhaps hidden vanities, and something else, some unknown motivation I felt in him. I wished I understood that motivation, it was important.

"We're good then," I said after Mora exhausted his comments. "Let's move in the equipment ASAP."

I close connection and dialed Cruiff's number at Lockwell.

"You've been out for a while, stranger," he said.

"Just settling into the new life, " I said. "How far are you in our little project?"

"Done, bubba."

"That includes the geometry cuts I asked you for?"

"Done, like I said. Come over and check it out, and tell me if you want anything else."

I checked my wristwatch.

"I'm on my way," I said.

***

When I entered Cruiff's office, he took his feet off his desk, sat straight and pushed a thin data disk case towards me.

"What's in there?" I asked.

"That's the geometry data from your model," he said and twisted his computer screen towards me. Displayed on the screen was the three dimensional layout of the new engine concept.

"That's how your baby looks like," he pointed to the screen. He worked the computer showing the virtual slicing of the engine model along the locations I had given him. It was all first class accurate work.

I thanked him. "I may need you to do the same with the data measured by Hoover," I said. "Once he's ready with the measurements."

He smirked.

"Hoover is ready," he said. "I looked at his data and it looks good. I've even extracted the coordinates you need, just like I did for this model here. There is one problem, though."

"There are always problems, aren't they?"

He laughed dryly, "The data is going to go under wraps. Varese wants restricted access."

"How restricted?"

"Lockwell confidential."

I understood. I wasn't a Lockwell employee, only a contractor paid via Jackobs' agency. Lockwell had the right to withhold data considered a trade secret and marked Lockwell Confidential. Varese was legally allowed to withhold the actual coordinates.

"I see," I said, and left the matter linger in the air.

Cruiff closed it: "Sorry, stranger," he said. "It's outta my hands."

"I understand," I said. "I'll work on it."

"One more thing," Cruiff said.

"Yes?"

He took a few moments before talking.

"There is a new guy around. Up there, rubbing elbows with McNutt, Varese, and the rest of them."

"What about him?"

He stayed silent again, as if waiting for something. I heard voices and steps muffled by the plastic carpet, people passing by Cruiff's cubicle, talking.

"He's a hatchet man," Cruiff said after the people were gone. "Everything that's not MORPHEM or an active paying contract is getting slashed, cut, amputated. Lockwell's books will smell like roses. The way it looks to me, the company is up for sale."

"Is there a buyer?" I asked.

"No idea."

Only a big corporation, I thought. One with some appetite left for acquisitions.

"I know nothing about it, Bob," I said.

"Thought you should know," Cruiff said.

I nodded and mocked a military salute towards him, and rushed out of Lockwell. I held the data disk in my hand as if it was made of thin glass.

The sun was setting over the hills towards the Pacific as I hit the packed freeways. I leaned forward over the Mustang's steering wheel and watched the sky while caught in a crawl between a Volkswagen and a pick-up.

2 4

By the time I reached Pasadena it was dark. In the Old Town, people living on credit card debt dined at the sidewalk tables, laughing, waving their hands, postponing tomorrow.

My house was dark. Only a thin thread of light came from a crack in door of Jane's room. I pushed the door open, slowly. She was lying in bed, eyes closed, facing the ceiling. For a moment I held my breath. She looked the same way she did the night I found her unconscious from the overdose.

But this time, she opened her eyes and turned her head towards me, without a word. I sat on the edge of the bed and we watched each other in silence. She smiled, got up and sat on the edge of the bed by me, her legs tightly crossed underneath, as in a Lotus yoga exercise. She did it with ease and mobility as if made out of rubber. She touched my shoulder.

"Let me buy you dinner tonight," she said. "Or get a drink someplace. I still owe you some money."

She had a smile I hadn't seen before, as if light was coming from within her. I was tired, but that light was giving me strength.

"I'd love a drink," I said.

She smiled, jumped off the bed and stretched, a gracious unwinding coil, breasts pushed against the black shirt.

"Give me ten minutes," she said, and kicked me off the room.

***

The place was called the Viper Room, a joint in West Hollywood owned by an actor, with live music concerts every night. Its entrance was on a narrow side street coming downhill from Sunset. The street sloped down so much the entrance was one floor lower than the club's main room, which was at Sunset level.

We got in and walked through a narrow corridor, Jane still laughing at the bouncer who had ID-ed her. A flight of stairs led upwards from the entrance corridor to the main room. There was a bar at the lower level, underneath the staircase. We ordered drinks from a sleek bartender who had some trouble finding the vermouth bottle for my Manhattan. Noise was coming from upstairs: strong bass, muffled by the walls. Jane didn't look comfortable. It didn't seem her kind of a place, although she had chosen it for the evening. We went upstairs.

The Viper Room proper was just that: a large room with a raised small concert stage on a corner and a long bar along one of the sidewalls. Opposite to the bar there was one single row of tables, the rest of the room just bare floor, people standing, listening, clapping, waving and shaking butts and shoulders. It wasn't my kind of music: a dissonant strong punk-rock type. Slim and sweaty, the band leader was playing guitar and doing vocals as well, jumping left and right with dilapidated excitement. The strong stage light underlined the worn out features of his face. The bass player was a fat guy with some white make up on his face, mascara on his eyelids and shades of dark blue around his eyes. His face was streaked with dripping sweat. He had a peculiar way of throwing his face at the mike, doing some sort of a second voice for the slim band leader.

I took Jane to the wall opposite to the stage, and just leaned against it. The band finished the piece. The crowd cheered, applauded. The band leader laughed and said something to the bass player, off the mike. They both laughed.

"We love the ladies!" the band leader cried on the mike, pointing to the front row of the crowd. He spoke with some Brit accent, real or fake. The indicated ladies made as much noise as they could. The way they looked, the sentiment declared by the band man was either platonic or perverse.

"Our next song is called 'Reverie'", the band man said, and they immediately started playing it. The reverie consisted of lots of drums beaten crazily, frantic bass, and synchronized cries from the leader and the bass player.

It kept like that for several minutes, when I felt a hand on my arm. Jane made a sign towards a side door. I followed her through the noise. People were getting out for a smoke through a door that seemed to be leading out on Sunset Boulevard. Two bouncers were guarding the door.

"Hand!" one of them yelled at me.

"What?" I yelled back.

The bouncer pushed the door open and followed us out on the sidewalk and then closed the door, cutting the noise down.

"You guys out for a smoke? Lemme stamp your hands."

"Forget it," Jane said, "We're leaving. Thanks."

The man shrugged, banged on the door for someone to open it, and got back in without a word. We stood on the sidewalk, watching the traffic on the street.

"I'm sorry," Jane said.

"Why?"

"This was a bad choice."

I grinned. "I loved the ladies," I said.

"Yes, fuck them. How about we try a place of your choice?"

There was no place of my choice. I didn't care. I was there on the sidewalk, free, alive, with a plan for tomorrow. I felt an exhilaration of just being on that sidewalk. With my arm around Jane's shoulders, I leaned down gently and quickly, tilted her weight on my arms and lifted her up. Somehow, it was that gesture of lifting Jane in my arms that defined me and her, everything else about us was unclear, unknown, lived one moment at a time. The feel of her body in my arms, the work of my muscles, her weight, neither light nor heavy, just right. Beyond the gesture, I wanted to fire up that hidden light I had seen in her eyes just hours before.

I searched for her lips while holding her. She answered in a surprising way, swinging off in my arms and wrapping her legs around me, raising her face above mine, while embracing me back in a girlish way, like a teenager.

"At least they make good drinks, judging by their effect" she said. "Where is your car?"

I drove us back to Pasadena listening to jazz on a Long Beach station. Jane kept touching me; my arm, my fingers, playing with my hand, her fine long fingers intertwined with mine for a moment, running up my forearm the next, never leaving me. The feeling was electric, a fairy-like fluid coming out of nowhere and invading the insides of my body, my mind reduced to just witnessing it. Love is both a chemical state of the brain and the formula of magic. I let it flow in my blood, absorbing it.

We made love fast and with hunger, as if driven by a necessity to consume the unbearable peak in the electric fluid flow. And yet, there was no sense depletion, afterwards, but rather a new sort of magic where only a peak had been consumed by climaxes, a depth of magnetism remaining. We spent hours in the dark embraced, listening to each others' breaths, feeling each other's warmth.

Yet, I fought to maintain lucidity. I thought about the lively light in Jane's eyes, the flow of warmth coming from her. I had felt it all again, when she had made her typical gesture of taking my hands and caressing her breasts and her belly, holding my palms on her skin. Even then, I still felt layers of protection covering her thoughts from me. I let the unknown joy flow through me, clearly aware that I still didn't know her, clearly aware that I still didn't know what that magic really meant, that it may only last a day, a week, a month, and so be it.

***

The phone rang at dawn. I heard it in my sleep.

"It's for you," Jane said, and shook me lightly.

She pushed the telephone receiver on my hand. "Can't figure out what the guy says," she said.

I growled a hello on the piece.

"I need to speak to Matei Salajan" a man said, in Romanian.

The voice speaking my old name forced me awake. "Speaking," I said.

"Matei, this is Chris Popa. Old buddy, if you remember, it's been a while."

I searched my memory, in silence.

"Christian Popa," the man spoke again. "Perhaps you remember, Careni airborne, Class of '84 at the Polytechnic."

Christian Popa. A shadow in my memory, a college mate from the Polytechnic Institute in Bucharest, a man I hadn't seen in more than twenty years. How did he find me? Why?

"Chris, yes, I remember of course," I said.

"Glad you do," he said. "I know I'm coming out of the blue, but I need to ask you a favor."

"Where are you calling from?"

"I'm in Bucharest"

"I see. What can I do for you?"

"I'm planning a trip to Los Angeles. I'll arrive on May 30th. I'd be very grateful if you could wait for me at the airport."

He was uneasy, and the request sounded strange.

"Do you need a place to stay?" I asked.

"Matei, all I need is less than half a day of your time," he said. "But it's important for me."

"When will you arrive, again?"

"May 30th, that's Monday next week."

"OK, I'll write this down."

"Thank you. I'll call again with my flight info."

"Chris, one question."

"Please?"

"How did you get my number?"

He laughed, still uneasy. "I asked around. Someone in Montreal had it, I believe."

He thanked me again, and closed connection.

I tried to remember more about Popa. We hadn't been too close back in our college days, although we had served together in the Romanian military before college. Nothing special in that, it was the case with most of my male college mates. At the time, the military service was mandatory in the old country, starting right after high school. For those admitted to colleges the service was shorter and the military used to group the boys from each college on the same base. Personally, I had found the regular service too dull and boring and had applied for paratrooper training, together with many others. Popa had applied as well and made it through the qualifying tests, but his preferred activity during the whole service had been to ditch everything he could and just do nothing. Later in college we met at several parties and in classes, but that had been all. I had lost track of him immediately after graduation.

I took the call off my mind and focus on the main task of the day: starting the computation work with Stefan Mora.

2 5

"What's on it?" Mora held the disk by the edges and examined it on both sides. The disk reflected sunlight on his face, and gave it a strange transparency. It was early morning and our office in the Diamond Inc building was getting plenty of the early day sunlight.

"Coordinates," I said. "Engine geometry data."

His eyes left the disk and locked on me.

"You said Lockwell lost the CAD files."

"This is a different design."

"What design?"

I carefully took the disk from his delicate grip and examined its surface myself, playing with the reflected light.

"My design," I said.

Suspicion wrinkled the skin on his forehead.

"I hope you're not delusional and wasting my time, Salajan. You don't have a design."

I pushed the disk into the computer reader and worked the keyboard. The screen filled with a crude wire-mesh image depiction of the engine model.

"This is the engine as it should've been designed," I said, and moved the image on the screen, bringing up details. "I can't guarantee it would've produced the performance we wanted, but it wouldn't have exploded."

Mora examined the screen carefully.

"Who generated this design?" he asked, dryly.

"I did. It's my design."

"What about the one that exploded?"

"We'll have the coordinates soon. We'll run the simulations on both cases, and compare. I need to understand what happened during that test."

He curled his lips in deriding contempt. "It's your money," he said. "Let's get to work".

We began working at two separate terminals, splitting the tasks: I worked on the simulation code, while he proceeded to build the numerical model of the engine design. We were both remotely logged into the Columbia computer systems at the NAS center, three hundred fifty miles north.

I transferred the computer code files through a secure file transfer protocol into the NAS machines. The code had to be *recompiled*: translated into the machine language the NAS massive machines could understand and run. The code was written in a standard programming language, and translation was done on the NAS machines, using their specific code translators, the machine *compilers*.

In spite of the standard language, specific details in the NAS system began blocking the compilation. The code had to be adjusted. After each attempt at compilation, a long list of errors and warnings kept filling up the screen. I was familiar with the process: after making the corrections, the compilation had to be restarted from the beginning. Over, and over, and over again.

Mora began building the computational engine model, sector by sector, creating the virtual detail information of the MORPHEM engine core geometry. He ported the models from Cruiff's data disk into the NAS system and began translating them into algebraic language the computer system would understand.

The work was intense, yet captivating. The day passed fast. Late afternoon we walked out of the building to a burger joint. We ate the grease in silence, thinking about work, and returned to the office without delay, and without much talking.

I launched a new compilation job and new error list scrolled on my screen. Debugging was just code detective work, figuring out which subtle part of a routine broke the syntax rules understood by the machine. Patience was the secret. The screen scroll started again. I let the lines fly and waited.

My screen scrolling stopped. The error on the top of the list was a trivial one this time. A format incompatibility. I opened the code source file with the faulty line of code, corrected it and then initiated the compiling sequence one more time. Lines scrolled again fast on the screen. Subroutines were compiling one by one, on and on. One minute passed after another, but the scrolling kept going. I was following the lines with tired eyes, waiting for the new error list, but the scrolling went on. It kept going until the magic word showed up on the screen: *Linking*. The whole code had been compiled, and now, its many parts were being logically linked together into a machine language code able to run the complex calculation in the visceral elements of the NAS Columbia system.

"Stefan," I called Mora. "The damn thing compiled."

He quickly rose from his chair, and came to look over my shoulder. He watched the screen lines, indicating the successful linking.

"Yeah," he said, "You got it".

"What's your status?"

"Come over and see. Almost done as well."

I followed him to his terminal. He turned the screen so I can watch. He was assembling the grid system. Computer simulations of physical processes such as plasma and fluid flows are done by filling the space volume where these processes take place with fine virtual meshes woven through algebraic numerical coordinates. The MORPHEM's inner core had become a dense collection of nodes in a grid of millions and millions of points made visible by graphical interface software.

"I've modeled all the engine details in several hundred grid zones. You can see them here as wire meshes of different color. You can zoom in and view through the volumes"

Mora explained as he was rotating the images on the screen.

"Right now I am connecting them into one large system," he said. "I gotta set up the boundary conditions for each zone, and this takes time because I must double check everything."

I watched him work. He was telling the computer, in mathematical language, where the walls were, where the inflow of fluid was coming from, where it should discharge, where the energy fluxes were generated and how were they expected to propagate in the engine core.

Once the conditions were set, we started verifying everything again. It was tedious work. I followed everything he did, every connection, every set-up. It took another two hours and I found no error. It was all accurately done. Mora was one of the best professionals I had worked with.

"Now, last but not the least: the domain decomposition," he said. "We need to set this up by hand."

The domain decomposition was the key for the power held by the supercomputer system. The immense amount of spatial nodes filling the inner details of the MORPHEM engine core was being broken down into thousands of adjacent chunks. Each chunk was assigned to one particular processor of the thousands processors the NAS Columbia machines were equipped with. Each such processor was instructed where its domain is, exactly which are the coordinates it must work on, and which are the neighbor processors it should exchange information with. The trick was to assign each processor an even amount of work, such that all processors would work in a balanced way, and not wait on each other before exchanging information during the computations. Each of these fast electronic brains would be instructed by the code executable what to do with the numbers, and how to exchange data with the neighbors. The huge task of calculating the intricacies of plasma flows through the complicated geometry of the engine core was thus being broken down into several thousand small portions, speeding the calculations enormously.

"It's all set," Mora said, leaning back on his chair. "I'm queuing the job"

The way to run codes at NAS was in the so called batch mode, very much like in the old days of mainframe computers. The commands instructing the computer how to run the code - for how long and with how many processors - were written in a script file. Running the script would submit our job into a queue. If the supercomputer system had the requested memory and free processors available it would start executing the code immediately. If not, our job would wait in the queue until some of the running jobs will finish and free up resources. It was the way things were done in the times before the personal computers, before windows based systems, before the Internet. Except one detail: the NAS system computing power had been unimaginable in the old days.

Mora operated the keyboard.

"I've set it up to run a hundred iterations," he said and pointed to the lines on the run script. "A hundred iterations it's just a test. If NAS is that good it would take up to an hour to complete this test job."

He hit a key. The job was queued.

"How long a wait?" I asked.

He listed the run queue on the screen.

"I don't know," Mora said. He pointed to a list on the screen indicating that several large jobs were already running, keeping the processors busy. The MORPHEM job was next. We had to sit and kill time. My concentration dissipated. Mora began reading NAS documentation. I laid back and closed my eyes. Minutes passed, then an hour. I needed a drink, and thought about having a bottle handy in the office and then discarded the idea.

Mora returned to his chair, and checked the NAS queue again. The MORPHEM job was still waiting. Then, he suddenly got excited, watching the screen.

"Hey, we're on," he said. "It's running".

He typed again the verification commands. His face seemed puzzled.

"It disappeared!" he exclaimed. "For a moment I saw the code on the 'run' state, then nothing. What the fuck?"

"Check the log file."

"Log file says it executed OK."

We both watched the screens confused.

"Check the result files," I said.

The code was instructed to write the solution into a set of result files, one for each of the several hundred zones.

Mora typed the commands. He watched the screen for several long seconds. Suddenly, he snapped his fingers.

"It completed the test run! Everything is there: one hundred iterations in practically no time".

He looked at me, excited and in the same time tensed.

"This is super-power here!" he exclaimed. "I'm fucking God here, Salagen!"

I watched him, thinking.

"You're no God, my friend," I said. "You've just got a toy way bigger than ever before. Please use it to tell me how my engine works."

2 6

Back at my Lockwell office someone knocked lightly on the doorframe. Xiao Lin stood by the threshold of the open door, holding his porcelain teacup in his hand.

"Xiao, please come in," I invited him, and rose from my chair.

He walked in, with his usual restrained smile.

"I must make you an invitation," he said in his mumbling way, and then he stopped at the sound of steps rushing in from the hallway.

Bob Cruiff burst into the office. He eyed Xiao Lin and me in a quick glance: "You guys busy?"

Xiao smiled courteously, without a word.

"Something burning?" I asked Cruiff.

He grinned, "Varese's ass is burning for sure. He came to me for some nice picts on MORPHEM and he needed it pronto. I gave him the stuff on a memory stick and he took off to the HQ right away. That reminded me I haven't seen Jenny in a long time. I stopped by and said hello and saw there a bunch of suits, folks I haven't seen before. Know anything about this?"

Cruiff's cool was hiding anxiety. His interruption made Xiao postpone the completion of his unexpected invitation. The way Xiao had acted, the invitation was important, but Cruiff's apprehension made him close on himself, waiting. He was going to wait until all the fuss and agitation would be over. That was his way.

"Don't know about any suits," I told Cruiff.

The phone rang. Double rings, an outside call.

I picked up

"Stan Jackobs here," a voice said through the metallic sound of a mobile phone in bad reception. "I'm on my way to Lockwell. I called McNutt's and Garland's offices and can't get anyone but some clever secretary. I'm informed there is a meeting there between Lockwell and some outside people. Just what the hell are you guys doing over there?"

I looked at Cruiff and said: "No idea, Mr. Jackobs."

Jackobs replied something I didn't understand. The connection was breaking again. I waited.

"Meet me at your headquarters building," Jackobs' voice came back clearly again. "I should be there in about fifteen minutes."

The connection went off. Cruiff's eyes were on me. Xiao was studying his cup, still leaning against the wall by the door.

"Everybody seems angry about these visitors," I said flatly. "Why are you angry Bob?"

He grinned broadly, showing a row of strong teeth.

"Why should I be angry?" he growled. "None of my business these fuckers want to sell the company."

"Lockwell is in a mess right now," I said. "Who the hell would want to buy it?"

He shook his head.

"When I hired here, sonny, there were only cornfields around. That's many years ago, before your ass got into this country. Way back when this country was good for something."

He dug in his jeans pockets for his chewing gum.

"Times have caught up, as we've been here asleep," he recited, focused on the unwrapping of a blade of peppermint gum. "You look around now and it's all malls and office buildings left and right of this place."

His grinned again, looking me in the eye as he placed the gum in his mouth.

"We're sitting on a hundred million dollars worth of prime time real estate, stranger. With business potential towards a billion or more. Whoever wants to buy us doesn't give a shit about rockets. Know what I'm saying?"

I had no idea. Maybe it was true.

"So, you gonna to join the little jamboree?" Cruiff asked.

"Master Jackobs wants me there."

"Good, follow you master. Go and dance. Stop by afterwards and lemme know what's up." He turned around to leave and stopped to look at Xiao. "You gonna stick around here or do some work, bubba?"

Xiao nodded and smiled towards me as an excuse. He walked out after Cruiff.

I left in time to intercept Jackobs in front of HQ. Jenny was sitting very upright at her oversized desk with the attitude of a model posing. She turned her head towards us at the exact angle for a half profile and smiled.

"Good morning gentlemen," she greeted us and showed us her very white teeth. "How can I assist you?"

Jackobs cut her off. "Where is the meeting?" he asked with no protocol.

Jenny's smile froze, but remained in place.

"Right this way, Mr. Jackobs, in the Conference Room One, please follow me."

She rose from her chair, her clothes instantly arranging their fabric in perfect folds as if by magic. She had pronounced the conference room direction with proper intonation and in capital letters. She was perfect.

She opened the conference room door and stepped in ahead of us, holding the door open.

"Please come in, gentlemen," she said loudly. Her hand was extended in an inviting gesture, the way a stewardess would invite you take a seat on the business class. She was doing a good job. Inside, McNutt got her warning. He showed up at the door with an inviting gesture.

"Stan, please come in," he invited. "Matt, take a seat."

He was all sugar. I looked at the suits in the room, expecting Bronson and his men. I recognized Jim Garland, sitting on a chair away from the meeting table, relaxed. Varese was standing by a wall screen filled with plots and diagrams, dressed in a brown suit lacking the type of perfection found in Jenny or Jackobs. Besides the Lockwell men there were five other men in the room. I didn't know any of them.

"Great to have you here, Stan," McNutt said volubly, inviting Jackobs towards a chair. "We couldn't reach your office this morning."

He swept the room with a large gesture of his hand.

"An opportunity arrived to have some key people in the launching industry as guests here at Lockwell," he said and motioned towards the men at the conference table.

"Let me do the introductions."

He pointed towards two men at the table on his left. "Stuart Greene, Director of the Advanced Propulsion Directorate at the NASA Marshall Space Flight Center, and Tom Alvaro, Chief Research Scientist in the same group."

The two indicated men grimaced a smile. Greene was tall and thin, with carefully combed sandy hair, prominent cheekbones and strong hands. The other one, Alvaro, was dark haired, slightly overweight, with sophisticated features and fine hands.

McNutt switched to the opposite side of the table. "Jeff Stone, president and CEO of the Pratt & Whitney Rocketdyne division of the United Technologies Corp, and James Adams, director of the Advanced Propulsion Directorate at Rocketdyne."

The two men responded with the same amiable grimace. They were men in their sixties, yet showing full vigor and energy, carrying themselves with weight. I knew why. Pratt had bought the Rocketdyne division from the Boeing Corp only a year before. The merger had made P&W Rocketdyne, known as PWR, the main North American producer of large liquid propellant booster rocket engines. The Delta and Atlas family of heavy launchers and the Space Shuttle were powered by Rocketdyne engines. That made them the de facto contractor of choice for many of the engines needed for the Space Exploration Initiative launched by the US president two years before.

McNutt turned towards a tall man seated at the head of the table. "We owe the opportunity of this gathering to Dr. Scott Stirling," he spoke with reverence, indicating the tall man. "Dr. Stirling is the president of the Stirling Consulting Group, a think tank and consulting firm in the field of aerospace and defense business. Scott had the excellent idea of this visit here."

Stirling smiled slowly, with quiet and relaxed confidence. He sat on his chair, leaning backwards, fully relaxed, yet with sharp focus on his eyes. His hair was all white and carefully combed backwards, his face tanned, and the skin on his neck rough and wrinkled. His tan and an apparent flexibility of his body made him appear less old that he probably was. The look on his eyes suggested a keen interest for the universe around him, but also a prudent and careful watch.

McNutt placed a hand on Jackobs' shoulder. "Stan is one of the key people we're working with," he said. "Stan's understanding of new technologies such as MORPHEM and his vision for the future have generated the unprecedented progress in propulsion development here at Lockwell."

The NASA and PWR men watched Jackobs like poker players to whom a new player is introduced.

McNutt finally turned towards me. "Also, this is Matt Salagen, senior scientist engineer who is the liaison with Stan's office here at Lockwell."

The men's eyes brushed past me. All, except Stirling's eyes. He nodded slowly, and took his time to study my face.

His focus got distracted by Jackobs, who spoke without hiding his irritation.

"Before anything, gentlemen," Jackobs said, "I need to ask for your security credentials. The MORPHEM data I see on this screen requires certain clearances."

That got the men's full attention.

McNutt fended off for the whole group. "We're all cleared Stan," he said. "We're discussing here the technology breakthroughs enabled by the MORPHEM."

He switched quickly from defense to sales. "Scaled up versions of MORPHEM engines can place heavy payloads on low earth orbit at very low cost. Also, we can basically achieve Single Stage to Orbit operation for manned space vehicles. A revolutionary Space Shuttle."

It was true, if a large MORPHEM engine worked.

The price man has to pay for placing an object in space is a large amount of energy. That energy means fuel. The heavier the payload, the more fuel needed, and even more fuel to lift the weight of the extra fuel, and so on. And if one builds a large rocket to carry all that fuel besides the payload, there will be a large dead weight of empty tanks to be carried in flight after most of the fuel is burned.

The solution to this problem came in the form of staged rockets. Instead of one large rocket, the idea is to build several rockets on top of each other. At launch, the lower stage fires first. That stage must be the most powerful, as it must lift up itself, the stages on top of it with their propellants, and the payload. After the first stage burns its propellants, it is jettisoned away from the rocket. Simultaneously, the next stage ignites its engines. And so on, the stages are used one after another, accelerating the top section of the rocket, which carries the useful payload, be it a communication satellite or a crew, into orbit.

"The shuttle concept is dead," Greene said. "Back in the late 70's when we designed the Shuttle, it was based on the promise of vehicle re-usability and low cost. It's not low cost. It takes four billion dollars per year to operate it. That's why we're gonna go to the Moon old fashion style, with expendable rockets."

"MORPHEM can change every paradigm in the game," Varese intervened from near the screen, and then walked to the table and joined the group. "Reusable or expendable rocket vehicles, it doesn't matter."

"The discussion is premature," Jackobs said. "This technology is being re-evaluated."

"Very good point," said the NASA man named Greene. "Your performance is on paper. How mature is this technology?"

"You guys had an explosion with this thing, last year," said one of the Rocketdyne men, Jeff Stone. "I haven't heard much more ever since."

McNutt addressed both Jeff Stone and Greene with a sad smile. "It comes with the territory," he said. "You know it very well, Jeff, just how many J-2's did you guys blow up back in the old days?"

The J-2 engines had been used in the upper stages of the Saturn-V rockets for the Apollo missions to the Moon in the 1960's. Forty years later, NASA was re-utilizing a modernized version of the engine, the J-2X, for the new Ares rocket of the Constellation space program.

"True," Stone said. "We blew up a couple of them. But it was a different era, different dynamics of the industry. Today, this industry has become very intolerant to failures, even in the development stages."

"We lost our guts," intervened Jim Garland from his back seat. His resonant voice made the point stronger. "This is a risky business we're in. These damn engines discharge a controlled burst of energy, tons, and tons if it. You do a mistake, thinks blow up. That's the way it is. What's the alternative if we adopt no tolerance to failure? Stop making rockets? Buy them from the Russians? From the Chinese?"

The NASA director raised his bony hands in the air, palms up.

"It a question of budgets, Mr. Garland. Current budgets allow for very few mistakes. The costs for designing, making and testing rocket engine components has, well, sky rocketed. A development failure, such as an engine explosion on the test stand is becoming more and more prohibitive, in terms of both budget and schedule."

"The F-1 and the J-2 engines for the Apollo missions were designed with slide rule for calculations," said the NASA man named Alvaro. "Even during the Shuttle Main Engine development in the 70's there was a lot of testing, not as much prediction. Some explosions happened there as well, right?"

Stone nodded. "That's right."

"But now we have all these computers," Alvaro continued. "We can predict things, run simulations, analysis, solid modeling, computational fluid dynamics, finite element stress analysis, everything is modeled and analyzed in detail. It is normal to tolerate less catastrophic mistakes."

Garland shook his head. "I would agree if you just did the same things all over again. You're talking about chemical rocket engine design. It's been done for more than fifty years. But MORPHEM is a new technology. New physics. You got to damn try it, and try it again, if it's so promising. Yet, it is new physics, with its possibly unexpected effects. What do we do, then, one failure and we shy away? "

"No, perhaps you don't," Greene answered, "if you're confident that the chunk of physics works as you think it does. But it doesn't make sense to attempt use it on a manned mission from the start, doesn't it? It's like putting astronauts on top of German V-2's"

"We did just that with the Mercury missions," Garland pointed a finger at Greene. "We put men on top of a Redstone rocket for the Mercury program. The Redstone was nothing but a redesigned V-2."

"That's right," Jeff Stone said. "I guess we did."

"And we took that risk," Garland continued his point. "Why? Because the Russians had beaten us to it. They were the first to place a man in orbit, that fellow, Gagarin. Our national prestige was down. We had to catch up, and we did, all the way to the Moon."

"Times have changed Mr. Garland," the NASA man said. "Currently there is no pressure for such risks. All developments for the Space Exploration Initiative are based on proven technology. There is no reason for unnecessary risks."

"And there is not much money either," Garland pounded. "These are not the times of the Apollo program. How many employees did you guys have then?" he asked Jeff Stone.

Stone nodded again, "During Apollo, Rocketdyne had over twenty thousand people employed."

"And how many right now?"

"Less than four thousand, both Florida and California operations."

"Here we go. You guys at NASA are also down by one third of the personnel as well. And I don't see any government budget increase for the Space Initiative. How are we supposed to do it?"

"We can do it in an intelligent way. We already have assets. We have the Space Shuttle technology which is well proven in terms of propulsion. And there is the full experience of the Apollo program. We don't need to reinvent the wheel."

"We've been asleep for more than forty years in terms of manned space flight technology," Garland said. "When we landed on the Moon and designed the Space Shuttle we were ahead of the world by forty years. Instead of going ahead, we slept for forty years, and the world caught up with us."

Stirling laughed at Garland's words, silently, shaking his head. It was his first visible reaction.

Greene, the NASA man was irritated. "I believe that is a strong statement, Mr. Garland, and quite a bit stretched," he said, coldly.

McNutt threw a cold but pleading glance at Garland. He didn't want any of the NASA people upset.

Garland ignored him. "We assume we have the supremacy in aerospace technology", he said. "It may be true this year, next year, maybe another three years. It's not going to last longer, if we move at the present pace with research. The Chinese are coming from behind, and with vigorous development. They can afford it, their engineers are cheap and willing to work. Chemical rocket technology it's only text book physics, with some proprietary expertise. The whole rocket race is in materials and manufacturing technology, which is a very diffusive type of information. Fifteen years ago, the Chinese were only good at manufacturing sneakers and toys. Now they're in full development for manned missions to the Moon. I heard your NASA administrator speaking at the Joint Propulsion Committee meeting. He thinks the Chinese are going to beat us to the Moon this time."

"Their capsule is based on modified Soyuz technology," said Greene. "You cant' have much control when the technology is not genuinely yours."

"That's naïve," Stirling said, finally participating to the discussion. His voice had a resonance similar to Garland's, yet without the roughness. "The Chinese are acquiring know how on critical technologies at unbelievable rates. They've learned to use that huge market of theirs as leverage to force foreign companies to share technology. The laws of economics dictates that no large corporation can afford to stay out of the Chinese market, be it a US, European, Japanese, South Korean, and yes, even Taiwanese corporations. The Chinese play the game with the high tech corporations: you either set up joint ventures and share know-how with the them, or you're blocked out of the Chinese market."

"But we have export control regulations, the ITAR regulations" said Stone. "No specific propulsion related know-how can possibly be transferred."

"Not directly," Stirling said. "That's why they're doing homework on those text books Mr. Garland was mentioning. It's only a matter of time for them to gain expertise. The Chinese also learned to target dual-use technologies, technologies that are used for civilian products but can be converted to military technology. Among which, metal alloys, metal manufacturing, and so on. I agree with Mr. Garland. The Chinese have a good chance to beat us to the Moon."

"What do you think we should do, Mr. Garland?" asked James Adams, the Rocketdyne chief of advanced propulsion development. He had followed the discussion calmly, playing with a beautiful golden fountain pen.

"What we should do?" asked Garland, rhetorically. "We should aggressively investigate new concepts, and protect them while doing it. We need intelligence, creativity, and competence."

"And of course, money," Stirling laughed, calmly. "And it's a government job, to shell this money out. If you look at the rocket business, last year, the Russians scored the best. Twenty-one launches total, three of them commercial American payloads, and other three supply flights to the International Space Station, partly paid by the good old Uncle Sam. The United States had twelve launches, out of which one was a Space Shuttle launch, and two of them Sea Launch launches, basically Russian rockets flown by Boeing. The Europeans had five launches, three of them with American commercial payloads. The Chinese had four launches, and the Japanese had two. This is a very frugal piece of statistics, gentlemen. No industry can be sustained at this pace, unless there is strong government support."

"We must not forget the private sector," said Greene.

"The private sector only does what makes sense economically. What is the market impact of the space programs? The commercial sector that uses space launching services, the telecommunications, is not growing fast enough. The Space Shuttle missions, the International Space Station missions, the astrophysics research on the Hubble Telescope, all these missions produce extremely interesting scientific data, which, unfortunately, reduces to just pretty pictures in the news, as far as the large public is concerned. A new type of marvel dish washer detergent could have more impact, if you ask me."

Tom Alvaro laughed. Greene, his NASA boss smiled coldly, leaning back on his chair.

"How do you know that marvel dish-washer detergent won't come precisely out of some Shuttle, or the International Space Station experiments with colloidal mixtures in weightless environments?" Alvaro asked, still smiling.

"I'm afraid not," Stirling answered calmly. "Don't get me wrong, I am among the ones to appreciate the space effort, the astrophysics research, the missions to Mars, everything. One whould be too narrow-minded to overlook the importance of these activities, and to overlook the fundamental research in general. I believe, for example, that one of the most unfortunate decisions our government made was the decision to give up the Super-Collider project in Texas. That saved what, a billion dollars? That's half of a B2 bomber. Meantime, we're working with the Europeans at CERN, in Geneva, Switzerland to run experiments in fundamental particle physics, sharing costs anyway. The amount of opportunities lost here will never be estimated correctly. On the other hand, we have invested heavily into the International Space Station, which ran over budget many times. Yet we still fail to convince ourselves that the station was an important enough achievement. We beef up otherwise moderately interesting experiments and push them up on orbit just to prove, politically, that the station is of great value. In my opinion it's a wrong approach. The station will only prove its value with better thinking."

"I find your views extreme, Mr. Stirling" replied Greene. "It seems to me you're minimizing very important and essential effort and work."

"Well, maybe I do it, a bit, do take it to heart," Stirling laughed. "I'm just making a point. I put some of my hopes into this Space Exploration Initiative. This initiative is about forty years overdue. Commercially, it is a useless enterprise, if you try to measure its direct output. The real important outputs are the indirect effects."

"Such as?" Greene asked.

"Technology development. Materials, computers, all sorts of devices which will find their way into the commercial market. People well trained into sciences and management of complex projects. Jobs. Accountability. You guys at NASA have been producing paper studies for too long. Now you'll have to fly people to the Moon and back twice a year. There is no room for incompetence there. No room for mistakes."

"But that takes money, Mr. Stirling," Jim Garland said. "Our government lives on credit, and is entangled in the Middle East and financial crises. The Apollo program couldn't have happened with this kind of funding."

"Very true, Mr. Garland. The Apollo program costs compare with formidable efforts such as the building of the Panama Canal. In today's money, the peak NASA annual budget was in 1966 at around thirty billion dollars and most of it dedicated to the Apollo program. The today's NASA budget stands at sixteen billion annually and a significant part of it just keeps the NASA going."

Greene and Alvaro did not comment. They knew the numbers. Stone and Adams gave Stirling a strange look. The industry men didn't want any confrontation with the government agency.

"I see you industry folks upset," Stirling said and gave another slow, silent laugh. "I have some news for you, it's good or bad, depending which side of it you examine. The US government cannot afford to drop the Space Exploration program. Why? Because there is a huge Chinese tidal wave coming from behind. We here in the US gotta start moving, otherwise we risk paying the price for those forty years of sleep Mr. Garland was talking about. The Chinese are currently employing two hundred and fifty thousand people in their rocket development industry, with more than forty thousand of them highly specialized scientists at doctorate level of education. The have a manned space program for the Moon in the works and some other good stuff coming."

Adams turned his golden pen around on the table, thinking aloud: "What's is it at stake for them? Why such a huge effort?"

Stirling smiled. "Prestige, Mr. Adams. National prestige. The European and the Russians are not sleeping either, gentlemen. The European Space Agency just decided to join forces with the Russians and help finance a new thing called The Joint Crew Transportation System. I expect Russian French and German to be spoken on the Moon, besides Chinese."

The industry and NASA men in the room stood hard faced. None of them enjoyed Stirling's words.

"Besides prestige, there is no real commercial pressure to go seriously into space," Stirling continued, seemingly amused by the reaction. "The pressure will be of political and military nature. I see a military race for assured access to space much sooner than making marvel detergents on that space station of yours, Mr. Alvaro. It is for staying ahead of this new challenge, and for new and versatile military space vehicles that the MORPHEM technology presented here may be applied, gentlemen. It is a non-conventional technology which allows one to get ahead of the pack."

Stirling eyed McNutt and Garland as he rested his hands calmly on the table suggesting he had finished his speech.

The NASA man, Greene was paying attention this time.

"Is the program funded at present?" he asked towards McNutt and Jackobs.

"Yes," McNutt answered, quickly.

Jackobs was more reserved. "At present, the program is in a particular phase of technology re-assessment," he said.

"Any NASA money?" Greene asked his man, Tom Alvaro.

"No, we don't participate."

"Are you going to propose this engine in conjunction with any particular vehicle configuration?" Jeff Stone asked. He had become alert, relaxation gone. That was the reason he was at Lockwell, to assess the situation. MORPHEM could become a serious challenge for his corporation if taken too seriously.

"It's premature," answered Garland instead. "There are some options, but we'll keep them in the drawer until we see the thing working."

"Going back to the performance," Greene spoke, "what are those predictions based on? Your prototype had a destructive failure; did you collect enough data to base some predictions on it?"

Varese gave me an ugly look. McNutt saw it and glanced at me as well. I understood. They didn't want me to speak. Jackobs ignored the exchange.

"The predictions are based on isolated component testing," answered Garland again, "The plasma temperatures, the electromagnetic field intensities, coupled with our modeling. We're pretty confident in these numbers, once we'll get the full engine to operate. Once we secure the right funding we'll definitely make it work."

His confidence impressed everybody in the way he wanted.

"Can we get some copies of these charts?" asked Greene.

"We'll e-mail them to you" McNutt assured him.

"Cc me as well, please" Jeff Stone requested.

"We'll do," Varese said.

The men gathered their notebooks and briefcases. Stirling stood up.

"Just a moment gentlemen," Jackobs finally said, forcefully. Stirling sat back down, but no surprise showed on his face.

"I'll be short and straightforward," Jackobs said. "There is a rumor of a Lockwell sale. True or not, the situation is as follows:

Lockwell is under government contract to fully investigate the details and capability of the MORPHEM technology. There are sensitive issues related to this contract that cannot be discussed here. Consequently, any sale attempt at this point will not receive government approval."

There was dead silence for several long moments.

Then Stirling moved and stood up again.

"Anybody knows a good steak place around?" he asked jovially. The men pretended to relax and laughed. Varese said he knows just the right place. Out in the hallway Jackobs whispered something to McNutt, steel faced. They both headed towards McNutt's office.

"Dr. Salagen," Stirling called from the hallway, hands in his pockets. He slowly walked towards me and placed a hand on my shoulder, driving lightly, merely suggesting I should walk along the hallway with him.

"I got a chance to read some of your earlier reports on MORPHEM," he said as I obeyed his arm. "Impressive data."

"Thank you."

He suddenly stopped and faced me.

"But very empirical physics," he said.

He was watching me very carefully.

"Perhaps so," I said.

"How do you plan then to develop a full engine?"

"It's not my call and not my plan, Dr. Stirling."

"But can one be developed?"

It was my turn to scrutinize him.

"With enough testing, and tolerance for accidents, yes," I said.

He handed me a business card. "Perhaps we'll have the opportunity to discuss it in detail," he said.

There was a special wisdom in Stirling's way of dealing with people and I liked it. "Perhaps so," I said.

"Would you join us for lunch?"

"I'm afraid not, Dr. Stirling, too much work lined up for the day, still."

"In that case, it's been a pleasure, Dr. Salagen."

Nobody else paid attention to my humble person. Stirling turned to join the rest of the group for lunch.

***

I walked to Cruiff's office in A-25.

"McNutt was trying to push MORPHEM to the NASA," I told him.

Cruiff smirked.

"Did they buy it?"

"There is nothing to buy. But McNutt and a guy named Stirling there got them thinking."

Cruiff looked at me. "Stirling?" he asked, "Scott Stirling?"

"Yes, I think that was the name."

Cruiff laughed slowly, thinking.

"Stirling in one of the brains in this industry, sonny. He's been around for ever. He's a gray eminence with the defense business. Who got Stirling in this?"

"No idea. It looks to me McNutt knows him personally."

Cruiff nodded. "Well, that's interesting.   What about you? Where are you in this?"

"If they sell MORPEHM into a NASA program it's fine with me. But there are issues with this program which will prevent any sale."

Cruiff was silent for a moment.

"Issues?" he asked

"Issues of all sorts," I said. "What about that beer, stranger?"

"Any motherfucker time you want, my man."

I gave him a US Marines salute and left.

I remembered Xiao. His cubicle office was empty. I found him in the coffee room. With his slow motions, Xiao was filtering tealeaves in his porcelain cup.

"Thought you've left," I told him. "Sorry about earlier, we got interrupted."

"That's all right" Xiao said, smiling.

"You mentioned an invitation?"

"It's a bit cumbersome," he muttered. "I was asked to invite you to a *dimsum* this weekend, if you're available. Some people who want to meet you."

He was smiling nervously. The typical mumbling of his speech was more marked that usual.

"What people, Xiao? Friends of yours?"

He smiled, uncomfortable.

"It's a bit complicated to explain," he spoke hesitantly. "They are associates of some associates of some people I know. I didn't know if you are available, but I was asked to ask you anyway. "

I felt a cold ripple along my spine. In a flash, I recalled the face of the Asian man thrusting himself against the censored face of the unknown woman and the burst of fire chopping the Chevy Impala. You, the quiet Xiao, I thought. Do you know anything about those people?

"Where is the place?" I asked him.

"It's a restaurant in Monterey Park. It's called The Ocean Star."

"When?"

"Would Saturday morning work for you?

"Saturday is fine, Xiao. What time?"

"I suggest ten thirty to eleven. Traffic is very bad around Monterey Park on weekend."

"Then, Xiao, ten thirty to eleven it is."

27

The city of Monterey Park was baking under a hot Saturday morning sun when I turned left on Valley Boulevard coming from Rosemead. The Mustang's V8 idled while crawling on Valley in dense traffic.

I knew the city. East and west of the Rosemead Boulevard backyards radios filled the air with a mixture of Chinese tunes and *corridos*, but towards east, deeper into Monterey Park, there were no more *corridos*. As there were no more English labels on the produce at the neighborhood supermarkets. Only Chinese. Monterey Park is the true Chinatown of the greater Los Angeles.

The Ocean Star restaurant parking space was packed. I kept driving along residential streets east of Atlantic. It took more than three blocks to find a parking spot by a small park.

I was early for the meeting. I waited in the car, engine shut off, windows rolled down, listening to the street and city noises. Several old Chinese men were executing a Tai-Chi routine on the park's grass. Half of the houses around were old and small chunks of the American dream built by lower middle class people in the 60's and 70's, populated at present by Chinese immigrants. The other half were newer houses, built with more largesse by Chinese families with larger budgets, extra floors added, all finished with good paint and expensive outside lighting. Their architecture was nondescript, as if improvised, with the apparent objective of adding as many rooms as possible.

An old Chinese woman passed on the sidewalk pushing a small cart half filled with groceries. Her walk was tired but steady, the walk of an old woman for which life is but a long difficult road, not yet at its end.

That corner of Los Angeles had lost its geographic identity. It was no longer an American place. It wasn't any place of certain identity, as its identity was being reshaped by immigrant Asian cultures settling in. And the fact made it back, an American place.

I got out of the car, and walked towards the restaurant. Farther down the street, a large blue sedan was trying to squeeze itself in between two small old cars at the curb.

Once inside the Ocean Star lobby I lost track of geography again. I could've been anywhere from Shanghai to Singapore. A large and noisy crowd was waiting to be seated. I was one of the few non-Asian men in the packed crowd, everyone talking loud, vividly yelling or laughing, all in Chinese dialects sprinkled with English. Two large TV sets on an adjacent waiting room were broadcasting shows, news of an Asian channel on one, the other a Chinese version of Jeopardy crossed with Who Wants to be a Millionaire.

I elbowed my way to a front desk where hostesses were taking new names on a large book while scratching out the names of parties seated already. From time to time, a voice called numbers on a speaker system with enough amplification to cover the noise of the crowd. The hostess asked me something I couldn't understand.

"Xiao Lin!" I shouted over the noise, "the Xiao Lin party!"

She didn't understand. My pronunciation of Xiao's name was probably wrong. I wrote the name down. She talked fast in Chinese to another woman wearing the red uniform of the restaurant's employees. The woman looked at me while listening, and answered something, short.

"You wait," said the first hostess. "Please wait."

I waited. On the TV screens some Asian troops were training with determined faces, then some diplomats wearing suits, descended from shiny cars, shaking hands. On the other screen the show was impossible to follow. I couldn't guess who the show hosts were and who were the guests. They all seemed to have great fun nevertheless, the laughing was non stop.

A young Chinese maître-d' came out of the restaurant, browsed the crowd and quickly locked on me.

"Dr. Salagen?"

"Yes."

"Your party is waiting, please follow me sir."

He turned around and led me into the restaurant. The noise did not diminish once inside, it only changed in nature. The restaurant was large, filled with round tables seating ten or more people, all packed. Everybody was talking loud, eating, laughing. Waitresses were pushing carts with steamed *dimsum* dishes around the tables, moving fast, making quick and efficient stops at each table on their way.

The Chinese man led me to a side of the restaurant where he pushed a narrow sliding door. It took me by surprise. I didn't realize a door was there.

"Please, sir," he invited me in.

Once I entered, he pushed the door closed from the outside, and the noise died.

Three men and a woman were sitting at a table. One of the men rose at the sound of the door. It was Xiao. He pushed his chair away, and with a gesture of his hand invited me at the table with his typical restrained smile, the gaze of his eyes guarded and careful.

"Matt, welcome," he said. The other two men rose. The woman lifted a pair of black eyes and watched me with a slight smile. The Asian features of her face dissolved beautifully into her exquisite pale white skin, graciously arched full lips, and rich, long black hair.

"I'm glad you made it," Xiao said. "Let me please introduce you to Feng Zhijian, and David and Evelyn Chang".

The man named Feng was short, stocky, with a wide face, rare hair and severe features. He was wearing a gray business suit, the shiny expensive kind people buy from Hong Kong or Singapore, with a look on the border between elegance and bad taste. The other man, David Chang was taller, an academic type with distinguished features, designer frames on his eyeglasses and full hair with a good cut. He was wearing slacks and an elegant light beige coat over a simple white t-shirt.

The one in charge was Feng.

"I am glad we have the opportunity to meet you, Dr. Salagen," he spoke volubly. "I have asked my friend Xiao Lin here to offer us this opportunity, and I thank you for accepting the invitation. But please, do sit down."

We all sat. The seat saved for me was in between Xiao and Evelyn Chang. Feng Zhijian sat across the table from me.

"Did you find parking all right?" he asked.

"Yes, thank you, a few blocks away," I said. "Too busy here."

Feng laughed.

"Yes, pretty busy here, we had to make arrangements."

He fiddled with the menu.

"I always come to this place for *dimsum* when I'm in town," he said. "It's one of the best. Do you like *dimsum* Dr. Salagen?"

"Occasionally," I said. "I'm never quite sure what to order."

The woman laughed. She knew how, the sound of her laughter was good, musical, feminine. The men followed suit, laughing politely.

She leaned towards me and touched my forearm. "Then, Dr. Salagen, if you allow me, I would be glad to order for you."

There was very little scent coming from her, no perfume.

"Thank you," I said.

She laughed again, nodding. She did her part well; the atmosphere in the room was relaxing. The man named Feng seemed to be reading the items on the menu with certain familiarity with the restaurant specialties. Evelyn Chang took her offer seriously and opened her menu towards me. I hadn't opened mine, and glanced at hers, written only in Chinese, without English translations.

"This is a soup of herbs," she said, pointing to a place amongst the ideograms and reading the item aloud. "It would be, I suggest, a good start."

I said OK. She crafted me a sequence of dishes. A waiter came in through the sliding door, as if summoned. Feng Zhijian and the Changs ordered in Chinese. Evelyn put her hand on my upper arm and began speaking to the waiter, making it obvious that she's ordering for me. Xiao ordered last, as if reluctant to speak his mother tongue. Hearing him speaking Chinese made me suddenly feel insecure, as if abducted on an alien ship in the middle of a bad dream. I studied Evelyn Chang profile. I imagined her nursing an infant or discharging an Uzi from the back seat of a Toyota, pulverizing the Chevy on Slauson Street. She seemed perfectly capable of both.

The waiter left. Feng seemed to prepare to speak again, his severe face changed to an amiable grimace, eyes flickering.

"Again, I must express to you, Dr. Salagen, that I am very glad you accepted this invitation," he began. "My friend Xiao was suggesting you may refuse it, given your full schedule."

He had a strange way of emphasizing the expression '*my friend Xiao*' with a meaning I couldn't guess.

Feng continued: "I believe it is fair to say that we work in the same branch of business, Dr. Salagen. I am talking about plasma physics. While we will delight ourselves with some excellent food, I hope to be able to explain to you a bit about our work, and why we searched the opportunity to meet you. I also hope that you will find this meeting interesting from your point of view as well".

He spoke correct English, with well exercised American accent, yet retaining the typical Chinese pronunciation in r's and ch's.

"Speaking of physics," David Chang spoke, "Only several weeks ago I read two of your early papers on intermittent plasma confinement and found the work very interesting."

I watched him closely, masking my distrust.

"The American Physical Society reports?" I asked.

"Precisely those."

"Are you working in the field?"

"Yes," he said. "Five years at UC Berkeley, got my Ph.D. in 87. A couple of years of research at MIT, then on my own."

I searched my memory and couldn't remember any particular report or paper with a David Chang among the authors. On the other hand, papers are being published by the hundreds every year. His English was fluent, with only a slight accent.

"What about you, Mrs. Chang," I turned towards the woman on my left. "Do you work in sciences as well?"

She laughed again.

"I work with numbers, Dr. Salagen, but only those that really matter. The esoteric nature of physics is too complicated for me. I prefer the naked reality of finance."

She spoke fluent English, with no effort, as if she grew up in the States, her voice bearing a deep feminine resonance, a Chinese version of Garbo.

"Banking?" I asked.

"Venture capital. Feng and David may have these great ideas, but they're worth nothing without solid investment. I'm taking care of that."

The sliding door opened again to allow our Chinese waiter in. He pushed in a small cart filled with steamy silver pots and started distributing the dishes. I tasted my soup. It was, in fact, delicious.

Once the eating started, the dishes kept rolling. The Changs ordered wine, a chardonnay. Evelyn explained the dishes to me. She delicately offered me samples of the small *chow* snacks, *war teep* wrappers, and the sesame seed meat balls. Feng told stories from his travels. He seemed to be traveling often to Asia and Europe. Too much travel, for a scientist. Clothes too shiny for a scientist.

On my right, Xiao kept quiet, almost a non presence.

The Chinese waiter seemed to have been summoned again. Feng ordered tea and coffee, and produced several Cuban cigars, from the breast pocket of his shiny coat. I refused. Feng and Evelyn Chang lit up. It was against city ordinances, but a room air control system seemed to be picking up the smoke with no trouble.

"Dr. Salagen," Feng spoke again, "Please allow me to bring up physics again. I read your papers as well, the reports David mentioned here earlier. You are trying to apply the intermittent plasma confinement to propulsion. It is visionary, definitely, but, in my opinion, it limits its potential".

"What do you mean?" I asked.

"Frankly, there is only one client for the propulsion application, and that's the government" Feng explained. "No corporation or venture capital would invest in it, unless just redirecting funds from one of the government agencies. Would you agree?"

I shrugged: "Seems a reasonable assumption."

He laughed, softly, satisfied.

"But there are valuable commercial applications, Dr. Salagen," he said, smoothly. "Applications which can easily attract funds, royalties, profits."

I leaned back on my chair and sipped some coffee.

"What sort applications?" I asked.

David Chang spoke instead of Feng: "How about something as simple as welding?"

I was puzzled. "Welding?"

"High speed plasma metal cutters, to be exact," Chang explained. "Do you have any idea of the time and energy spent by shipyards, steel mills, by the whole industry that deals with cutting large dimensions of steel plates? The amount of resources spent is tremendous."

The field was completely unfamiliar to me.

"I fail to see the application," I said.

"I can provide documentation," he offered. "There is a large variety of plasma cutter equipment on the market already, and have been there for years. However, I did some calculations, assuming a scaled down intermittent plasma cavity similar to the one you propose for a plasma engine core, which has also the ability to focus the jet into a very precise and narrow area. The amount of energy spent for cutting steel plates can be reduced by more than half, in some cases by almost eighty percent. If you apply this to several hundred million dollars spent in the industry per year, you can guess the figure."

I rested my elbows on the chair's armrests, locked my hands together and rested my chin on them.

"OK," I said. "What's missing, then?"

Chang glanced quickly at Feng. His wife drew smoke from the cigar, blowing it out slowly. Her lips were sensational.

"I'm not going to beat around the bush, Dr. Salagen," Feng said. "If you'll analyze the application on your own you will realize immediately that the key to success is to obtain a stable plasma cavity. The current technology uses a blunt electrical arc to heat a jet of fluid and blow away locally molten metal. If we replace the arc with a cavity of intermittently confined super hot plasma, the benefit is enormous both in energy efficiency and in the quality of the cut."

I watched him carefully. Somehow, I had expected something like this, but the concrete form of the approach was appalling. It saddened me that Xiao was part of it. I had always liked Xiao, and I still felt this was not something he would do unconstrained. I felt the need to cut the whole story short.

"I understand the physics," I said, interrupting Feng. "I still don't understand is what prevents you from going ahead with this, and what is it exactly that you need from me."

Feng recoiled slightly from my blunt question. He quickly glanced at Xiao. Evelyn Chang drew smoke from her cigar. I felt a wave of ice coming from her, something even more dangerous than Feng's severe personality could generate.

Feng marched forward.

"Dr. Salagen," he said, "let me make you this offer. We have several funding openings lined up, and we're dealing with something that is no more than textbook physics. However, time is of essential value in our project. I can offer you a half of million dollars lump sum payment plus percentage participation for providing the scaling principles of an intermittent plasma confinement cavity for this application. Please examine this opportunity carefully. It is, in my opinion, extremely lucrative for all of us."

I watched their faces, each, one by one. I felt my blood pulsing in my ears. I rose from my chair.

"I must thank you for this wonderful brunch," I said, my voice flat. "I cannot accept your offer Mr. Zhijiang. You will have to do that textbook physics on your own. For now, I wish all of you a good weekend."

I pushed away my chair, and walked towards the narrow door. It opened before I touched its handle. The Chinese waiter was there, in the door, smiling courteously and blocking my way.

"Dr. Salagen!" a voice called.

It was Evelyn Chang. I turned towards the table. Feng sat, red faced, while David Chang had the expression of an extra left without his script instructions in a B series. Feng barked something in Chinese, apparently towards Xiao. Xiao mumbled something back, in a vaguely defiant manner.

"It has been a pleasure meeting you, Dr. Salagen," Evelyn Chan said, her deep voice at its full charm. "Perhaps we'll have the pleasure again."

The waiter said something, smiling, and cleared my way. I walked back into the restaurant's noise, then outside, on the sidewalks. The sun was hot, scorching the city. I walked the three blocks distance towards my car ignoring the heat, watching my back. The sight of my Mustang was a relief. The machine was a trusted friend, a familiar object. I reached for the keys, still watching my back.

28

"Dr. Salagen?" a voice called behind me, while car doors slammed. They were white men, blond, tall, dressed in dark blue suits. I glanced up the street. The blue sedan was still there, squeezed between two small old cars, the men inside it just sitting and watching.

"Yes," I said.

One of them came close and showed me a badge. It was a large piece of metal stuck to a black leather holder. I knew nothing about badges.

"You need to come with us, sir, right away," the man said and pointed to their car, another blue sedan looking big and powerful.

I thought of Xiao, sitting there at the table, silent, almost sad. I didn't feel any anger at him, somehow I couldn't. The others, the man named Feng and the Changs were probably going to leave unperturbed. Feng Zhijiang in his shiny suit driving an even shinier car. All they had done was make a commercial proposal. All I had done was refuse it.

"What about my car?" I asked, "I don't want to leave it here."

"Jim!" the man called over his shoulder.

Another tall blue suit came close.

"Give him the keys," the first man ordered me. "He'll take care of it."

The keys were already my hand. I handed them to the man named Jim.

The sequence of facts accelerated as soon as I got in their car. The two men on the front seats didn't seem to care what I do in the back seat. The car immediately sped up as the driver vigorously maneuvered on the city streets. He was skilled in using the quiet power of the car to fight his way in the traffic. We quickly reached the 10 freeway, and, to my surprise, the car engaged on the east bound ramp, away from the LA city. I expected they'd take me some place downtown.

The car swung strongly and engaged an exit ramp. I didn't understand where they were taking me. We had only gone a few miles on the freeway. I searched the streets. We were in the city of El Monte. The driver took the Santa Anita road, and then turned the car off the main street into a wide open field. *El Monte Airport* was lettered on a road sign. The man in the front seat raised his hand and talked into a small radio. The radio beeped.

As we turned the corner of a hangar, I heard the beat of a rotor and whistling of engines. It was an ugly military helicopter. The car drove straight to it, we all got out of the car and the men pushed me into the aircraft, which was speeding up its rotor. The men slid the doors shut and pulled back from the helicopter as it took off. Inside the helicopter, a man wearing a grey uniform and sunglasses yelled at me to buckle up.

I felt caught in the teeth of an immense machinery system. Confusion fully took over weariness. For a while I tried to follow the route. The helicopter first flew west, then north, through the mountains. I gave up and closed my eyes. The helicopter vibration and its strong side swings made me regurgitate food. I kept swallowing. The restaurant encounter had already detached from reality, entering the sequence of bad metaphysics belonging to the past.

We were flying over the Mojave Desert. Somewhere, nowhere. Mojave Desert is a big place. Some French friends of Christine had visited once, a few years back. We had taken the pair on a trip and had driven through the Mojave for a while. *"Where are we?"* the French man had asked me after the arid landscape bored him. *"Mojave Desert,"* I'd said. He'd asked the question a few more times, and had gotten the same answer. Then, he'd kept his mouth shut for a while. *"And where are we know?"* he'd asked after another two hours. *"Mojave Desert"* I'd said, one more time. The Frenchman had exclaimed, *"It is tres big, this desert"*. *"That's right"* I'd said, *"fucking big"*.

We landed, all of a sudden. It wasn't any particular place, just the arid desert and a military Hummer vehicle waiting there. Then I looked better and saw hangars and some buildings farther east.

The man in the grey uniform handed me to the two other men dressed in fatigues who had been waiting by the Hummer. They asked to see my identification. Then, they ordered me to get into the Hummer. The vehicle had incredibly small passenger room. I hold on tight while it bounced hard over dry dirt. The vehicle entered a building resembling a hangar and followed a track marked with paint on the floor. We stopped in front of a double metal door where an officer was waiting. Better uniform, higher rank, the man was cleanly shaved, looking competent.

The Hummer driver got out of the car and reported my name to the officer who examined me with an air of urgency.

"Major Tom Brodsky," he introduced himself. "Please follow me, Dr. Salagen."

He quickly turned around and rushed me through the door into a long corridor ending on another large metal door. I forced myself to walk as fast as he did. At the end of the corridor, he keyed in a sequence of numbers on a security pad and opened the door with a swipe of his badge, inviting me in.

The room we entered was very large and almost in the dark. Several wide TV screens were lit on a wall to the right. The screens were showing maps, and images of people sitting at tables, shuffling papers and looking at other screens.

"0-2-5" a voice said, broadcasted loud on a speaker system. It had the background noise of a space communication or an aircraft transmission. "Negative, repeat, negative" the voice came again.

"Negative, confirmed. Failure to intercept," another metallic, clearer voice announced.

A rumor of worried men's voices spread through the large dark room. The officer named Brodsky frowned. He took me to a conference table on the side of the room opposite to the TV screens. Lamps on the table were lighting precise spots underneath them, enough to read a document, if necessary. The faces of the men sitting at the table were in the dark. Most of them, as I could guess, were wearing military uniforms.

"They brought Salagen," Brodsky reported to one of the shadows.

"Have him sit down at one of the stations," the shadow ordered. "See what he needs."

Brodsky turned back to me.

"Please take a seat here," Brodsky said, pointing to a desk in a row, in the center of the room.

I decided to wake up, break the surreal.

"Major Brodsky, is that your name, sir?" I asked the man.

"Yes," he confirmed, surprised.

"Why was I brought here? What exactly is happening?"

He watched me, puzzled, trying to understand.

"You weren't briefed?"

"Briefed?"

He thought he understood, but wasn't sure. He turned around towards the table, uncertain of what he should do, when another shadow there moved, rose, came closer and became a tall man offering his hand. The face looked familiar in the scarce light, but I couldn't associate a name to it.

"I had them bring you as urgently as possible," the man said, shaking my hand. "Come, let's sit here," he continued, indicating the same console desk Brodsky had invited me to sit at a minute earlier.

The tall man bore an intense yet quiet sense of urgency. Frantically, my mind was searching for the identity of the man. As I sat down, another officer placed a stack of papers on the desk. My memory jolted.

"Stirling?" I asked, unsure of my finding, "Dr. Scott Stirling?"

He looked at me slightly puzzled, and hazily guessed my state of confusion.

"Yes, don't you remember, Dr. Salagen? We met last week at Lockwell."

He watched me again, thinking. "In fact," he said, it is after that meeting that I took the liberty of adding your name on a list of experts that are to be called when certain situations occur. And we do have a situation, right now as we speak, Dr. Salagen, that's why you've been located and brought in."

The desk had telecommunication equipment and a computer screen embedded in a panel. On the screen, small windows were reproducing the images from the larger TV screens on the wall.

"0-2-6" another metallic voice said on the speaker system, with the same background of crackling noise as before. "Negative, repeat, negative".

"Negative, confirmed. Failure to intercept," the other voice echoed. Stirling listened and frowned as Brodsky did before, and voices in the room grew increasingly alarmed.

Stirling began explaining, speaking fast. "Here's what's happening. We first spotted this thing at 11 a.m. this morning. Commercial pilots reported a condensation trail at very high altitude northeast of Guam. For some reason they were intrigued by the contrail. US Pacific Command verified it with the civil traffic controllers, the military traffic controllers, everybody, it was neither a commercial flight nor any other flight that was known to have that route. Besides the contrail, not much of detection could be achieved. A radar station on Midway Island had picked up something, unclear. Whatever it is, it's coming fast at us. Here is a data sheet. We tracked the object again when it passed slightly north of Hawaii, on a course east. Roughly 65,000 feet altitude, air speed close to Mach 3. Way beyond passenger liners and even jet fighter altitude. US Pacific Command's Air Force sent a few F15's from Hickam in Hawaii with high altitude intercept missiles, but all they observed was the contrail. Only the NORAD is able to track it. As I said it is hard to track, it shows on and off the radars. Also, apparently it is steadily increasing speed. We tried three intercepts so far, you've just heard the communications related to the fourth, all failed. We don't know what the nature of this object is. Very weak radar signature. Our surface to air and air to air intercept technology doesn't seem to work on it, so far."

I listened to him perplexed.

"You guys brought me here for something like a UFO?" I interrupted him.

He frowned.

"This is no fucking UFO. This is very much a piece of hardware made by humans, and probably not very sophisticated ones. It's a combination of revolutionary and rudimentary."

He grabbed my arm.

"Dr. Salagen, I'm familiar with the concept and all intelligence on your MORPHEM project. I know there are people out there who made it work, and they may be using it as we speak. Do you understand? We've got to know if there is any chance the object we're tracking is powered by something like MORPHEM. How do we shoot it down? We need to know fast, this thing is going to cross the west coast line in less than thirty minutes, and we don't know what's carrying on board!"

He reached on the console and operated a keyboard showing familiarity with the equipment. Numbers showed on the screen and a map was displayed.

"The object has reached airspeed of over Mach 3," he said, and turned towards me.

Low frequency vibration noise came from the ceiling.

"We're scrambling our F-15s here" Stirling said, looking up.

I understood the urgency and the tension, but I was lost. The surreal had transcended into a vicious reality which still smelled of a bad dream. I made an intense effort to focus, concentrate on the puzzling elements of that reality, on the nature of the danger, and examine it with cold technical reasoning.

"What's the size of this object, do we know?" I asked Stirling.

"No," he answered. "Here is the only information we have" he brought a few images on the screen.

Satellite images, hastily shot from low earth orbit by spy birds, processed by computers on the fly. A vague dark shape followed by a very long, narrow bright trail. I shook my head.

"It can be anything," I said. "If it uses MORPHEM technology, it produces water: some of the hydrogen fuel is used in straightforward combustion, it reacts with oxygen and produces hot steam. That's why such a rich condensation trail, the object itself may be small. Why is it so hard to intercept?"

Stirling made a nervous gesture. "We're damn blind shooting. The NORAD did some sort of a telemetry to calculate where the object moves, then we shot at the position with sea based SAM system. Somehow, both thermal and electromagnetic tracking technologies used by the surface to air missiles are failing to find the thing."

Someone made a change in the speaker system of the room, and a flow of voice communication burst out. Tensed voices of command people overlapped noisy aircraft transmissions. NORAD people were talking to people at the Pentagon. The sound level went down. Stirling listened then turned back towards me, flexing his jaw.

"Can you estimate how far this thing can go, what's its possible payload size, what to expect?"

"I'd be just guessing."

"Guess your best, and fast."

He meant it. The pressure and tension in the room had become more obvious to me, people moving fast from one console to the other, the intercom voices.

One more time I forced myself to concentrate. I laid down a set of assumptions, sizes and amounts of hydrogen fuel that could be carried. But the actual thrust, the possible performance of a

MORPHEM-like system was impossible to guess, if I didn't know its size. I worked numbers chasing my tail in assumptions, growing dizzy, feeling the pressure invading and blocking my brain. I couldn't think.

Size, sizes. You have one thing, and you want to make it bigger. You take the blue prints and multiply each dimension by an enlarging factor, and you get a larger thing, scaled up from the initial one. Scaling, that's what Zhijiang wanted as well, the scaling principles for the MORPHEM cavity, because a straight dimensional blow-up or shrink-down was not working for MORPHEM, its geometry had to be changed in a certain subtle way, using a method I had constructed empirically. The Lockwell people didn't understand the scaling problem. The MORPHEM explosion at Lockwell proved

The graphical chart with the exponential growth of energy just before the explosion during the MORPHEM tests came suddenly in my mind. Growth. Energy, increasing until becoming uncontrollable. The unknown flying object was accelerating steadily. Energy, it was flowing more energy, more power. How to perturb that energy, to make it unstable?

"Stirling!" I called. His head jerked, his eyes fixed me, expectantly.

"We need to hit this thing with focused radio frequency" I said. "I don't know how. We just need electromagnetic radiation in the radio or microwave frequency range, tons of it, as much of it as it is possible, a blast".

He weighed my words and picked up a phone from the console desk. I heard him speaking but didn't understand his words. I just felt exhausted.

"Yes, focused microwave beam," he said in the phone and placed it back in its cradle.

We sat and waited. Sweat had mixed with dust on my hands and I wished I could wash somewhere, but I didn't move, didn't speak. Time passed. No intercept messages came on the speaker system. Somehow, the motion in the room had died. Lights were blinking on consoles, screens changing colors, people's faces lit by lights from the console lamps, lips moving in front of microphones.

"2-0-6-3-5" a voice said in the intercom, "abort mission confirmed."

It was an aircraft transmission, judging by the noise. More voices confirmed aborted missions.

"What's happening?" I asked Stirling.

He shrugged.

"They're clearing the air space."

"Japan Air Lines 6-0-2-5 diverted south," an operator voice started but it was cut off by the invisible operator switching channels on and off somewhere in a control room.

Stirling nodded.

"Clearing the air of commercial flights as well. All bets are on you, Salagen, you and your radio frequency idea".

"What are they going to use?"

He shrugged again.

"Something that needs clear air space, so it doesn't kill innocent people."

We waited. More transmissions came, illegible for me. Numbers and jargon. Chunks of intense communication traffic, making their way into the room's speaker system by rules of choice I failed to understand.

Suddenly voices erupted, overlapping, calm but rushed voices, trained operators quoting numbers and words, faster, nervous, in an accelerated carousel of sounds. I opened my mouth to ask Stirling again, but the expression on his face stopped me. He had placed his hands spread on the console, and bowed his head, listening, his jaw muscles pulsing.

Then the flow of voices stopped. Only rare short communications followed. Confirmations and numbers. Stirling operated again the console terminal, switching window after window on the screen. He exhaled, leaned back and patted me on the shoulder.

"No more trace of that shit," he growled. He kept switching images operating the keyboard. "Gone," he said, "doesn't show anywhere on any radar screen. Good job, doctor."

My arms and legs felt heavy, as if full of lead.

"Can someone fucking explain to me what happened?" I whispered to Stirling.

He laughed, slowly, softly.

"I just passed your idea, nothing more. We're in a secondary command center, the really big shots are somewhere in Colorado. They used your idea, and, apparently, somehow it worked."

"Where are we here?" I asked him.

He laughed again.

"Mojave Desert," he answered.

"Mojave is a fucking big place."

"We're on the south-east corner of the Edwards Air Force Base"

"I see," I nodded with unexpected relief. The place seemed more familiar. I knew the base.

Stirling tapped lightly on my shoulder. "Brace yourself for a long night, doctor. Debriefing and analysis".

For several blurry hours faces on the screens kept reporting, and other faces kept asking questions. Somebody said my name. It was one of the faces on a screen with a hard mouth. The face repeated my name and Stirling shook my shoulder.

"Yes," I said, "could you repeat that, sir?"

The face's mouth hardened even more and spoke again. "It has been your suggestion to use intense radio or microwave radiation on the target. On what assumption was your suggestion based?"

A small red light came on the console desk I was sitting at. Simultaneously, my face appeared on one of the large TV screens next to the one with the face interrogating me. I contemplated myself fascinated, as if a different man was on the screen. That man was older than I knew myself. He needed a shave, and some sleep. The face of Matt Salagen on the screen opened his mouth to speak, and I collected my thoughts.

"Dr. Scott Stirling here made the first suggestion that the object was powered by a propulsion system similar to a system I worked on for a number of years. That system is based on strongly ionized gas, working with electromagnetic fields of microwave frequencies. The device is very hard to control, very unstable. It can either die, loosing power, or deflagrate. Last year, a prototype exploded on the test stand displaying what seemed to be the latter situation. Very preliminary analysis I did on the test results made me think that an addition of outside energy could render any similar device strongly unstable. Hence my suggestion."

There was silence. The face on the screen conferred to someone unseen.

"Are you able to provide a quantitative analysis of these assumptions?" the face asked.

Geometry, I thought. Hoover. Get me Henry Hoover's measurement results.

"I need support for obtaining some measurement data from the Lockwell corporation," I said, "I may be able to provide analysis".

"What sort of a support is it necessary?"

"I will communicate that through Dr. Scott Stirling here."

Stirling nodded. "I can take care of that, general" he accepted.

I looked at the screen and noticed for the first time that the man on the screen was old and had blue eyes. He was conferring with someone on his left again.

"We need a report ASAP," he said.

"You'll have it, general," Stirling said, and nobody questioned him.

I leaned back on the chair, and let reality further detach from my grip.

2 9

"The data is confidential and proprietary," Varese declared. His face had gotten a shade of green induced by a ferocious and hardly controlled fury. "Your review of this data is not necessary, Salagen."

Henry Hoover sat at his large impeccable desk swinging slowly on a comfortable leather office chair. His eyes scanned Varese with calm, expressing no emotion, like a naturalist examining a lizard.

"Check with McNutt's office," I said. "I have all the approvals in place."

"Bullshit!"

There was another moment of silence. I weighed Varese's fierceness. He was throwing all his weight into covering the fact that he had scaled up my early small scale engine into a large, full scale MORPHEM, without understanding the physics.

Hoover's gaze came again upon me. I was a second lizard and I was supposed to fight the first. But I was fed up with both him and Varese.

"Henry," I said, "be kind enough and push that phone of yours towards me, please."

Hoover's swinging stopped, and the hairless eyebrows went up again. Slowly, he pushed his desk phone towards me.

"All yours."

I lifted the receiver and punched McNutt's internal number. Jenny answered in the most melodious voice she had produced that month.

"Jenny, this is Salagen," I said sharply. "Put me through, please."

"Dr. Salgen," she sang, "I'm afraid Mr. McNutt has stepped out of the office, may I take a message or would you like his answering?"

"Just cut the shit. Put me through"

"I'm not sure I like your tone, Dr. Salagen."

"This is above your head, Jenny."

I heard static on the line and silence for e few moments.

"Perhaps I could check again," she finally said. "Just a moment."

"McNutt," a voice said, thickly.

"Sir, this is Matt Salagen. I'm at the PMR section in Henry Hoover's office. Present with me are Henry Hoover and Paul Varese. I am officially requesting access to the MORPHEM PMR measurements no later than today, close of business time. I need the data transferred in the format agreed upon in the contract, and in its entire content. There have been recent developments that support my access to this data, and to my knowledge you have been briefed. I am requesting a timely cooperation on this."

McNutt cleared his throat.

"Gimme Varese," he said.

I pushed the receiver to Paul Varese. For a second he was reluctant to take it. Slowly, he forced his hand to move, grab the receiver from me and lift it to his ear. He listened, stone faced. His eyes lost focus, looking somewhere beyond the walls.

"They can't," he said. "I don't accept this."

He listened for a few more moments, then, suddenly, he threw the receiver on the desk, turned around and left without a word.

Hoover picked the phone calmly and listened.

"Yes," he spoke into the mike. "No, sir, this is Henry Hoover. Yes, it's all done and complete. Yes, good day sir."

Hoover placed the received back on the cradle and watched me with disdain.

"You'll have it, Salagen" he said. He straightened in his chair. "Anything else I can do for you?"

I sat down on the edge of Hoover's desk.

"Where is the data, Henry?"

"You're a pushy fellow, aren't you Matt?" Hoover asked. He seemed frustrated. I watched him with curiosity.

"What's your stake in this, Henry? You've been alienating Varese ever since I've known you two, so OK, you don't like him, but there's more stuff bothering you. What is it?"

He laughed with no joy and pulled the computer keyboard closer to him. He eyed me, before typing.

"I've been in this business for twenty years plus, Salagen. I didn't make it to the big league level, but I know my job really well and I'm not afraid of any type of reptile in this company. And all these twenty years I saw management growing more and more incompetent, greedier and greedier. Budgets being cut, and cut again, doing less with a dollar and all my American machines getting worse with every replacement and in the end having to replace them with foreign ones, Japanese, then German. On top of that, I have to watch folks like Varese rolling their egos all over the place, squeeze what they needs out of anybody they please to squeeze. As far as I can see it, you seem to be picking up at the game yourself, son."

I opened my mouth to protest his last statement but he raised his hand, and pointed to the screen of his desktop while typing several lines on the keyboard.

"Here is your data," he said pointing to a list of names on the screen. "This is a secure website designed for exactly this type of exchanges. Here are the folders and here is a list of files and format descriptors. That includes some data files Cruiff has made per your specification."

I examined the content of the screen. The data had been uploaded a day before. Hoover had done it without waiting for Varese to authorize it.

"My obligation was to upload the data here," Hoover said. "You need to get your own authorized access to download it and use it. Anything else I can do for you?"

"No, Henry, that's fine," I said, "I do have access here, I'll pick up the data from my office."

I shook his hand.

"Thanks, Henry" I said, "This is an excellent job."

"Just fuck off," he said.

3 0

Outside Hoover's office Lockwell's grounds appeared deserted, the gray buildings grumbling in their gloomy language of electric fans and AC compressors. I headed to my office.

My cell phone rang.

"Dad!" Julie's voice streamed full of joy, the moment I opened connection. I calculated the time in France; it was evening.

"Julia," I spoke softly as I stopped and sat on a thick duct running parallel to the alley. "How is my girl?"

She didn't respond right away, fussing with her phone in silence, letting me listen to the buildings for a few moments.

"I just miss you, dad" she said.

"I miss you too, Julia."

"I'm glad you do. She misses you too, you know?"

"Who? "

"I know who. Mom. She misses you too. She keeps a picture on her desk, the one with both of you on your friend's boat. I saw her once looking at it for a long time."

Images, memories. Christine, looking at our picture. Jane forcing my hands on her breasts.

"Life can be strange sometimes, Julia. Many times, a moment, something you see, something you observe may be interpreted in many different ways. You'll understand when you'll be older."

"I understand now, dad."

I smiled. "I know you do, Julia. But you'll understand more, later."

"Dad," she said and then hesitated. "Is there someone else?"

"Someone else?"

"I mean, someone else, with you."

I swallowed with a dry mouth.

"Yes. And no."

"I want to know about the yes part."

I laughed softly.

"I'm not sure I really know who she is, Julie. She's young, charming, and strange. Her name is Jane."

She remained silent for a while. The buildings told me with their dull compressors that I'm an idiot to confess Jane's presence to my daughter.

"Would I like her?" she asked.

"I don't know, Julie."

"Would she like me?"

"Yes."

Julie paused again.

"I won't tell mom. Not yet, OK?" she said, after a while.

"There is nothing to tell, Julia. My God, it's so good to hear you. I miss you, I miss my little girl."

"I'm not that little, not anymore, you know it very well."

"Well, you are to me, in a certain way."

A silhouette came out of one of the buildings and started walking towards me.

"Speaking of little girls," I said, "how is school going?"

"It's going fine. They're crazy here. I have twice as much work as back home. They make everything so complicated."

The silhouette was John Meinhardt. He was getting closer.

"Keep at it, Julie. I told you it's gonna be tough for a while."

"I'm glad you taught me how to think, dad. If I do the good thinking everything is easy, really, all except the stupid literature classes."

"Then work on that one. Remember? The more difficult a thing the more pounding you're giving it, right?"

She laughed.

"Yup. I'm just lazy sometimes."

"Well, don't be, ever. I gotta go, Julia. Please write, ok?"

"OK, love you dad. She misses you."

I hesitated.

"Then, say hello from me."

I closed connection right at the moment Meinhardt stopped in front of me. He waited for me to pocket the phone.

"I got a few hardcopy reports I need you to take a look at," he said. "Otherwise I'll trash them."

"Sure," I said. "Don't even joke about trashing."

He laughed.

"I wasn't joking. I'm swamped in these papers. Anyway, did you see Xiao anywhere today?"

A cold wave passed though my spine.

"Haven't seen him," I said, carefully. "Why?"

"Just asking. His wife called a few times."

"Mei Lin? Why did she call?"

He shrugged.

"Looking for him. He wasn't anywhere in A-25. Anyway, gotta go. The reports are on your desk. They're just prints, no electronic copies."

"I'll take a look."

He left and I rushed towards my office in the A-25. The Space Shuttle calendar hung crooked on the wall. I sat down at my desk and thought about Xiao Lin with that old stab feeling jolting again through my stomach. My last image of him was from the moment I left the private room at the Ocean Star.

I pushed the reports left by Meinhardt on the floor and logged into my computer and accessed the website with the measurement data uploaded by Hoover. The data was all there, tabulated in rows after rows of numbers. I called Mora at the Diamond office.

"Please go to a terminal," I said, when I heard his morose voice.

"I'm sitting at one", Mora said.

"Go to this website," I gave him the address and password and heard him operating the keyboard.

"What am I looking at?" he asked.

"Engine geometry as tested. The one that blew up. How fast can you make a model from it?"

"Let me download all the data. I'll take a closer look. If the measurements are complete, I mean if I don't have to guess contours and dimensions where the probes may not have had access, I can model it in two to three days. Otherwise it'll take a lot more time."

"Take a look and let me know. I may help with the missing contours."

The office door opened slowly, with a strange and measured motion. Quietly, Bob Cruiff came in. He moved slowly, measured, the same way he'd opened the door. His eyes were blood shot. He closed the door with care, all the way, insulating the two of us from the rest of the crowd in the building. Without a word, he grabbed a chair and sat down, placing his elbows on my desk, palms together, fingers intertwined.

"I'll call you back," I told Mora and hanged up without listening to his answer.

Cruiff leaned forward and locked his eyes on me, powerfully, without a blink.

"I want you to tell me what you know about Xiao Lin's whereabouts," he said in low voice. "The exact truth, son."

I cringed, watching his eyes, locked into mine.

"Xiao?" I asked. "What about Xiao?"

He placed his hands on my desk and thrust his body forward with unmistakable determination. "You fucking with me?" he asked in a mad whisper.

There were both fury and fear in him, ready to burst out.

"Do I look like I'm fucking with you? What about Xiao?"

"Damn it Salagen!" he slammed his fist on my desk, "I'll find out! I'll find out, you motherfuckers, even if I'll have to squeeze it out of every fucker in this damn place!

"Find out what, Bob?"

He watched me with hate. And still, fear. Moments passed in charged silence.

"They pulled Xiao Lin up from a ravine along the Los Angeles crest highway this morning," Cruiff spoke, and kept his eyes locked onto my face. "All of his body twisted and broken. Xiao Lin is dead."

It was as if we stopped breathing, both of us, in perfect killing silence.

"How did it happen?"

"He rolled over the edge on the crest highway. They found his car all the way down propped on the rocks."

"When was this?"

"Late morning today. Mei has called the cops yesterday and reported him missing."

We watched each other in silence. Images, again, screaming in my head. Feng Zhijian, with his severe face and his stupid shiny suit, him and the Changs, sitting there at the table with Xiao. I'd left Xiao there with them, sitting quietly at the table.

"What was he doing on the crest?"

"No idea. He's been missing ever since Saturday."

"Saturday?"

Cruiff nodded. He spoke carefully, slowly.

"Salagen, you are the last one to have seen him alive on Saturday."

Again, our eyes scanned each other.

"What do you know about Saturday, Bob?" .

He slammed his palms on my desk again.

"You think we're fucking idiots here? You think all that shit with MORPHEM is such a tight secret? There is plenty of rumor and talk on the hallways."

"What does that have to do with Saturday? Is Xiao involved in the MORPHEM mess?"

"You tell me, Salagen. I was very close to Lin. He did nothing wrong, he never played the shit games people play in this place. He's is dead now, and I want to know what happened even if I have the squeeze all of you motherfuckers one by one."

"Why are you scared, Bob?"

He froze. His bloodshot eyes hesitated.

"What kind of a fucked up question is this?"

"It's in your eyes Bob. Why did you destroy the MORPHEM CAD files? It couldn't have been anyone else. It was you who destroyed the files and all the back-ups."

"You're full of shit Salagen!"

"Am I? You're the only one likely to know how to wipe those files, I thought about this for some time now. I may speak with an accent, but my brain works. Who made you destroy the files?"

A jaw muscle pulsed on his face.

"Salagen, it's not a big secret, but few people know this: I own about ten percent of Lockwell. I want this corporation alive and doing what it does best: rockets. Call me crazy. If this company is sold, I collect a few million. I don't want it and I don't need it. McNutt was trying to sell the company even after the test fiasco on account of MORPHEM designs and patents. The shit with the CAD files had blocked it. I welcomed the whole thing."

"You didn't answer my question."

"I don't give a damn on your question."

"If that's how you want to play it… What did Xiao tell you about Saturday?"

He pupils contracted as his face froze back into stone lines.

"You guys met on Saturday with some friends of his."

"Friends? He said friends?"

"No. He didn't say friends. Who did you meet?"

I blocked the question, "Did Xiao know who busted the CAD files?"

"What the fuck is this, a third degree?"

He stood up, as if ready to hit me.

"I'm not your enemy, Bob," I said. "I left Xiao alive and in good health on Saturday, and haven't seen him ever since."

He scrutinized me, weighing his trust and distrust.

My cell phone rang. I ignored it. The ringing stopped, but none of us said anything. Then, it rang again. I picked up.

"Matei," a voice said, in Romanian. "Glad to get you, old pal."

"Who is this?"

"We talked a while ago, remember? Chris Popa?"

"Chris Popa," I repeated. "For God's sake. Where are you?"

"I'm at LAX, just like we discussed. You forgot."

I had no time for him.

"This is a really bad time," I said. "I apologize. Please take a taxi. I'll give you an address."

"No, please," his voice got tense. "I'm only staying a few hours in town, Matei. I'm heading back to Europe tonight. One more time, I hate to impose on you, but it is extremely important we meet in person."

"I see," I said. The feeling that Chris Popa was important slithered up my spine and into my mind. The surreal. The tickling sensation in the back of my head. "Please wait at the terminal," I said. "It'll take me about an hour to get there."

"Thanks Matei," he gave me the terminal information.

I flipped the phone shut.

"What was that about?" Cruiff asked. "Can't you speak English?"

"Forgive me," I said. "It's an old pal from the old country, he's at LAX. I was supposed to pick him up and forgot."

"You're leaving?"

"Just for now. I'll be back before close of business here. I'll make some phone calls see what I can find out about Lin."

"Who you're gonna call?" he asked. "What's your plan?"

"I have no plan. I'm searching, just like you do. Give me a phone number I can reach you at."

He wrote his numbers on a notepad and turned to leave. I ripped the page of the pad and pocketed it. One more time, we weighed each other's eyes. None of us said anything.

31

I parked in the Terminal 3 parking lot, checking for the blue sedan that was always following me. It was nowhere in sight. Just airport security everywhere.

Popa was pacing the floor by the carousels. I recognized him before he saw me. The man was fit, even athletic, dressed in a beige summer suit. His skin was dark for a white man, giving him a Mediterranean look. When he spotted me he smiled widely, offering his hand.

"Matei!" he exclaimed jovially, "Good to see you after all this time. I'm sorry to impose on you like this."

I shook his hand, "Welcome to LA!"

We complimented each other on being trimmed and fit. Behind the words, he was scrutinizing. I invited him towards the exit, but he stopped me.

"I'm sorry for the hassle, but I've got a problem," he said. "They lost one my suitcases. I have filed a form with the airline, I need to inquire again, could you please wait for a few more minutes?"

I nodded, mutely irritated. Popa left for the airline counter. I tried Bronson's phone number and got his answering. I waited and then tried the phone number again, in vain, and then waited some more. I searched for Popa, and I saw his beige suit in the crowd, approaching.

"I am really sorry to abuse your schedule like this, Matei, my luggage is on its way here, it'll be here in a bit over an hour. Please allow me to invite you for either late lunch or early dinner, anything you may prefer."

His eyes were studying everything, my presence, the crowd. He had come with a definite purpose. I let him lead the moves. "I could grab a bite," I said.

"Thank you, I really appreciate your patience, Matei. You know the airport surroundings, any place you may enjoy? My treat, please."

"Steak OK with you?"

"Steak sounds just perfect."

I found a steak joint across the street from the Airport Hilton, on Century. The kind of place with worn out carpets and tired waitresses serving breakfast all day. We got a table by the window, facing the boulevard. Popa ordered beers, but I switched mine with a coke.

"Excuse me for a moment," Popa said and left towards the restrooms. I saw him pulling out his cell phone from his coat's pocket.

Minutes passed. Everything felt strange. Air seemed partially depleted of oxygen, people's faces look like fish in a dirty tank, hunched over their tables and waited by mechanized rubber androids with a million fine wrinkles on their gray skins. My coke tasted as if poured from a two litter bottle opened a week before.

Popa came back, rubbing his face. He glanced at his wristwatch.

"It's two in the morning for me" he apologized with a smile. "Jet lag."

"You came through New York?"

"Chicago. I switched both flights and airlines there," he explained, "That's where they misplaced my suitcase."

"Did you fly in from Bucharest?"

"Montreal, actually."

"What brings you to LA?"

"Actually, it's business," Popa said.

He sipped from his beer. A waitress came to take the orders. We were easy customers, steaks. She smiled and produced a thousand extra wrinkles on her gray cheeks.

"How is business, back in the old country?" I asked Popa after the waitress left.

"It depends," he said. "Aerospace is down to a minimum, if that's what you're asking about. It's a small country."

On the sidewalk outside the restaurant, a thin man dressed in a gray suit walked slowly while peeking carefully inside the restaurant. He noticed me and Popa, and looked carefully at Popa. Popa turned his head slightly and looked back at the man. He remained motionless, just looking at the man, almost annoyed, but somehow acknowledging his presence. The man entered the restaurant and got seated at a nearby table, ignoring us. I watched

Popa, intrigued. He was calmly spreading butter on a piece of bread.

"What I'm saying," he continued, "is that, in general, an engineering job doesn't pay anymore at home, Matei."

I focused back on him. He was completely ignoring the presence of the man in gray.

"So, what do you do for a living?" I asked.

"I quit engineering," he said. "Instead," he continued carefully, "I found a very decent job in the intelligence business."

"Private business?"

He smiled. "Government," he said.

"You're working for the Romanian intelligence?" I asked, and sensed again the surreal in the air. I'd learned to smell the surreal over the years, it always announced havoc.

"This seems to have a bad rep," Popa said, smiling politely. "I read it by your reaction, Matei. You're thinking the old Securitate, the whole shit. It's not like that."

I felt adversity towards him.

"What is it like, then?" I asked him, coldly. "Help old ladies across the street?"

He ignored my irony. "The very first assignments I got into were anticorruption sting operations. We nabbed some guys, pretty high on the ladder, nabbed them well. Some of them worked their political connections and got out. Some others got jail time. I felt I was doing something good. I really did."

He ate a piece of bread. I strongly felt I needed to leave. I didn't want anything to do with him.

"You said you came here on business," I said. "What business is that?"

He eyed me, chewing slowly, swallowing.

"I came here to talk to you, Matei," he said.

Something clicked, strongly, right behind my head. Hot air pressure hit my skin. Popa jerked violently. A stain of blood flowered on the right side of his chest. He tried to rise from his chair when the clicking sound came again. The bullet hit him in the face and he fell on his back, knocking off his chair.

The following seconds extended to infinity. The air felt completely depleted of oxygen. I fought for breath, fought to move, run, escape. My eyes recorded what they saw, but my motion was slow as in a bad dream.

The man in the gray suit was standing. He was clumsily reaching inside his coat.

Simultaneously, a hand landed on my left shoulder, and a strong arm grabbed around me.

The man in the gray suit straightened his arm. The barrel of the big handgun he was holding was pointing at my chest.

I forced myself down. The strong arms locked on my throat and shoulders and didn't let go. The man in the gray suit fired his gun. It was no longer a clicking noise, but a sharp blast. The arms holding me down suddenly released their grip.

In accelerated time frame I turned around, and dropped to the ground. I saw the man who tried to immobilize me holding his shoulder and dripping blood. The man in gray fired again, and my assailant fell on his back, thrown by the impact of the big caliber slug.

Women voices screamed crazily. A man's voice yelled an order and a high cadence submachine gun burst in a cracking sound. The volley of slugs ripped through the coat fabric of the man in gray and jerked his body in a fractured motion. He was dead by the time he hit the floor. His gun bounced on the carpet towards the middle of the aisle.

A forgotten instinct suddenly dictated me to move. I rolled towards the gun, picked it up and kept rolling, knocking down chairs and a table. Adrenaline took over my brain, handling the surreal as if it was natural fact. I kicked another table down as my instinct told me again to roll, jump and move.

A silhouette of a man holding a weapon registered in my brain through the corner of an eye. I fired at the silhouette. Voices kept screaming. People ran towards the exit, shadows on the corners of my eyes. I kept searching for the aggressors in the crowd. The man with the weapon showed up again from behind a rolled down table, but held his fire. I spotted him more precisely, adrenaline pumping harder. My eyes collimated into his hiding spot, my arm lined the gun firmly. I fired one round after another, not thinking, just precisely acting. I fired until the gun clicked empty.

There was motion behind me, a chair moved and hit a table. I turned.

A short and wiry man darted towards me. He was holding a weapon, like a short rifle. His hands and arms made a fast move, like a magician doing a gig. The rifle became something like a bat that he swung at my head. I raised my arm, and took the blow in my forearm flesh. Pain was sharp, intense. I pivoted towards left and kicked the short man in the chest with my right foot. The blow lifted his lightweight frame and threw him back over the tables.

Then, for a brief moment, I heard nothing. Nobody was screaming, nothing was moving or shooting anymore. Only muffled traffic noise was coming from outside.

And then, too late, I heard a faint noise on my right, someone moving fast and agile. Before I had time to turn, nothingness hit me.

3 2

I came back to life and saw nothing. Panic hit and I tried yelling with no sound coming out of my mouth. My arms jerked, only to realize they were grown into my body. I felt like a plant grasping to breathe. I shook my body hard, and my repeated attempt to shout produced only a faint moan, and then lack of air made me loose conscience again.

And again I came back to life. My nose, I realized, my nose was the most important part of my body. It was grabbing air and letting it go to my lungs. It's a vital part, the nose, I told my brain, let's concentrate on using the nose best possible.

I was wrapped in tape. Tape around my arms, legs, upper body. Tape on my mouth. Some sort of a fabric wrap was covering my eyes tightly. From what I could feel, I was laying on a soft horizontal surface, like a bed, or a couch. I had to keep focusing on the nose, keeping panic under control, just trying to breathe.

Time was no longer a dimension. It had become everything. I started listening to my heart beats and count, figuring out the difference between seconds and hours, between hours and what seemed like days. It didn't matter, nothing was happening, except the fight for one more breath, and another one more.

A long dimensionless time elapsed. The sign of it was an urge to urinate. I tested holding it, giving time its dimension again by counting heart beats. One hundred of them turned out to be manageable. A thousand heart beats, a trip to infinity. A millennium of empty black nothingness filled with urine. I let it go. The jeans became warm and wet under the tape, then cold and wet. My nose, that precious instrument informed me of the smell.

I decided to dream, and dream hard. The warm sand in the dark at Point Dume, the weapon pointing to my head. The dilation to infinity of that moment. Had I pressed the trigger? I couldn't remember. Heart beats passed. Hours passed.

"Yes," a muffled voice said, behind a door, or a wall.

I discovered sound. There was sound. Distant traffic, a helicopter. And a muffled sound of a voice, probably in a different room. Time came back to some more meaningful dimension.

Several seconds to say a word, another second to take a breath. Real seconds.

"Yes, we do have him," the voice said. Was it English? Romanian? What was it? I remember heated arguments with Christine, not knowing which language we were using for shouting.

"That's difficult," the voice said again. "We can't move him like that."

I kept listening for more, but nothing more came. Very faint, a TV or radio show, behind some walls.

I listened hard until I grew tired of listening; my own heart beats became again the only meaningful noise. Time became again dimensionless, and the obsession for air and breathing took over.

Little by little, another quantity crept into my dark dimensionless time. It was pain. My arms, my legs were growing num via pain. Pulsing pain was coming and going at random on the right side of my head. The pain kept my mind gruesomely busy fighting it, fighting the lack of air, and ultimately, fighting fear.

A door opened. There were feet stepping in, floors creaking. There was a whisper, words I couldn't understand. Two arms lifted me and made me sit. A hand reached behind my back and the tape covering my mouth was removed in one sudden pull. It hurt. The eye cover was removed next. My vision was blurry. The cover had been pressing hard on the ocular globes. Something cold touched the right side of my head, and found the hurting spot. I growled, jerking my taped arms.

"I'm only cleaning the wound," a man's voice said. "Stay put, don't give me trouble."

I forced my eyes to focus, with no success. There were three people around me, dark figures wearing some sort of face masks, dressed in black. The one in front of me was reaching the right side of my head. I could feel the smell of his breath mixed with perspiration. The other two were standing behind him at some distance, as if prepared for any reaction I may have. The nurse man finished his work and moved away. One of the two other silhouettes came closer.

"How do you feel?" a man's voice said from behind the mask, "I am glad you are not seriously injured, just a scratch on your head, you seem to be in good condition?"

I didn't respond. I didn't figure I had to.

"Are you in good condition?" the man repeated the question. "Do you feel OK?"

I fixed my blurry sight on the masked face. But I said nothing. The masked face cleared his throat.

"You know," he said, reproaching, "we need some cooperation from you, and I'm afraid I can't offer you too many choices. If you're feeling good, you're useful to us and things will be OK. The other option is a shot in the head. So, before anything else, one more time, do you feel OK, can you hear and see me?"

"I've been better," I said.

"Well, good," the man said. "You have that little wound to your head, and we were just worried."

The nurse man approached and reached again to the side of my head. He grabbed my head with one hand holding tight. I felt a light touch on my left ear and heard a beep.

"Temperature normal," the man said, and stepped back.

Nothing happened for a few seconds. There was hesitation from their side as well. The masked man in front of me stood still. The one that was playing nurse came close again, and I felt the cloth covering my eyes again.

"Let him breathe," the man closer to me ordered, "fuck the tape. Give him the shot."

A sting in my arm. Then a thickening dark fog, falling on my mind.

33

I came back to life and didn't pay attention to breathing. It was just there, normal. Just numbness mixed with pain in my arms and legs. The jeans stank. My mouth felt dry.

I let time pass, fighting pain and fear. A sense of desperation was growing. Everything that I was had become noting but a bundle of taped limbs and clothes smelling of urine. Somehow, I felt, I was important for these people, yet the value of the human entity named Mathew Salagen or Matei Salajan had been erased from the ledger of the earth.

Suddenly, a man shouted something, behind a door. The voice seemed full of shock, and urging action, but the shout ended in a gurgle. The fast cracking sound came again, the same weapon I heard at the restaurant. It came slightly muffled, from the other side of a closed door. Another man cursed. The curses ended in a strange noise, air being forced out of the lungs though one's vocal chords in a long moan of death.

I forced myself to roll off the surface I was lying on. I fell on the floor. Just then I heard the door kicked opened and the cracking sound blasting in. Bullets ripped cloth and hit objects above my head. Feet moved fast, voices growled and cursed. Multiple metal clicking noises repeated fast several times. A man's voice sighed. Bodies dropped on the floor. Feet stepped closer to me, unevenly. One more strong click, and someone fell on top of me. I shed the sudden weight and rolled away from under the inert body.

All sounds ended. There was silence, broken only by faint noises from far away behind the walls, behind closed doors and windows. The floor creaked, under silent foot steps. I felt a presence, inches away from me. Two fingers touched the jugular artery on my neck and rested there for several seconds.

The touch and the presence shook the insides of my guts. I couldn't tell why. It wasn't fear. A sense deeper than mind and brain had felt something, a piece of hidden knowledge throwing my body into convulsion. I yelled and rolled on the floor trying to touch that invisible presence, incapable of anything except a worm crawl. My taped legs slipped on a viscous patch, and I stopped moving. The air was full with smell of blood. Death was around me, I felt it.

I rolled on one side, and I started crying. I cried with tears and moans, a long, unstoppable crying. I heard car engines and the rush of steps approaching, but couldn't stop crying. Steps and voices filled the room, hands lifted my body and removed tape after tape, and then my eye cover, while I was still weeping.

Only later, in the ambulance, I quieted and listened to the growl of its engine and the rumble of its tires, letting myself rocked by the vehicle's swings, thinking of nothing.

34

The hospital bed was good and hard. Its comfort, the immaculate white of its sheets seemed unreal. There was again a sense of life in my body, the sense of fresh blood pulsing through my veins.

Someone moved closer to the bed. A hand lightly touched my face, followed the contour of my neck, collar bone, and then slipped caressingly on my chest. I didn't know how she got there, why, I didn't care, I grabbed Jane and embraced her with all my strength, holding on to her as if holding on to life.

"It's OK, take it easy babe," she said. Her fingers pulled my hair, her mouth came on mine swallowing my breath. "It's OK," she repeated and poured her scent on my nostrils.

I partly let go of her, made room for her on the narrow bed, and kept her body embraced. Time had the dimension of Jane's breaths, and I wasn't counting. Then the sedatives took me out for a while.

When I opened my eyes, Roger Bronson was standing besides the bed. Jane was crouched on a chair by the wall, watching a nurse dressed in a pale green uniform reading the monitors next to it.

"He's in good condition, just very exhausted," the nurse told Bronson. "He's good for debriefing."

Bronson moved his eyes from the nurse towards me. "How are you, Dr. Salagen?" he asked. His voice was calm, flat.

"I'm all right," I said.

He looked at me, thinking. Slowly, he stepped closer to the bed.

"We'll have to do a debriefing," he said. "There is a significant amount of information and facts we need to sort out."

"Xiao Lin," I said. "What happened to Xiao Lin?"

His eyes looked at me, but focused somewhere else.

"Dr. Lin's death is only a part of the things we need to sort out, Dr. Salagen."

He headed for the door. Hand on the knob he turned towards me and eyed Jane shortly.

"Your friend, Miss Brayton here, asked for the permission to stay here with you, and we assumed that would be all right with you."

I looked at Jane. She flipped the pages of a magazine and ignored Bronson.

"Thank you," I said.

***

I got discharged in the morning. Seen from the outside, the hospital had the appearance of a small private clinic. The building had no particular inscription. As I was watching the façade, a young man dressed in a blue suit and looking like an android stepped out of a blue sedan parked in front. He walked around the car and opened the rear door.

I invited Jane in. "No," she said. "Go ahead. There's law and cops waiting for you at the house. I'll catch you later."

I got in the car and the android drove away, smoothly and with very precise motions. Two large sedans were parked in front of my house, Crown Vics smelling of law. My Mustang was parked on the driveway. It sat there, still cold from the night, with dew on the rear window. It had been towed back from the LAX.

Bronson was waiting in front of the house holding a yellow envelope which he handed to me when I got out of the car.

"Some of your personal objects, Dr. Salagen," he said. "They were recovered from the location."

I opened the envelope. My wallet and my keys.

"I thought it would be a good idea to do the debriefing at your house if you don't mind the intrusion," Bronson said.

The oddity of the proposition was lost in my apathy.

"Fine with me," I said and unlocked the door.

Two more men showed up from a second Crown Vic and walked towards us with their eyes trained on Bronson like hounds waiting for their master's gesture. Bronson gave them orders over his shoulder, "No interruption unless necessary. Low key, please." He then followed me in the house.

We settled in the living room where Bronson's assistant produced two small recorders, and a notebook. He turned the recorders on, laying them on the coffee table.

Bronson asked the questions. Name, address, the intro. The recorders, with their small red lights captured every sound of my voice, each breath, each hesitation.

He debriefed me about the Ocean Star meeting. Date, time, location, participants. Physical details about the man named Feng Zhijiang, and the couple, David and Evelyn Chang, their eyes, hair, hands and clothing. Then, the conversation sequence, phrase by phrase. Xiao Lin's words, his attitude.

I brought up the trip to the airbase in the Mojave, but Bronson seemed uninterested. He switched the questioning to the events at the LAX. I described Christian Popa as he was when we first met in the Romanian military and college and what I could put together about him when he arrived at LAX. Then, for several times, I recalled the fight sequence at the LAX restaurant, each time in more detail.

The time spent as a captive, however, was on a different metaphysical plane. In my mind, that time had been warped beyond reconstruction. I had no clear perception of the length of time I've been held captive.

"Three days, Dr. Salagen," Bronson said. "Three days."

I weighed the duration in my mind. It was irrelevant. Three days or three years. I told him about the voices, and the radio or TV shows heard through the walls. Bronson caught it. His assistant refreshed the tapes into the recorders.

"Please recall, again, in as much detail, the phrases you overheard, the voices," Bronson asked. "Take your time."

I closed my eyes. "Someone said it was going to be difficult to move something," I said.

I thought about the darkness, the tape wrapped around my body. I understood, suddenly. "They were talking about me," I said. "They were reporting they got me and it was difficult to move me."

"Move you where, Dr. Salagen?"

"They didn't say."

There was a moment of silence. A strange retroactive anger was choking my throat.

"Why was I kidnapped, Bronson?" I asked. "Who were those people?"

Bronson exhaled.

"Professional kidnappers," he said. "Cooperating with local sleeper elements unknown to us. Disciplined, no phone trace, no rumor in the regular underground."

He rubbed his face with his palms and then opened his briefcase and extracted several large pictures printed on glossy photographic paper. He pushed them towards me. The images showed a long wooden box, photographed at different angles. One detail image showed several rows of holes drilled into the wood. Two small fans, similar to those used for cooling computer cases, were mounted on the wood panel on top of the holes. Another detail showed the bottom of the box where a layer of plastic foam had been glued to the wood. The meaning of the images hit me with delay.

"A cage?" I asked. "They were going to put me into this cage?"

Bronson rubbed his temples again.

"There is a strange mixture of rudimentary and sophistication in this operation that puzzles me, Dr. Salagen. As I said, the team left no trace. They had knowledge of the environment, knowledge of communication technology, and discipline. On the other hand, there are more ingenious ways to have you transported, methods requiring both sophistication and money. Interestingly enough, we were watching precisely for those methods, say any transport of some medical emergency nature. Yet, for some reason, your captors had chosen this rudimentary method, this box, which actually may have worked. But I fail to understand the reason behind the choice for the rudimentary, if it was shrewdness or lack of resources."

A theory versus another. My life, in the middle.

"What do they want from me, Bronson? Fuck the academics, just give me some facts I can understand!"

"I don't know!" he snapped. It was the first time Bronson had snapped in front of me. He calmed down and continued: "We didn't capture any of them alive."

Voices at the door interrupted him. The two hounds he had left on guard outside opened the entrance door and let in a short, dark skinned man, dressed in black jeans and a leather jacket. I didn't like the way that man entered my house. His walk felt as an intrusion. Then, I recognized him: Ben Balder, the CIA man from the Lockwell meeting.

He grabbed a chair without much protocol and without asking permission, and sat down across the coffee table from me, setting up his own recorder on the table. He opened a handheld device and played with the pen on its screen, and then raised his head and drilled holes into my face with his beady eyes.

"I'll skip the introductions, Dr. Salagen," he spoke flatly. "You know who I am, and you understand you're being debriefed on matters of importance to national security."

He read something on his gadget and then asked: "When did you do your military service back in Romania?"

I hadn't expected a question in that direction.

"It's been more than twenty five years," I said.

"Can you be more precise?"

"I'll have to check the dates."

"It's all right," he declined. The device in his hand emitted a beep as he moved the pen on it.

"Where was it that you served?" he asked.

"An airborne division."

"Located where?"

"City called Careni."

He nodded, and made a note.

"The Careni Airborne. Can you name some of the people that were in your unit?"

"I'm bad with names."

He watched me coldly.

"I'll read some names from a list here. Just confirm if these people served with you in the Careni Airborne"

I shrugged. He read the names. Christian Popa was the last name he read.

"How many of these men are currently living in US or Canada?"

"Most of them," I said.

"How come?"

I shrugged. "Competence, I presume."

"Do you care to explain?"

"We were all put through five very tough years of college after the service. One of the best and toughest departments in the Polytechnic. Whoever made it through those five years and graduated became very employable in any engineering job, anywhere. Since life back in the old country sucked, people emigrated."

"Are you in touch with any of these people?"

"Not really. There is a newsletter published in Montreal, and there is an annual meeting also in Montreal. I never attended."

Balder pulled a picture from a folder extracted from his briefcase and pushed it towards me.

"Do you recognize this man?"

I was a standard mug shot of a younger Chris Popa looking in his late thirties.

"That's Chris Popa," I said.

"What do you know about this man?"

I repeated what I had told Bronson earlier and went again through the details of the LAX restaurant fighting

"He specifically stated he works for Romanian intelligence?"

"Yes."

"Did he explain what his business was in the US?"

"He said he came here to talk to me, and right then he was shot."

Balder raised his eyes from his gadget and watched me carefully.

"That is a very interesting situation, Dr. Salagen" he spoke, touching his lips with the thin pen. "The Romanian Intelligence Service, the SRI, has confirmed that Mr. Christian Popa worked for them, but insisted that Mr. Popa had no assignment here whatsoever."

Balder let his words hang in the air. I said nothing.

"Dr. Salagen," he continued, "where did you work in Romania, prior to your leaving for the US?"

"The National Institute for Science and Technology, the Propulsion Division"

"What sort of an institution was it?"

"A government owned research and development organization."

"For how long did you work there?"

"About seven years."

"Can you describe the employees?"

"Half very competent people and half very connected people, not necessarily incompetent, but living well and doing very little work."

"Any person you may remember specifically?"

"Like I said, I'm bad with names."

Balder grinned.

"You remember Popa's name, now, don't you?"

I let it pass. He fiddled with another folder extracted from his briefcase.

"Were there many of you who had served on the Careni Airborne working for the institute?"

"Yes, some."

"Do you know of their current whereabouts?"

"No."

He studied my face again, his lips curled in a sneer. "I was hoping you could help me with some information," he spoke and kept the sneer on his face. "There are a number of these former colleagues of yours which seem to have vanished, Dr. Salagen. There is no trace of their lives any more."

"I don't understand."

"I'll explain it to you. We've obtained intelligence on about a hundred colleagues of yours, Dr. Salagen. About seven of these men have vanished. There is no record of their lives. They don't spend money, they have no bank accounts, there is no death certificate, no new medical record. Nothing. They stopped leaving any trace of existence about five or six years ago."

I shrugged. "If you're using Romanian records, you my find several other thousand people like that. It's not the most organized country in the world."

He went quiet for several moments. He extracted another folder, and verified the recorder. Its red light shone bright, unforgiving.

"Dr. Salagen," Balder restarted, "please explain the nature of your relationship with Dr. Xiao Lin."

I glanced at Bronson. He sat on the couch watching Balder with no expression on his face. Bronson's assistant was carefully studying the east wall of my living room.

"We worked together at Lockwell," I said.

"For how long have you known Dr. Lin?"

"About ten years. Maybe more."

"The two of you socialized?"

"To some extent. I have been invited to his house several times, and the other way around. I know his wife, Mei."

"Did you collaborate with Dr. Lin on any project outside your work at Lockwell?"

"No."

"Did you share with Dr. Lin any special information regarding your work, additional information than what was required for your regular work?"

"I don't know what you mean by additional information. We worked together, we shared whatever information necessary. We both had the proper clearances."

Balder made a note on his notepad.

"For how long did you know Feng Zhijiang?" he continued.

The name brought ice in my veins.

"I first met him last week," I said.

"For how long did you know David Chang, or Evelyn Chang?"

"I first met them, last week."

"Have you ever met Feng Zhijian, David Chang, or Evelyn Chang under a different name?"

"I've never met these people before in my life."

"Are you sure, Dr. Salagen?"

I stood up. "Get the fuck out of my house!" I said.

Balder smiled. He slowly stood up. He weighed me with narrow eyes for a moment, then grabbed his recorder and walked away, without a word, reached the door, opened it and walked out of the house.

Minutes of silence passed. Bronson cleared his throat.

"What the hell was that, Bronson?"

He raised his palms up in the air, "I've only known Mr. Balder for a short time," he said. "I assume he's a good professional. Although," he gestured with his hands sideways, "he's got his own ideas, his own priorities."

"I won't take that crap," I said. "Besides, I'd like to get a few answers myself."

He gestured again with his hands.

"Do ask," he invited.

I sat back down.

"Was there an autopsy done on Xiao Lin? What happened to him?"

"Contusions to his head, multiple fractures and severe internal bleeding. It is the latter that killed him. We found no trace of any chemicals in his blood, except some regular medication and a very small quantity of alcohol"

"Do you really believe it was an accident?"

"Frankly, no," he said. "I'm just answering your questions."

"How do you know the men at the LAX were professional kidnappers?"

"Fingerprints and files from the Interpol. Of the four bodies recovered from the restaurant, two are still John Doe's, no papers or any ID on them, no identification based on fingerprints, nothing. We assume they were local sleepers of some sort."

"What about the man I shot at?"

"Possibly one of the dead. Both of the unidentified men have been shot with a Glock 45. We found the gun on the floor, empty as you recall that you've emptied a gun. Some of the fingerprints on it are yours."

"There was a man in a gray suit. Who was he?"

Bronson smiled, bitterly.

"Identified as an employee of the Romanian Consulate General in Los Angeles. Your friend, Popa, must have asked for some cover, someone to watch his back. On papers, the man was working security at the consulate."

I recalled the man's clumsy action, the volleys of slugs hitting him.

"What sense does this make?" I asked.

Bronson shook his head.

"There was a mistake on our side when you were freed. One of the operatives was excessive, and your captors were all killed, unfortunately."

One of the operatives. The silent footsteps, the two fingers pressed on my neck searching, making sure I'm alive. Anger and helplessness burst into my chest, at the recollection.

"This is absurd!" I shouted. "Xiao Lin killed! Chris Popa killed! All these people killed! What for?"

Bronson watched me, expressionless again. He grabbed a small briefcase he had brought with him, opened it, and took out a sheet of paper. He held it, hiding its content from me before talking.

"Let me show you something, Dr. Salagen" he said. "We recovered the lost luggage of your friend, Mr. Christian Popa, and we made a thorough search of it."

He handed me the piece of paper.

"We have found this hidden within a double layer of covers in the suitcase. This is a copy, the original is preserved elsewhere."

I looked at the paper. There was a picture printed on it, and the image stopped my breath. It was the image shown by Yvette Nahman during the Lockwell meeting: the image of the alien MORPHEM-like engine decrypted by the NSA. I carefully studied the piece of paper in my hands. Christian Popa had carried it in his suitcase. And, perhaps, he died for it.

"Dr. Salagen," Bronson spoke with a new tone in his voice, "I believe that we are long overdue in clarifying several details from your past. For example, we need your help in clarifying the whereabouts of a man named Victor Petrescu."

Bronson had even pronounced Victor's name correctly, as in Romanian. No English 'r's, the correct "u" at the end of the name. A buried past, left behind, was coming back to life, haunting.

"Where did you get this name from?" I asked

"Please turn the page on the other side," Bronson said.

Two names were handwritten on the back of the picture print. The first one was Victor Petrescu, underlined. The other one was also a Romanian name, Cornel Oniga.

"We did some research, Dr. Salagen. There is a Dr. Petrescu authoring with you two reports published in the Journal of Applied Physics published by the Romanian Academy of Sciences. One publication in 1986 and the other in 1988. There is no record of anything recent by Mr. Petrescu. There are many Cornel Oniga's but none of them seems to have anything to do with you or your work."

I held the piece of paper, studying Victor's name, scribbled on it.

"Victor Petrescu was an old friend," I said. "He's been dead for sixteen years. Never heard of Cornel Oniga."

3 5

I waited for the night to get deeper and listened to the nightly breath of the city. Distant freeway rumble, passing aircraft, and occasional wails of sirens mixed in the fluorescent darkness of greater Los Angeles.

I chewed on a cheap cigar, re-lighting it from time to time, steadily drinking scotch in amounts insufficient to get me totally drunk. Just keeping myself mentally num. Memories from the past came alive, together with strange dreams dreamt with open eyes. Old nightmares resurfaced and began haunting.

I fought them with whisky and smoke. It felt like holding a stomach full of a toxic load and delaying the puke. But it was pointless. It had been pointless all along, holding it all in my mind for years. I had to unbury everything I had left behind and try to find my answers. I had to revisit the past and obtain closures. Thinking about it, after so many years, it seemed so simple and so logical a decision it amazed me for how long I had been delaying it. I had to go back to the old country.

As I finally made the decision, gusts of Santa Ana winds began blasting. The wails of the wind echoed through the house. I longed for Jane, longed for a soul.

From a drawer of my office desk I extracted an old address book. Old numbers, scratched and overwritten with newer ones filled the pages. I found the number I wanted and dialed it. The night was closer to dawn in Montreal. Someone picked up after many rings.

"Who the hell is this?"a sleepy man's voice said.

"It's Matei," I said. "Sorry to bust like this in your pinky dreams."

"Matei," the man's voice said. "What the fuck." Then he recoiled, and laughed. "Fuck man, it's been years. How the hell are you? Do you know what time it is?

"I know and I'm sorry. I need to organize some logistics."

"I see," he said. "Wait a second."

I heard a faucet and a clink of glass.

"All right, old bugger," he said with a refreshed voice. "What can I do for you?"

"Do you still own that place in Bucharest?"

"Yeah. You taking a trip?"

"Looks like I have to."

"When was the last time you went there?"

"'95. You remember. When my old man died."

"You need to be off the radars, still?"

"As much as possible"

"I see," he said. There was silence for a while, he was thinking.

He continued. "There is a guy, renting in my place. He's out on a job for a few weeks, is that enough?"

"That would do."

"How soon are you leaving?"

"As soon as I can."

"I'll send you a key overnight."

"Things OK with you?" I asked.

"Almost divorced," he growled. "She's the same bitch as always, but it's been twenty six years and it's just hard to part ways. You know how it is. How's Christine?"

"She's back in France. We did part ways."

"Oh boy," he said, and laughed softly.

"That's life, old chap. One more thing. I may need a car in Bucharest."

"I'll send you to some people. Cash only and a big deposit."

"All right. Thanks. Sorry for waking you up."

"That's OK. Good hearing you."

"See you, old man."

He snorted. I hung up.

A little red light was blinking near the scotch bottle. The answering system, left unchecked for all my days of missing. I poured a drink while he machine rolled the messages. Chris Popa's voice came back from the dead and told me he was in Chicago, in between flights. Good bye, friend. I never liked you that much, but I wished your fate was better. Mora, at increasing levels of impatience. Cam's voice, quietly asking "*Matei, where are you, what's going on with you?*".

Then, someone's breath, and a voice: "*Where the fuck are you?*"

I froze.

Cruiff.

I replayed: "*Where the fuck are you?*"

I drained the glass and poured the rest left in the bottle, sat down and kept drinking, feeling tired but no longer shaken. The scotch worked quickly, filling my arms with lead. Outside, the winds had stopped and the LA was changing its nightly breath into the dawn noises of a new day.

3 6

Xiao Lin smiled in my dream. He was holding his porcelain tea cup, smiling, standing by a fountain.

I woke up to a sunny and strong morning daylight. I took a shower and then dialed all Cruiff's numbers. His voice on the answering systems came flat and professional, consistently the same on each number. I placed the telephone back on its cradle.

Outside, two Crown Vics stood guard, one in front of the house and the other parked further up the street. I got into my car and worked the ignition of the Mustang's V8. At the sound, two men jumped out of from the Crown Vic parked closer and waved me to stop. One of the men came to my side window and said, "We'll need an itinerary, sir."

"Mine?"

"Yes sir. You'll be escorted at all times."

I gave them the directions to Lockwell and dove off. The two cars moved swiftly in front and behind my Mustang. They kept close all the way through the freeways.

At Lockwell, Cruiff's office was empty. Everything looked as if he'd just stepped out: papers scattered on his desk, a blueprint unfolded with a mechanical pencil left on top of it. Yet, the cubicle smelled cold.

I called Meinhardt. "Haven't seen Bob lately," he said. "You guys all vanished. Bob was upset with Xiao's accident. He was talking about taking a few days off. What happened to you? I haven't seen you in days either."

I made up a story, and thanked him. From a Lockwell directory, I wrote Cruiff's home address and then left.

***

Cruiff's house was surprisingly bourgeois, on a street with high priced properties, manicured lawns and shiny cars parked in the driveways. Beautiful wooden patio furniture was spread through a small garden in front of the house. The tall curved wall hosting what seemed to be a staircase inside was decorated with a large and beautifully worked stain-glass window.

I rang the door bell, and waited. Nothing moved inside, nobody came to the door. I knocked and yelled. There was no answer.

I felt watched. The front door of the neighboring house opened. A dark haired woman came out, dressed in sweatpants, sweatshirt, sneakers, as if ready for a gym session. She was Korean or Chinese. She greeted me politely, with a smile, waiting.

"Good morning," I said. "Do you know Bob? The man who lives here?"

She came closer, and nodded again.

"Mister Robert," she said. "He is not home."

Her eyes examined me flatly from an amiable face.

"I work with Bob," I said. "I need to talk to him."

Smiling politely, the woman glanced quickly at the blue sedans and the men inside.

"A friend of Mr. Robert died," she said. "Mr. Robert said he will be away." Her smile remained tight on her face.

"Did he say where he's going?"

She smiled, shaking her head.

"I'm sorry, I don't know."

I thanked her and walked back to my car, thinking. Before getting into the Mustang I walked to one of the escort cars and gave them the address of the Pasadena office. I needed to see Mora.

From behind the wheel, I turned and watched Cruiff's house one more time. The woman stood there, by the front door, smiling, watching.

***

Thoughts kept rolling on my mind while forging the Mustang South on 101 towards the junction with 134. The escort car behind me flashed its lights. I was speeding. I slowed down and exited 134 at Harvey, driving along Colorado to the office building.

Stefan Mora was in. He returned my greeting with a dark look.

"Where the fuck have you been?" he asked.

"Personal problems, "I said. "Sorry for the lack of contact."

He looked me over while brewing coffee.

"Nice vacation," he said.

I didn't answer. He poured fresh coffee in two mugs.

"Can you give me un update with the simulations?" I asked.

He walked to one of the terminals.

"Grab a chair," he spoke over the shoulder.

He typed several lines and started the graphic modeling code.

"First of all, geometry," he started. "The data you've send me was good, just a few things to patch. I was able to make a model in two days."

"What the status now?"

"I'm running both cases: the model you say should work, and this second one that blew up."

"From what you have so far, can you tell the differences in operation between these two engine versions?"

"I'm still crunching numbers. I'd need about two more weeks."

I closed my eyes. How long a week was. People die and people vanish, in a week.

I asked him, suddenly: "Remember Petrescu, back at the Institute?"

He seemed surprised. "He died, back in '89 didn't he?"

"Yes. I was just thinking about him the other day."

"I remember him. Tough drinker."

"Ever heard of a guy Cornel Oniga?"

He hit the return key, eyes on the screen, cursing.

"It got stuck again," he said and turned towards me. "Who?"

"Cornel Oniga."

He shrugged. "Never heard of him. Why?"

"Someone was asking."

"Who was asking?"

"Doesn't matter. Too many memories from the past."

His eyes became two narrow slits, watching me coldly.

"As far as I'm concerned, the past is dead," he said.

I rose, ready to leave.

"How is Cam?" I asked.

"She's fine," he said.

I stood silent, not knowing what to say. I walked to a window and watched the traffic on 134 for a minute.

"I'll be away for about ten days or so," I said.

Mora frowned. "I see. Traveling?"

"No, not really," I said. "Some treatment I should've gone through a long time ago."

"Have fun," Mora said and swiveled around on his chair and began working the computer keyboard.

Out on the sidewalk, I lit up a cigarette again, facing the street. The men from the two escort cars were out on the sidewalk, talking. One of them saw me and they all turned their heads. I kept standing, undecided, rolling thoughts in my mind under their waiting eyes.

I needed help. And there was only one man able to provide it.

3 7

There was a black SUV parked in front of the gate on Citrus street. Its presence made me ring the bell instead of using my key. The gate buzzed open and a man came out of the house and waited for me on the entrance steps. It was Ernesto.

"Good timing," he said and invited me in. "Mr. Mason wants to talk to you."

"How is he doing?" I asked as we entered the hallway. The black statue reflected a sunray on its left hip and made me rest my eyes on it.

"Mr. Mason had a surgery last week," Ernesto said and led me up the stairs. "He is recovering."

I understood the truth about Hal's condition as soon as I saw him. He seemed to have had lost half of his weight, the skin on his face had darkened and wrinkled even more, his eyes sunken into deep hollows. He silently greeted me and nodded towards Ernesto who understood the order and left the room. Hal pointed towards the bar where a bottle made of dark and thick glass stood prepared. I fixed our typical drinks and handed Hal his glass.

"How long did they give you?" I asked, flatly.

He laughed silently and sipped one drop. His hand shook on the glass.

"Two months, the most," he said. "I believe it's much less that that." His voice was calm, as if the matter did not concern him.

I drank, fine scotch with subtle taste, an Aberlour.

"I guess you have a story to tell?" Hal asked, adjusting the chair back to a resting position.

I gave him the whole film of events, the LAX, the captivity, the rescue. He listened with his eyes closed, without asking any question until I finished.

"Killing all of your captors was a big mistake," he spoke and pressed his lips in a severe line. "Any possible trail to whoever was behind it is gone."

He lifted his glass with a swift motion and was about to sip another drop when the coughing started. He couldn't control it. I rushed to him and leaned his chair back further. His hand reached for the oxygen mask. I pressed it on his mouth. Gradually, he suppressed the cough and remained motionless, breathing, his eyes closed, the skin on his face darkened even more by the rush of blood.

I sat on the couch and waited.

Minutes passed. Hal's breathing continued normally and I thought he had fallen asleep. Then, his hand searched for the control panel of the chair and adjusted it back into an upright position.

"I should let you rest," I said.

He rejected my words with a nervous gesture.

"I'll rest plenty, soon enough."

He focused his eyes back to me. "Why do you think someone wants to kidnap you?"

"I don't know. That's what bothers me, I make no sense of it."

"What's your instinct?" he asked, sharply. "Forget logic."

He was suddenly focused, his eyes trained on me so intensely I avoided them.

"It may be linked to the Chinese," I said.

"The Chinese?"

"They've made me an offer," I explained. "The contact was a Chinese guy I used to work with at Lockwell. He invited me out to a place in Monterey Park. Two men and a woman; they made an offer for my engine, disguised as an offer for some commercial technology, but it was clear what they wanted. I refused."

I recalled for him the Ocean Star meeting. He listened without moving, absorbing every word.

"Fascinating," he spoke, his eyes lit by an unknown passion. "They know they have a revolutionary technology in their hands. They also know the design they've got is wrong, it blew up in their faces. And they understand they can get the correct principle only from you. How did they come to understand this?"

"I'm not sure I follow you."

Hal watched me and grinned.

"You're still so young," he said. "Let me explain it to you: I am convinced beyond doubt that the Chinese have obtained the engine design plans from Lockwell. Perhaps your Chinese friend or somebody else there had provided them with the CAD files. Lockwell's engine blew up in a very peculiar way - you have that satellite observation indicating it was something like a small nuclear detonation. The Chinese engine blew up the very same way. Do you agree?

"Yes," I said.

"Then, here is the interesting thing: nobody at Lockwell came searching for you after their engine blew up. On one hand their internal politics was more important than clarifying the design and on the other hand none of your colleagues was convinced you hold the key to the correct design, even if you initiated the whole project. In other words, Lockwell didn't trust your competence. So if the Chinese have their man inside Lockwell, that man would not advise them to search for you in order to get the correct design. But they did search for you. How did they know?"

"I'm not sure I hold the correct design, Hal. That's why I'm trying to do all this research."

He shook his head.

"You're missing the point," he said. He rested against his chair, exhausted, his passion diminished. "I could use a few more drops," he said and pointed his chin at the bottle.

I rose and fixed his drink. He held the glass so his lips could touch the fresh ice cubes and let the vague taste of scotch through.

"There is another development, in parallel to all this," I said.

"What development?"

"A high altitude cruise missile was launched towards the West Coast the same day I met the Chinese. I got picked up right after the meeting by a bunch of suits and taken to a Mojave air base to assist in the intercept. I have strong reasons to believe the missile was powered by propulsion of the MORPHEM kind."

He nodded slowly.

"I saw a report on it," he said. "Do you think it had anything to do with the Chinese people you met?"

"No. That's probably a coincidence."

"Probably," he agreed. "NORAD people have tracked back the trajectory. The missile was launched from a pirated trawler which was scuttled shortly after the launch."

"Who launched it?"

He shrugged and exhaled air, tired. His black eyes filled suddenly with sadness, a moment when his steely self control faulted.

"I may not live to find out, Matt. I am tired, and I'm dying."

I took his glass, refreshed the ice cubes and wetted them with scotch. As I handed it back to him, I gently squeezed his shoulder. He grabbed my forearm and held it.

"Whoever published the engine picture on the internet has provided the system for the missile attack," he spoke and kept holding my forearm. "All these years I fought against proliferation of weapons of various sorts only to see them popping up more and more, everywhere, pointed against this country."

He released my arm, and gestured towards the couch. "Please sit down," he requested, "I want to discuss your course of action."

I obeyed. There was still scotch in my glass and I drained it.

"How did your debriefing go?" Hal asked.

"I told them the same things I just told you now."

"Who was in charge?"

"Guy named Bronson, FBI."

"Anybody else?"

"Some other guy from the CIA, name is Balder. He's pushing some shit on me, no idea why."

"What about Bronson," he asked, "you trust the man?"

"Yes, to some extent."

Hal watched me intensely again, studying my face as I played with the ice cubes in my glass.

"So, what now?" he asked.

I placed my glass on the coffee table.

"I'd like to ask for your help," I said. "That's why I'm here."

He smiled with subtle satisfaction.

"Finally. Go on."

"You asked me what my gut feeling is. I feel I need to go back to the old country."

"Why?"

"I left unfinished business there, Hal, you remember. My instinct tells me I must go back and search for some closure."

"What sort of closure?"

"I'm not sure. I thought that everything I left behind is dead and buried. For many years I felt there is no going back. But now I feel differently."

"It could be dangerous."

"I'll take the risk."

He nodded, and his eyes lost their focus as he weighed things in his mind. He grabbed his glass and closed his eyes, resting his head back on the chair's head rest.

"How can I help?" he asked.

"Logistics," I said. "I'm under continuous and open escort surveillance."

"What do you need?"

"Help me get out of the country. I have arranged a place in Bucharest where I can lay low."

He opened his eyes, and fixed them on me, his gaze intense, scrutinizing.

"What do you want to do in Bucharest?" he asked.

"Poke around. Try find some people I used to know, listen to them talk."

He pursed his lips in grimace of doubt.

"I can have one or two men come with you," he said.

"No," I refused. "I need to go by myself."

He watched me, thinking, and then nodded slowly.

"Maybe your instinct is right," he said, and his eyes lost focus again, his brain at work. "The root of many things is probably back there."

He sipped more of his drink. "I've come to learn," he continued, "that every piece of a circle you leave open during your life time, will come back at you for some closure. Each closure eventually becomes another circle which needs a continuation, but it all comes back to you, nevertheless. Maybe you left many things open back there, Matt. No matter what you do, they'll come back to you for that closure, one way or another."

"I don't know about circles," I said. "I just feel I gotta go back and bury the dead for ever."

He moved his chair closer and faced me intensely.

"I'll help you," he said. "I hope you understand what you're doing. This game is deadly. While you're searching for what you want, there are people out there searching for something they want, hard and tough people ready to do anything for their purposes. I want you to be careful, and ready to withdraw from any situation likely to get complicated. There are professionals that can take care of those situations."

I shrugged. "Of course, I understand."

"My suggestion would be to take someone with you."

"Take who with me?"

He put his glass on the desk, tired, loosing breath.

"Someone that'll slow you down, someone that'll make you think twice, prevent you from rushing into anything," he said, softly.

"Jane?" I exclaimed, the name almost escaping my lips by itself.

"Yes, someone like that."

"Yeah, but, she's… I cant' associate her with something like this. Doesn't fit."

"You'll be surprised at what fits or doesn't fit in a story like this," Hal said. "Why don't you just ask her?"

He was growing tired, speaking with great effort. I rose, ready to leave.

"Wait," he stopped me and indicated the couch again. I sat again.

He moved his chair towards the computer and started typing. A calendar window popped up on the screen. He operated the keyboard stopping to think every few moments. After several minutes he produced a print-out and handed it to me.

"Read and memorize these instructions," he said. "You're going to meet Ernesto at the location written there. Have the luggage ready and leave it in your car, the trunk and doors unlocked."

I read the set of instructions a few times.

"Ask the girl to come with you," he insisted. "If she comes, make sure she's got a passport. Whether she'll come or not, the instructions remain the same. Clear?"

"Clear."

There was silence again. I rose and offered my hand. He smiled, warmly and grabbed it with both hands.

"Thank you Hal," I said, and felt my throat dry and hurting.

"Make it a good trip," he said, for a good bye.

3 8

The 737 touched down at the Henri Coanda International Airport in Bucharest half an hour before midnight, arriving from Amsterdam. The cabin was packed with Romanians collected in the Netherlands from everywhere on the globe. Lost in the crowd, a handful of foreigners had spent the three hours of the flight silently nibbling a drink.

Jane had endured the whole trip with silent and efficient resilience. Back in LA I'd asked her is she would like to come with me and she'd said a simple yes and readied herself for departure in no time. We had tricked the feds at the rendezvous place with Ernesto, a mall. Ernesto had led us to a waiting car whose trunk miraculously contained our luggage. Jane had remained indifferent at the scheme. "You gonna leave you car back there?" she'd asked, pointing to the mall's parking lot. I'd said "Yes," and she'd shrugged the matter off.

The 737 taxied to the terminal. At the customs, I let Jane go ahead on one waiting line and I picked another, separating her from me. She went ahead without hesitation. I hailed a taxi, once outside and loaded the luggage in the trunk.

"Where to?" the driver asked in English. "Hilton? Intercontinental?" He smiled, weighing us carefully.

"Just take us home," I answered in Romanian, and smiled. I gave him an address in Cotroceni.

He laughed broadly, uneasy.

"You got me fooled, boss. You look like the others, the guys from the outside. Cotroceni it is, then, boss. That'll be sixty euros."

"Make that thirty, friend," I smiled.

He grinned, and turned back to his wheel, ready to start.

"Thirty it is," he said.

He exited the airport and took the Ploiesti-Bucharest highway. I recognized some of the landscape, but most of it was changed. The city had changed, as seen though the taxi's windows. New malls and steel and glass office buildings.

We approached Cotroceni along Stirbey Voda, an avenue reminding me too little of my student years. I had walked that route hundreds of times returning from a late drink in town, shaking of cold and wishing I was in my bed in the dorms. There were many more trees lining the road, then.

"Here," the driver said, stopping the car. "I got you and the lady home."

We got out, walked around the vehicle and grabbed our duffel bags from the trunk. Jane moved as if synchronizing with me, smooth and efficient. I had expected complaints from her about the discomforts of the trip or about such strange stops at odd locations in the middle of the night. Instead, she stood by the luggage, on the sidewalk, waiting for me to make my moves.

I handed the driver three tens and a tip.

"Thank you, boss" the driver said. "Any help with the luggage?"

"No, thanks, we're fine."

He smiled and nodded, walking around the car and getting back into the driver seat. His walk was slow, and his glances at us often, as if he was curious to see which house, which door or which gate were we going to enter. We didn't enter any, just waited patiently for him to leave.

The streets were deserted. Only once in a while a car would pass. I looked up a little map I'd brought from LA.

"We need to carry these for a block or two," I told Jane, pointing to the luggage. "Is that OK?"

She said OK. My duffel bag could also be carried as a back pack; I strapped it on and helped with hers. Two short blocks down the street, I found the address. It was one the houses built before the last world war, with cubed volumes and large spaces. A real estate fortune on the local market. The nouveau rich would hunt such properties, acquire them and remodel in an opulent manner. No sign of that was showing on the house. Everything looked in good condition, but old and ordinary. I rang the bell by the gate. After a while, a crackled voice answered on an intercom. I explained who I was.

"You came for the car?" the voice asked.

"Yes."

"Come in," the voice said, and the gate buzzed open.

The man was in his fifties. He was heavy as only a former sportsman or a former military man would grow heavy; a thick body without hanging fat. His movement still suggested considerable strength, but he was tired, unshaved, and apparently very used to giving cars to strangers in the middle of the night.

"Who's your reference?" he asked, opening an old notebook.

I told him the name of the contact in Montreal. He wrote it down.

"Your passport," he demanded.

He opened the document looking for the name with a routine motion, knowing where to look. He handwrote my name on his notebook."

"The money," he demanded.

I have him the envelope prepared. It was thick. He looked inside.

"US dollars?" he grumbled. He shook his head irritated, and counted the cash with the speed of a bank clerk. "Fifteen hundred is the cost for ten days," he explained pocketing the cash. "You keep my car more, I keep more. The rest is for possible damages. Don't fuck with the car. I'll check it when you return it and I'll keep whatever extra I think it's gonna cost me to fix it."

He gave me a set of keys and took me to an old Jeep Cherokee parked in the back yard. There, the house had another gate accessing a small street behind it. He pressed a button and rolled the gate open. I loaded the luggage in the Jeep and drove off. The car was old but in good condition, its suspension acceptable, given the bad roads.

The place I needed to reach was located on the western side of the city. I had forgotten the streets topology and got lost, hitting potholes and dead ends of roads in work. Then, all of a sudden, things came back in my memory and I found the correct route.

The building was located near a large intersection with a wide underground passage. Street names had changed but the surroundings looked the same. It was a four stories concrete building, hidden from the main boulevard behind taller twelve stories apartment blocks.

I parked the car at the curb, lucky to find a spot: the place was packed with vehicles parked at odd angles at the curbs so as to fit as many as possible in the tight space available. Most of the windows on the buildings around were dark, except a few lit by the flickering light of TV screens.

The keys I'd received from Montreal worked right, one for the main entrance, the other for the apartment door. The flat had a bedroom and a living room, a separate kitchen and a bath. The belongings of the tenant were scattered al around, but in relative good order. An old picture of him was hung, framed, in a corner of the living room where a table was used as an office desk. He was holding hands with a woman. I remembered the man, looking at the picture, and I realized I remembered the woman too, although I couldn't recall the names.

Jane briefly studied the bedroom, unpacked as little as necessary and got in the shower. I washed my face at the kitchen sink, and dried up with a paper towel. The night view from the kitchen window consisted of dull concrete, the walls of the taller buildings around. It felt as if two huge trap doors had closed behind me at the airport, and there was no way back out unless I found the secret key for those doors.

In the bedroom, the bare light bulb on the ceiling hurt my eyes. I lied down in bed, facing the crude light and the empty walls. Reality had a slippage factor. *"What the hell am I doing here?"* I whispered to the air. *"And where the hell am I?"* It wasn't the past, and it wasn't the present. Somehow, the former had been altered by the latter, and that placed me in a time no man's land.

I closed my eyes, focused, and began remembering.

39

December 22, 1989
National Institute for Science and Technology
Propulsion Division
Bucharest, Romania

"It's going to be a big mess," Victor Petrescu said.

In the dark, hidden by the window, we watched the soldiers running out of the barracks, grouping and lining up in platoon formations. A rush of khaki uniforms, the barks of an officer.

"Alarm drills," I said.

"The second one in the last hour. They keep the men on the edge."

Our office was located in the rear side of the Institute grounds by the engine test stands. Its windows faced the barracks hosting the Securitate[4] infantry troops in charge of Institute's security. It was still early morning and the sky was pitch dark. No other Institute employees had arrived yet.

"Radio Free Europe is in continuous broadcast," Petrescu said. "Timisoara has fallen, they say."

It was against the law in Romania to discuss Radio Free Europe broadcasts. Petrescu trusted me and I trusted him, but sometimes Secu would bug offices, especially in defense enterprises like the Institute. But that morning, it didn't matter much. Secu was likely busy with whatever was brewing on the streets.

"Fallen to whom?" I asked.

"They say troops had fraternized with the population. Civilians and military are shouting anti-communist slogans all over town."

"I wonder, how much of this is true" I said. "Other rumors I heard say there are several thousand dead."

Petrescu frowned. "A lot of it is true. Otherwise you wouldn't see these guys so nervous."

---

[4]   The Romanian Department of Homeland Security during the communist regime - the Securitate was the secret police spying on the citizens for signs of dissent. It also had a branch of infantry troops in charge of security for defense R&D enterprises. In street jargon, the people referred to the Securitate with the nickname of "Secu"

We sat in the dark, silent, watching.

"Did you go downtown, yesterday?" Petrescu asked.

"I did," I said, lowering my voice. Did you?"

"I didn't. I spent the night listening to the Free Europe and Voice of America. The Bulgarians showed some stuff on TV."

"What did the Bulgarians say?"

"All Romanian borders are closed. They showed trucks lining up at the border crossings, waiting. They also showed Ceausescu's big popular meeting yesterday when the crowd went crazy."

"What did they show?"

"They replayed our TV broadcast. Something made a big loud noise. The crowd panicked, and the TV transmission went off. It came back after several minutes, with Ceasca[5] making promises to the crowd, whatever he could think off. He had his people all in front of the crowd, making nice and waving flags and banners for the cameras, but you could see the crowds in disarray behind them."

He stopped; someone was walking noisily on the outside alley. It was a woman, from another group, arriving early.

"Lots of things don't make sense," I said. "Suddenly we have protests in Timisoara last week, something unheard of in this country. And with that mess in Timishoara, Ceasca goes to Iran on a state visit. Was he nuts? As if he thought all is well and under control. Was the visit so important that he had to take the risk? Then he comes back, and organizes this big mass demonstration of yesterday. He forces all these people gather in one place, for the cameras, here in Bucharest. And during his speech everything goes crazy. He lost control?"

"Someone played him on this one," Petrescu said. "People close to him."

"Who? What do you mean?"

"I wish I knew. Someone inside Secu but also connected to an outside hand, probably the Soviets."

He started pacing the office. I looked out the window. The soldiers had broken formation and were lining up for the morning meal.

---

[5] One of the nicknames used by the population for dictator Nicolae Ceausescu.

"Ceasca's being set up by his very own people," Petrescu continued. "Not the first line of power, those will fall with him. The second echelon, guys whose names we don't know, yet. Folks with good connections to the outside, to the Soviets, or to the Americans, maybe both."

He placed a cigarette in his mouth, but didn't light up; smoking was prohibited in the test stands. I was about to say something when I heard steps on the stairs leading to the office. We waited in silence.

A tall and heavy man dressed in a thick fur coat entered the office and turned all fluorescent ceiling lights on. Petrescu squinted his eyes, watching the man with disdain. The man fumbled around his messy desk and found a good spot for his heavy briefcase and then took his time arranging the pillow on his chair.

"Let it be light, comrades," he joked for a greeting and laughed by himself. He appeared preoccupied with the objects on his cluttered desk. "Did you guys listen to the Free Europe last night?" he asked matter-of-factly.

I didn't answer. Petrescu growled at the man, "We do not listen to capitalist American propaganda, comrade."

"Yes, yes, of course," the man grinned. "Timisoara is down, Bucharest is next, they say," he continued, ignoring our coldness. He took off his heavy coat. It was an expensive coat, with a rich fur collar.

"They're pushing like hell," he said and glanced at Petrescu, a quick and furtive look of a scared man, before reverting to his usual grumpy posture. "The will of the masses, freedom, what a piece of crap!"

He kept speaking, as if not only for the benefit of me and Petrescu, but for a larger and invisible audience. He opened his arms wide and gestured with them while he spoke:

"George Bush[6] meets Gorbachev in Malta, all in secret, on a war ship far from anything that can eavesdrop on them. They have a little cup of coffee, maybe with a little something in it, and they set-up the

---

[6] On December 2nd and 3rd 1989, US president G.H. Bush met USSR leader Mikhail Gorbachev in Malta on board the Soviet cruise ship SS Maxim Gorkiy, anchored off the coast of Marsaxlokk Harbour in the Mediterranean island of Malta. The meeting is considered to mark the official end of the Cold War.

whole game. And then, all of us, the fart Soviet satellite countries start shaking. First, Hungary opens borders with Austria. Then, trains full of East Germans start heading down to Budapest and then straight to Vienna. The Soviets have troops in Hungary but they don't move a finger. Czechoslovakia is awakening again, and the Germans are talking about reunification. And finally, the fucking Berlin Wall goes down. How much bigger of a set up you want? You have to be blind not to see it. We, in this little spit of a country don't even count more than a checkmark on a list, this idiot of ours here has his days numbered."

I watched the man and said nothing. His name was Adrian Durlic and we suspected him of being a snitch for the Secu. His objective may have been to provoke comments from us and report on them. But there was something else in his voice, reconfirming the moment of weakness I'd observed a minute before: the man was scared.

He ignored our cold silence, placed a cigarette in his mouth and left to smoke it in the designated smoking area.

"The motherfucker is right," Petrescu said in low voice, following Durlic with his eyes. "Or rather he's spreading the rumor he's been told to spread. Either way, Ceasca is being set up."

Petrescu had repeated his theory several times already, but I wasn't that convinced. At the age of thirty, I had been born in a communist country and had been raised under communism. Communism seemed to me clad in concrete, an ever lasting evil.

"We'll see what happens," I said.

We kept watching the Secu troops outside. Like any Romanian defense enterprise, the Institute was guarded by Secu infantry troops. Such troops were a derivative of the regular infantry but subordinated to the Romanian Homeland Security Department, the Secu. Their training was better than the training of their regular Army counterpart.

"I was here late the other night, working," Petrescu spoke again. "They brought extra ammunition loaded in bakery trucks."

"Bakery trucks?"

He shrugged.

"Secu's idea of secrecy, I guess." He turned towards me and asked in a low voice: "Tell me what happened down town, last night."

"I was at the University Plaza," I said. "Troops everywhere. Anti terrorist units, USLA[7] guys lined up with shields, keeping the streets blocked. The crowds filled the streets wherever there was access. Lots of students, regular folks, many retired men. Something interesting though, on one hand the students were friendly with the troops, exchanging cigarettes, lighting up and talking over the shields held by those USLA boys, but on the other hand there were groups of men whistling and booing the troops. They looked like teams of sportsmen, or military guys dressed in civilian clothes. You may be right, it looked like someone wanted to get some action going, provoke. Late in the evening, a military truck ran into the crowd. Accident or by intention, I couldn't tell. Big commotion, anyway. I got out of there just before shooting started."

"Shooting? Who fired?"

I shrugged.

"No idea, I got out. Some say the troops, some others say there were snipers on the roofs, or even guys within the crowd shooting people in the back with silenced guns. I heard someone in the subway this morning saying they were washing the blood off the floors at the University station. Too many fucking rumors."

Petrescu grinned bitterly.

"Secu is spreading the rumors. It's their method of intoxication. I stick to what I said, Ceasca's being set up."

We had to quit our discussion. The rest of the employees started arriving for work. There wasn't much eye contact and talk between people, just apprehension.

"Matei," Petrescu whispered, "let's get our engine stuff in order. We have parts for two engines in crates, and the one installed for testing, let's secure everything, pack the documentation and put everything under lock. That is now, pronto. Then, wait and see what happens."

---

[7] USLA - Romanian Special Antiterrorist Units during communist regime.

Our engine was our life. Known as Motor Racheta cu Fortaj Electromagnetic[8] *or by its acronym, the MRFEM engine was our baby project. We had struggled with the inept Romanian research and development system to get it off the ground. We had started the project in a low key, low budget, let's-see-if-it-works type of effort. It had quickly evolved into a full program because it worked well, and we managed to get further support by pulling connections up in the Romanian Communist Party. MRFEM became the main research program carried by our branch of the Institute. Petrescu was in charge of the testing work and I was in charge of research, both guarding our technology know-how with tenacious passion. The third man, Adrian Durlic, had been attached to our project management group with the task of spying what we do and capture the expertise. At least that was our suspicion. But the man was incompetent; the only problems he could create were of political nature, if he was an informer as we suspected.*

As if attracted by my thoughts, Durlic returned from his smoke and walked into the storage area to observe what we were doing. Our physical effort of packing, carrying and stacking the crates with engine parts and materials was not to his liking. He decided we don't need any help. He returned to the office and planted his ass on a chair and pretended to read a report.

We finished the stacking, locked the metal doors and returned to the office to organize the documentation left there. Petrescu and I were the only ones working. After some initial apprehension, the rest of the people in the office had started discussing the political situation, heating up to arguments, beating fear with words, caring less and less about informants or hidden microphones.

Suddenly, Petrescu stopped from his work and listened to engine noise coming from outside. Through the window, I saw several black government cars driving through the inner yard and stopping at the entrance of our building. Petrescu leaned out the window and looked, carefully.

"Watch out," he muttered quickly. "Lock the archive."

---

[8] Electromagnetically Enhanced Rocket Engine – in Romanian

"It's locked," I said.

Footsteps echoed on the walls of the concrete staircase. Several people were coming up. The whole office went silent, people busying themselves with paperwork, blueprints or reports. The door opened, and a group of four men dressed in suits walked in. The man leading the group wore a dark blue suit of good quality and kept his shoulders straight, with military demeanor. His skin was dark as if suntanned and the hair on his skull was black with only a few traces of gray, naturally curled but cut short. His severe eyes were partially masked by gold rimmed prescription glasses with shaded lenses which he adjusted again and again on his nose in a nervous habit. He walked into the office and swept the place with his eyes in a careful and intense inspection.

There was dead silence. The man glanced quickly at his three subordinates and they immediately took positions by the staircase door, the door accessing to the test stand and the equipment room door. Those men were young, rugged and athletic, dressed in cheaper suits.

"Report," the dark man demanded.

The male employees in the office saluted, military style, and the women just watched, frozen.

Adrian Durlic reported in a quick phrase that all people were present for duty at the Test Stand Number 1. In spite of the rough, military style, his voice was humble. The man flashed Durlic with a look that had the power of carbonizing. Then, he inspected the room one more time.

I kept my eyes on the floor and didn't move. I knew very well who the man was: a powerful and dangerous apparatchik, formerly the Director of the Institute. He had sacked many, some in the management, some simple researchers like me and Petrescu. He had climbed the ladder from the management of the Institute into the position of Deputy Minister for Heavy Industry. People had nicknamed him "The Bolshevik" for his ruthless manner, yet Petrescu, in one good moment of inspiration had shortened the nickname to Bolek[9], and the new nickname had caught with everyone.

---

[9] The name of a cartoon character popular at the time in the Eastern Block.

Bolek was not the typical incompetent apparatchik: he held a doctorate degree in Aerodynamics and the military rank of a colonel. Politically, he was a shrewd operator with a very enigmatic personal agenda: he had destroyed many careers of people he didn't like and managed to destroy or stall many efforts meant to generate indigenous Romanian propulsion, even projects that may have benefited his own career. There were rumors that Bolek was in fact a KGB mole, part of the political control mechanism the big brother USSR was employing in the satellite communist states. We strongly suspected that Adrian Durlic was Bolek's man.

The previous year, as if just to confirm some of our suspicions, Bolek had disappeared, suddenly, and rumors circulated that he was investigated by the counter-intelligence branch of the Secu. However, someone high in the government had gotten him out. Bolek had showed up again, and worked his way back up the ladder. He'd pulled one of his tricks to climb even higher. He'd spread the news that one of the newest planes in Ceausescu's fleet had excessive engine vibration, and arranged that the piece of news hits Ceausescu himself, using his connections in the dictator's entourage. Then, he'd made a big show out of a bogus technical investigation of the alleged vibration. He'd buried the reports indicating that nothing seems to be wrong with the engines and had issued another report directly to the dictator claiming success in resolving the issue with indigenous engineering talent under his - Bolek's, direct technical leadership. The trick had worked. The dictator liked the report. By the following fall, just weeks prior to the anticommunist uprising, Bolek had been made full member of the Central Committee of the Romanian Communist Party. He was prepared to rub elbows with the first line of power in the country.

The morning arrival, however, was not typical Bolek routine. I felt it had something to do with the MRFEM project and the political situation in the country. Bolek had shown very strong interest in the MRFEM project as soon as the project had gained traction. That's when Bolek had inserted his man, Durlic into the team. And that morning, I felt Bolek was more dangerous than ever. And for that reason, I kept studying the office floor.

As if reading my mind, Bolek walked closer towards me and Petrescu and stared at us through the shaded lens of his gold rimmed glasses.

"Status report on MRFEM," he demanded. His pronunciation of the acronym was MORPHEM.

Petrescu arched his back and fixed his gaze somewhere far ahead through the wall. "Test stand work proceeding as planned, comrade Minister," he reported. "The main hydrogen tank is completed and under testing. All parts and documentation packed and archived under lock, given the events and the situation."

Bolek took a sudden step forward, closing into Petrescu, one inch from his face. He arranged the shaded glasses on his face with a hand displaying prominent knuckles, as if made from roots of trees.

"What situation, comrade?" he asked icily. "What events?"

He kept his gaze on Petrescu for several long moments, in dead silence. Then, he turned towards the rest of the office and spoke powerfully, "You must be aware that anyone who spreads false rumors only facilitates the work of foreign spy agencies trying to undermine the achievements of our communist country."

After letting his words make their accusing effect on everyone, he eyed the locked door of our archives.

"Continue your daily work, comrades. And since you are so worried about the MORPHEM project, comrade Petrescu, the documentation and engine components will be at once transported into the official archive and special storage space of the institute. These three men will provide help," he pointed to the men in suits.

I looked at Victor, trying to weigh the situation quickly. Moving the archive was something we had opposed all along and until then, Bolek had been careful in his attempts to force our hands.

"Comrade minister...," Petrescu started, but the door burst open, and another man in a gray suit ran in.

"Forgive me, comrade minister, we need to leave right away," the man said, barely catching his breath.

Bolek turned towards him, raising his eyebrows. He seemed to understand the nature of the emergency. He raised his hand and pointed his root-like finger towards Petrescu's chest.

"*Carry on as ordered,*" *he demanded.* "*These men will remain and help.*"

"*Comrade minister, with all do respect,*" *the man who had rushed in intervened.* "*We need all the men.*"

Something changed on Bolek's face. Like a freeze on his face. He glanced around, frowning. Then, without a word he turned and rushed out, followed by all his men.

Petrescu and I exchanged a glance. What was that? And another set of footsteps echoed on the concrete staircase, one of the intern engineers bursting in, red faced, his eyes gleaming, out of breath.

"*People from the factories around are gathering out on the street!*" *he said with intense excitement.* "*They're out in front, big marching column. They're calling for us!*"

I felt a strong rush of adrenaline. The factories next door meant a lot a people. More than four thousand people.

"*How much more do we have to do here?*" *Petrescu asked.*

"*We're done, everything is locked,*" *I said.*

"*Then let's go in front see what's happening.*"

I got my coat and left with Petrescu. The rest of the people in the office followed us. Most of the Institute employees were in the front yard, quietly watching the crowd outside the gates. The slogans against Ceausescu were breathtaking. The crowd's shouting voices propagated in strong sound waves, a people's thirst for freedom breaking loose. A fence made of wrought iron and Secu sentinels separated us from the crowd outside.

Some of our intern engineers demanded exit access and suddenly walked towards the gate. The soldier there raised his hand, and brought his AK-47 in ready position. Only feet from us, the Director of the Institute was nervously watching. The Secretary of the Institute's Communist Organization was next to him, red faced, perspiring, in spite of the cold.

The man in command of the Secu troops came from the barracks walking fast and arranging his cap. He had the rank of a major, and we all new him simply as "Major". He had been there in command for many years.

"Comrade major," I called him as he walked by me and Petrescu, and he stopped, surprised, watching us, eyebrows raised.

"Yes, comrade engineer?"

"Those kids by the gate, comrade major," I said in lower voice.

"What about them?"

"They're kids, comrade major. They want to get out on the street. Some of us may even want to join them as well. What are you going to do? Would your men open fire on us?"

He looked at me stone faced, and then smiled slightly.

"My mission is to take care of this institute, comrade engineer. What's on the street it's not my concern. I'm only concerned with individuals who may want to enter these premises without permission or proper passes. Those who want to get out are not my business."

He walked to the gate and raised his voice.

"Men, listen up! Our mission is to guard the Institute. Only people with proper access documents can come in. Whoever wants or needs to exit is free to do so. Open the gate."

The Director protested. The Secretary rubbed his face with his gloved hands.

The young men from the Institute walked out. One of them turned back and faced us. His eyes found me and Petrescu. I knew him, he had graduated the previous summer and his wife was pregnant in the fourth month.

"Matei!" he shouted, "Victor! What the hell, guys? This is it, let's go!"

I felt a shiver down my spine. Petrescu laughed with no joy.

"Decision time, old pal," he said, and sucked air strongly through his teeth. "How many times, in these fucked up lives of ours will we have a moment like this?"

I listened to the sound waves from the thousands of people shouting the rhythmic slogans. I watched the faces of the Institute authorities, the AK-47's in the soldier's hands. There are moments when you make decisions with your brain, other moments when you just do it with your guts.

"What the hell," I said. "Let's go."

We both stepped towards the gate. Strong rumor of voices rose among the small crowd in the yard. Some other men followed us.

"Write them on the list," I heard the Secretary saying to an aide. We had crossed the red line.

40

December 22, 1989
On the streets of Bucharest, Romania

Out on the boulevard we joined the crowd. We found people we knew, and joined hands. We were about twenty men and women among the thousands in the crowd, all shaking out of fear, excitement, the feeling of no return; we all had been written on some black list or another.

After marching for a few blocks, a salvo of rifles reverberated through the buildings ahead of us. Cries came from the front of the column, "They're firing at us! They're killing us!"

Petrescu grabbed my shoulder and pointed to tracer bullets flying up in the sky.

"Calm down!" he shouted. "They're firing in the air!"

Other people saw that too. The crowd began shouting the slogans again. The rhythmic sound waves of voices reverberated from the buildings against the echoes of the weapon fire. Somehow, it felt as special power against the guns.

A new salvo came. More tracer bullets flew high in between the walls. A heavy truck came from behind, slow, blowing its horn and gently parting the crowd.

"Get ready, kids," the old man at the wheel shouted. "Look behind. They're bringing in the tanks."

I looked back, behind the truck. The crowd obstructed my view, but stronger and stronger I heard the sound of engines and tracks hitting the pavement. Suddenly, the tail of the marching column got scattered away. The mass of bodies which had been obstructing my view dissolved.

I saw the tanks, dark forms of steel approaching in two columns. They weren't rushing it. Human silhouettes crouched behind the turrets.

Petrescu pulled on my shoulder.

"Don't play fucking hero," he said, quickly.

I didn't listen to him. I stood in the middle of the road, waiting for the tanks, Petrescu next to me. The people we knew were all lost in the thousands of silhouettes ahead of us. Another salvo came, and broken glass fell from the upper floors of the buildings around.

Victor pulled at my arm towards a hideout in between the buildings, but I shook off my arm and said, "Let me see their eyes."

The first tank of the column reached me. The gunner had lowered the barrel of heavy machine gun, pointing it to my chest. I looked for eye contact with the tank crews. The previous night, while trying to get out from the University Plaza, I had passed some road blocks manned by troops commanded by men dressed in inferior grade uniforms which didn't fit their rank. Their faces were old, well groomed, eyes too intelligent for the inferior rank. I suspected they were high ranking Secu officers disguised as army men. But the tank crews' eyes looked honest: military men with a mission, scared and confused but determined to carry it out. Behind each tank's turret, there were two infantry men. Those were also honest young soldiers, scared, grasping their Ak-47's and pressing their backs against the steel of the turrets.

"Don't shoot at the people!" I shouted. I held up my ID with my picture. Petrescu promptly imitated me. The men on the tanks couldn't see de details, but they could recognize the worn out document. In his latest TV speech, Ceausescu made reference to foreign spy agencies that were setting up the turmoil in the country.

"We're regular folks!" I shouted again. "Everybody there in that crowd is just the same. Don't shoot your brothers and sisters."

It was pathetic, but I didn't care. We were living a strange hour, like a bad movie with a bad script, but a great moment. I ignored the barrels pointing towards my chest. Victor Petrescu came up with cigarettes. He offered them to the infantry on the tanks. Most of them refused, but one of them reached for a cigarette.

The commander of the third tank yelled at me.

"Move away! We have orders to reach downtown, if you guys let us through, there will be no trouble!"

"There will be no trouble," I shouted back.

He looked severely at me, his tank already further ahead, but nodded and disappeared in the turret. Another salvo was heard ahead of us. The crowd seemed to have reached a standstill in front of who ever was shooting the salvos. The first tank reached the rear of the crowd and slowly penetrated through it. One by one, the tanks went through. Trucks carrying troops followed.

"It's going to be a long mess," Petrescu said, and lit up his last cigarette.

I lit up my last one. My hands were shaking.

"You had your hero moment," Petrescu said, "now let's think about what we do next. We're on the black list. If Ceasca gets the crowds under control and the order is restored we're in deep shit. We're on the list. We must figure out something, some plan."

I drew smoke. Suddenly, I felt I was in the middle of nowhere, having lost the sense of fraternity with the marching crowd and left with just bitter taste in my mouth. My whole life had changed in less than one hour. I didn't know what to expect, months of civil war ahead, being hunted by secret police, anything.

"It's going to be a long mess" Petrescu repeated.

***

He was wrong. The tanks and the troops had come too late for Ceausescu. About the same time the tanks had passed us, General Milea, the Romanian Defense Minister had committed suicide, after refusing to order the troops to open fire at the crowds. Later, rumors said he had been in fact assassinated. Either way he was left on a couch still alive, waiting to die with a bullet in him while a fresh successor took over. News of Army officers and soldiers fraternizing with the crowds of protesters quickly spread. The troops and tanks were ordered back in the barracks, while Ceausescu and his wife made a narrow escape taking off in a helicopter from the top of the Central Committee Building, just seconds before the angry crowd had reached the roof. By late afternoon, several possible government teams were proposed and dismissed in the middle of a generalized chaos, while the fate of the dictator was still unknown. The whole country felt like a bus running on an unknown road without a driver.

There was very little looting, people prevented that as soon as any attempt was made. Men and women on the streets were in a joyful trance, embracing at random, crying and walking the streets.

On an electronics store, several TV sets were on. We got in and watched over the shoulders of people who had gotten there before us. The national TV station was in disarray. Actors and news anchors in the TV studios were talking about freedom while various silhouettes crossed at random the field of view of the cameras. Some of the silhouettes carried rifles. **"Christ is being born again, on this land,"** *an actor declaimed.*

We remained in the store for the rest of the day, watching. There was nothing else to do. By evening, one more new government was formed. It seemed some final arrangement. Someone read the list of people in the new government. A mélange of political dissidents, known or vaguely known personalities, and a real guy in charge, acting with apparent modesty, a former communist activist, addressing people with comrade left and right.

"Isn't this the guy they say he went to college in USSR? Schoolmate with Gorbachev?" Petrescu asked. "He used to be some big shot in the Party, a while back, then he'd vanished."

"That's him," I confirmed. "I heard rumors about this guy way before this. Ceasca was afraid of him, but didn't take him out. He was scared the Soviets would come after him."

Petrescu laughed, "Looks like they came anyway."

We kept watching. The disarray continued. A man dressed in a general uniform was ordering moves of troops from certain military units around the city waving his hands in front of a TV camera. He was claiming the TV studios are under attack.

The man annoyed me. "Who the fuck is this guy?" I asked, louder that I intended.

A man in front of us turned around and eyed us closely.

"He's Army General Militaru," he answered. "Ceausescu kicked him out after Secu documented him a Soviet spy. That's who he is."

I didn't reply, just exchanged a glance with Petrescu. It wasn't clear if the man in front of us was a supporter of the general or was scoffing at him. Why would the man issue orders on TV? Didn't they have military communications? Then I realized that if the general had been discharged then he was no longer in command of anything, he was just creating chaos trying to break down the loyalty of the military chain of command. Or he was just trying to rally the army behind the new government.

The TV broadcast switched over to live cameras on the Palace Plaza where the new government was making public declarations from the balcony of the very same building Ceausescu had left by helicopter in the morning.

"Hold your fire! Hold your fire!" someone kept yelling, off the camera. Yet, we could hear shots fired.

"Who is firing? Hold your fire!" military officers were ordering from the balcony, yelling to the crowd.

But shots kept coming, intensifying. It wasn't clear from where. The members of the new government left the balcony. The cameras kept showing the Palace Plaza, vaguely lit by fluorescent lamps, firing continuing. It was a blind and surreal gun fight. Chips were being pulverized from the walls of the Museum wing of the old Royal Palace, hit by heavy caliber fire. Behind the walls, paintings by Rembrandt, Titian and Rubens were waiting to be destroyed.

Then the image switched back to the studios. People were running around, soldiers in uniforms carrying AK-47's moving in front of the cameras.

"We are under attack by terrorist forces faithful to the dictator," the discharged general declared, and kept waving his hands. His uniform, although genuine, seemed a costume. "Everybody, everybody, come and defend the new freedom, come and defend the TV station!" He sounded desperate and pathetic, but again, the moment was desperate and pathetic. He issued more orders to some military units he seemed to know. There was no way one could tell if he had any success with those orders of his. A TV camera showed some images from outside the TV building, and we could see tracer bullets hitting the walls. Some people in the store declared aloud they are going to head towards the TV station, and left.

I pulled Victor Petrescu out of the store as well. Out on the sidewalk he grabbed my arm.

"No more fucking hero shit, Matei," he started.

"Cool off," I stopped him. "Let's think a bit about us, me and you, what do we do from here."

He grinned.

"That's more like it. I thought you were going to the TV station with those folks."

"I would, if I were convinced I'd do any good. I'm not convinced. Meanwhile, we only have one asset, and that's the engine at the Institute."

His eyes flickered.

"We're on those people shit list, buddy," he said. "We can't go back, with all those Secu troops around." He wasn't very sure of his words.

"Let's get home, take a shower, and grab some clean clothes," I told him. "Let's wait through the night and start fresh in the morning."

"What if Ceasca gets the Army units in the provinces organized and is coming on to Bucharest to clean the mess?"

"If that happens, we head for the border, Yugoslavia, Hungary, wherever."

"Yugoslavia or Hungary? The fuck, just like that?"

"If you'll come up with something better, we'll discuss it. My guess is that we won't need to. I think you're right, this set up is too big to reverse."

He nodded.

"OK, so what do we do now?"

"Let's get home and pack some clothes. Then either I come to your place or you come to mine, and wait the night."

We found a man with a car working taxi services without a license. It was a common practice for people to make an extra buck that way, licensed taxis from the state owned taxi companies were scarce. The man asked us an enormous sum to get us home.

"There's shooting all over the place, either you take it or leave it, comrades," he said.

We paid him. Petrescu and I lived in different neighborhoods of the city, in small studio apartments, both of us unmarried. We arranged with the man to take Petrescu home first, then me.

The streets were in fact calm, with normal traffic, only perturbed by trucks full of people waving flags. The flags had a hole in the middle, where people had cut out the seal of communist government. The holed flag had become an instant symbol of the new freedom. Here and there, groups of people carrying similar flags walked the streets barely illuminated by rare fluorescent lights. Each time we passed such a group, our driver blew his horn and showed the victory sign, driving around the crowd. The maneuver worked perfectly every time. Ceausescu himself may have gotten away with it.

We stopped at a traffic light on a stretch of the road passing the north side of the Military Academy. The light was still red when gun fire erupted from somewhere on our right side. Our driver panicked and tried to gun the engine, but only stalled it. He cursed and started cranking the engine, while we peeked along the poorly lit side street to see what was happening. A shadow ran towards the car, awkwardly. Before we could react, the shadow jumped on the hood of the car, small fists beating on the windshield.

She was a girl, no older than eighteen. Her chest was full of blood, but not hers. She was crying hysterically, pulling us towards the side street from where the shots had come moments earlier. Three bodies were lying on the ground. She pointed to them continuing to cry and speaking unintelligibly. I kneeled down. They were young boys, her age. Petrescu checked them.

"Dead," he said, and moved to the next one. "Dead," he said again. The girl cried in convulsions.

"They asked for directions," she said through the sobs. "They stopped the car and asked for directions, and when we got closer they shot at us with a machine gun! Why? Why? Why?" She lost her breath and bend down, desperately crying.

"Quick," Petrescu said, "This one is alive. You!" he ordered the driver who was scared to death, "Bring the car here! Get that engine going!"

"What do you want to do?" the man asked.

"What are you a fucking idiot?" Petrescu yelled. "Let's get the kid to the hospital!"

The man stepped back, in the dark.

"I don't want to get involved," he mumbled, "I'm an honest man, I have no business with this. I don't want blood on my upholstery."

Petrescu stood up quickly and grabbed the man by his coat.

"You motherfucker, give me the keys!" he ordered.

"Give them to me" I asked, and grabbed the keys. I got the engine going and backed the car on the side street. We loaded the young man on the back seat, and managed to find room for the girl, beside Petrescu and the old man.

I drove back, down the hill, towards the Municipal Hospital. The ER was packed. Orderlies and ER nurses took the young man on a corner of the room but didn't seem to be able to do anything immediately. People with gun shot wounds were being brought by ambulances continuously. Petrescu fought his way towards a group of doctors and yelled at them. After an argument, they got the boy in the operating room.

"Can you stay here with him?" I asked the girl. Her face was white, she could barely speak. She only nodded.

"Can you call parents, relatives?"

She nodded again, and gained some strength at the idea.

Petrescu tapped on my shoulder. He had an Army sergeant with him, with a notebook.

"I have to identify you, comrades," the sergeant said.

I gave him my ID. "You have two more bodies to take care of," I told him.

"Wounded?" he asked.

"Dead. Shot on the sidewalk."

"They can wait, then," the sergeant said.

I gave him the location while he was writing down our names and ID numbers with a shaky hand. A woman was crying next to us.

"We were just walking," she said, "Doru wanted to get out, we live by the North Railroad Station. Shots came out of nowhere, and he just started loosing his balance. Is that leg of yours? I asked him, does it bother you again? I asked him, but he said nothing and fell to the

ground. And he's just gone, he's gone, my Doru, all gone." Her words became unintelligible and her body shook in convulsions. The sergeant eyed her with tired compassion.

"Snipers," he said.

We left and found our driver sitting in the car, sobbing. In the strong light by the emergency room his thin face appeared wrinkled with confusion and fear. The man was wearing a worn out coat, ripped at the elbows. I gave him back the keys of his car, and searched my pockets for cash.

"This is for your trouble, old man," I told him, forcing the bills in his hand. "Just take us home."

4 1

December 23, 1989
Ghencea
Bucharest, Romania

I choose to spend the night at Petrescu's place; it had become too dangerous to move around town. Petrescu lived in Ghencea, a section of Bucharest home of two large military bases. The choice left both of us without sleep: the bases came under attack and intense gun fire ensued. Compact volleys of tracer bullets kept hitting the skies all night, originating from everywhere along the boulevard. Intense barrages of 7.62 mm caliber from the AK-47's and heavier bark of 22 mm guns from the turrets of armored vehicles.

At dawn the fighting decreased in intensity and gradually stopped. Then, sporadic gunfire returned, erupting at different distances further away.

The enemy remained unknown and faceless. Secu, the Army and the Police had openly declared themselves on the side of the new government. They all seemed to be fighting blindly against ghosts. The TV station kept referring to the unknown enemy as 'terrorists'. Generic and convenient, no other detail. Rumors abounded instead and were dutifully spread by the continuous TV broadcast.

The main rumor said the unknown fighters were special troops loyal to the dictator, trained in secret bases unknown to the Army, Secu or Police. Other rumors elaborated on the identity of the special troops: orphans extracted from the many orphanages of Romania and raised and trained in those special military bases, brainwashed into believing that the dictator was their only parent and benefactor, and made ready to die for him. Some of the snipers and shooters had been captured, but once the reporters searched for them, they found no trace of the prisoners and only misleading information instead. One of the snipers had been apparently wounded during capture and hospitalized. Once found on a hospital bed by reporters, it turned out he couldn't speak Romanian. A new rumor spread: an Arab dictator, close friend of the Ceausescu's had send terrorist troops in support of the

Ceausescu couple. A voluntary fighter defending the TV station could swear he'd heard Arabic over the radio communications. Later in the morning, the mother of the presumed Arab terrorist came to his hospital bed and revealed they are simple Romanians from a village around Bucharest, and that the young man is mentally retarded, not being able to speak any language, neither Romanian nor Arabic, or anything else.

In this chaos, soon after dawn, Petrescu's phone rang a few times. He picked up the third time, carefully. The Institute operators had received orders to gather all the employees at their working places in order to organize the defense of the institute. "Defense against whom?" asked Petrescu. "Against the terrorists", came the answer.

"What if it's a trap?" I asked him. "We go there and they just lock us up for joining the demonstration, yesterday?"

We thought about it, and discarded the idea. The mess had gone just too deep for that.

There was no public transportation or taxis. We walked. Along the Ghencea sidewalk lay the night's casualties. Corpses of men dressed in the Patriotic Guard[10] uniforms were scattered on the sidewalks, several of them in grotesque positions: rigor mortis plus freezing had stiffened their legs in a bent position. Some of the dead had been rolled after freezing, probably being searched for documents. Those bodies were left with twisted stiff legs raised in the air. As we walked and watched, a military patrol stopped us and checked our ID's. We showed our Institute ID's which were issued by the Ministry of Defense and had a good resemblance to the ID's issued to the Army and Secu personnel, inspiring more respect. It was a trick both Petrescu and I used to employ with train conductors, when rushing to the stations too late to get tickets. The conductors were easier to bribe that way. As the soldiers carefully read the ID's, we kept watching the corpses.

"Are you pitying those motherfuckers?" one of the patrol soldiers asked following our stare. "Fucking curs! They have extra layers of clothes, different uniforms underneath the Patriotic Guard ones. Our

---

[10] Troops made of regular civilian people organized in military organizations at their work place. The Patriotic Guards have been formed following Ceausescu's doctrine of defense of the country by the whole people. Their training was minimal.

uniforms, army infantry. They're no fucking Patriotic Guards, they're no infantry, they're terrorists!"

"But who are they? Where are they from?" Petrescu asked.

The soldier spat on a side and ignored the question, with a dark light in his eyes,

"You can go now," he told us. "Don't spend too much time around here, it's not safe!"

At the institute, the Secu troops were in full battle gear, manning trench posts along the wall facing the boulevard, guarding the gates, and operating military radio communication equipment which had been installed over night. The Secu men were nervous. They ID-ed us several times, and then opened a wooden crate smelling of timber and oil and armed us with two brand new Ak-47's and ammunition clips. In the labs, most men were awkwardly carrying the heavy rifles along. Black and white TV sets were switched on here and there, people silently watching the chaos settled into the whole country.

On the TV screens we could see enthusiastic young men bringing fresh bread to the troops defending the TV station against faceless inexistent people who managed to kill. Actors, TV anchors, celebrities and reporters kept working on a continuous and improvised broadcast. Just days before, the same people had been producing rigid, stale and boring shows loaded with official communist propaganda. Each of them had dropped the rigid face mask, talking and behaving like normal people. The men were unshaved, tired, and eager to shake off their previous image.

The new government had named itself the National Salvation Front. The man in charge, the former communist activist turned revolutionary, seemed to be the new leader. He had teamed with people from the former communist elite, themselves turned reformers and revolutionaries but dragging shadows behind them. Until the previous day, all these people had been largely unknown. A younger and handsome man wearing a plain sweater seemed to be second in command after the old activist. He also belonged to the former communist elite, yet an elite of a very different flavor than the quasi-illiterate brand characteristic to the entourage of the Ceausescu's. A university professor and researcher, the young man spoke live in telephone interviews with French and Italian journalists, speaking fluently both languages. After years of dumb incompetence at all government levels, his presence on the TV screens was refreshing and somehow comforting.

"Remember what I told you?" Petrescu asked me. "The second tier of big shots. Let's go to our office, we can set up a TV over there."

4 2

December 23, 1989
National Institute for Science and Technology
Propulsion Division
Bucharest, Romania

We verified the wooden crates with the MRFEM documentation
and the crates containing the engine parts. There was a test engine
prototype installed on the test stand and parts for two more engines, all
well organized with tables listing the crate numbers and their contents.
We knew the MRFEM project carried a special value that should be
recognized no matter how the political situation was to evolve. I
dreamed for a moment. What if a new society was to emerge, one that
would value all the opportunities, where private initiative and a
healthy scale of values would structure the society in a fundamentally
good way? Was such a thing possible, after so many years of illogic
government? Hidden hopes deep inside my chest told me yes. My brain
said no.

Petrescu brought a small TV set he'd gotten from the girls in the
design group next door. The morning time passed, measured in chunks
of news on TV. There were reports of a gun battle near the Otopeni
International Airport during the night. There had been a large number
of casualties from friendly fire, the result of a tragic radio
miscommunication: troops being brought to help the defense of the
airport had been mowed down by the very troops they were coming to
help. Each party, separately, thought it had engaged a large terrorist
group. Stranger news came from the Air Defense section of the Army:
a large number of air targets had been recorded on the radar screens.
Some of these targets had been engaged with SAM fire, and in several
instances the objects proved to be balloons carrying long metal stripes.
In most cases the targets were just fake spots on the radar screens
generated by electronic jamming. Somewhere, there was a mysterious
enemy operating. Who was that enemy? Why were those targets
detected outside as well as inside the Romanian borders? We watched

the news in silence, and, by instinct we strapped the rifles tighter on our backs.

Shortly before noon, the door opened with a vigorous bang. Adrian Durlic walked in, followed by three other men dressed in blue overalls. We hadn't seen those men around before.

Durlic walked straight to Victor Petrescu and asked sharply: "Where is the key to the storage facility, comrade Petrescu? Please present the list of inventory in the test facility and storage area." He had an air of authority I'd never seen displayed by the man before. The object of his request was the database list with the MRFEM crates and their content.

I raised my eyebrows and didn't move from my chair but rather got a good grip on the rifle. No matter which political system we were in for the moment, I wasn't going to accept any authority from a monkey like Durlic.

"What do you need it for?" Petrescu asked, surprisingly amiable.

Durlic frowned and eyed the large padlock on the door of the storage area.

"Orders from the headquarters to secure the MRFEM contents and transport them to a safe location. I'm coming straight from the office of the director. This must be done immediately. There are two trucks with escort on their way and these men have been sent to help us."

Petrescu had a dreamy face, smiling vaguely at Durlic. "I am not sure I follow you," he spoke slowly. "We need to transport the MRFEM contents to a secure location? Let me see, perhaps a location guarded by troops within a clear defense perimeter? But wait, we are already at such a location."

"I don't have time for your humor, comrade Petrescu," Durlic snapped.

Petrescu slowly stood up. I remained on my chair.

"I'm not your fucking comrade," Petrescu said with an icy growl. "Get these monkeys out of here," he added, indicating the three men in blue overalls. "Touch a crate, and I'll blow your head off. Is that clear?"

Durlic stiffened. He was a tall and heavy man, six five and close to three hundred pounds. I could sense aggressiveness in the other men; they didn't seem typical technicians or Institute workers.

Durlic stepped towards Victor Petrescu. The other three men walked sideways, spreading around the room. I quickly leaned forward on my chair and produced the assault rifle on my chest. I armed the weapon, placing a bullet in the chamber. The sound made all of them watch me. A second similar sound came from Petrescu, his weapon ready on his chest as well. Everybody became motionless.

Then, Durlic carefully stepped back.

"Comrade Petrescu," he said, reproaching, "comrade Salajan, let's take it easy... There is an order from the headquarters, I mean, comrades, it's a job, OK? MRFEM is a government property! After all, what's the problem? It's an order, we load the stuff and off it goes, we don't need to worry about it anymore."

Petrescu watched them from under his frowned eyebrows.

"Nobody moves, not a finger, not a hair," he said, and walked closer to one of the men in blue. "You! Give me your badge, slowly," he asked the man. "You, others, just breathe." He checked with me without turning his head, "Matei?"

"I'm on it," I said, the rifle ready. "I'm their very close friend."

Petrescu picked the plastic wrap the man was carefully handing him. The typical Institute badges were simple pieces of paper, with the name and location of the person's job typewritten, a mug shot glued on a corner, with the official stamp of the Institute imprinted over the whole thing. The piece of paper was placed in a support made of plastic which quickly showed signs of wear, scratches and bents.

"That's an awfully nice and clean piece of plastic," Petrescu said to the man.

The man stood quiet. For several moments there was no sound, no motion in the room, just the TV on a desk rambling. The gun shots from far away battles outside had become part of the background.

Durlic tried to protest his way out. "You guys are just crazy!" he vociferated. "You've always been nuts, you two. And now you got some fucking new toys!"

He backed towards the door as he spoke. *"I don't know who you think you are, or what you think you're doing, but I'm going to report back that we can't accomplish the mission because of you two people gone nuts."* He addressed the other three: *"Let's go, men, let the fucking headquarters take care of it."*

We let them go.

"Who do you think wants this stuff so bad and why?" Petrescu asked, looking for his cigarettes.

"Bolek," I said. *"That's why he came early yesterday morning. Although, I don't understand, it's a fucking chaos now, what does he care anymore?"*

Petrescu grinned.

"MRFEM is an asset," he said, *"He wanted it all along. We may need to take turns and do watches. We have plenty of water, we just need some food and coffee"*

As if to exemplify his determination to live in that corner for many weeks to come, he rested his head against the wall and closed his eyes. I relaxed and switched my attention back to the TV.

***

The night came, with rumors that the Ceausescu's had been captured. Most people left the Institute and went home. Strangely, among the chaos and shooting, the subway trains and the buses were operating, stores were open, and people on the streets were carrying small fir trees. The next day was Christmas Eve.

4 3

December 24, 1989
National Institute for Science and Technology
Propulsion Division
Bucharest, Romania

Jet engine noise woke me up during Petrescu's watch. I raised my head from my improvised bed on the floor and saw Petrescu wrapped in blankets, propped on two chairs. He jumped off the chairs and ran to the windows, looking out at the skies. Twice during the night we had heard similar jet engine noises.

"Did you see it? " I asked. "Did you see the markings?"

The unspoken thought was that it could've been the Russians. The fate of Prague in 1968[11] was still a fresh reference.

"I didn't see it," Petrescu said, while turning the volume up on the small black and white TV. On screen, someone was talking about safety instructions for the civilian population of Bucharest, how people should prevent snipers from taking shelter and hide on the rooftops of their apartment buildings. Then the discussion was interrupted for an important announcement.

The TV anchor, unshaved and with dark circles around his eyes read an official communiqué from the new government: the dictator Ceausescu and his wife had been captured and were held at a military base in the city of Tîrgovişte. An hour later the station reported that the news of the capture also brought an intensification of fighting all over Bucharest. Other news followed, most of them rumors broadcasted as usual, read from little notes with no verification. One such piece or information claimed that the base where the Ceausescu's were held captive was under intense attacks, by the ubiquitous ghost forces. Reports from other cities around the country talked only about sporadic fighting, if any.

I prepared coffee using an electric plunger, while watching the continuous TV broadcast. They showed chopped footages with images

---

[11] After Czechoslovakia attempted to reform its communist system, USSR invaded the country in only 48 hours on August 21-22 1968.

from downtown, shot hours before. The National University Library had burned, thousands of valuable manuscripts transformed into ashes. The terraces on a building next to the Atheneè Palace hotel were being pulverized by heavy machinegun fire.

Suddenly, Petrescu stood up.

"*For Christ sake, we have a big problem here,*" *he said.*

I raised my eyebrows, over the coffee mug.

"*The hydrogen tank,*" *he said, the statement by itself self revelatory.*

I froze. He was right. There was an obvious danger and we had completely forgotten about it. We had filled the large capacity tank two days before the unrest, for testing. The tank contained liquid hydrogen at -253 degrees Celsius, had triple walls and was well insulated. The calculated dormancy – the time it took the liquid hydrogen to warm up and start boiling was about four days. Then, the evaporation rate was about 4% a day. It could take many days for the tank to empty.

"*If they shoot at it and it blows up, we're toast.*"

"*Damn,*" *Petrescu started pacing the room.* "*We gotta inform the military command here! Organize some defense. Make sure they know not to hit it*"

"*We lock up here and go,*" *I suggested.* "*The main doors are made of steel, they'd need a pick hammer to get in. If Durlic comes with more men and tries to break in we'll stop them. We'll keep watch from somewhere else.*"

"*All right,*" *Petrescu approved, grabbing his coat and his weapon.* "*Let's go.*"

We locked the test stand and left. Several fliers were flapping in the wind, tucked to doors and windows. Someone had called a meeting with all of the scientists and engineers in the main building. We found our way into a small and crowded auditorium. It was cold, and people had kept their coats on. A few men carried rifles, seeming inconvenienced by the weapons. A man was speaking, standing and gesticulating with his hands.

"*I had to do it, comrades*" *he was saying.* "*The director called me to his office personally, and there he was, the Minster of the Interior himself, with his son. I was ordered to write the young man's doctoral dissertation, I was ordered! I want you comrades to know, I had to do it."*

Rumor came from the crowd. "What did you get for it?" someone shouted. "That fancy apartment of yours?"

"Nothing!" the man cried in his defense, "I got nothing, except I kept my job. But I want to expose these abuses! These people have no right to lead this institution anymore."

"Yes," people shouted. "We need to elect a good leadership, by vote, comrades."

"Can you cut this shit with comrade?" some one else replied with a strong voice. "Communism is over, how about dropping this comrade shit?"

Everyone approved. The TV anchors had been already changing the word comrade with Mr. or Mrs. It sounded new to people's ears.

"There is something else you need to know," another man intervened. "I had to lock up four new computers last summer at the chief stress analyst orders! He was afraid to let the young engineers use the computers because he didn't understand anything they did. He ordered me to lock-up the equipment. Here, I have the key, I can show everyone!"

I looked at Petrescu. He made a sign towards the door. We got out.

"This is not a meeting, it's a fucking confessional" Petrescu said. "Let's go to the main gate. Secu has a command post over there."

The main gate had been organized by the Secu troops with military destinations. A storage room held ammunition; the office space had been divided between transmissions and a local command center. Since most of the walls were basically large glass windows, they had been partially covered with stacks of sandbags.

Handcuffed to the bars of the storage room protection door was a man dressed in a navy blue parka and black pants. Through the open parka, his shirt appeared dirty, hanging on him. His blond hair was in disarray, and his gaze lost. One of the soldiers seemed to guard the man, while some people from the institute were watching at some distance. A woman stood in front of the prisoner and gesticulated with her fists.

"You son of a bitch!" the woman yelled in the man's face. "You crazy bastard! What did you think you're doing? Kill all of us?"

At the sound of our steps, she stopped and glanced around. A short and wicked light gleamed in her dark eyes and went quickly away. She was giving a show there. We knew her. She used to be beautiful years before and still had some leftovers: arches of grace still preserved on her overweight body and legs with the cambered fine calves of a good fucker. The woman was intelligent, shrewd, and well connected. She was famous for easily opening any door all the way up to Bolek's office. She was also pimping for some of the men at the top, using a service apartment of the Institute.

"Who's this guy?" Petrescu asked her.

"This man?" she turned, emphatically, to the rest of the small crowd. "This man!?" She threw her hands in the air. "He's a terrorist! You want to see how one of these terrorists looks like? Look at him!"

The man ignored her, his eyes unfocused. He had the appearance of a mentally disturbed person.

"What did he do?" I asked her.

"He was spreading some sort of a powder in the ventilation system," she explained. "They saw him around the factory buildings first, then he jumped the fence over here, and these boys got him," she made a gesture of sympathy towards the soldiers. "He was trying to kill or intoxicate everyone," she added, with a flash of a dark and dramatic look at the man chained to the bar door.

"Powder?" I asked, perplexed. "What kind of powder?"

"Hell knows!" she cried, and swept the hall with her eyes, forcing the people present to bear witness to her righteous indignation, and, inherently, bear witness to her dedication to the good of the new world that was in the making.

Petrescu went to the man and pulled his parka, searching his pockets. They were empty. He grabbed the man's free arm and forced his palm up towards the light. The man groaned and jerked his hand, but weakly, with no strength. The skin on his hand was red, but it could've been just the effect of the cold, the soldier's hands looked very much the same. The chained man started laughing stupidly, watching the ceiling. Petrescu turned his back on him.

I turned to the soldier guarding the prisoner.

"We need to find Major," I told him. "Where can we find him?"

"Try the barracks," the soldier said.

"What are you going to do with this man?"

He shrugged. "He's crazy. We called headquarters, they're going to come pick him up."

"Please see that he's treated properly."

He nodded, with an obvious lack of interest.

Major was in his office. It was the first time we have ever walked inside the Secu barracks. Major had been in command there for as long as we could remember.

He didn't seem surprised at our visit. He was tired, but in good control of his demeanor. Petrescu explained the hydrogen tank problem.

"Can't you do something about it?" Major asked. "Pump the fuel out? Dump it?"

"We can't," Petrescu explained. "The installation is designed to supply an engine with fuel, through the engine's own pumps. But we can't start the engine now. The tank is only discharging through special vents, at slow rate."

The officer stood up, paced the room, then took off his cap, and sat on his desk, facing us.

"We can only hope for the best," he said. "There's nothing we can do. If somebody attacks and shoots in that direction, they'll hit the tank and that's it. I can't tell them, hey folks, don't shoot the tank, let's fight on the other side of the yard. It doesn't work that way. Besides your tank, I have other headaches; hangar number four has two mobile launchers, all armed and ready to go. They have seals on the launch switches but you can take those out with a pair of pliers. Forty eight rockets a piece. They had been prepared for testing. All we could do was to siphon out the fuel from the trucks' tanks. We cannot disarm the launchers. The people in charge of the project didn't show up, and they don't answer the calls at home. Those launchers, fallen in the wrong hands can do some real damage."

"Forgive me for asking, Major," I spoke, carefully. "Who are those wrong hands? Who are we fighting, after all?"

He didn't answer immediately. He rubbed his face, with two rugged hands, the hands of a tough peasant, used to hard work and hard weather. His hair was white and cut very short. It occurred to me that Major may be much older than he looked, maybe just close to retirement.

"I have three children," he said. "My wife is a teacher. You kids can bear witness that we're doing our duty here." He exhaled, and put his office cap on the desk.

A long burst of a heavy 22 mm echoed from several blocks away. Major seemed to ignore it, yet, he absently removed this gun from his holster and checked the ammunition in it.

"I don't know who is it we're fighting," he spoke, "I don't really know what's out there. We have our orders, but nothing beyond that. We're here with you, the people. The Army, the regulars are with you, the people, as well. With us, with the revolution," he corrected himself. "We're just fighting the terrorists, loyal to the dictator."

Petrescu looked at him, and sat down on a narrow bed placed by the wall.

"Let's just cut the bullshit, Major," he said. "You got a family, a life. Plenty of reasons to play it straight. Whatever it's happening now may turn the other way around tomorrow. We don't mind bearing witness to your dedication, but just cut the bullshit"

The officer fished a cigarette from a pack and lit it. He realized he didn't offer, and raised the pack towards us. It was a pack of cheap cigarettes, no filter. We all lit.

"It's not that simple," he said. "Nobody knows how to play it straight. Not at my level, anyway. All these events in Timisoara, you think they got started just like that, people rising against the authority spontaneously?" He smiled bitterly. "The people of this country have been enduring communism for decades, everyone was unhappy, but it's hard to stand up all of a sudden and start fighting and protesting. It has to be triggered. Somehow, it had been triggered."

I inhaled acrid smoke from the cheap cigarette. If felt strange to me to talk to a Secu officer and speak my mind.

"You guys in the Secu took care of protesters and dissidents all these years, didn't you?" I said. "But now, who triggered what?"

Major narrowed his eyes. He shook his head.

"I'm an infantry man," he said. "I don't work for the Directorate that deals with dissidents. But I have my sources of information in the department."

"You want us to believe what Ceausescu said, that foreign spy agencies are at the heart of all this?"

"Ceausescu isn't stupid," Major retorted. "We had precise reports: a ten fold increase of tourists coming from the USSR. Men crossing the border into Romania, driving Russian made cars, Lada's. Two to three men in each car, thirty to forty years old. Some of them crossed into Yugoslavia, but returned just prior to December 17th, when the troubles started in Timisoara. Yesterday, a column of five of those Lada's approached Bucharest from the East, and didn't stop at a check point. We had men at a roadblock there with an armored transport vehicle. They opened fire with the 22, destroyed three of the cars. Those folks had weapons in the trunks and two Romanian army uniforms."

"So it is these people that we're fighting against?" Petrescu asked. "What's their objective?"

"I'm not saying these are the people we're fighting. They were part of the triggering mechanism, that's what I'm saying. The truth is I don't know what's happening now. I'm just taking my orders while trying to think. Who is it to trust, up there? I don't know. Who are these new guys, declaring themselves the new government? I don't know. Militaru, that army general making this fuss on TV is a soviet spy. His dossier is several inches thick."

"So what do you say we should be doing?" I asked him.

"Don't let anyone you don't know on these grounds," he said, and put his officer cap back on his head. That suddenly made him less human and more of a regimented element of power. But he spoke softly. "God help us," he said.

He got his coat, and walked towards the exit.

"Make sure you get everyone out of those test stands, and block access. Whatever happens, happens, but let's just try have as few casualties as possible. Understood?"

He assigned us to the improvised command post at the front gate. The small room by the soldier's booth at the gate had two military narrow beds right by the large glass walls. We settled there and brought our TV, coffee and water.

"You trust Major?" I asked Petrescu, while lying in the narrow bed. He was setting up the TV, fiddling with the antenna.

"He's honest," he answered. "But he is brainwashed by his many years on the job. Keep your eyes open."

"Hard to do it on an empty stomach," I said. "Let's find some food."

The soldier who had guarded the presumed terrorist was now in charge of the gate.

"We need to get out and shop for some food," I told him.

"That's okay," the soldier said. "But leave your weapons here," he asked. "It's for your own good. We really cannot stop you from carrying them, but if you meet another military patrol, they may open fire on you if they see you armed. So leave the weapons."

We left the weapons and had the guards lock them in the ammunition room.

In a store half a block away, we found freshly baked bread, cheap salami and red wine. The store was busy, with a long line of people waiting to buy food. In spite of the wait, people seemed happy. There were heated discussions about political parties newly created or revived after four decades. A man came into the store carrying a Christmas tree with small and rare branches. It was a last minute cheap purchase, but the man's face was content as he waited patiently in line. The scent of the tree engulfed the store, mixing with the aroma of fresh bread. I remembered the actor on TV, the day before, saying that Jesus is being born again on that land. I sensed the deep hope carried by the people around. A deep feeling of hope and freedom. A blonde girl was watching me. I smiled. She smiled back.

"Let's go," Petrescu pulled on my elbow, pocketing the change returned by the salesgirl. "I'm fucking hungry."

There were a few benches on the sidewalk. We chose one and sat down. I broke the bread and slid slices of salami in between the warm bread chunks, improvising crude sandwiches. We ate hungrily, passing *the wine bottle back and forth. Bursts of gunfire kept erupting from several blocks away, and I realized that I paid less and less attention. We walked back slowly, enjoying the winter sunlight.*

Once returned to the small room by the gate, I curled down in the narrow bed, wrapped in two blankets, with the assault riffle next to me. Somehow, I stopped worrying. I had been infected with the sense of hope and freedom from the street. The Russians didn't come. For the moment, we were free. Somehow, all the mess was going to be sorted out and over. I closed my eyes and let the day light pass into the dark of early evening. It was Christmas Eve.

The government announcement came in late evening. In the quiet parts of the city, people were returning from churches, families were around the tables filled with the best food they could improvise from the limited supplies available, kids were waiting to open the frugal presents their parents could afford.

The TV anchor was an older man, bearing a sense of authority. I remembered him from the time I was a teenager, he used to be the news anchor for the daily news then, the TV Journal.

"The dictator Nicolae Ceausescu and his wife Elena have been tried and found guilty for genocide against the Romanian people," the old anchor man read from a stack of pages in front of him. "The dictator and his wife have been sentenced to death. The sentence has been executed."

A carol followed. An old Christmas blessing song. All of a sudden, I had taste of rot and bitter in my mouth. I was reluctant to believe the announcement. It felt cheap and stupid.

"What was this shit?" Petrescu shouted at the screen. "Is that fucking it? Grab the old sonofabitch and put a bullet in his head? " His face was pale. He sat down on the bed. "This is shit!" he repeated and cursed.

We waited. A second carol followed. Then, stupidly, a Mickey Mouse cartoon. And then the image of a Christmas tree decorated branch, shown for minutes. And then the old anchor man appeared again, and read the same announcement.

"Something's not right," Petrescu said, and his voice sounded different than the one I knew. "I was stupid enough to start believing,"

he went on. "Earlier today, eating on the sidewalk I just felt good. The people's hope around us, it was good and genuine, and it was contagious. I let my fucking guard down."

"I feel the same," I said. "I don't like this, either. But anyway, let's wait. Maybe there is a reason."

Petrescu didn't answer.

It is then when I felt the surreal, for the first time. The perception of surreal, when evil is hiding in plain view. On TV, another carol ended. It had been the Madrigal choir, a good recording. Then, a Popeye cartoon followed. We watched the screen without moving, waiting for more news. The soldiers on duty were also watching, standing on the hallway. Each of them seemed grim, uncomfortable. Another carol came, followed yet by another cartoon.

After that, the old anchor man showed up again, and repeated one more time the announcement. He added that a videotape from the trial was on its way to the TV station. Terrorist snipers still surrounded the station, he explained, the transport will be made by armored vehicles.

Each minute of the night passed painfully slow. We stubbornly kept waiting, motionless in front of the small black and white screen. The sequences on the screen was almost clockwork: the announcement repeated, a carol by the Madrigal choir, and cartoons: Donald Duck, Mickey, Popeye, even and old Woody Woodpecker. And again the announcement and the whole cycle would repeat.

"Fuck man, not this way," Petrescu growled from his bed. He seemed affected more that I would've thought possible, I always considered him a cynical. "It's like having all the Nazi guys taken into a back alley and strangled, instead of Nuremberg," he explained. "No sense of cleansing, no justice served, just an additional killing."

And then, deep in the night, a tape rolled on the TV screens for several minutes. The sound track had been removed. Everything was silent. Ceausescu came out of an armored transport vehicle, weakened, holding his fur cap. In spite of some physical weakness, he was holding himself straight. The tape skipped to showing a corner of a classroom where two narrow desks had been arranged in an L shape. Behind the L, Ceausescu and his wife, still wearing their winter coats, sat and argued mutely with unknown people behind the camera. Every once in *a while, Elena Ceausescu would wave her hands strongly, and in those moments, one of the dictator's hands would touch her, stopping her, stopping her words. With the other hand the dictator made repeated dismissive gestures towards the people behind the camera. His face, despised and hated for decades, had lost the seal of power. It had become the face of a cornered man, knowing that's the end of his rope, playing his exit from history. The recording then skipped again. It showed the outside yard of a military base. The objective's lens approached a wall. When it got closer, I realized what I was watching. Crumpled, at the base of the wall, were the corpses of the two Ceausescu's, riddled with bullets, contorted, blood soaking their chests. Then, the tape ended. The image with the globe hanging from the Christmas tree branch replaced the view of the two corpses. My eyes still saw the image before, the two contorted bodies. I wanted to freeze the image, examine it carefully, understand what had happened, the meaning of it all. But it was all gone.*

4 4
December 25, 1989
National Institute for Science and Technology
Propulsion Division
Bucharest, Romania
4:30 a.m.

Chatter of intense radio communications woke me up. Victor rolled on his bed, re-wrapping the blankets around him. His breath was steamy in the dim light coming from the hallway.
"*Move! Move!*" *a voice ordered, sharply.*
I rose from the narrow bed and looked. A young lieutenant, rushing the soldiers. The men grabbed clips of ammunitions handed by someone from the storage room and were rushed outside, in the dark.
Petrescu raised his head, awakened.
"*What the hell is going on?*"
"*I don't know.*"
The metallic voice of a radio transmission came from the improvised communication center. Static covered the words. The operator asked for a repeat. The transmission repeated: "Enemy vehicles…at kilometer one… the city… approaching from the west, the Institute is possible target… " Hisses were breaking the communication.
"*Get going!*" *yelled the lieutenant and pushed the rest of the soldiers out through the gate. He quickly checked the clip of his own assault rifle and prepared to follow his soldiers.*
A man ran across the wide inner yard and rushed to the lieutenant. It was Major.
"*What the fuck is going on?*" *he barked at the young officer.* "*Report!*"
"*Radio report of a column of enemy vehicles,*" *said the lieutenant.* "*They should be here any minute.*"
"*What enemy vehicles? Who are they?*"
"*Don't know, comrade Major. But they're about to arrive.*"
The lieutenant was scared. Major weighed him with a quick look, and rushed to the radio operator.

"Where did you get the communication from?" he asked the operator and shook him by his shoulder.

"I'm not sure, comrade Major."

"What the hell you mean you're not sure?!" Major yelled savagely. "Where did the transmission come from?"

A roar of engines came from outside. I froze. Three standard armored transport vehicles took the exit from the boulevard and came straight for the gate. The lieutenant rushed outside in the dark and started barking orders. Major left the radio operator and went to the large glass window inspecting the arriving vehicles with a hawkish eye. The first transporter stopped right in front of the gate. Several hisses came from the radio. A clear voice came through. Someone laughed and said, "I hope these motherfuckers have something warm to eat and something to drink, I'm hungry, I'm thirsty and I'm tired." The radio hissed, and the voice continued, on a different tone, "Institute, this is lieutenant major Rosca in command of the patrol unit two...."

A storm of fire broke outside. Intense automatic fire covered the transporters. Tracer bullets centered on the first vehicle. Ricochets were flying in all directions. The voice on the radio started cursing. After several seconds of confusion, the first vehicle backed up and collided with the one behind. All three of them tried maneuvering. Then, they opened fire with the 22's. The glass wall got shattered and pulverized by the heavy caliber fire. I rolled on the floor and Victor pushed me into a corner, protected by the lower portion of the concrete wall.

I started shouting. "Hold your fire! They're our guys! They're our guys, for God's sake, stop, stop! Hold your fire!"

I kept yelling in vain, already knowing I had no chance of being heard.

"RPG! RPG!" the lieutenant voice yelled from somewhere in the night.

Engines kept roaring. I risked raising my head carefully and looked towards the street. The rear armored vehicle had backed up all the way into the boulevard and was covering the whole area with heavy fire. The one in the middle tried a tight turn and collided again with the first one which was maneuvering as well, then ran into a tall road side shoulder and rolled on one side. Its belly became exposed, facing the gate.   The front vehicle managed to turn around. It tried positioning so as to protect the one that rolled over, but it was too late. An RPG hit the exposed belly of the rolled over transporter and exploded. More RPG's hit. Machine gun fire roared continuously. Flames engulfed the transporters. Those machines weren't designed to take RPG fire. Yet, the small turrets kept returning fire, spraying heavy caliber rounds at random towards the gate. Victor pulled me down once more. I lay on the floor, among sharp pieces of broken glass, searching for Major. He was lying on the hallway floor, his body twisted, partially propped against the wall. He'd been hit by the first bursts of 22's shot by the confused gunners in the transporters.

The battle seemed to take for ever to end. Slowly, the intensity of the machine gun fire diminished. With no previous combat experience, the soldiers were scared, afraid of anything that moved. All three armored transporters were burning. Now and then, a long burst of gun fire erupted, followed by yelled orders to stop. Ricocheted bullets hit the walls. An order was finally given to inspect the carbonized vehicles.

I got up, carefully. Victor did the same. I walked to Major's body, rolled him on his back. He was dead. We stood and watched. I felt like running to the soldiers and explain the tragic mistake, make them understand they've killed their own. Yet, I didn't move, just stood there watching.

"This is strange," Petrescu said and turned towards me. "All that radio shit, did you hear?"

"I heard. I wander if they could reach the hydrogen tank, with those 22's?"

Victor raised his head, with a strange light in his eyes.

"The test stand!" he exclaimed. "All the way in the back, with all this farce here."

He grabbed my arm.

I understood his thought. "A diversion."

"Let's go!" he said.

We grabbed our weapons and left. As soon as we turned the corner of the main building we saw a line of four trucks and an armored transport vehicle parked in the back by the test stands.

Silhouettes of men in officer uniforms stood by the trucks, while men in soldier uniforms were loading up the trucks.

Victor grabbed my arm. "They're getting the MRFEM parts. The documentation," he said, with a low growl. "They're cleaning the place!"

He looked at me with desperation. "That massacre, by the gates!" he cried. "That whole shit, by the gates, was just a diversion." He suddenly grabbed my shoulders and shook me. "Do you understand?! Do you fucking get it?!"

I understood. The dark alley felt like a fast rotating carousel, things seemed to be whirling around me, I was dizzy, yet knowing where things are, feeling my arms, my feet planted on a hard surface that wasn't going to stay put. I scrutinized the trucks, the people around them . One man turned around and looked at us. It was hard to make distinct details in the crude fluorescent light coming from the tall posts, yet, I recognized Bolek.

"It's him!" Petrescu exclaimed, making the same recognition in the same moment. He brought the Ak-47 into ready position, and pulled out the ammunition clips from the pockets of his parka. He looked at me while arming the weapon.

"Don't let them get to me before I finish," he requested.

"What do you want to do?" I asked, already knowing the answer.

"I'll blow the tank on them!"

I grabbed his arm. "It's not worth your life, Victor!"

"Let me go!" he shook his arm off my grip and adjusted the strap on his rifle again. "This is a big pile of shit," he said. "This whole thing, everything that happens. People fooled, killed. Lives don't count. We don't count. But fuck them. I will count, this time. Let me go!"

He grabbed my shoulders and looked into my eyes. He wanted to add something, then gave up and ran towards the east side of the test stand facilities.

I stood, watching, paralyzed. I knew Victor will die in the next several minutes, but the thought refused to articulate.

The events rolled and forced me to act. Victor ran in the dark, his body merely a shadow. Suddenly, a long burst of gunfire erupted from that shadow. The tracer bullets trajectory showed the target, red burning spots flying in the air towards the hydrogen tank. At the sound of gunfire, the men loading the trucks entered a frantic fast motion, like cockroaches discovered on a filthy floor when lights are turned on. Response gunfire erupted, this time tracers searching for Victor. During dilated seconds measuring a warped time, I could still see where he was, running and firing. The hostile tracers seemed to find him, yet not quite, as his own firing kept going. Voices barked by the trucks, engines scrambled.

I raised my weapon and armed. Reality and thought disconnected even more. At whom was I to fire? Why? Those were my people, other men, obeying other orders, yet we were all the same. But they were trying to kill my friend who was racing to his own death.

From the distance, Victor shouted something, and fired another long burst. A rain of tracers searched again for him, in response.

I shut off my mind and opened fire, yelling an illegible and desperate cry, hands cramped onto the weapon, trigger fully squeezed, the noise and rhythmic kick of each fired shot streaming a special energy out of the weapon and into my arms. Still, from a vague residual connection between reality and consciousness, I raised the barrel, sparing the people. My fire went high, hitting the sky and empty walls.

Fire came back, searching for me. The trucks loaded with MRFEM crates gunned their engines and moved away.

My gun emptied. I replaced the clip with shaky hands and armed.

One more burst flashed from Victor, now somewhere close to the tank. A flow of tracers searched for his silhouette, fire spots hungry for flesh. I screamed and opened fire again. A bullet hit me in the left leg. My gun kept firing as if independent of my will, the noise indistinguishable from the reverberations echoed by the walls. Another bullet found my hip. And another one hit me in the shoulder spinning me around.

I fell to the ground. My body shook in shock, the pain still dull.

I suddenly felt cold. Machine gun roar kept filling the air, while engines screamed, gunned hard. Loosing consciousness, I could only watch the sky and the flow of tracer bullets shot high.

Then, I heard the deflagration. A strong flash of light illuminated the tall poplar trees lining the boulevard, and the tall buildings by the boulevard. The explosion shook everything. The cold air was swept away by the intense heat of the shock wave produced by the blast, windows were shattered and the ground shook.

He did it, I thought, he hit the damn tank.

The last thought I could remember.

4 5

The Institute buildings stood dull under the hazy noon light while heavy traffic on the boulevard filled the air with intoxicating fumes. Exhaust gases blended with spicy smoke from small grill joints set on the sidewalks.

I watched the soldier guarding the gate. His uniform had a new cap design, the old look of the soviet block replaced by a mixture between regular infantry and police.

"What is it with this place?" Jane's eyes came in front of mine, juxtaposing her face over the view of the old institution. "You're watching as if in a trance, Matt."

Her presence made me feel the truth of my alienation. Years have passed. I was now a stranger, one of those to be kept outside by the guard in the booth.

A man walked out through the gate after exchanging a few words with the soldier. He walked towards me and studied me carefully.

"I'll be damn if it's not you, Mr. Salajan," the man exclaimed.

He offered his hand and I shook it and used the moment to study him. I recognized him. He used to work there as a machinist. I remembered him younger and thinner, with a bit of an edge. Now, he had gained weight, his face was tired, with swollen bags under his eyes.

"Good to see you," I said, unable to remember his name. "It's been some time. How are the things?"

He laughed amiable, but with little joy.

"How can things be, around here? Down. That's the only direction we know."

"Why is that?"

"Eh, Mr. Salajan, it's a long story. Don't you know our people here, the good Romanians? You've been gone a long time, you may have forgotten. You don't even look like us anymore. When I saw you a moment ago, haircut, glasses, these clothes, I said to myself this is some foreigner, what is he doing here, and I looked better and it was you."

I gestured towards the gate, "Are you still working here? How is business?"

"Here? Don't work here no more! What to do here?" He laughed bitterly. "The lathes are gone. The machines are gone. Most of the equipment is gone."

"Really?" I raised my eyebrows. "How come?"

"He he, Mr. Salajan, I told you you've been gone too long. Where could they go? Sold, that's where they went. Some folks filled their pockets. What do they care you won't get no contracts anymore, they got their houses, their cars, the hell with the rest."

He threw his hand back, indicating the institution.

"It's all broken to pieces, all independent, small outfits. Salaries are budgeted from the government. Peanuts. Some sectors got privatized and now they store underwear and coca-cola on the premises."

"Sounds pretty bad," I said.

His lips stretched a smile of disappointment while he was slowly shaking his head.

"So, what were you doing in there, then?" I asked him

"Oh, just getting some paper work I need from personnel. Like I said, I don't work here anymore, I'm in sales now."

"Sales?" I smiled to him. "What are you selling?"

The man threw a quick glance at me, checking.

"Kinda everything," he smiled, and his eyes went blank. "A little bit of this a little bit of that, it works. Better than here," he jerked his thumb dismissively towards the gate.

"Who is he?" Jane asked, leaning on my shoulder, smiling. I jerked, slightly. I had disconnected again from her presence. I touched her arm, smiling.

"He's a former worker here. He tells me everything is gone and dust is settling on empty rooms."

She smiled.

"This is my friend, Jane," I introduced her to the man. Jane offered her hand.

The sound of English spoken between me and Jane made the man feel as a host. He ceremoniously took Jane's hand, and kissed it. By the local customs and manners, it was a sign of consideration, of politeness. He let go of her hand and smiled, checking her, nodding.

"You got yourself one of those foreigner women, Mr. Salajan. Not bad at all, please tell the lady she's very beautiful, if you don't mind me saying so, sir."

I translated. Jane kept smiling, calmly, a mask on her face.

"Where do you live, now, Mr. Salajan?"

"California," I said. "Los Angeles."

"Aha, America," he exclaimed, and laughed, nodding, with an attitude implying I must be rubbing elbows with every Hollywood celebrity he knew from the movies. "What are you doing back home, here, Mr. Salajan?" he asked. "Just visiting?"

"Yes and no," I said, watching him carefully. "I may be looking to do some business as well. See if I can find some cheap good quality work for some contracts I have."

He got focused, instantly. "Contract work? What sort of work, Mr. Salajan?"

"Complex metal parts," I said. "Stuff that needs a lot of machining, tons of labor. You know what I'm taking about? If you remember, years ago, those complicated parts for the engines. That kind of stuff, that's what I'm looking for."

He frowned, "You can't do it here no more, Mr. Salajan," he said bitterly. "I told you, all the machines are gone. You may get something done at the factory, there over the fence, but it's hard, they work for foreigners now, not much room for anything else."

I watched him. He hadn't let go of the opportunity. He was waiting.

"What if I wanted to make only a few complicated parts, say two or three of them? Would that be possible?"

He rubbed his chin.

"It might. You'd pay in dollars or euros?"

"Whatever needed."

He looked along the sidewalks, and down at his shoes.

"Where are you staying, Mr. Salajan? Is there a telephone number I can reach you at?"

"I'm staying at a friend's house" I said and I gave him the number of the pre-paid cell phone I'd bought earlier in the day.

"I'll give you a call, if I find something" the man assured me, and said good by, kissing Jane's hand again. He turned around and walked towards the subway.

I turned back, for one more glance at the Institute. The soldier at the gate was talking to a young woman, smoking and gesticulating with his hands.

***

City traffic proved to be a challenge. The number of vehicles on the roads had increased ten fold compared to the old times. I used the stops to watch the landscape: a large concrete building left unfinished from the old times and flanked by newer glass and steel additions. Across the street, a McDonalds. The burger joint, surrounded by a perfectly kept green lawn looked like a publicity poster transplanted from the normal reality into a strange dimension. Or maybe it was just my warped mind incapable of grasping the present. The old country had changed and I was still anchored in the past.

I parked the Cherokee and played tourist. I rediscovered streets, corners of buildings, memories. It felt good. Every city has a smell of its own. The smell of Bucharest had changed, but not completely, there were still some traces of the old city in the new one. The pulse of the streets was very intense. Traffic was fast, new cars mixed with old and decrepit vehicles. Mini-malls had been built with tinted glass and steel structures, contrasting with the old, badly kept buildings. The mixture of new and old was dominated by the frantic fast rhythm, yet there was enough of the old to help me remember.

Jane's hand was in mine, I realized, and had been there for most of the walk. Her resemblance to the other woman of many years ago came at me stronger, a resemblance that had first struck me in LA when I'd first seen her at the coffee shop, and which I had forgotten. I stopped and embraced her, lifting her slightly off the ground so I could feel her special warmth. I kissed her. She responded well, yet without understanding the special moment, the special feeling. The moment belonged only to me.

We were in front of an old inn, a landmark of the cityscape, hosting restaurants, a bar, several shops, and too many memories. I dragged her in.

"Let's have a drink here," I said. "A good old fashion cognac."

"We didn't even have lunch, Matt."

"You want lunch?"

She smiled slightly, shrugging.

"I don't care."

Alcohol did me good, tempered my inner beats. I called the waiter and asked for a pack of cigarettes. He brought a pack of Camels and we both lit. After the interdictions in the bars of the healthy conscious LA it was even more relaxing to have a smoke with the drink.

"All right," Jane leaned forward over the small table and fixed me with her black eyes. "What's so special with this place? I feel it in you, it's very strong."

She surprised me. It was for the first time she showed she payed that sort of attention. No longer the strange wonderful creature of the wild, she was a woman getting involved.

"Years ago, in this place," I began, "a woman I was desperately in love with has told me she was going to marry another man. I haven't seen or heard of her ever since. Now, I am strangely happy to be here with you."

"What was her name?"

I drew smoke, exhaled.

"Carmen," I said.

Jane's eyes gleamed as if she smiled, but she didn't smile. She leaned over the low table and kissed me slowly, without an embrace, just pushing her lips into mine, playing with her tongue on mine, and slightly sucking my breath.

"Here," she said, pulling pack. "The spell is broken."

Is it really?, I thought.

But for a moment, life felt good.

4 6

I placed the cheap cell phone on the kitchen table, waiting. Outside, the morning light grew stronger as the sun rose from behind dense packs of concrete buildings. On the stove, water started to boil in an old and dented coffee pot. I mixed four spoons of coffee and two of sugar in the pot, an *ibric*, avoiding making noise.

Jane was still asleep. We'd made love during the night. She'd initiated, as if trying to shake something out of me. It did me good, some of the acute anxiety was gone. She couldn't remove the root of the past. She couldn't remove my awareness of the shadows. The shadows, somewhere, watching, waiting for my move, while preparing their own.

The phone rang. I picked up quickly, suppressing the sound.

"Good morning Mr. Salajan" said the voice of the former Institute machinist. "Sorry for calling so early, is this a good time?"

"I'm having coffee," I said.

"Aha, OK, OK," he laughed. He repeated the '*OK*' as if it conferred him a rank of complicity with whatever enterprise he thought I was into. "Mr. Salajan, regarding the problem you mentioned to me yesterday, I asked around a bit, I thought I may be able to help."

So fast a catch, I thought, my instinct recoiling, *or just scammers?*

"Which problem?" I stretched.

He got worried.

"The parts you need manufactured, you mentioned that yesterday," the man said, uneasy.

"Ah yes, I remember."

He laughed, nervously.

"As I say, I asked around, and I found some people for your job, I wonder if you'd be interested to meet them sometime today."

"Is this a private firm you're talking about?"

"Something like that, Mr. Salajan, they'll explain. It depends on the job you need, how complicated it is, materials, and so on. It's more like an ad-hoc consortium of people, kinda getting together for one job."

"That's a bit unusual," I said. I laughed slowly, dryly, thinking. I still couldn't remember the man's name. "How do I know they can deliver what I need?"

"They did jobs like this before."

"They did this sort of jobs before?"

"Yes."

"Well, let's meet them. I want to see some of those jobs they did. I want to know how long it took for each of them. Money, we can discuss."

"Good, good, we're on, then."

He gave me an address of a joint, for lunch. I knew where the location was, but the name didn't tell me anything. A new restaurant, probably, among the many that had popped up in the city.

***

"Let me drive," Jane said.

We'd come off the apartment building and instinct told me again we're being watched. I stood by the Cherokee, head down, pretending to untangle my keys while glancing around. One car, had parked under the rare trees not too far from my jeep. The man at the wheel was smoking, waiting. Further away, across the narrow street, another one, a cherry red Opel with tinted windows. It felt wrong, parked there, wheels turned away from the curb.

"It's a zoo on these streets," I told Jane. "You sure you want to drive?"

She slowly drew the keys from my hands.

"Yeah, I'm sure," she said.

She proved it. She drove fast and found her way easily. It was as if she was testing herself, testing the foreign street environment in a professional way. She parked, squeezing the Jeep in between two Renaults, right wheels on the curb.

Out on the sidewalk she gave me back the car keys, patting the Cherokee on its hood.

"I guess I know too little about you," I said.

She smiled. "Stunts are part of my job description" she said, and she wasn't smiling anymore. I looked at her, and I understood she had opened a small door for me.

I'm bad with women. Two stories in my life, both fucked up. I had loved once, deep and total, and I've been carrying a residual of that love ever since. Years later, Christine was a pragmatic choice which turned out to be wrong. Or maybe she had felt those residuals and chose to devote her energy to her career, and then quit me as soon as I was too deep in my own troubles. After those many years, Jane's physical resemblance with Carmen was enticing. Like an elixir of youth, her presence felt good, but I felt her closed, and I let it be that way. And suddenly, she opened that small window.

A large luxury sedan interrupted my thought. The car drove by, fast, blasting a powerful horn at a stray dog. I searched the streets. No shadow car I could spot. It meant nothing. The shadows were there, somewhere.

My new friend, the machinist, came out of a restaurant terrace spread over the sidewalk at the street's corner. It was the restaurant he had indicated as the meeting place.

"Welcome, welcome," he said, and raised his hands sideways, turning the gesture into an inviting one. "The weather's good," he invited, "should we sit outside?"

I had no objection. The man kissed Jane's hand, and invited us to a table. Then, I remembered his first name. Marian. A male name, in the old country. We sat down and Marian's cell phone rang.

"Yes," he said. His voice was flat and steely. "They're here. Yes sir."

He turned towards us, and the steel was lost in his voice when he asked what we would like to drink.

A large Mercedes drove by, and slowed down while passing the restaurant. Inside the car, a man raised a dark object. Light reflected on lenses. The car sped up. Marian didn't seem to have noticed. Jane's smile remained unchanged.

We waited for another ten minutes. Marian played host and offered new drinks. I politely refused. Jane's drink was untouched.

The Mercedes, the one before or a similar one, came back and stopped. Two men dressed in suits came out of the limousine and walked towards our table. They seemed cut from the same human material: overweight but strong, large but compact bellies carried with a rough walk, bulldog cheeks, thick necks, fat overflowing the shirt collars, tight mouths and small eyes buried on piggish faces of prosperous tough creatures. One of the men was carrying a briefcase.

Marian the machinist rose and did the introductions. We shook hands. The men kissed Jane's hand. She seemed to have gotten used to the custom.

The man with the briefcase opened it and gave the other one a small dossier. He opened it, displaying a first page with my picture taken minutes ago from the passing Mercedes. The next page seemed to be a photocopied form with an old mug shot of mine on its upper corner. It looked like one of my old employment forms from the Institute.

"You've been away for a long time, Dr. Salajan," the man said, raising his small eyes towards me, impenetrable, weighing me, opening the moves.

"Sixteen years," I said.

The man waited. Nobody said anything. I slowly brought my hands together, on the table, and watched the lead man. He grinned, slightly.

"Sixteen years is a lot of time, Dr. Salajan. This is the Balkans here. A lot of things are happening. This country has been sold over and over again, like an old debt for collection. We're a NATO country now, ready to re-enter Europe soon. All sorts of people come here with all sorts of ideas. Better make sure we're doing business with legitimate partners. You follow me?"

I nodded.

"Good," the man said. "So who are we dealing with?"

"You're dealing with me," I said carefully. "I run a small business. I had some innovative ideas for aerospace products which were run into the ground by a corporation I worked for. Now, I am trying to apply my ideas on my own, but I need to keep the costs down."

He weighed me again with narrow piggy eyes.

"We're a long way from California, Mr. Salajan" he said.

I shrugged, "Distance is not a problem. I'm looking for cheap labor on quality work. I thought of the Institute."

"Why the Institute?"

"That's where my heritage is. Besides, I want a partner who operates in the culture of quality assurance typical to the aerospace industry. But I ran into Marian, and he's telling me the capability is lost at the Institute. He's also saying your group may have the manufacturing capability I'm looking for, and honestly, I doubt it."

He pulled back his shoulders and frowned, burying his pig eyes deeper in the fat of his face. "What makes you doubt our capabilities?"

I took a sip from my coke.

"When an industry goes bust," I said, "its culture goes bust as well. Maybe you guys have some good machines here, some x-ray inspection equipment there, maybe even digital measuring equipment somewhere else. But the culture of making a part strictly per spec and deliver it with its documentation, that culture is hard to maintain."

He grinned and moved his hand, as if inviting me to come to his fat chest.

"How many parts and how much money we're talking about?" he said.

"Three parts," I said, and thought carefully of the MORPHEM's core parts.

"Only three parts?" he asked, losing his mask, genuine disappointment on his face.

I nodded and threw another card.

"Yes, three parts, about $500k a piece."

He glanced at me, turned around and yelled for the waiter. "Mineral water!" he barked. He turned towards me.

"People around here pull stings of a half million daily," he said. "Taxpayer's money, foreigner's money. It's easier than struggling to machine a complicated part."

I placed my hands on the table and grinned at him and said, "Then, we'll finish our drinks, I'll go my way and you go yours."

He leaned back and laughed loudly. His companion did the same. Marian smiled broadly, with a confused face. Jane stood up and went inside the restaurant for the restroom. The two men glanced at her hips, furtively.

"Gimme the case," the lead man said, and grabbed the briefcase handed to him by the other man. He took a pile of five or six dossiers from the briefcase and placed them on the table."

"We're professionals," he said to me, and opened the first dossier. "You want fucking top quality stuff, we've got it. Here are some of the projects we did. The customers prefer anonymity, for various reasons. I trust you may prefer anonymity as well, and we guarantee that."

We unfolded the blue prints from every file. Most of them were various types of complicated gear boxes. The blue prints had their cartridges blackened out. I studied the drawings while the men explained manufacturing details. I was puzzled. Why not setting up a standard firm? I looked at the blue prints again. Helicopter and small turboprop gear boxes, speed boat gear parts. Anonymous.   It was the Balkans. Somewhere, someone was operating a small pack of aircraft and boats, off the books, off the records.

I unfolded the last blue print. The drawing showed a hydraulic rotor with contorted blades like long sheets of metal wrapped in spirals around a cylinder. I held my breath, it couldn't be. My heart pumped hard, yet I didn't move, aware that my hands may be shaking.

Jane came back. The men raised their heads to watch her hips again. I studied the drawing, absorbing everything, details, hand scribbled notes on the paper, the blacked-out indicator box, hoping for more information. The men turned towards the drawing again.

"This is a strange part," I said, slowly. "What is it?"

Marian the machinist laughed.

"Man, that was a bitch of a job, tough part to make, and those folks from Bukow, what a bunch of motherfuckers, measuring this, measuring that, checking everything, a real bitch of a job."

He stopped. The other two men were watching him with their beady eyes, their faces dark, dead. Marian's laugh distorted into a panicked grimace.

I removed the drawing, discarding it on a side.

"I'm more interested on casings type of work," I said, distracting their attention from the strange drawing, and the men turned back towards me. "What I need is more complicated than what you have here. Imagine something as complicated as this one," I unfolded one of the first drawings. "There are more side volumes, stuff that needs welding. Special welds, all inspected, x-rays, the whole lot." I drew some vague schematics on a napkin.

The flush of technical details took their attention away from Marian's goof. His big mouth had revealed the location of the client. I felt perspiration on my back. The strange rotor shown on the blue-print was the liquid hydrogen suction pump of the old MRFEM engine. I had found the hot trail. Someone in the northern city of Bukow had the part manufactured by the two tough alligators sharing the table with me. I didn't ask for more details. More inquiry, I felt, could be deadly.

***

"Who were those people?" Jane asked, after we left.

I was driving.

"I don't know," I said.

She rolled down the window, and lit up a Camel.

"Do you have a plan for whatever you're doing?" she asked.

I avoided a yellow Renault squeezing itself in between my Cherokee and a tramcar.

"No," I admitted. "Or, maybe yes. We'll travel north."

"Why?"

"These guys told me something about a firm in the city of Bukow. I need to check it out."

She drew smoke from the cigarette, and watched me. I felt her gaze like heat on my chin. She kept quiet for the rest of the drive.

4 7

Jane stood naked in the doorframe of the narrow terrace. The hotel room was on the last floor, nothing but the sky and several satellite dishes above it. Sunrays and a nice breeze of cool air competed for her pink nipples.

I rolled in bed. I was also naked, lying on several layers of newspapers bought earlier in the morning.

Ten floors below, the city of Bukow exhaled breaths dense with car exhaust. The city was packing close to half million people in a tight network of narrow streets and densely grouped concrete buildings. Its existence was driven by a compact and dense network of businesses and interests, an incomprehensible web for outsiders or uprooted wanderers like me. The local newspapers, however, were a gold mine for getting an insight into the tangled web. It was election year for the local governments and a good amount of dirty laundry was being washed in public. The two days we'd spent in the city had been just a succession of reading big batches of print, besides lovemaking and frugal meals.

"Can you get Chinese anywhere around here?" Jane asked, lighting up another Camel. Her posture in the window was absolutely wonderful, a perfect animal, confident of its environment, alert, but not afraid.

"Haven't seen any," I said, and unfolded another piece from the early morning batch.

She came to me and rolled me on my back, mounting me like a wrestler, but in slow motion. She caressed my hair, examining my face, playing with my gold necklace, bending to bite my chest. I enjoyed her without arousal, saturated.

"What's wrong with your nipples?" she moaned. "You never let me touch them. Most of the guys I knew were crazy about it."

I grabbed her hair and moved her head around with gentle force so her lips would slide along my chest and my belly. I made her give me oral sex on my limp organ and when I grew hard I moved her off. She let herself driven, with a moaning laugh.

"You should let me play to the end," she said, rising her head up, holding herself with her hands on my chest, looking me in the eyes. "What the fuck are we doing in this city?"

"Looking for someone. Or something. Or both."

"Who?"

"I don't know."

She bent and kissed me.

"You don't know," she said, keeping her mouth on my lips, breathing. Her breath smelled of tobacco.

"No."

"You're a fucked up case," she said, and went back to the window. I returned to reading.

The city was networked in a mafia like structure. With few exceptions, all businesses were lined up with the party in power and the mayor's office. Most of the scarce capital flowing around was public funds, channeled by the mayor's office to his own businesses. Cronyism and corruption seemed the standard. But most of it was linked to road and building contracts mostly, uninteresting. I was interested in the larger outfits: an aircraft and military factory complex, a large petrochemical group. The aircraft factory was traded publicly. The petrochemical group was held privately, owned by sharks of a much higher caliber than the mayor's crowd. I searched the newspaper for names. Some of them rang bells from the old times, the 1989 coup. A man who used to run Ceausescu's weapons export agency. Another one who'd been running a front for the same agency in Cyprus. They were old, rich, badmouthed in the press and envied just the same.

The last paper in the batch was a business daily gazette published in Bucharest. The lower end of the cover showed a picture of an elegant couple exiting what appeared to be a private jet. A small insert directed the reader at page 10. I turned to page 10, and I read the column.

Reporters and law enforcement have been waiting equally impatient for the return from London of Mr. Raoul Conta. Naturally, the paparazzi had prepared their cameras for capturing the images Mr. Conta's arrest. They were disappointed. The police was there only to humbly salute Mr. Conta and to make sure he safely reaches the small motorcade awaiting for him with their engines on, ready to take the multi-millionaire to his residence in the city of Bukow without delay. We are sure that Mr. Conta had business matters which could not suffer any postponement.

The behavior of the authorities only shows one more time the emptiness of the official declarations by our toothless government. Mr. Conta's debt to the government is calculated at more than three hundred million Euros based on several sources from the Financial Guard's office who wish to remain anonymous due to the sensitivity of this matter. The same sources speculate that Mr. Conta's trip to London had the objective of perfecting the sale of his oil refineries to a consortium owned jointly by British Petroleum and KazMunai, a company based in Kazakhstan. The sale could raise the funds necessary for Mr. Conta to clear the debt accrued in various unpaid taxes. Analysts in the oil industry appreciate, however, that the value of Mr. Conta's assets has been eroded by lack of upgrades and investment. The Bukow refinery, the smallest in the string of installations owned by Mr. Conta, has been closed for more than five years and in spite of repeated statements expressing Mr. Conta intention to significantly upgrade and restart the facility, nothing has been done.

Mr. Conta has been accompanied in his trip by his wife, Mrs. Carmen Conta.

I studied the picture. Conta's face was hidden behind designer sunglasses. The man was overweight but wore one of those expensive suits that would make a camel look good. His wife was tall, a mature beauty, her hair cut very short and her elegant haute couture deux-pieces showing a sportive cut. She had offered the cameras a greeting smile.

I touched the page slightly, with my fingers, examining it carefully. The woman's eyes were just two dots, on the small print. I threw the paper aside.

"Let's try look for your Chinese food," I told Jane.

She extinguished the cigarette.

"Lemme take a shower" she said.

***

There was one Chinese restaurant in town, on the north side of the city where you wouldn't normally look for a restaurant. The place was almost empty. No one was doing any seating. We chose a table on our own and a dark haired Chinese waitress appeared from behind a red curtain and came to us. Her genuine ethnicity took me by surprise. I was expecting some surrogate. Ethnic diversity was norm in LA, but here, in the heart of the old country, I found it odd.

"You speak very well the language," I told the waitress, "how did you learn?"

She forced a smile. "I practice," she answered.

"With your husband?"

"My husband is Chinese. I speak with people around."

"Are there more Chinese people around, in the city?"

She disliked the question.

"There are a few, yes," she answered, carefully. She smiled again. "Did you decide on the menu?" she asked.

Jane asked her if she spoke English. She didn't.

When food came, no chop sticks were offered, just regular cutlery. The waitress brought them after we asked. The food was greasy, Cantonese style. We ate and left.

I drove to the southern part of the city on the main road. Traffic was slow, the city streets too small for the number of cars on them. Somewhere, close to a cemetery, a funeral procession blocked the traffic and everyone just sat in the cars waiting, engines idling.

"Where are we going?" Jane asked, rolling the window down, and lighting her tenth Camel of the day.

Exhaust from a diesel blasted through the car window on her side. She ignored it, and kept smoking.

"Diesel and tobacco, I missed that," I grinned, and took the cigarette off her mouth and place it in mine. She let me draw a smoke, and took it back.

"I want to take a look at the aircraft factory," I explained.

The traffic got moving. After about four miles, I turned right, on a narrow uphill road, leading to the factory. The enterprise used to repair MIG's. In the old days it had another, more secretive section, where they had been making rocket launchers, some of them exported to the Middle East and African countries. I wondered what was left from that part of the factory. Would anyone there need a part for MORPHEM hydrogen suction pump? And if so, why would they need those alligators in Bucharest, and not use their own machines?

It was midday and not much activity could be seen. A poster of an F-16 was glued on a fence. I turned back. I had no idea what I was expecting to observe, perhaps repeating the experience at the Institute's gate in Bucharest, when Marian the machinist showed up, bringing the strange clues that led me here.

But there was nothing for me at the factory's gates. I drove back into town.

48

I parked the Cherokee across the street from the hotel entrance and surveyed the vehicles around. It had become a habit.

"I'll see you in a bit," Jane said, "I need to buy stuff."

She slammed the door and left.

We hadn't exchanged a word while driving back from the factory. I'd been deep in thought, once again disconnected from her presence. She seemed to have gotten used to my slipping in and out of reality, entering trances and visiting my strange times in the past. How deep these lapses of attention may have been upsetting her, I couldn't know. She'd never said anything about it. She had her own strange reactions, hours of silence when she seemed to be punishing herself for her brief moments when she opened to me. Those moments seemed to be a strong interior need of hers, which for some reason were forbidden to her.

I jaywalked to the hotel entrance. There was a main entrance, and another one, about a hundred feet to the left, leading into the hotel's main restaurant and café-bar. I headed for the restaurant entrance, when I felt the warning vibe again and stopped. Motionless, heart pounding, I looked around.

A man exited the restaurant and walked across the wide sidewalk towards a black sedan which came and slowly stopped at the curb, waiting for him. The man was about my height, fat, with a slight limp. He had dark glasses hanging on his wide face like two dark patches. I couldn't distinguish any of his face features, except the bulldog cheeks which seemed a ubiquitous feature for most local men aged past forty. He was partly bald, the type of baldness one gets after a hair disease or a head injury. There was something about the unknown man that had triggered the warning feeling. I watched him as he opened the back door of the car and got in with moves that seemed to be causing him pain.

And then, I felt a strong presence on my right. I turned. Standing on the stairs leading to the hotel's entrance, an elegant woman watched me with a face that seemed frightened. I searched her face, intrigued by her emotion. She was the woman in the newspaper picture, the wife of the powerful local oligarch. She kept staring at me intensely and without a word. A man came close to her; a bodyguard with a tough face and dead fish eyes, throwing me a short glance with annoyed surprise, is this bug any trouble for you, he seemed to be asking. The woman waved him away with a move of her hand, and walked towards me.

"Matei," she said.

If I had any hesitation in recognizing her, the voice cleared it. The voice had not changed in twenty years. The voice who had whispered songs onto my ears, the voice who said love is coming my way. The voice that had said farewell.

"Carmen," I said.

"My God," she muttered, as if merely for herself. "Why did you come?"

It was as if I didn't hear her words, I didn't pay attention. My eyes were now absorbing her features, rediscovering, her lips, her eyes, the noble line of the nose, all changed by years and made part of the mature and exquisite woman in front of me.

"I'm searching," I said, speaking slowly, in somewhat of a slurry, not sure of what I wanted to say. "I'm looking for myself," I said, feeling stupid, yet realizing that it was true; a simple revelation.

Her face changed expression as if discretely taking a decision, forcing a relaxation of features, a smile. She offered her hand, and I kissed it politely, holding it for a second, as if her unknown decision gave us plenty of time.

"Your hair is gray," she said, her eyes searching, her smile touching a note of sadness. "But you didn't change at all, Matei. Ah yes, I see these lines," she continued, and touched my face, lightly. "Ah, this unforgiving time."

"Time has been generous with you, Carmen," I said. "I saw your picture in one of the newspapers here and you looked wonderful. You did change, but there is nothing wrong with the change."

She laughed, without shaking the note of sadness.

"It's been many years," she said. "When did I see you last time?"

Her eyes changed their light in a way so familiar I almost missed it. Surrounded by perfectly applied shades of makeup, her eyes were the only part of her that were still young, crossed by changing lights, expressive or hidden, just as I knew them.

"It's been a long time, Carmen, I forgot."

I remembered as well as she did. But she didn't allow herself to be aware of her remembering, as if it wasn't quite related to her, as if the farewell she had bidden me at the inn in Bucharest had been someone else's moment, not hers.

"Anyway," I said, "how is life?"

She laughed, slowly, this time cryptically, a cold, social laugh.

"If you've read the newspapers," she said, "that pretty much sums it all up. That's my life. I have two boys, seventeen and fourteen. I keep them away from most of the circus, although they can read, and they have their own minds to use and judge. But I manage to keep them away as much as I can."

Her directness surprised me. There was something like a veiled warning in her words.

"I've settled down abroad," I said, for lack of anything else to say. "I live in California."

She flashed me with a quick look, her face unreadable.

"I know," she said, and looked at her wristwatch. Behind her, the bodyguard had leaned against a wall smoking a cigarette, waiting. She continued with a voice so low I could barely hear, "I'll have to talk to you again, later, I have no time now. It's very important, Matei. Please wait in the hotel. Don't move around too much. I'll look for you as soon as I can."

"Why? When?"

"Please. As soon as I can."

Someone gently grabbed my right arm, and embraced it. I hadn't heard Jane's steps and I hadn't felt her presence until the moment she'd touched me.

"I'm back," she said, leaning against me, continuing to embrace my arm. The embrace was something more than a woman's instinct to mark territory, it felt as a diversion. Jane's eyes watched Carmen like hunter's eyes.

"This is Jane," I said, but Carmen interrupted with a quick wave of her hand.

"I really must run," she said. She threw a quick smile at Jane, and flashed me one more time with her eyes, just like moments before, then she turned around and walked away at a fast pace, producing that good and special sound of a woman with her heels on the pavement.

Her bodyguard jerked away from the wall, threw the cigarette on the street and walked after her. A dark blue BMW pulled at the curb, the bodyguard opened the back door for Carmen, and then got in the front seat. The car took off fast, cut in front of the slow traffic, powerful, impertinently turning in a sharp U-turn.

Jane had let go of my arm and watched the departing car. I searched her features for the resemblance she had with Carmen, the young Carmen of years back. It was there in her, yet I couldn't identify any specific features, the nose was different, her mouth was smaller, the lips in a perfect and delicate shape different than Carmen's wide sensual lips. The resemblance was valid in general, not in any particular feature, yet such a strange coincidental bridge over two different worlds, two different times. Was there a meaning to it, I asked myself, and if it was, how much did it matter? My train of thought got blurry, and I felt the shirt on my back was soaked in sweat. The encounter had shaken me. I hadn't expected it.

Jane grabbed my arm.

"Let's go upstairs," she said, pushing me with calm determination, without tenderness.

We rode the elevator watching each other under the strong fluorescent light, without speaking. Once in the room, I dropped the key on the small counter and opened the balcony door, letting the sounds and smells of the city come in. I searched the counter for a drink. Behind me, I heard Jane dropping something on the floor. I turned. She was packing.

"What are you doing?" I asked, perplexed.

She stopped and came next to me.

"You're getting close to the end, Matt," she said. "Close to the end of whatever journey you're on, close to some end. I feel it, I know it. I've seen this before. I have a good instinct for it."

I touched her shoulders.

"Maybe so," I said, "but whatever it is, why do you have to leave?"

"You need to be alone for it, Matt. And I have my reasons."

She went back to her packing and finished quickly. I realized how little luggage she had with her, and how fast she was. In a minute, she was done. She came and kissed me. It was a long and strong kiss, lacking the erotic intensity she had with me before. It came from somewhere deeper inside her.

She let go of me and turned away. I tried to put aside the emotion brought by the encounter with Carmen, trying to focus on Jane and her decision to leave. So sudden, so unexpected, it hurt.

"Where are you leaving like that?" I asked her, feeling the seed of desperation. "Do you need the car? Should I give you a ride somewhere?"

"No," Jane said, "I know my way."

She grabbed her duffel back, and opened the door.

"Hang tight in there, cowboy," she said, and left.

49

I sat on the bed feeling the seconds passing by. Jane's departing steps were still echoing in my mind. The fat man limping to his car, the encounter with Carmen, Jane's sudden farewell, they were all playing again and again in my brain, chopped, discontinued, mixing with information and images from the newspapers and memories from twenty years before.

The emptiness of the room hit me. Emptiness is a universal void; it tastes the same in Los Angeles and in the Balkans, in the city of Bukow.

I rushed out of the room, through the hallways, calling the elevator. It was slow, or stuck somewhere. I ran down the stairs, loosing count of the floors, bursting out on the hotel lobby and running out on the street.

Where could she be? Waiting for taxi? Had she taken one already? Where?

I looked around and up and down the streets and then gave up. Jane was on her way to wherever she wanted to go. She was gone.

I went back to the room, lit a cigarette and ripped the cork seal of a new bottle of Johnie Walker. I drank and let the adrenaline dissipate away, thinking.

An end, Jane had said. Something had been waiting for me in that city, and now I was there. The shadows were ready for me.

So be it, I thought. I, too, was ready for the shadows.

***

The Camel smoke felt stale in my mouth. Deep in the night, ten floors below, the city was winding down its noises. The hours since Jane had left felt like years. The days spent in Bucharest had blurred in my memory. It was as if I'd traveled from my house in Pasadena straight to that empty hotel room in Bukow. In between was just the memory of the old times mixed with a vague perception of the new country with its people ready to forget the past and the history again, too busy building the future, hungry for life, hungry for money, fresh vigorous vegetation covering old ruins.

I threw the stub out in the dark. It made a quick arch in its downward trajectory. I lit another cigarette, and inhaled fresh and sweet smoke.

I thought of Hal Mason, the dying man to whom I owed my new life, and who owed me his life. There were many questions I had to ask him and never did. Throughout our years of friendship I've been accepting the side of him he offered me. I'd never inquired about the other side of him, his network of contacts, the security surrounding him. I was reluctant to find out because I was uncomfortable with the answer, as if I had sold my soul and didn't want to know about it. Fate made it that he was on my side, and that was enough. Fate also made it that Hal was a Jew, and I was a Christian. The same fate that had made us take turns at holding each other's life in our hands.

A deep thundering sound interrupted my thoughts. Lights were moving fast on the sky, ascending. MIG's from the airbase on a night exercise.

I lit up another Camel and sat down on the balcony's floor. My thought went back to Harold Manson and how I met him.

50
June 14, 1990
Downtown Bucharest

I emerged from the subway and noticed the air was full of smoke. I hesitated by the station's exit. The surreal, again.

After three months spent on various hospital beds I had returned back to work at the Institute and found new faces, new management. They'd told me all MRFEM materials had been destroyed in the explosion. The dead had been identified and the corpses buried fast. Victor Petrescu was dead and buried.

One piece of information I'd obtained said the Ministry of Industry's Central Archives had received copies of all the blue prints and spec books for MRFEM. Accessing them needed special approvals since the materials were classified as weaponry and defense. I had submitted my request for approvals and waited.

Meanwhile, on the streets of Bucharest, the feeling a freedom had degenerated into a feeling of deceit. The smart and the skeptical had begun to understand the farce played in December. Since then, the city had become a political cesspool. Hundreds of new political parties had mushroomed. Dubious investors arrived from abroad bent on scavenging the left-over communist economy. The National Salvation Front, which had acceded to power during the events in December 1989, wanted to stay in power. Street demonstrators wanted free elections. The hundreds of new political parties wanted a piece of the pie. The game was tough and it was played through the manipulation of the people on the streets. And there, on the streets, a nation awakened after decades of communist repression was eager to discover freedom.

*A marathon protest against the new government was being held in the University Square. It had been going on for months, uninterrupted. Students and intellectuals blended with pick-pocketing gypsies and ex-convicts. At every corner, paid political agitators gave speeches. The government tried in vain to disperse the crowd. It couldn't. The marathon protest had become a symbol against the authors of the bloody farce they called **the revolution**.*

I had been oblivious to most of the turmoil and managed to get all the approvals needed to access the MRFEM blue prints. With the forms stamped and signed in my pocket, I stood by the metro station exit watching the blackened sky, listening. There was no noise, no fighting, no gun fire. I headed towards the Central Archive's building.

The offices were closed, the building's doors locked. The entire place seemed deserted. Across the street, were the archives of the former Securitate, a large building with a dome on the top. I discovered the source of the thick smoke: the dome was on fire. Large flames billowed towards the sky as a crowd was watching. Firefighters came, but the crowd barred their access to the building. Let it burn, the crowd yelled. It was a strange crowd. They didn't seem like regular folks but paid agitators again. A group of them tried to ram a minivan into the main door. An effort stupid and pointless, the vehicle could not reach up the dozen stairs to the door. A helicopter came and flew very low. Nothing else happened. The building kept burning, the group continued their futile assault. The firefighters timidly opened a hose line and sprayed the flames. The crowd let them do it; it was too little, too late.

I walked away from the fire. Two miles down the road, infantry troops were waiting besides armored transport vehicles, smoking cigarettes, killing time.

I kept walking towards downtown. Suddenly, the street filled with men dressed in dirty dark clothes wearing helmets and armed with bats. I heard a warning and I stepped out of the street into the arcade of a store. Two other men hiding there as well said the dark men were coal miners. They had been brought by special trains into the city and instructed by the National Salvation Front to restore order.

I peeked at the dark silhouettes. Coal miners had a tradition of radicalism. During communist time they had almost removed Ceausescu from power with determined strikes. Now, it seemed, the National Salvation Front was using them. I watched them roaming the street. They carried thick pneumatic hoses taken from the mining equipment. Made of rubber with steel inserts and fittings at the ends, they were perfect weapons.

The arcade was not safe. One of the two men dashed towards a narrow side street and vanished. The other one, young, dressed in jeans and sporting a beard hunkered down deeper into the niche. The best way to draw the miner's attention.

A couple of greasy dark men approached. One of them grabbed the man muted by panic and body searched him. That miner didn't look as genuine as the others, the dirt on his face seemed as fake as if made up with shoe wax. He found a piece of paper in the man's backpack read it and then hit the bearded man hard on the head. The victim howled in pain and held his head, while the fake miner showed the piece of paper to the other miners. The paper seemed a political manifesto. It made the miners angry. They started hitting the man with the hoses. They clubbed him down, full of blood, and then dragged him and threw him into a minivan collecting arrested people.

I didn't move. I heard on my left the clink of those hoses. A miner with a worn out face pointed a blunt index finger at me: "Got some identification?"

I got the Institute ID out and showed it to him, holding it at hip level, hoping the ID would work again its deceitful appearance..

The light in miner's eyes changed. He eyed my short haircut and his voice changed the tone into one of complicity.

"You with the teams?" he asked and let the hose just hang in his hand, no longer a threat.

"What kind of question is that?" I said. "Weren't you instructed?"

He suddenly humbled.

"I missed the instruction. They got us straight from the shaft."

"When did you get here?"

"I got only on the third train. Some **ortacs**[12] who were at the instruction told us what to do while we rode south."

"Carry on," I said.

The miner jerked his hand in the direction where the young man had been dragged full of blood.

"Students and intellectuals," he said and spat on the sidewalk. "We'll take care of all of them. We're good people, sir."

---

[12] Miner's slang for team-mates, in Romanian

I searched for a way to leave, but then, a glimpse of something happening down the street changed my fate.

There, on a narrow street, another group of miners had surrounded a man with gray-white hair whose face had whitened out of fear. He saw death coming.

I reacted by instinct, before logic could preclude my reaction, just acted. I forced my way in the middle of the miners, next to the old man. He seemed fragile, scared, but alert and aware. He carried a video camera in his hand.

"I need help," he said, in German.

"Are you press?" I asked him back, in German as well. "Give me your pass, take your pass out!" I urged him. He took out a blue passport. I'd never seen an American passport before. But I recognized the eagle, nevertheless.

"Back off!" I yelled at the miners. They were pressing us with their chests and more were coming, surrounding us.

"Back off!" I yelled again and raised the man's passport, open. "He's an American!" I shouted. "Do you want to get us in trouble? The National Salvation Front needs America! It needs the USA! Back off!"

Somehow, it was the right thing to say, the right tone.

"He's got a camera!" one of the miners said. "Whoever has a camera is an enemy of the state, that's the instruction."

I told the old man to hide the camera, in English this time. He put it in a backpack. The pressure of the chests around us had diminished. A miner asked for my ID, making sure. I showed him my Institute ID again, in the same manner as before. The man got confused because it was a government issued ID, but not the kind he was instructed to obey. The conjecture was murky, and the man wasn't sure of his orders and from whom to take them.

"I'll take care of this man," I charged, and slowly led the old man away from the center of the group. Each miner we passed on the way out had to be slowly pushed away by thrusting my left shoulder forward while dragging the foreigner behind me. The miners seemed reluctant to let go of what seemed like good and proper prey. We made it through the pack and kept walking. Danger was still there, my guts

screamed, death is still just one second away, just get out, get out.
Behind us, the miner who ID-ed me was talking in low voice with three
others, operating what seemed to be a walkie-talkie. The rest of them
eyed us with suspicion.

"Get a car," the old man said, in a flat voice, yet urging. "No
matter how, get a car," he repeated.

There were several cars parked around. Some had the windshields
broken, chunks of glass spread on the front seats and around on the
pavement. I considered short wiring one, but gave up, it would look
very suspicious, and they'd get us before I would be able to start the
engine.

"Get a car!" The old man repeated and I saw the miners
insistently looking at us while the one with the radio was talking
vigorously on the device.

An unmarked police jeep arrived and stopped several feet away. A
plainclothes cop got out and walked fast towards the man with the
radio while the driver descended and remained by the car, playing with
the keys. He seemed relaxed. I weighed his strength; he was a stocky
guy, slightly shorter than me, with a big belly but strong shoulders.

I led the old man towards the driver who looked at us with some
surprise. He paid more attention to the old man and the back pack he
was holding. I shifted my weight and kicked him hard on his balls. I
freed my right hand from holding the old man and hit the driver in his
face. He fell back, dropping the keys. I picked them up and yelled at the
old man to get in the car, but he was already running around it. I got
in and started the engine, almost stalling it. Several silhouettes came
running towards the car as I was flooring the gas pedal and the
windshield broke under the blow of one of those pneumatic hoses. Gun
shots cracked from behind. The bullets impacted on the metal frame of
the car. The engine went crazy at high revs and we picked up speed and
distance. One slug cracked the side view mirror.

"Where?" I yelled at the old man. "Where should we go?" I
shouted the question again, feeling the absurdity of the situation, it was
my city and he was a foreigner who wouldn't know a thing. Yet the old
man fished a piece of paper with an address and gave it to me, grasping

my hand, making sure I get the piece of paper without loosing it in the stream of air coming in through the broken windshield.

I didn't quite know where the address was, only guessed it. It was a risk to keep driving that jeep with the broken windshield, but there was no alternative and I kept speeding through the city, avoiding the large boulevards, taking small narrow streets.

I'd found the address after sweeping around Dristor. It was an old house in the middle of a development built before the war. A man was smoking a cigarette in front of the house, sitting on a bench. He jerked up at the sound of the engine and searched the jeep with his eyes, focusing on the broken windshield, recognizing the foreign man in the front seat. He shouted something and two other men opened the dusty metal gates painted in green, while he energetically signaled me to drive the car in.

The gates were closed behind, and an old discolored cover was thrown over the jeep. Someone took me inside the house. The old man vanished somewhere. I sat on a couch. The scars from my healing bullet wounds were hurting. It felt just like before the fuel tank explosion, months before, when reality seemed to have disconnected from my conscious thought.

Then, the old man came back in the room and sat in front of me. Someone gave me a glass and I drank the alcohol, burning my guts.

"My name is Harold Manson," he said. "I am deeply grateful to you. I owe you my life. What is your name, please?"

I told him my name.

"Thank you," he said. "You must listen to me very carefully, Matei. At this moment, you must make a very important choice. You can try slip back into the city, and hope they don't have a positive ID on you and you'll be able to go on with your life. Or you can decide now to come with me. I am able to offer you asylum in the United States of America. Do you have family here?"

"Just my father," I said. "I'm not married."

"Then," Mason said, "you must decide now."

Someone filled my glass again. I drank. It was whisky of some sort. I finished the glass, and closed my eyes.

"Yes," I told the old man, "I'm coming with you."

51

More thundering sound came from the west. The MIG's kept taking off and landing on their night practice. Down below, on the street, two drunks were yelling at each other.

At three in the morning local time it was early afternoon in LA. I dialed Hal Manson's number. Ernesto's voice answered.

"Ernesto, this is Matt Salagen" I said. "I'm calling from abroad. Is Mr. Manson in?"

"Mr. Manson is resting, Mr. Salagen"

"How is he?"

"Not too good, Mr. Salagen."

"I need to talk to him, Ernesto. It's important."

"Let me check, please," he said.

I waited.

A click came on the line, and I heard Hal's heavy breath.

"How is it going over there, Matt?" he asked. It was a real question, not a greeting. "It's a good thing to keep in mind these phone lines are not secure" he added.

"I'm following a strange lead," I said. "Someone ordered a part from my old engine design here somewhere. I had the girl, Jane with me. She left yesterday."

"She left?" he asked, without appearing surprised.

"Yes. That's what she felt like, I suppose."

"Where are you now?"

"I'm in a hotel room, thinking about the past."

He coughed and spat.

"Go on," he said.

"Hal, I am at a point here where I need to clarify a few things. Don't know how to explain, it's just for me."

He laughed slowly.

"I understand," he said.

I focused on my words.

"Back in June 1990. Why where you in Bucharest right there, by the archives?"

His echoed heavily through the satellite intercontinental link.

"At the time," he explained, "several weapon technologies had showed up on the black market. Some of them had been traced to Bucharest. Those technical archives contained blue prints from several institutions in Romania. I was looking into that."

He had been waiting for my question. He didn't need time for recollection. The questions were long overdue.

"Was there anything like MORPHEM that had been offered on the market?"

"No, not at the time."

"Has it been offered later?"

"Yes."

"When?"

"Last year."

"By whom?"

"We don't know."

"Any link to Bucharest?"

"No. No clear link to anywhere."

"It that related to that picture?"

"Please remember," he interrupted, "the phones are not secure."

I recollected my thoughts back to the Bucharest moment.

"Back in 1990, when we met, where you then involved in anything against the government in Bucharest? Or in support of it? Were you part in any of that manipulation?"

"No. We tried not to interfere at all, that's why I chose to go investigate by myself."

"Who were the people in that safe house?"

"They were part of my rescue team. I always used to have one in place. As you saw for yourself, it has been put to good use."

"Is anything that happened then linked in any way to what's happening now? To my trip here?"

"In part, yes."

"How?" I asked. "What is it that I must know, Hal? What's the truth in all this?"

"Nobody knows the full truth, Matt," he said, and all of a sudden the city night noises seemed to have vanished, all of a sudden there was a deep silence, as if the only important element in the whole universe was Hal's voice on the telephone. "You can never know the full truth, Matt, I told you before. Nobody can. You can know only that part of it that you are able to understand."

He erupted into coughing. It was a long burst. The old man fought for his breath.

"I'll have to go now, Matt. Call again, whenever you can."

He closed connection.

I threw the cell phone on the bed. I reached the pack of Camel, but it was empty. My mouth was stale. In the bathroom I brushed my teeth watching the lines on my face in the neon light.

5 2

The tree in my dream was in full bloom, its flowers blue with shades of purple. *Perhaps a magnolia*, I thought in my dream, but its scent was too strong, a sweet dangerous warning.

A cold hand touched my face.

I opened my eyes and saw nothing; the hotel room was in the dark.

"Please get dressed," lips whispered, touching my ear. The perfume was strong, the touch of the lips unknown. "Pack some clothes. Please hurry. No lights. Don't make noise."

I did what the lips told me. The woman stood in the dark, waiting. I threw some clothes in a bag and she grabbed my arm and pushed me towards the door.

She was dressed in jeans and a leather jacket, light boots on her feet. Practical, but still full of feminine elegance, it was her style. *How did she get in the room?*

"How…" I started asking, but she covered my mouth with her hand and dragged me further towards the stairs.

"We need to leave," she finally spoke, on the way down the stairs. "You need to leave town."

"Why? What the hell is going on, Carmen?"

"I'll explain," she said. "We'll have to take your car. Why did your wife leave?"

"My wife? You mean Jane?"

"The girl. She left."

"She's not my wife. How do you know she left?"

"You're being watched. She's not your wife? Who is she?"

We kept walking down the stairs, quietly.

"A friend."

A man was vacuuming the floor in the lobby. He eyed us with tired curiosity.

She knew her way; we went through the restaurant kitchens and through a back door and we were outside, in the cool night air.

"Where is your car?" she asked.

"Here at the curb. You said I'm being watched. Who's watching me?"

"I'll explain," she said. "But now we must get your car and leave."

She pushed me along the sidewalk. I found the Cherokee squeezed in between two small Hyunday's.

From the darkness of a passage a man appeared and approached us. He nodded towards me with a servile smile. It was the body guard with dead fish eyes. Up close he seemed thin and light weight.

"All's well, Mrs. Conta," Dead Fish said.

"And the others?"

"No move, no transmission. It worked fine. As far as they're concerned this baby is still asleep."

The street was deserted. The city felt alien. I felt the need for a weapon. The Beretta was in a drawer, in a room, in a house, ten thousand miles away. Carmen's presence felt alien as well. Only a vague connection was left to the ghost of a woman I once loved beyond limits.

I unlocked the car and we got in, Carmen in the front seat, the bodyguard in the back. She led me along a series of narrow streets. No headlights were following. We joined the main route south over a passage bridge and switched to a beltway road west and left the city.

The road passed through farm fields and then rode uphill along the winding road crossing the Magura Hills. After five or six miles Carmen told me to turn left on a side narrow road. Winding through pockets of timber trees, the road passed several luxurious properties. She pointed to one long driveway through the trees. I drove though a wrought iron gate and stopped the jeep in front of a large, two story house.

She led me into the house where she turned on a few lights, dimmed their intensity and made a mute invitation to a set of comfortable couches. I sat down. Dead Fish had remained outside.

We sat quietly. Questions were spinning in my head but I let Carmen speak first.

"Why did you come here, Matei?" she asked with a tired voice. "The understanding was that you shouldn't come here. I asked Chris to explain it to you."

"Chris?" I jerked, "Chris Popa?"

She watched me, confused.

"Yes," she confirmed. "He did find you, didn't he? Why would you have come otherwise?"

"You sent Chris Popa to talk to me?"

"Yes."

"This was more than ten days ago, Carmen. Didn't you get any news?"

"What news? Chris knows not to call me. Every phone I use around here is bugged."

I leaned towards her. "Carmen, Chris Popa is dead. He was shot at the Los Angeles airport, right after he arrived. He was shot in front of me, by people who then kidnapped me and kept me wrapped in duct tape for three days until I was rescued."

She looked at me without a word. Then, her face appeared to be decomposing. It expressed pure terror. In a sudden motion, she buried her face in her palms, shaking.

I grabbed her by the shoulders and forced her face me.

"Why did you send Chris? What the hell is going on? The fuck, Carmen, what's all this?"

She stood up, her face recomposed, expressionless.

"We must leave now!" she said. "We must leave!"

The door opened. Dead Fish came inside walking without noise. Carmen turned towards him.

"Get my bags!" she ordered.

Through the open door, a faint car engine sound came from the night. Dead Fish stood in the doorway, motionless.

"I told you to get my bags!" Carmen yelled at him. "Move!"

The man didn't move. The engine sound came closer. I stepped towards the door trying to listen better. Dead Fish punched me hard on my stomach. The blow broke me in half. I lost my breath and dropped on the floor gasping for air. Carmen charged at Dead Fish, but he brutally threw her back on the couch.

"Don't do anything stupid, Mrs. Conta" he hissed. "The orders are to wait here."

Seconds passed. Air came back into my lungs. I remained crouched, resting my right arm against the floor underneath my belly, gasping, careful at Dead Fish in case he intended another blow. He was watching me, ready, but listening to the approaching engines as well. I forced the air out of my lungs and filled them up again.

I held my weight on my right hand and pivoted swiftly around it. My legs sheared Dead Fish's feet off the ground. He fell on his back and hit the floor hard. I rolled and jumped on my feet half a second before he did. He was still getting up when my foot smashed his face with a *mai geri* kick. His neck bones gave way. Dead Fish fell on the floor and crumbled like a dirty shirt.

Carmen was next to me, breathing hard, grabbing my arm.

"My bags," she said rushing the words.

"Forget the bags," I said and ran out of the house, dragging her behind.

I backed the jeep through the gate trying to decide a route.

"Is this road dead-ending?" I asked Carmen.

"Yes. It ends in into the hills towards the village," she said. "We need to get back to the main road."

The option was not available. A pair of headlights approached from the main road, followed by another pair. They appeared to be powerful cars, Benzes or BMW's.

I turned the jeep around, towards the hills, and floored the gas pedal. After half a mile, the road ended into a construction site for a new property. I charged through a gap in between piles of construction material, switching the Cherokee into four wheel drive. The cars behind shot through the same gap and rushed in pursuit gunning up their engines.

I raced uphill on smooth grassy dirt. Engines screaming, the chase cars tried to get ahead and block the jeep. We hit moguls of dirt and the slope became steep. The headlights behind bobbed violently and the chasing cars wavered and stopped one after another. The Cherokee shook hard, the suspension creaked, but with traction on all four wheels the jeep pushed ahead.

"Where to?" I yelled at Carmen, and suddenly, I remembered Hal, sixteen years before, passing me the crumbled paper with an address.

Carmen didn't pass me any address.

"I don't know!" she cried. "There are just hills and ravines ahead!"

Suddenly we reached the peak of the hill. I had no time to break. I got a short glimpse of the city lights towards east before the car dove into a steep slope downhill. I fought to control the car and avoid rolling over.

Gradually, the slope flattened under my wheels. The jeep rolled on a dirt road. Scattered houses showed up on the beams of my headlights.

We were at the edge of a village. I stopped the car, switched the lights and the engine off, and rolled the windows down. For a minute, I listened to the night. There was no engine sound, no shouts, no traces of headlights or flashlights. Somewhere far way, a bark of a lonely dog.

I turned the engine on but left the lights off. Putting the jeep gently in hear, I drove carefully away from village, deeper into the hills, guessing the path in the faint starlight.

"Where are you going?" Carmen asked.

"Trying to get lost," I said.

After getting far enough I switched the lights on and gunned the engine. I looked Carmen over, aware of her silence. She seemed in shock. Her jaws tight, the skin of her face pale, she clenched on the support handle of the jeep.

I shook her with my right arm. "Who are we running from, Carmen? What's happening?"

She looked at me with the same expression on the face she first had when she learned Chris Popa was dead. She didn't answer. I kept driving, eyes on the dirt road.

I focused on thinking. Whoever and whatever I had been searching for had found me. The shadows had caught up with me and attacked. I was on a road to nowhere. The people hunting for me had more resources.

I stopped the car and turned the engine off again. I rolled the windows down completely and forced myself into *combat breathing* to remove the excess of adrenaline. I began noticing the smell of dust mixed with fresh scent from the trees. The surroundings felt strangely quiet, cricket bugs and birds as the only background sound.

I turned to Carmen again. "I need to know what's going on," I said, keeping my voice low. "You gotta talk to me, Carmen. Those men behind, they'll catch up with us, sooner or later, and I need to know."

She bent and held her head with her palms, without a word.

I reached and forced her back on the seat. "We've got no time for this quiet drama, do you understand? Can we get help from the cops? Or do we need to avoid the cops?" I gave her a hard shake. "I need to know!"

She looked at me as if I was crazy to hold any hope.

"Raoul works with Ukrainians," she said. "They're brutes. And Raoul has networks of people everywhere. He's part of a group, people from Bucharest. They control everything and they're ruthless."

The name reverberated in my mind. Raoul. Raoul Conta, the man in the newspaper picture, next to her, wearing the expensive suit. The tycoon. Her husband.

"Ukrainians?" I asked.

"Yes. They're ruthless, and they do the dirty work."

"What do they want, Carmen? Why did you try getting me out of town?"

"They want you. It's something Raoul has been working on for the last several years"

"What do they want me for?"

"It's for this project. You know something they need, Matei. They have an obsession on you, and they've had it for a long time. There is a huge amount of money at stake and they'll do anything for it. Do you understand? They have no limits, and in this country there is nothing you can do to stop them."

"What about the cops? Can we go to the cops?"

She sighed, closing her eyes. She spoke with her eyes closed.

"The cops are slow, and he's got that covered too. We go to a local cop and when he reports to the city Raoul is going to get the news, he's got people working for him."

I searched for a solution in my mind. We had to get out of the country. I pulled out my cell phone. Faces and names of people came to mind, people that could help. Hal Mason. Roger Bronson. People who were ten thousand miles away. The cell phone had no signal.

"Do you have your passport on you?" I asked her.

Her eyes blurred. She produced a passport from a pocket of her jacket.

"We gotta find a way out of the country," I said, and at the very same moment I felt an opposite instinct: I suddenly understood who had ordered the engine part from the shady bunch in Bucharest. There was a part of me urging me to run, and a part of me determined to stay and find out why Conta was so desperate to get me. Why would he need me, if his MORPHEM engine was working?

5 3

I didn't pay attention to the two wheeled cart stopped by the side of the road and the peasant bent on the harness, fixing something. But just as I reached the spot, the horse cambered and pushed the cart on the jeep's path. I steered right and half rolled into the long ditch parallel to the road. The Cherokee shook hard and reached a dead stop, throwing us against the seatbelts.

The peasant grabbed the reins and cursed. The animal shook, nervously, as if ready to camber again.

The jeep's engine had stalled. I carefully restarted it and shifted gears in reverse. But as I slowly backed the car off the ditch, the steering felt crooked and sluggish.

I got out and inspected the front wheels. The right wheel was bent and stuck at an awkward angle. It had hit a massive boulder protruding from the ditch, full impact. I reached under and shook the suspension. The front arm was broken.

"How bad is it?" Carmen asked. She had walked around the car and leaned down, watching my face, trying to read the sentence in my eyes.

"Fucking dead," I said. "Broken."

We were trapped. I read it on her face as she could read it on mine.

The peasant came closer.

"The damn horse," he swore, "it's a bad one, this one. I am very sorry, dear sir, I am very sorry."

He looked at the crooked wheel and nodded with compassion.

"I'll go down to mechanic shop, by the church," he said. "There is a man there, Neagu Toader, he's working those tractors you know, he'll help you. You'll see, he'll help you, he's good, Toader, I'll bring him here."

Without waiting for an answer, he got in his two wheel cart, grabbed a small whip and jerked the reins, whistling at the horse. The animal took off, as if motion was what it needed most.

We were left alone in the morning sun, in the silence of the unknown village. The surreal of rural background noise against the sense of danger. Dogs were barking far out on the hills. Someone

in a house nearby started crying. A child, begging for something.
A woman's voice answered, tenderly. Slowly, the cry stopped.

I suddenly I felt again that I was being watched. I carefully
surveyed the place around. Dusty houses, wooden fences in need
of repair, patches of cultivated land, the hills. On the porch of one
of the houses, an old woman with a brown head scarf was staring
at us.

Engine sound came from the hills west of the road. A healthy,
well kept small engine, a small blue Toyota SUV coming from the
right side of the road rolling down along a path no wider than a
hiking trail. It crossed the road and disappeared behind houses and
trees.

The silence came back. I found a fresh pack of Camel in the
trunk and lit up. Carmen sat in the front seat leaned back against
the headrest, eyes closed. I looked at my watch. Minutes passed.
Time measured in smokes drawn from the Camels, the first sweet
smoke from a fresh cigarette following the bad sour smoke from
the finished one, poison packing into my lungs.

An old engine coughed down the road. There was a farm
tractor approaching, its diesel breathing hard at low revs. It was a
relic from the communist times, a standard tractor used for
plowing.

When reaching within feet of the Cherokee, the tractor driver
did a quick, skilled u-turn and backed the tractor right in front of
the jeep. He cut the engine off, came out of the cabin, and jumped
down on the road's dirt. A thin and short man, aged anywhere
between forty and fifty, dressed in dark and oily cotton clothes,
obviously a work outfit.

"Heard you're in trouble," he said and eyed me and the jeep,
seeming eager to inspect the car. His face was full of fine lines on a
skin marked by hard weather, two small blue eyes flickering under
graying eyebrows.

"You heard right," I told him. "Are you Toader?"

"Yes dear sir, that's me, Toader Neagu."

"Well, thanks for coming. Can you fix this?"

Toader turned towards the jeep.

"Broken wheel, eh?" he asked, rhetorically. "Let me see here."

He quickly dropped on the dirt and crawled under the car.

"Aha," he exclaimed from under the Cherokee. "Broke it right in the middle."

He jerked the jeep's suspension parts, shaking the car. Carmen woke up from her light sleep on the front seat. I put a finger on my lips for her.

Toader spoke from under the jeep, "Forgive me for saying so, sir, but you should take better care of this car. This is a good car, everything here is good stuff, but these arms are old and worn out. That's what happens with our roads. Look at these here, they're torn, waiting to break."

He took his time and shook every little piece of the Cherokee's front suspension. He seemed to take pleasure in that. Finally he came out from under the jeep and stood up.

"I'll try patch it," he said, shaking the dust off his hands and clothes, "Let me get you off the road. I'll take you to my shack, and try some welding there. But it's only so you can get to the city somewhere, only that. You follow me, dear sir?"

"Yes," I said, "that's fine. Just fix it the best you can,"

Toader got back into the cabin of the tractor, started the engine and backed the tractor close into the jeep. The rear side of the tractor had a hydraulic mechanism used for handling a plow. An improvised device like a bar with rubber pads had been welded onto that mechanism. He backed the tractor, operating the hydraulics to lower the bar and pushing it under the Cherokee's front bumper. Then, he jacked the hydraulics up, raising the jeep's front wheels off the ground. Leaving the tractor's engine on, he jumped off the cabin and secured the connection with a steel cable.

"I need you to stand on these cable loops here as I drive sir," he told me, indicating the bumper. "I'll drive slowly and you need to keep your feet on the cable so it doesn't come off. Do you understand, sir? Like this."

He jumped on the jeep's front bumper, pressing the cable with his feet.

He noticed Carmen, sitting in the jeep with her eyes closed.

"The lady can remain there," he decided.

I climbed on the jeep's front bumper and placed my feet on the steel cable as he has shown me. I understood what he wanted: I was an improvised human safety mechanism for his towing system.

He got into the tractor's cabin and drove slowly down the road. The jeep bounced at every bump on the road, but the cable held, and I waved at him to go faster.

The mechanic's place was comprised of a small house, a shack, a small yard packed with another old tractor and an immense earth moving tractor of Polish make, a Stalowa Wola, another relic from the old times.

"What do you do with that?" I pointed to the Wola tractor which was two thirds the size of his house.

"I'm fixing it," the little man answered with a sly grin. "Good money. I got all the engine parts I need, two good tires, and now I'm rebuilding the hydraulics. It's going be as good as new. They're paying ten thousand Euros a month for a Wola with a driver, three six hours shifts a day at the quarry. I fixed it for less than thirty thousand and my cousin is gonna work it there. I'll get two more of these within a year."

I whistled. Not bad. The middle of nowhere was actually somewhere.

"How can you even change the tires?"

He laughed.

"The rims come apart from the sides. It's made smartly, for people like us, with little means. I can change all four tires in a day with my cousin. No sweat."

In spite of the tension in my guts, I laughed. He was a little devil of a man.

"What do they do at the quarry?" I asked.

"They're breaking stone for the new road. There's going to be a lot of work. It's that new road they're making with the Chinese."

I thought he said it wrong. The outside world was bursting again into the heart of my old country.

"The Chinese?"

"Yes sir, that's what I hear, some works with the government in Bucharest, the Chinese bring the money for the whole new road."

"Why?"

He shrugged.

"I don't know, dear sir, those boyars in Bucharest make the deals, and I am sure they've filled their pockets on this one as they always do, but thank God there is work for us here."

I helped him jack up the jeep on steel stands. It was good to have the jeep off the road. Forced by the accident, we had pulled a temporary vanishing act.

"You're welcome to wait in the house," Toader said. "Forgive the mess, it's just the two of us, myself and my woman, and I work a lot on these machines. And also, forgive the noise, I'm going to work right here."

"Thank you for the hospitality. How long is it going to take?"

He scrapped his chin.

"Well, I'm going to pull those parts off, and we'll know better. Meanwhile I'm waiting for that cousin of mine to bring back the welding transformer, he borrowed it and I told him to bring it back today."

It was going to take all day.

"If you're tired, dear sir, you're welcome to go in the orchard, this hill behind the house. There is a little shed there, it has a bed, it's clean, but you have to forgive me, there is no running water over there."

I looked up the slope. He was pointing to a long and narrow patch of land uphill, with the shed at the hill end of it.

"Actually that would be great," I accepted. "We've been on the road for most of the night, a little rest is welcome."

"Good," he smiled, seemingly glad at my acceptance, "I'll tell Maria to bring some clean sheets, for the bed."

5 4

I watched the cracks on the ceiling of the small cabin, lying in bed. The mattress was hard, the cover smelled of old dust, but the sheets were clean, smelling of lavender.

I closed my eyes.

I opened them.

Outside, the daylight was almost gone.

Carmen moved. She sat on the edge of the bed, watching me.

"You snore," she said.

My wristwatch read 7:12 pm. I got up and opened the door. The night was just arriving, purple twilight still lingering on the western edge of the sky.

"You should've wakened me up," I growled, my face buried on my hands.

"What for? He's not done with the car."

My throat was hurting, dry, roughed by thirst.

"Is there water somewhere?"

She rose.

"There is a well with a pump, I'll show you"

She was wearing one of my t-shirts. Her own white shirt was hanging out to dry on an improvised support. My bag was lying on a small wooden table, open. I touched her hanging shirt. It was still wet.

"I hope you don't mind I borrowed this from your bag," she said, arranging the sleeves of the t-shirt.

"I don't mind."

The water well was half-way between the cabin and the small house in front. There was a large tin can hanging on a hook by the pump. I filled it up and drank in long swallows, the water sweet and cold.

The man named Toader walked up the dirt path through the trees. He made a wide gesture with his arms.

"Please come have dinner with us," he invited. "It's not much, Maria put together a few things, please come, she'll be upset if you don't."

He eyed me in the dim light, and smiled.

"This air here is good, isn't it? Makes you sleep well."

The food was in fact good. The dish was a *tochitura*, pork meat in small chunks partly pan fried, partly stewed. It was served plainly with warm-fresh wholegrain bread and pickled green tomatoes I hadn't tasted since I was a teenager.

Both Carmen and I ate very little, however. The other guest, the local priest, made up for us. Toader's wife, Maria, seemed happy with the consumption. She kept busy bringing more food, slicing tomatoes. Her man poured some red wine in small thick glasses.

"C'mon, don't worry so much," he slapped lightly on my shoulder. "Tomorrow morning you'll have your car fixed."

He got up, walked to the monster Wola truck and picked an object from its wide read bumper. The object was the front arm of my Jeep's suspension.

"Look at this here," he said, showing me the part. "Stronger than before. Even if you don't find a new part to replace it right away, just align the wheels in the city at some shop, and go on your travel, I guarantee it's going to hold well."

He'd done a magic piece of welding and reinforcing work using additional scraps of steel. The part was three times heavier, but I agreed with him, it was going to hold. He read my face, slapped my back again and laughed wholeheartedly.

"See?" he exclaimed. "You'll just stay here tonight, you'll sleep like a baby. We'll make room in the house, that cabin is not that warm and good at night."

"No, please, the cabin is just right," I said. "If you only have an extra blanket."

He laughed, nodding, and filled the glasses again. The priest had finished his food and refused a third serving, but accepted the wine.

All sunlight had vanished from the sky, replaced by a myriad of stars. The village was quiet with my childhood quietness: distant noises of dog barking, cricket bugs and voices of people carried by wind.

***

The only source of light in the cabin was a candle Maria had given us. The tall narrow bed had been made again with crisp, white clean sheets. Two thick blankets had been placed on the bed, folded.

"Please bring me some water," Carmen asked, handing me an empty bucket made of cheap green plastic.

I filled it up with fresh water from the well and carried it back and placed it on the small wooden table.

From my bag she took out a small towel, soaked it in the cold water and slowly wiped her face and neck. Stretching her arm out the small window she squeezed the water off, then soaked the towel again and took the t-shirt off. She slowly wiped her arms, her breasts. In the light of the candle, her back appeared sculptural without loosing the magic quality of her gender, the essence of a woman defined by the contour of her shoulders, the jut of her shoulder blades and the fine line of her spine. With slow motions, she took the rest of her clothes off, and started wiping her skin.

I didn't move. The dim light, the tension, and the film of events of the last twenty four hours impressed the moment with a surreal dimension. The surreal again.

She turned towards me. Her breasts bore a mature beauty: large, only a bit sagging, at perfect distance from each other, with nipples well defined by their shadows in the candle light.

"Your turn," she said, and waited.

I accepted, without words. On close proximity, the warmth of her body radiated through my clothing.

"Take your shirt off," she said.

The touch of the wet towel was cold and rough. She cleaned my back, and my arms with the same slow and long motions she had used on herself. Her bare breasts touched me on and off, my arm at one moment, or part of my back the next. I felt her scent again, as if new.

She handed me the towel and went lie bed, her body language displaying her usual sort of detachment from reality, her way of inserting a protective layer of void in between her thoughts and the surrounding space, as if her mind was somewhere else; yet her motions were discretely languid, like a strange feline ready to mate for no other reason than for it was time to do so.

I took the rest of my clothes off and finished cleaning with my own motions, fast, efficient and thorough. As unpleasant the feel of the cold cloth was, as good the feeling of clean skin was after finishing. I laid in bed next to her, with my senses focused on her, waiting for her moves.

She didn't seem to have anything to do with the young Carmen I'd loved many years before. She was a good as a stranger. I thought of the time she left me. Her decision had come unexpectedly and with some cruelty. When she bade farewell, there was contempt in her eyes. Like she had made a much better choice, then.

Who was Raoul Conta then? Friends of friends rumored about her fastidious wedding, her eccentric dress leaving her back fully bare with flowers painted on the skin with glitzy paint. I had never asked the rumor bearers about who the man was, or his name. The pain of loosing her had faded away slowly, in time, day after day at work, in many drinking sessions with Victor Petrescu for a while, then, later, giving up drinking in favor of martial arts, yoga and physics. Years had passed and Carmen had become a warm but painful icon left in my chest, in my memory. And now, there she was: an older and very real version of her, breathing next to me, both of us bonded by fear, by the full uncertainty of the next day.

She rolled over me, her lips searching for my mouth. Her kiss was full, her lips soft and wide, tongue touches discrete. I embraced her slowly, strongly, fully aware the moment was exceptional, and will never occur again. The thought of danger, the instinct of survival got melted away and vanished. I explored her body and the taste of her in an abstract and dilated time away from immediate reality. Her breasts felt as they had looked earlier, in the candle's light, wonderful, mature, soft, the taste of her nipples good on my tongue. I felt her skin, smooth and tan, the muscles well kept by exercise and massage, the scent of pheromones starting to come out of the pores, mixing with the perfume fragrance she seemed to have placed everywhere on her body. I explored her with full fascination. I had been too young to know how to explore her years before, so even more I was deepening the ecstasy of doing it now.

I induced her first orgasm absorbing the sound of the deep moan with my lips. Her erogenous spots were deep, hard to reach, just as her motions were deep and strong in their length. Her half suppressed moans were loaded with a pure distillate of a woman, surprising my senses which were still bearing the memory of Jane's thin steely fiber and boyish womanhood.

We entererd a long and physically intense lovemaking; strange animals sweating, swirling the bed sheets, linked in a fight-like quest for a climax which arrived so gradually and so powerfully it left us in total exhaustion after it passed.

***

"Why did you marry him?"

On her side of the bed, she shook her head, rejecting my question.

"Don't ask me that. What did I know then? I was young, beautiful and confused, with plenty of choices. I just chose wrong."

"Yeah. But why him?"

"I don't know. Why didn't you grab me, like he did? He wanted me with no reserve, with little love and a ton of vanity. I was going to be his top trophy. I didn't know that. I just felt his determination and I liked it."

I rolled on my back. The sheets were still wet with our sweat.

"I was a poet, Carmen. I still am. I was waiting for you to flutter your petals, give me that little sign. I couldn't grab you without it. And you didn't give me any sign, ever."

She laughed, slowly, shaking the bed in that good intimate way when your lover is close. She rolled closer and kissed my shoulder.

"What did I know then? Life was confusing and there were all those men showing up, parading and spreading their feathers in front of me, confusing me even more."

"But you chose this man. Raoul Conta. Why?"

"I can't remember. He wanted me. He wanted me hard. He had power. He was sending his men to take me to him, drive me to the sea where he was waiting, all arranged in a good hotel. I liked that."

"He was sending his men? What men?"

"He was in the Securitate, pretty high up. You didn't know?"

I shrugged. "I only found out his name two days ago, in the newspapers."

She exhaled, wrapping the blanket around her.

I finally understood. I had been only a shadow in Carmen's life at the time. She hadn't pay attention to who I was, she didn't have time to sort her own life. Yet now, she knew well I had settled in California and what I was doing. Why?

"Why did you send Chris Popa to LA?" I asked her and suddenly brought back the reality left aside for several hours.

She rolled away from me before she answered.

"Raoul is working with a network of powerful people, very well connected. They're working on a system you developed years ago. It's very valuable, yet something went wrong, a few months ago, several people died."

I was listening with my eyes closed.

"What does he want to do with that system?"

"They want a larger device. But it doesn't work. They want you, because you did the physics on this thing they're making. It's about scaling it up."

The expression, which she used correctly, surprised me. It shouldn't have. Carmen was a chemical engineer by training. She could read blue prints and specs. She knew more than she was showing.

"How does Chris Popa fit into this?"

She rolled again, on her side. Her breath was reaching the skin on my shoulder.

"I sent Chris because I felt I should warn you, Matei," she said. "And I was going to make you a proposition, through Chris," she spoke as if forcing the words. "There is a more elegant way do business than kidnapping."

No, I thought, *please don't. Not you.*

"The man died, Carmen."

She embraced me under the blanked, shivering. I felt again the layer of void wrapped around her as thick as ever, and something else, hidden deep.

"I need to sleep," she said, her lips touching my chest.

She had closed herself in. I had to let go of my questions.

"Then sleep," I said, and it all became quiet, the night noises of the village coming in through the small window.

55

The morning air was cold and I rolled the Jeep's windows up. The car felt stable on the dirt road as we approached the main road west.

"Drive it with no worry," Toader Neagu had said earlier in the morning with a bit of a pride. "It's better than before you broke it."

He had assembled the jeep's suspension back as promised. With great reluctance he had charged me a hundred dollars for his work. We had become his guests and acquaintances, and he felt he's asking for too much. I doubled the amount, and asked him just to forget we stopped there. He refused.

"It wouldn't be fair to you, dear sir," he had explained. "The people in the village already know, they've been talking around."

***

The narrow dirt road made a tight turn. I took the turn, and a Toyota 4x4 suddenly blocked my way, too short a distance to avoid impact.

I slammed the brakes, trying to steer sideways. The Cherokee stubbornly slid forward, scrapped dirt and crashed into the Toyota head on. Another SUV came from behind and rammed into the Cherokee's rear. The jeep was trapped.

I pushed the door open with my shoulder and rolled on the ground. From the car behind, a man dressed in a blue gym outfit charged at me. I dodged him and hurled dust at his face. He cursed and stopped.

A second attacker kicked me on my right shoulder. The impact threw me against the jeep. I quickly slid sideways and dodged a second kick which missed and broke the rearview mirror. I rammed my head on the attacker's face. The cartilages of his nose felt squashed against my forehead. Hate and adrenaline flowed through my whole body. I kicked him hard but too high, chest instead of stomach. The blow threw him backwards, but he dropped on the dust, rolled and jumped back on his feet.

The man in blue charged again, still handicapped by the dust in his eyes. I aimed to take him out for good, but he'd done enough fighting to know; he blocked my kick, and hit back. We got into a body clinch. He grabbed around my neck and shoulder with his left while aiming a punch at my stomach with his right. More hate and adrenaline dissolved in my blood and gave me strength to twist my shoulders under his wrestler's half lock. I swung him around hard and threw him against the Cherokee. Another attacker came from behind and hit me. Both men tried blocking me in between them, yet I shook and pushed madly, buried my knee on one's groins, rammed my fists together in the face of the other. I heard Carmen screaming. More men attacked. Strong arms pushed me against the jeep. I pushed back hard, to no avail. Someone yelled curses. A gun barrel pressed hard on my face. I got hit in the stomach. I fell in the dust, grasping for air. The barrel followed my motion, pushing hard against my head.

Strong arms pulled me up and held me with my back against the jeep. Hate kept flowing in my blood, futile. I wished in vain to see each of those men burned alive. All I got was taste of blood on my mouth from the blows. Dust filled my nostrils. Balkan dirt, road dust, or sand at Point Dume.

I got surrounded by hard breaths of angry men. The gun pushed harder on my face. Seconds dripped slowly, mixing sweat and dust.

"Take him to the Rover!" the man with the gun ordered.

They pulled me up and dragged me towards a Land Rover.

"Get these cars running or tow them away!" the lead man ordered again. "Clean up!"

Plastic ties locked my arms and feet, followed by tape on my mouth. I was pushed on the Land Rover's floor. Men's feet pressed me down with smelly boots and shoes. The car roared its engine and left.

***

The ride was not very long. They forced me out of the car and dragged me into a hallway lit by fluorescent lamps. Thick ducts and cables ran along the walls. At a junction between the hallway and what looked like a boiler room there were two men dressed in suits, waiting.

The ambush man greeted them with a short jerk of his chin.

"We got the foreigner," he said. "The boss here?"

His accent in Romanian was very thick.

"He's on his way," one of the suits said, inspecting me. "Get him in the place prepared, let him cool off and clean him up. The boss wants to see him."

The men dragged me up several stairs to another hallway and opened a metal door to a small room. They threw me on the floor and locked the door.

I rolled on my back and stared at the fluorescent lamp on the ceiling. Adrenaline was long gone. I feared for my life in an abstract way, like it was somebody else's fate. There was something else brewing in my mind. What were these people after? I wanted to know. And where was Carmen? What did they do to her?

I closed my eyes and dreamt I was walking somewhere, meeting Carmen, talking to her, kissing her breasts, embracing her, realizing her body felt like Jane's, thin and tight.

Then I came back to reality, opened my eyes and stared at the same white fluorescent light again.

5 6

The metal door lock clicked and the door opened.

A tough face came over me. Bad breath blew in my face.

"I'm going to untie you," the face said. "You give me any trouble, I'll break your legs. Ponyo?[13]"

He pulled the tape off my mouth, just like the man in LA did, harshly, with a short brutal motion.

I laid still.

The man rolled me on the floor, and cut the ties off.

I moved carefully. Blood started flowing back normally through my arms and legs.

"I'll stand up, now," I said.

He stepped back.

"Go ahead," he said.

I stood up. The room spun a few times with me then slowly stopped. I noticed a leather couch in the room and a bare wooden table with a chair.

The man was blond, with cold blue eyes and a tough bony face. His skin had visible blood vessels, typical to hard drinkers. With his eyes locked onto me he stepped backwards and opened the door. Someone handed him a bag which he threw on the floor towards me. I recognized my bag.

"Strip!" the man ordered. "Get in there and take a shower," he added, and pushed his chin forward indicating a corner of the room behind me.

I turned. There was a small door on the opposite wall.

I stripped and got in the shower. The pipes hissed and discharged foul smelling air instead of water. Then, the pipe coughed out brown colored water full of rust. Slowly, the stream of water cleared. There was no shower head, just a jet of water.

The man stood in the small door frame, keeping his eyes on me like a robot. His attention was professional: he was a muscle man who'd learned to make no mistakes.

I dried and got dressed. The touch of clean clothes felt good.

---

[13] Understood? – Russian, street slang

The man opened the metal door and jerked his thumb back towards the room, inviting someone in. Another man came in, holding a camera.

"Where do you want him?" asked the blond man.

The newcomer looked around the room, and pointed to a wall. The blond man turned towards me.

"Go stand by that wall," he ordered.

I did what he wanted.

The man with the camera took a few head shots. He finished and left without a word.

"Come with me," the blond man ordered. "Walk and move smoothly, I scare easily, and I do ugly things when scared."

***

The building was part of some industrial complex. Raoul Conta's petrochemical plant, I guessed.

Fascination mixed with anger and fear. Something in my fate had drawn me back to that corner of the world. Another hidden and forgotten piece of my own past was about ready to get revealed and ready to pull at me like a creditor asking for his dues.

We entered a short hallway dead-ending into a mahogany door. A man dressed in a black suit was standing in front of it.

"Stop!" the blond man ordered me. I stopped, two feet away from the man in black. He was emanating scents of expensive aftershave and cologne.

"Here's Salajan," the blond man said. "What's the deal?"

"We let him in," the black suit said.

"What do you mean, let him in?"

The body guard raised his eyebrows.

"Let him in, that is, I'll open the door, he gets in, I close the door. What's so difficult?"

"That's the orders?"

"That's the orders."

The blond man shrugged, and leaned against the wall.

The body guard in black opened the mahogany door and made a sign, inviting me in.

I walked in.

***

The large room was empty.

It looked like an office. A thick, good quality carpet covered the floor. Opposite to the door was a large window. Leather couches were arranged in a tight square by the door. Beyond the couches, there was an L shaped modern office desk busy with papers, folders, and a computer terminal. Bookshelves covered one sidewall, filled with books and folders labeled by hand. The other wall was lined up with steel cabinets with strong solid locks.

I walked towards the desk. It was cluttered with technical notes, prints, forms. I examined the papers. Nothing meaningful.

Then, I noticed it.

A framed picture.

Carmen, when she was young. Carmen, laughing at the camera, her long hair partly covering her face. She was carrying a back pack while holding a stack of vinyl records in her hand. Dresden, 1983. It wasn't written anywhere, except in my memory. I had taken that picture.

I picked up the frame, and watched the picture closely, caressing the glass protecting it, trying to understand the mystery of time, how can something so far away in the past feel so fresh and present, real and surreal.

"Did you get a good fuck last night?" a voice growled.

I hadn't heard him coming. The man was heavy but moved easily. He bore the same toughness and sturdy weight typical to the men of power in the country, yet his eyes were different. Intelligent and treacherous, they had a subtle light, as if ready to spill humor and cruelty simultaneously.

He took the framed picture from my hands.

"She's a bit rusty now," he growled again. "She's put some godamn weight on her."

He looked at me and grinned.

"I got her in her prime," he said, his eyes flickering. "You should've seen her then, what a piece of ass she was!"

I hit him in the face, hurting my knuckles in his jawbone. The blow threw him back, but he was too stocky and too heavy to be knocked down with one punch. He hit back. Hate came back to me, overtaking exhaustion. I blocked his blow and hit him again.

It was a long fight. No body-guard showed up. We hit each other until growing num, thrashing the place. My hate got depleted. Any trace of energy I had, was spent. Conta's overweight and my blows took their toll on him as well, he got exhausted.

We stopped.

I sat on the floor, wiping blood from my face, watching Conta kneeling by a wall, leaning against it. His face was in no better shape than mine. We kept breathing, spitting bloody blobs on the carpet.

"Fuck you, Salajan," Conta said with his typical growl, suddenly forcing himself up. "You're an idiot."

He moved slowly, growling in pain, and opened a bar, grabbing a bottle of Johnny Walker and two glasses. He poured two stiff ones.

"Here!" he said, handing me the glass.

We drank. I needed the scotch. It filled the void left by the spent hate.

"What did you do with her?" I asked him.

"Carmen? Don't be a fool. She's bought enough insurance to be all right. I wouldn't touch her."

"What the fuck do you want from me?" I asked him, swallowing more scotch, letting it burn through my guts.

He threw his head back, in a burst of laugh, and drank his glass to the bottom.

"I want you to meet someone," he said.

5 7

Conta led the way. His body guard walked along his side. The blond muscle man walked behind me, stepping so silently I wandered from time to time if he was still there. We entered a staircase smelling of paint, chemicals and rot. Narrow stairs led downwards only. Four stores down, we reached a heavy, rusty metal door. Conta squeezed his large figure by the wall and made a sign to his bodyguard.

"Open it."

The man extracted a key from a small leather holster and introduced it into the metal door's lock. The lock made a smooth clicking sound, in contrast with the old appearance of the door.

One by one we entered a dark tunnel lit by bare light bulbs on a side wall. The smell of rot was very intense, water leaking from somewhere and dripping along the walls covered with mould. Yet the floor was clean and dry, the leaking water apparently collected by a drain system.

Conta's man unlocked another door at the end of the tunnel, letting us into a staircase similar to the one we came through. Mixed with other smells was a new odor, oddly familiar, although its familiarity remained vague, hidden somewhere in my memory.

We walked up the stairs and reached another short hallway. The walls were clean and covered with good paint. Ducts and cables along the walls were carefully painted in blue, yellow, green and red.

I suddenly recognized the smell. The mixture of chemicals, metal, special oils, hydraulics and other equipment mixing their odors in spite of the air filtering and conditioning systems. A propulsion test stand.

Is this the journey's end? The question came to me as fear and exhaustion mixed with excitement. *What was it to find, after all?*

Conta took the lead again. He walked to another metal door painted in light blue, opened it and held it open, inviting me in.

"Get in," he said, his eyes flickering.

I hesitated, and then entered.

First, I noticed the control desks with gage indicators for pressures and temperatures, the maze of lines and cables, several idling computers showing data acquisition software operating on their screens.

In the back of the room, a man was standing by a large desk lit by a lamp hanging low from the ceiling, some blueprints laid on the desk.

At the noise of my entrance he straightened his body, but didn't turn around, his back remaining towards the door. He was bald and chubby, wearing a corduroy jacket. There was something strange in his attitude.

Then, he turned slowly. He was wearing eye glasses with dark lenses, and I realized I'd seen him before. He was the man I had seen the day before getting into a car in front of the hotel, just before I had met Carmen. The same emotion I felt then arose in my chest again. There was something familiar about the man.

I stepped towards him.

His face had marks of surgery, or old injuries.

He took his glasses off.

I searched his eyes.

"Oh God," I said, a jolt firing through my stomach, "Victor."

He fixed his eyes on me.

"They told me they're going to bring you here," he said. "I was waiting. It's been a long time."

I felt tears, uncontrollable tears dropping.

"Victor," I said his name again, "My God, Victor."

His eyes stayed locked on mine. My emotion prevented me from being able to read them.

"For all these years," I said. "For all these years I have been thinking that I don't even know where you are buried."

He nodded, tightening his lips in a severe grimace.

"As strange as the circumstance may be," I said, "I am so glad to see you, Victor. I'm so fucking glad, man."

Victor Petrescu shook his head.

"Yes, the circumstances are strange," he said. "But they're generated by who we are and what we do, Matei. We create the circumstances. And it is interesting for me to see you as well, yet for reasons different than yours."

The coldness. I felt it only after his words. I finally read his eyes.

"What are you saying?" I asked.

He made a step away from the table. The move was slow, made with difficulty. With one hand he touched his body and then made a wide gesture.

"Look at me, Matei. I walk on two artificial legs, prosthetics. This left arm is a useless piece of plastic. Most of my skin is patched, it's been badly burned."

He paused, breathing with difficulty, very excited, searching for his words.

"I spent years on hospital beds hoping to hear from you. Here in the country, then in Germany. The crooks in Bucharest stole the money allocated for my treatment; I didn't even have enough food. I wasn't disappointed by them, somehow I knew, I understood what a big scam they played on us the night I blew up the tank. But I had been waiting for you, Matei, lying in those beds and waiting in vain."

His gaze on me was insane.

"But I didn't know, Victor! For all I knew, you were dead and buried. Records showed you were among the dead. I got three bullets myself while firing to cover you. I also spent three months on hospital beds, then, when I got out, I got into a situation when I…"

I hesitated. I still trusted Victor. Whatever strong resentments he may have had, I still trusted his character was straight; the suffering wouldn't have changed him. But there were the others in the room, Conta and his men. My encounter with Harold Mason was none of their business.

"My only choice was to leave the country, Victor," I said. "I left with just the clothes I was wearing, that's the truth."

"That's true," Conta's voice came from behind. "Our friend here was in a tough situation: he had just killed a police officer on duty, and he had to leave the country."

I jerked, and turned towards Conta.

"What the fuck are you talking about?"

He laughed, calmly.

"Don't play games, Salajan. In June 1990 you helped an unknown foreign agent to escape authorities by attacking a police officer on duty and hijacking his car. The man you attacked died of bullet wounds. There are witnesses and testimonies describing you hitting the officer. The bullets in the officer body have been shot using a silencer, probably by the agent you were helping. The jeep car you've hijacked has been found outside the city, burned. There is a file on you with the police, the SRI and other authorities which will be very eager to talk to you, doctor Salajan. There is no statute of limitation on those crimes, in case you're wandering."

I turned towards Victor.

"That's bullshit. It's not true, Victor. Whatever this man says, it's just manipulation."

Petrescu reached for the table again, holding his body straight.

"But is it true that you took the MRFEM project to the States and developed it there?" he asked.

"I didn't fucking take anything to the States. I left with just the clothes I was wearing and a bunch of handnotes, and I started a new life from scratch. In the States I worked for an aerospace corporation and yes, there I proposed a project based on the MRFEM principle and re-developed the concept. But that's the only thing I know, it is my profession, my life."

"But there it is, my friend," Petrescu said coldly. "You took our idea and built a new life, while I was rotting on those hospital beds, having made a pointless sacrifice."

I looked at the faces around. Victor's eyes were transfixed. Conta's presence felt like a deadly reptile waiting to swallow its prey whole. The musclemen were just waiting to see if their muscle is needed.

I felt dizzy, yet in more need than ever to hold it together.

Victor Petrescu was indeed dead. The man in front of me was only his shadow, having survived his idealistic and tragic sacrifice only to become a residual oh his own self.

"You were dead, Victor," I said. "Dead and buried."

I turned towards Conta.

"Let me ask you again," I said. "What the fuck do you want from me?"

Conta laughed, his eyes cold and dry.

"Now that we're all together, it almost feels like family, doesn't it?" he grinned.

Then he lost the grin, his face toughening, a tenacious rudeness surfacing in his eyes.

"Your only choice, my friend, is to repent and redeem your mistakes. If you understand that, maybe we can do some business of mutual benefit."

I weighed his words, read his eyes. Whatever I was to deliver, death was the only thing waiting at the end of my bargain.

I'm on the warm sand of a beach you can't reach, you motherfucker, I thought. *And if you'll ever reach me, I'll take you with me on the other side.*

5 8

Morning came slowly. I had no sleep. I paced the room, thinking.

Victor Petrescu was alive. But the mutilation he suffered and sixteen years of pain and resentment had changed him physically and mentally. The man I once had as a friend was dead.

I relived again and again that night of December 1989. I imagined, in thousands of versions, the one simple thing I could've done differently. Grab him, hold him, stop him. Everything would have been different. There would've been no Harold Mason in my life, no Christine, no Julia. *Julia! No, Julia must be!* That last thought came again and again and burned through my brain, through my guts. And then the tank was exploding again in my imaginary replay, while the bullets kept finding me again.

The memory was all too painful. Are sacrifices worth anything? Is saving the world worth trying?

The world always takes care of itself, pal. With, or without you.

***

In the shower, I waited for the brown dirty water to clear. I moved fast, cleaning, shaving, getting dressed.

Then, I sat and waited.

After another hour, the door opened.

Conta, dressed in a three piece blue suit, well rested and fresh, walked into the room ahead of the body guards, his eyes flickering more than usual. His aftershave smelled like a small tropical garden.

"Let's go to my office," he said. "I got some stuff for you there."

The office had been cleaned and put in order after the fight the day before. A TV set was running a Discovery Channel show.

Conta indicated a chair for me and sat at his desk, watching the TV screen. He seemed fascinated. I watched as well. On the screen, various species of fish were gulping each other. Then the image moved into a barren desert where a lizard snatched several insects, swallowing them. As it searched for yet another meal, a sidewinder viper suddenly uncoiled out of a hide in the sand and viciously bit the lizard. Slowly, the snake swallowed the agonizing lizard.

"It fascinates me," Conta said, gesturing towards the screen. "This is the simple essence of this world. It's just a long food chain, a cruel food market."

"Bruegel the Elder," I said.

Conta looked at me, surprised.

"Well, well," he exclaimed. "Good old education. Bruegel the Elder, The Big Fish Eat the Little Fish. It's been a while since I've talked to a cultivated, intelligent and sane man. Let me tell you this, Matei: there are great things we could do if we agree to collaborate. There is big money to be made and a very interesting future."

"You still haven't told me exactly what you need from me."

"I need you to listen, first of all," he snapped, irritated.

He walked to one of the shelves and grabbed a coffee pot from a filter machine.

"Coffee?" he asked casually, with the politeness of a domestic host.

I ignored the surrealism of the moment. Surrealism and altered reality had become the norms of my days.

"Please," I said.

We made the moves, sugar, cream. The overhead voice from the TV show was explaining how a snake bone system allows it to swallow the prey whole. I realized the show was a recording, not a regular TV broadcast. Conta muted the set.

"Do you like living in the States?" he asked me.

I raised my eyebrows, careful.

"I do," I said. "I had my problems there, just like anybody else."

He shook his head.

"Most people outside America don't understand what America is all about. They misjudge the reaction of the American public, the reaction of its political system."

He stood up and walked around, holding his coffee cup.

"I worked in the States for many years," he said. "I am very familiar with the life there."

I sipped some coffee. It was good and strong.

"What did you work in the States?" I asked.

He enjoyed the question; he wanted reactions from me.

"Intelligence," he said, grinning.

His frankness took me by surprise.

"Spying?"

"Yes. Interesting job. You'd be surprised how much you can learn. You eat in diners with average Joe's next to you talking weather, football and mother in laws, while you meet sources and find out shit that never reaches the public, follow policies in the making, decisions which are critical."

He poured himself more coffee.

"It's even more interesting today. The geopolitics have rearranged fully, did you notice? New game: capitalism everywhere. America is plundered by her own corporations. China, rising, accumulating wealth and power. Russia is reorganized, run by *siloviki*, former KGB folks; I used to run into them here and there. Capitalist systems but different: liberal America, where laws are for sale, and autocratic Russia and China, pragmatic and looking one hundred years deep into the future."

He watched me, yet through me, beyond the walls, captivated by his own lecture.

"We're living in a time now that's cruel but clean and simple. Only one thing matters: how much money can you make, how fast. That's all. Use the markets, sell. People compete with you, outsell them, blow them up, kill some of them, it's all fair game."

"What about the legal system? Ethics?" I asked.

He laughed, loudly.

"Laws. There were also laws during the time of the early Vanderbilts and Rockefellers. They killed and blew up competition, regardless. There were laws and rules of ethics during Yalta, when Churchill and Roosevelt sold the whole Eastern block to the Soviets[14]."

He drank more coffee, and glanced at me, watching my reactions.

---

[14] In February 1945, the leaders of the USA, UK and USSR, Roosevelt, Churchill and Stalin met in the Crimean city of Yalta and reached several agreements regarding the end of WWII. Among other agreements, USA and UK agreed to leave Eastern Europe at the discretion of the Soviets. This particular deal has been done with notes on one piece of a napkin.

"The laws are for the weak," he said, his eyes fixing me with their typical flicker. "And the weak cannot do anything except fucking cry to the sky and hate the strong."

He turned the sound on again on the TV set.

"But watch this," he demanded and fast forwarded to a section of the recording he wanted.

On the screen a Cobra uncoiled and spat a jet of venom at more than ten feet distance.

Conta laughed, excited.

"The weak can develop their own methods to fuck the strong," he said and locked his eyes on me. "Do you understand?"

"I don't eat much seafood and I hate snakes."

"Don't play fucking idiot! I'm trying to explain to you what the market is. And there is a big market. The hate for America, the hate for the strong, that's the big driver of this market. And the customers are the weak, the weak in need of weapons, in need of poison against the strong. That's where the money is."

I watched him carefully. Was he insane, or just carried away by his own verbal manipulation?

"You're talking about terrorist groups?"

He made a grimace of disgust.

"Did all that CNN brainwashing wipe your brain? You're using this shit labels. Terrorists. Remember our terrorists from December 1989? Did the public ever find out who the hell they were, after all the dust settled? Not a trace. Don't be an idiot. The Americans are just playing the same scare at a bigger scale."

"Then where is your market?"

He grinned.

"There are genuine parties out there, verifiable parties, which are interested. Not only interested, but very solvent and generous."

"You're placing yourself on the crosshairs of the biggest power on the planet, don't you realize?"

Conta laughed.

"That big power is growing feet of clay very fast, my friend. The world has the strongest weapon against your beloved America: globalization and economics. Besides, did you visit Washington lately? It's like the old Byzantine Empire, everyone is for sale, and betrayal is a daily routine. The multinationals are investing heavily in China and India and very little at home. They buy and bribe the politicians to be allowed to continue doing so. They bring cheap imports and sell for triple and quadruple the price, and pump even more money abroad. And the government sums all of it up and calls it gross domestic product and that's how they measure growth. The growth of their feet of clay."

He gulped the rest of his coffee, grinding his teeth.

"I'm not afraid of America. America is eroding itself very fast, my friend. All I'm doing is supplying products to a demanding market of clients who just want to accelerate the erosion."

"Let me ask one more time, what do you want from me?"

He leaned back on his leather office chair, thinking.

"The old MRFEM project, was it your idea?"

"More or less. I worked it with Petrescu"

"But you cooked the science in it."

"The most part."

"Can you make it bigger?"

"A larger engine you mean?"

"Yes."

"The proper term is scaling the engine up. It's not something I can do in several days. It may take years even with a large team."

"You want more coffee?"

"Excuse me?"

"Do you want more coffee?"

"Yes."

He got me some, and cleared his throat, continuously weighing me with his nervous beady eyes.

"We have some collaboration with a partner abroad," he spoke carefully. "The engine has been scaled up, re-designed at larger scale, but we had a problem with it."

"What sort of a problem?"

"It blew up. Petrescu says is something about an instability. He says you can understand it."

"Where was the large engine tested?"

"We didn't test here. Let's say it was abroad."

"Can I see the blue prints?"

He watched me intensely.

"So you're on?"

I shrugged off the question.

"I gotta see the blueprints."

He grinned.

"All right," he said. "If you make this work, you'll be set for the rest of your life, I guarantee it. Here, let me show you."

He opened a top drawer of his office desk, extracted a flat plastic folder and threw it on the desk.

"Open it," he asked.

I picked it up carefully. A passport slid out of the folder and fell on the desk. I opened it. It was a new Romanian passport. My picture appeared inside the document next to an unknown name.

"It's genuine material," he said. "That personal data will be entered in official archives."

I dropped the passport on the table, silent.

"I'm offering you a ton of money, a new identity, a fabulous life," Conta said. "There will be no trace of you, no questions asked, nothing.

"The US authorities are going to inquire into this."

"That will be taken care of. Right now, one doctor Matthew Salagen and his blonde girlfriend have departed our beautiful country and are traveling through Hungary towards the western part of Europe, leaving plenty of traces. They'll suffer a tragic accident, somewhere in the Netherlands."

His face suddenly lost joviality.

"That brings up a small matter," he said. "Where exactly did your girlfriend go?"

"What do you mean?"

"We have a problem locating this girl," Conta said, and looked up a piece of paper on his desk, "Jane Brayton."

"Leave her out of this. She's an actress from back in LA. We had an argument and she just left."

"We know she left," Conta said, coldly. "The problem is we cannot find where she is."

He smiled, a cold, cruel smile.

"It's only a matter of avoiding confusion. We have a doctor Salagen traveling west with a certain miss Brayton. I do have a doctor Salagen here with me, and I am making sure he is not going to create any embarrassing situations, like showing up in two different places at once. I need to make sure no embarrassing situation happens with this miss Brayton either. I'd appreciate your help on this, doctor."

I swallowed with a dry mouth.

"She's always been some sort of a nut head," I said. "I didn't even understand why she left. I'm sorry. I can't help you."

He scrutinized me thoroughly.

"All right," he said, "I'll take care of this miss Brayton issue. Let's work on that scaled up engine."

I closed my fists, controlling the shake of my hands. Behind me, the TV set emitted the sound of a rattler ready to strike.

59

The walls trembled slightly. Thudding vibration filled the dark control room as lamps fixed on the low ceiling began pulsing red light above our heads.

A closed circuit TV monitor showed several people laboring around a small steely device surrounded by a maze of ducts and cables. It looked like our old MRFEM engine. We were separated from it by a wall made of reinforced concrete. It felt as if something evil was brewing beyond the thick wall. And in spite of the wall's thickness, if the device exploded during testing, we would all be taken to hell together.

"Purge pressures," Petrescu spoke in a microphone.

"Gage, point zero three four atmospheres," a loudspeaker answered.

"Purge time?"

"Thirty minutes,"

Next to me, the muscleman was nervous. He didn't like the flashing red lights. His instinct knew danger; it was telling him his ass is seconds away from possible oblivion. Yet, face perspired, jaws muscles flexing, he wasn't loosening his focus on me.

The engine test had begun shortly after I had been brought in, straight from Conta's office. Warm helium and nitrogen gases were being pumped at low pressure through the various ducts and tracts of the engine. The gases would purge out any trace of moisture and prevent atmospheric water vapor from penetrating into the engine ducts and cavities. Moisture is a perfidious danger to the cryogenic engines: water gathered in small pockets and cavities at the joints and seals between different parts freezes at cryogenic temperatures. Dilating ice initiates cracks on the metal. Then, when the strong stresses kick in from high pressures during operation, ruptures can occur and generate an explosion.

"Ready for chill down," a voice announced through the speakers.

Petrescu nodded. "Chill down in five. Get out of there."

The nervous tension in the control room was high and steady. Victor kept his back at me, reducing my presence to that of a non-participating witness. But he didn't loose for a second the awareness of my presence.

One by one, three men came out of the test cell through a narrow steel door which seemed borrowed from a submarine. Each of them scrutinized me with hidden curiosity. Then, they each nodded a discrete greeting.

I realized I knew all of them. We all had crossed paths back in college in Bucharest or in the industry over the years.

The men started operating the controls. I knew the sequences by heart. Valves closed, shutting down the purge gasses, while other valves opened, releasing liquid hydrogen and liquid oxygen through the engine. Before firing it, the whole structure had to be adjusted to the low temperatures of the cryogenics.

"How do you get the propellants?" I asked Petrescu.

He jerked and turned around, glancing at me only for a moment, before focusing back on the test controls.

"We've modified some of the refinery small tanks to hold cryogenics," he said, his back at me. "We make the cryogenic propellants here."

"You do this test in the middle of an operating refinery?"

The question annoyed him; he exhaled, as if tired. "This refinery has been closed for several years," he explained. "We've designed a compact mobile platform. We use it for making the cryogens based on water electrolysis and gas liquefaction. And we deliver the platform with the rest of the package."

"What package?"

"I'll show you. This is the second package we're working on."

I watched the men, working. The team was well trained, the men were good. The test facility reminded me of Bronson's words: a fascinating mixture of rudimentary and sophistication.

From my experience, the chill-down was going to take at least an hour before all segments of the engine would reach the same very low uniform temperature.

I engaged Victor. "I understand you worked on a scaled up engine. What happened to it?"

"Who told you about the large scale engine?"

"Conta said you have a design for it from some collaboration outside. He told me it blew up and I should look into it. I told him I needed to see the blueprints and any test data you may have."

Victor turned towards me on the swivel chair.

"So you're on with us? You'll be working on this?"

I looked him in the eye.

"Do I have any other choice, Victor? Why do you think they brought me here?"

Petrescu frowned. He stood up, leaning against the chair, watching me intensely.

"Why they brought you here!? You fool! It was me! I told them to get you here. I told them you know the physics of this stuff, and we can make it work if you cooperate."

"You told them to bring me here?"

"Yes!"

"In a box?"

"A box? What the hell are you talking about?"

The other men glanced at us, listening.

I forced my voice calm and flat.

"Do you have any data records from the large engine you've tested?"

Victor examined the gages and the computer screens on his console.

"Keep the chill down going," he ordered the men. "Let me know if there is any problem, I'll be here in the back."

He turned towards me.

"Come with me," he said, and led me towards the back of the control room where he opened a metal door.

I followed him. The blond muscle man grabbed my arm and stopped me from entering. He peeked through the door.

"What do you want?" Petrescu asked him, irritated.

"What's in this room?" the muscleman asked.

"File cabinets and computers."

"He doesn't go anywhere without me, ponyo? Get it to your head, and don't make me problems."

Petrescu didn't reply. He elbowed the blond man away and entered the room making a sign for me to follow. All three of us got in.

The room was indeed filled with file cabinets, two office desks, computers, and one large drafting board.

Victor Petrescu extracted several blueprint rolls from a large drawer. He placed them on the drafting board after adjusting the board to horizontal position.

I unfolded the drawings. They were cross-sections, technical blueprints for a whole, large scale engine assembly. I studied every detail, making sure.

The drawings showed the Lockwell design of their failed engine.

"Where did you get these?" I asked Petrescu.

"It's an outside collaboration, that's all you need to know. Why do you ask? Have you seen this design before?"

"Yes."

"This very design?" Petrescu asked again, an odd anxiety growing in his voice.

"Yes. This design originated with the firm I used to work for."

His face whitened. "How do you know?"

"Just days ago I examined dimensional measurements . Were did you get these drawings from?"

"Conta told me this design came from the Fengyuan Institute in Beijing," Victor said, his face white, transfigured. "I know for sure the Chinese have manufactured the parts, I saw it assembled."

"Where did you test it?"

He answered with reluctance. "I had to travel. That engine blew up. Several people died."

"Xi'an," I said. "Base 067. Were you there?"

He nodded and moved his good hand over his body.

"Some of these injuries are old, some are new."

There was silence. The muscleman kept his eyes on us, not really understanding and not caring to understand, just making sure I am at a location he could control.

"Did you speak to the Chinese about me, Victor?"

"What do you care? You want credit now?"

"It's not that. But it's important for me to know."

"Yes. I told the Chinese what I told Conta: they need your expertise.

"How did you make the connection with the Chinese?"

"Carmen Conta."

"Who?"

"Conta's wife, Carmen. She brought the connection."

His words hit me in the stomach. Carmen.

"I don't understand, Victor. If you collaborate with the Chinese, why hide like this?"

"This work is not for the Chinese," he said.

"Who is it for?"

"I'll show you later."

He suddenly wavered on his feet. He rested against the drawing board and felt around for a chair dragging it towards him and almost collapsing on it. He reached his breast pocket and produced a plastic container with pills and a flat flask. He popped two pills and swallowed hard from the flask. He appeared to be under both excessive mental stress and physical pain. And we were in the middle of a dangerous test under his direction.

As if reading my thought, Victor glanced at the wall clock, checking the time. He leaned back on the chair, relaxing.

"Years ago, Matei," he began speaking, "I got back from those hospitals abroad and I had nothing. Indeed I was officially dead and buried, like you said. The new managers at the institute gave me the runaround. There was some disability pay available but it was hard to get without connections. My apartment had been allocated to some other people."

He wiped his forehead with the sleeve of his shirt.

"It was Bolek who found me. After December 89 he'd dropped that communist party activist shit and was all business. He got me working on this. As much as I despised him, he got me a purpose, something to hang on to, a reason to live. It took me several years to put together the original MRFEM engine from the parts transported from the institute by Bolek's men that night. Some of the parts had to be re-manufactured. But we put it together, and used the spare parts to make a second one. The one we're testing now."

He turned towards me.

"Remember when Bolek came at the Institute that morning, on December 22nd?"

I nodded.

"He had traveled with Ceausescu to Iran, several days before, between 18th and 20th of December 1989. Some deal was made on the MRFEM. The Iranians and other parties were very interested. Bolek had sold them the MRFEM project as a done deal, as if the engine design was finalized and in production. He kept the contacts in the Middle East and he still does. He brings in the deals."

"Bolek? How old is the son of a bitch?"

"He's over seventy. Conta joined in later. It was him to offer the option to work and test here, hidden. Bolek and Conta knew each other from before. You can't do such research and development officially anymore, we got cut off from all the arms deals we had, even with legitimate governments. Carmen Conta brought in the Chinese, I don't know how and where from. I don't care. You're saying these Chinese blueprints are your design? Did they steal it from the States? I don't give a damn. All I'm interested in is to make this engine work, it's the only thing that keeps me going. It's the only thing keeping me away from putting a bullet in my head."

I looked at his face. Brothers in fate. Until when?

"You need a beach for that, brother," I said.

"What?"

"It's a thing about dying my good friend. You need the proper place. There is a beach I know back home in California, a wonderful place to die at sunset."

He looked at me, without understanding.

"Now that you are here, Matei," he said, "either you help me, or fuck off. That's all."

The metal door opened.

"We're about ready" a man said, through the open door.

Petrescu turned around, painfully.

"I'm coming," he said, and he stood up.

***

A sound like a whimper flew through the strong steel structures holding the engine. The next second, the sharp noise of shockwaves hit the surrounding walls and penetrated to us through the wall. The flexible cables around the engine jerked, as the device produced its first spit of thrust. Ice formed during the chill down on various fixtures detached and flew away carried by the strong air stream entrained by the engine's jet. As steady chemical combustion settled, the engine exhaust became transparent, almost invisible: hydrogen burns in oxygen without obvious flame producing transparent, superheated steam.

The electromagnetic enhancement picked up and started growing steadily. The engine thrust started increasing as its jet plume on the monitors elongated, achieving a stronger and stronger blue glow due to ionization. After a minute, the small engine, no larger than a helicopter engine achieved hard thrust, as much as an engine powering a 747.

"Getting full reads," one of the test men announced.

Ninety seconds more went by on the digital clock.

"All right, data is good. Shut down," Petrescu ordered.

The controllers operated the valves. The flow of propellants was cut-off in special sequences, while purge gases started flowing at high pressure just seconds prior to propellant cut-offs. Within several seconds, the engine sat quietly on its fixtures, vapor of hot gas surrounding it, evacuated by purges and ventilation.

One of the men whistled. Others clapped their hands. I felt relief myself. Something had been achieved. A technical success. For a second, everyone had forgotten about the darkness.

"Wrap up," Petrescu ordered, and then turned towards me and said, "Let me show you the package."

6 0

Victor led me through the submarine-like steel door into the engine cell. Instead of heading towards the test cell, he walked to a wall steel panel and pulled a large lever on its side. The lever opened a steel door which seemed to be an emergency exit. It led out onto a metal stair case. I stepped on the steel stairs and then I looked up, with a jolt in my chest. There, above, was the open sky. There had been less than forty eight hours since my capture, less than forty eight hours since I had seen the sky for the last time. It could have been ten years as well.

I filled my lungs with the fresh air. I felt the smells of the city, the smells of normal life.

The muscleman pushed on my shoulder. "Move."

Victor had walked further ahead. I caught up with him. We crossed the cracked concrete pavement of several alleys. In between the concrete strips, overgrown grass and thick weeds covered the land.

We headed to a group of massive circular reservoirs of the kind used for the storage of crude oil, rusty and seemingly in need of repair. Once close to the rusty wall of the leftmost reservoir, Victor extracted a small plastic box from his pocket. It seemed a garage opener remote. He pushed a button on the box. A large trap door opened in the rusty wall. It had been well camouflaged by the streaks of rust.

Victor walked in through the door. "Come in," he called.

The muscleman waited for me to go in. He wasn't nervous. That place, he seemed familiar with.

I entered.

I found myself in a tall narrow room lit by fluorescent lamps, and surrounded by clear, thick plastic sheets falling from the ceiling.

Petrescu triggered the door mechanism and closed it. Suddenly, a strong gush of air started sweeping the room.

"Clean your feet!" Petrescu requested and pointed to a rectangular device on the floor.

I understood. It was a cleaning room. I stuck my foot into the machine opening. Brushes started scraping my boot and part of my jeans while air was sucked through a vacuuming device.

After cleaning, Victor led the way through the plastic sheets. We emerged into the circular space inside the reservoir. The floor was paved with smoothed concrete painted over with industrial strength gray oil paint. Strong fluorescent lamps flooded the space with light. Yellow scaffolds of different sizes were placed in the middle of the circular space.

Fixed in the scaffolding at shoulder height elevation, was a sinister object painted in dark green. It looked like a mixed breed between a delta wing jet fighter and a torpedo. About twenty to twenty five feet long, without a cockpit, it looked like a blind and sinister worm of death.

I examined the fuselage. "A cruise missile," I said.

Victor patted the missile with his good hand.

"Once piece of an ugly baby," he said. "That's the package, a P-15 naval missile. Vintage USSR design by the Raduga Bureau."

He turned towards the fuselage and patted its metal again.

"Only one single moment of fame for this baby," he continued. "1967, at the end of the Six Days War. It was the only hit the Egyptians scored against the Israelis. The Israelis maneuvered an old WW II destroyer around Port Said and it got sunk by a couple of these."

He began walking around the missile explaining in loud voice.

"Lots of P-15's around. Russian export versions mostly, you find them in Egypt and Syria. You can get Chinese made copies around too, the HY-1's, cheap. They're old, ineffective and use some really nasty liquid propellants: amine and nitric acid. Nobody likes them."

He grinned. "Ideal material. Everybody is getting rid of them."

I looked around. Three men dressed in dark overalls stood by one of the scaffolds, waiting. They were careful but relaxed, exchanging a few words among themselves.

I felt the metal on one of the missile's wings. Riveted aluminium.

"What do you do with the P-15?"

Victor pointed to the nozzle mouth opening at the end of the fuselage.

"Replace this old engine with a MRFEM. The P-15 has the perfect dimension. The tanks and the ducts must be changed and adapted to cryogenics, the force fixtures must be replaced, but it all fits perfectly. After the first one fired, we received strong demands for one more. Conta is pressing hard for it."

"One of these was fired?"

"Yes, the very first one. With pretty interesting results."

"When and where did you fire it?"

His reluctance returned, with a trace of hostility. But he decided to talk.

"It wasn't here, and I didn't participate. We packaged everything together and sent it away. We told them they would fire at their own risk. I trained some people in the test stand, and off they went."

"What people? Romanians?"

"No. They spoke Romanian well but they were not Romanians."

"Where did they fire the missile?

"Somewhere Far East," he said. "Over the Pacific."

"Do you have flight data?"

"No. There is no flight instrumentation, too expensive, too complicated. This is tinkering, not scientific engineering. We got some visual observations, and, actually, some things we found out from the Chinese, those were very interesting."

"Did the Chinese fire it?"

"No. There was a different party that fired. We just let the Chinese know ahead of time about it, and they've tracked it. They've also intercepted American communications."

At the thought, he dropped his reluctance, preoccupied.

"There are some really strange things that happened during flight." he said. "The original P-15 was designed to be launched from a ramp by a solid fuel booster mounted under its belly. The missile is fired from a ship: it goes up at an angle pushed by the booster under its belly, then it levels off, drops the booster and flies at sea level on its own engine pretty much as fast as a passenger jet. It detects the target ship, homes in, and hits it. Forty to forty four kilometers max range. The original engine gets about nine hundred kilogram force[15] of thrust."

---

[15] 2000 pounds force

He paused, lost in thought. I stood quiet, let him spill out his thoughts. He continued, preoccupied.

"The MRFEM pushes ten times as much. With a MRFEM installed on it, the P-15 also has a much longer range. So I changed the flight controls: I set it up to launch and keep climbing to very high altitude and only there level its trajectory. This thing can fly into the stratosphere, and even reach orbit for all I know. Incredible capability. The problem is that it will melt in the process, or so I thought. My calculations show that once it goes past Mach 3 the heat on the wings and nose is more than these materials can take. But the thinner the air, the longer it lasts, that's why I wanted it fly as high as possible, to last longer."

He was now completely captivated. It was clear to me he didn't realize the full consequences of his work. The memory of my helicopter flight over the Mojave Desert came into my mind, the panic at the Edwards Air Force Base, the vague satellite pictures of the strange object approaching the West Coast.

"How was it fired?" I asked.

"A simple rail. It doesn't need its original booster, the MRFEM is at full throttle at the release time, it takes off like a bullet. They used a cargo ship."

"They? They who, Victor?"

"People with enough money and motivation. Stop asking that."

He followed on his previous thoughts.

"One strange thing I was talking about," he said. "The Chinese asked how we made the missile stealthy. They were very interested, they said the Americans couldn't shoot it down, their interceptors kept missing."

He turned his head watching me with a strong gleam in his eyes.

"Yes. It reached the American West Coast," he said.

He was proud. He was insane.

"What generated the stealth then?" I asked.

"I'm not sure. I thought about it. The MRFEM discharge is strongly ionized and I believe it charges the fuselage, or initiates some discharge, it creates some plasma gas layer around the body. Something that absorbs or scatters the radar waves and confuses the interceptor rocket guidance systems."

He snapped his fingers.

"And that's why it didn't melt and break from the heat right away," he exclaimed. "The discharge layer around its body reduces the friction with air. It's been documented before."

His excitement at the technical achievement was almost contaminating. What he said made sense. I looked at him, his face preoccupied, his eyes lit by the mad passion behind them. I was searching for the old Victor, my old friend. But we were no longer together at the Institute pushing science against a retarded communist system and sharing enthusiasm and passion for what we did. An abyss of too many years, too many injuries and pains, and too much thwarted history was between us. I didn't question his sanity, or mine. In different ways, we were both insane. Victor, kept alive only by the traces of science left in a project of possible murderous nature of which he was oblivious. And me, chasing my past, trying to unveil the nature of a cage I felt locked around me ever since I had followed Hal Mason. The difference between us was given only by residuals of belief in right and wrong I still carried in my madness. Victor, my dead old friend seemed to have lost that judgment ability altogether.

I grabbed his shoulders. "Do you understand what you're doing, Victor?" I asked, trying to shake him. He jerked and tried to push me back.

I didn't let go. "What sort of warhead was there? Who was to be killed? What was to be destroyed?"

He struggled off my lock, his good hand firmly grasping my forearm and pushing it away, the prosthetic arm clumsily pressing on my other arm.

I let go. He stepped back and steadied on his feet looking at me, through me.

"I don't know," he whispered. "I don't fucking know!" he yelled. "And who the fuck are you with these questions?! Go to hell!"

He slammed his fist on the wing of the missile and turned back, walking around nervously. The men in black overalls stopped talking, watching us, surprised. The blond muscle man stood several feet away. The argument between me and Victor did not disturb him. His focus stayed on me, steady.

I heard the entrance door mechanism buzzing and saw daylight coming through the square opening filtered by the plastic sheets at the entrance. Vague silhouettes moved fast behind the sheets.

Swiftly, four men emerged into the room. They hadn't bothered with the cleaning. Two of them walked fast towards the center of the large room, while the other two positioned themselves along the round walls securing the whole floor. The men were dressed in black turtleneck shirts and blue or gray suits, their hair cut very short. They made no noise, said no word.

Following them, Raoul Conta emerged through the layers of clear plastic into the missile room. His walk was slow, expectant, hands in pockets, eyes poking in all directions.

There was dead silence.

The two men in the center came closer. One of them was wearing headphones.

The other one raised his hands in the air and spoke very loudly.

"I request everyone stay where you are. We need to address a security problem we seem to have."

He seemed in the lead, not Conta. He spoke with an accent and rigid grammar. He eyed the blond bodyguard and pointed at me.

"You with him all the time?"

"In my sight all the time," the blond man said.

"And him?" the man in the gray suit made a sign towards Victor.

The blond man shrugged. "They did that engine test. They talked a lot and then he brought him here to show him around."

The man with the headphones raised his hand, suddenly.

"It came again!" he said. "It's from here somewhere. It was strong."

The lead man's face frowned. He came to me.

"Turn around!" he ordered.

He searched me thoroughly.

"Check the others," he ordered to the other men.

The men in black overalls were searched as well.

"Nothing!" the men in suits reported.

"What's the problem?" Victor asked.

"It's a security matter, Mr. Petrescu," the lead man answered, his courtesy cold. "Somewhere in here there is a tracking device. It broadcasts a signal at various time intervals. We don't know to whom, and why."

Victor frowned. He quickly looked at Conta who was standing in the middle of the floor, hands in his pockets, waiting.

The man with the headphones pulled a small device from his pocked and read its readings, concentrated. He turned around as if searching for good reception for the device. He stiffened, then he stepped towards me. His eyes searched my clothes, my hands, focused, thinking.

"Take your shoes off!" he ordered.

I took off my boots. He searched their inside, puling out the insoles. He produced a knife from his pocket and stabbed the foam of the insole of one boot ripping off the material. After repeating the operation on the second boot, he extracted a fistful of foam crumbles from it and dropped the boot on the floor. With great care he opened his palm and sorted through the small fragments of foam on his palm, extracting a small black patch. He studied the patch, then he turned towards the lead man and handed him the black patch. Conta walked slowly approached them. There was dead silence in the room.

"It's an electronic beacon," the detection man explained. "It sends a signal at various time intervals depending on how fast it's charging. And it's charging when he walks."

Conta took the small black device from the other man's hand and studied it slowly, weighing the significance of the finding.

The two security men looked at me, their eyes suddenly filled with cruel cold ferocity. The lead man came to me, his face one inch from mine, his eyes lit with dark brightness. He breathed in my face.

"Who do you work for?" he asked in a whispered hiss. "Who sent you?"

My mind emptied.

"I work for nobody," I said. "Nobody sent me."

"You will sweat it out, my friend, along with your blood, so spear us the waste of time and talk. Who sent you? Who do you work for?"

"Nobody sent me," I repeated.

The other man came next to me. They grabbed my arms and forced plastic ties on my wrists and tied them to my throat with more ties.

I didn't fight. There was no point. I focused in avoiding suffocation.

The lead man ordered something to his other two men, several barks in a foreign guttural language.

Conta raised his hands sideways requesting attention.

"Listen everyone. Proceed to evacuation. Everybody out, secure and lock all exits."

He turned towards the security men.

"You! Take everybody to the test stands. Victor, please go with them. I'll take Salajan with me."

The security men didn't like the arrangement. They scrutinized Conta with squinted eyes, but said nothing. Conta made a sign to the blond muscle man and handed him a set of keys.

"Koseak, you'll drive."

The security men pushed me through the plastic sheets, and out through the square door. Outside, two SUV's and one large Mercedes sedan were parked on the dirt strip by the reservoir's wall. The city was out there, oozing its scents in the air. Suddenly, I felt exhaustion instead of terror. I had lost track of facts. Reality, for once, had beaten the surreal. And death was close again.

"*Let it come,*" I thought, "*Fucking hell, let's get this over with.*"

61

Koseak got the Mercedes moving. The group of cars headed back towards the building where the MORPHEM test stand was hidden. The first SUV ahead had reached the building already and the second was almost there. The bodyguard stepped on the gas and the Mercedes jerked forward. It bounced over the pavement of the decrepit alleys, shaking hard when the wheels alternatively met concrete and dirt. The ties around my throat choked my breath.

Three other SUV's emerged from the deserted refinery installations and rushed to the oil reservoir where the missile was hidden. Silhouettes of men carrying rifles came out of the cars and moved around the reservoir taking defense positions.

Conta's face came next to mine. Mixed scents of exotic after shave and bad breath hit my nostrils.

"Remember one thing, Salajan," he said in a growling whisper. "I can cut deals. I have the right cards in my hand. I can cut a deal with whoever sent you here. All I need is the right approach. Let me know who sent you, and I'll figure out the proper approach. It's gonna be good for everyone. Including yourself."

I turned with difficulty towards him, watching him without a word. His mouth was grinning and his eyes had their typical intense flicker. But confidence was gone from that flicker.

We reached the building. The technicians in black overalls were already going up the steel staircase escorted by one security man and led by Victor Petrescu towards the emergency access door.

Conta got out of the car.

"Leave me the keys in there!" he ordered the bodyguard. "Get Salajan out."

Koseak came and grabbed my arm, pulling brutally. The ties choked again my throat. The security men waiting by their SUV's watched and grinned.

A sudden cry came from one of them. He bent, grabbed his belly, and his hands reddened with blood. The side windows of the car behind him got pulverized in a thousand small chunks.

The other men crouched, guns in hands.

A silent salvo of bullets hit the vehicle again, with a rippling sound of metal hitting metal.

"Snipers!" Koseac yelled from the depth of his lungs. "Snipers!"

He viciously dragged me towards the stairs. Without any warning sound, his arm got shattered into strips of flesh and broken bone. He didn't get to feel the pain. Another bullet pulverized the right side of his head, hurling him against the wall.

The remaining security men rushed up the steel stairs. Conta threw himself into the driver seat of the Mercedes. The car jerked and took off, throwing off dirt from the spinning tires.

I rolled on the ground pulling at the ties around my throat to avoid choking. I pushed with my feet, crawling on my back towards the base of the wall, searching for protection.

Hand guns started popping in rapid fire from the steel stair case above, chaotically and with unknown efficiency. The attackers remained hidden, firing with perfect stealth.

Across the dirt fields and alleys, guns started barking around the large oil tank as well. Automatic rifles, firing in frenzy.

A man's arm holding a handgun extended over the rail of the staircase platform above my head. Its wrist twisted the gun downwards. The barrel pointed at me.

I jerked and rolled to my left. The gun above fired, slugs drilling the ground inches away. I kept rolling at random, with desperate vigor, fighting for breath as the weapon above kept fieing, the bullets searching for my flesh. A new ripple of slugs hit the steel stairs above and the arm holding the gun disappeared. I rolled back, tight against the wall.

The shooting around the reservoir diminished in intensity. Several more isolated shots came, and then there was silence.

Blood dripped on my leg from the stairs. It was warm. I pulled my leg away. The drip became a steady thin red stream, pooling on the dirt.

Fast steps approached in a run. A silhouette bent over me and a face painted in black and green studied me. A short knife cut the ties around my wrists and throat.

"What's in here?" the face asked me in a calm whisper. "What's in this building?"

The words had been spoken in English, with clear American accent.

"Oh God," I said. Uncontrollable relief forced my body to give in, for a moment. "Jesus Christ," I cried in a whisper.

He pulled on my shirt.

"What's in this building?" he asked again.

I refocused.

"It's a test stand."

"You hurt?" he asked.

"No."

"Good. My name is Porter. From now on you stay next to me, no matter what happens."

"My name is Mathew Salagen. I was kidnapped."

"I know who you are. Let's get movin' !"

I stood up and looked around. At various distances along the building several other men dressed in camouflage gear were crouched in firing positions, weapons ready.

"Is this the only access?" the soldier asked, pointing to the stairs.

"There is another access, from underground."

He turned around and mumbled. He was speaking on his headset. The group of men changed their configuration in silence, fast, efficient. Two of them climbed the building with the agility of monkeys, using the ducts and pipes and their fixtures for support, avoiding the stairs.

"Watch out for the blast," the soldier warned and pushed me against the wall.

The blast threw a jolt through the whole network of steel pipes, platforms and walls. Weapons fired. More men rushed though the stairs. Muffled gun shots came from inside the building and then stopped. For another minute nothing happened, then, the sound of another, weaker blast came.

"Come with me," Porter said and headed towards the stairs.

I followed him, careful at my steps, barefoot. On the first platform, the corpse of the security man who fired at me lay on a side, pools of dark red blood spreading on the steel plate around him. I stepped around the corpse.

Two other men lay dead further up along the steel steps. One of them was dressed in black overalls. He was lying there in fetal position, a grimace of pain frozen on his features.

"Come on, let's move," the soldier urged.

The emergency steel door had been torn off and twisted by the blast, its blackened residuals still holding on the hinges.

I grabbed the soldier's arm.

"Careful. There are fuel ducts inside. They're probably depleted of propellant, but there are tanks of liquid hydrogen and oxygen in there. Watch your fire. We can all be blown up into vapor."

"Thanks," he said, and mumbled instructions in his mike piece.

"And one more thing," I said holding him back. "Don't fire at the men in black overalls, they're engineers, they're not armed."

"Yeah," he said. "Now, let's get movin'."

The fourth security man lay on the floor squeezed in between two thick ducts, riddled with slugs. Hundreds of empty shells on the floor poked at my bare feet.

The small steel door accessing the control room had been blasted as well. I followed Porter inside with the strange hope that I would not see corpses anymore, that Victor and his men were alive.

They were. Cornered on the extremity of the control room, facing the wall, hands on the back of their heads, the two surviving technicians and the three engineers I met earlier during the engine test stood quietly under the watch of two commandos holding their weapons ready.

Victor Petrescu had collapsed on the chair at the control table, his good arm holding tight against his thigh. The fabric of his pants was imbibed with blood.

I rushed to him. His face seemed in shock, oblivious.

"Victor," I called at him. "You're hurt, man. Let me see how bad it is."

He watched me with unfocused eyes, without a word.

Another soldier came next to us. He was a thin and agile man, carrying a sophisticated sniper rifle on his back while holding ready a small submachine gun fitted with a silencer. He pulled an elastic bandage from a small pack he was carrying and handed it to Porter who threw it at me.

"Wrap his thigh real tight," he instructed. "It'll stop the bleeding."

I ripped off the fabric of Victor's slacks. A prosthetic leg with a mechanical knee joint was strapped on his thigh. His leg had been amputated several inches above the knee. The mechanical joint was deformed by a bullet hit. Another bullet had ripped through the flesh and muscle of his thigh. I unstrapped the prosthetic leg and wrapped Victor's thigh the best I could.

"We'll have to get him to a hospital ASAP," I said.

The soldier nodded, but said nothing.

Several other troops were moving fast in and out of the test cell. I glanced at the main TV screen which was still on. Their shadows were moving fast around the MRFEM engine.

They were planting explosives.

"What are you guys doing?" I asked Porter, intrigued. Suspicion began curling inside my guts. "What the hell is going on?"

He was watching the door, tensely listening to his ear piece.

"Shut up!" he said.

I rose on my feet, ready to demand an explanation.

"Just shut the fuck up!" he urged in a whisper, and something in his tensed voice made me freeze.

A man dressed in the same type of camouflage outfit entered the room. By the way he moved and behaved he seemed to be the man in charge.

"Which one is Salagen?" he asked.

Porter jerked his head towards me.

The lead man came to me.

"I need some information and I need it fast," he said, his tone of voice harsh, expecting compliance.

I didn't answer. The curling feeling in my guts intensified to a spasm.

"The missile hidden in the petroleum tank," the man spoke, "does it have a warhead installed?"

"I don't know," I said. "Probably not."

"Are there other materials hidden in any other reservoir?"

"I don't know."

A soldier carrying a black case came from the test stand, placed the case on the control desk and opened it.

"Carl, the charges are set," he reported to the lead man. "Forget the rest," he added. "We blow up the reservoir and this stand here, they're out of business."

The man named Carl turned and watched him, thinking.

"Lemme sort these guys out," he said.

We all waited. I tried to step forward, ready to ask Carl to get Victor out for some treatment, when I felt the grip on my arm. Porter made a discrete negative sigh with his head.

Carl walked to the group of prisoners standing by the wall. He tapped one of the men oh his shoulder.

"You, what's your name?"

The man turned around.

"Don't turn, don't move!" Carl yelled.

The man understood English. He obeyed.

"Just state your names," Carl said.

Each man was asked his name, some of them twice. Carl was careful, concentrating. He seemed to have memorized some list of names, and mentally checking each man's name against it. He had problems with the Romanian pronunciation of the men.

"All right," Carl said. He jerked his head towards his aide. "All set here?"

"All set," the aide said. "But we gotta clean up the personnel first."

"I know. Set up the timer."

"How much time you need here?"

"Set it for ten minutes. Local interventions must be on their way, there is not much time."

The aide worked on the black box.

"Ten minutes, counting," he said.

Carl eyed Porter and the soldiers guarding the prisoners. "Listen up," he called. "All of you, get to the reservoir on the double. Finish the job there."

The two men guarding the technicians stepped back, moved their weapons on the straps towards their backs and left the room without a word.

Carl's aide remained. He behaved like a very close buddy of Carl.

"Porter, you two get moving as well," Carl ordered.

Porter didn't move. The sniper didn't move either. Porter's body showed a false nonchalant relaxation.

"Don't fuck with me, Carl," he said.

The feel of danger fell hard again on my instinct. Things didn't make sense. I didn't move, didn't speak. The surreal. The real. Aberrantly intermingled.

"You two want to have fun and watch?" Carl asked with a grin.

Porter narrowed his eyes.

"Watch what, Carl?"

Carl threw a short hoarse laugh. He stepped to the middle of the room. His aide man came next to him.

And reality slipped. My eyes recorded, yet my brain refused to process the record right away.

Carl and his man raised their compact machine guns. The weapons silently coughed in rapid cadence. Streams of hot slugs bit and ripped off flesh and bone in the bodies of the unarmed men standing with their face against the wall. Some turned and raised their open palms against the slugs and got cut in half by the volley of lead. The guns spat their load till the end of their clip capacity, when all there was left were bloodied bodies on the floor.

Carl and his man moved fast. Hand guns in their hands they shot each victim in the head at close range emptying their clips.

My breath had stopped. The air around me became a red blur. Desperation and anger filled my chest and spilled out in mad fury. I cried from the depth of my soul and charged at Carl and his man. They turned and fired their guns at me, both clicking empty.

I grabbed Carl and threw him against the test stand console. His back hit the metal edge and he gasped in pain. Carl's aide threw a hard punch in my stomach. Panting and still raging, I charged and rushed him against the wall. His back crashed hard against the concrete, but not hard enough. His knee hit hard on my plexus and took out the rest of the strength and breath I had. Carl kicked me hard on my ribs. They both grabbed me and threw me against the wall. I fell on floor, depleted.

Breathing hard, they watched me with dead eyes and grabbed fresh ammunition clips from their packs, replacing the empty ones on their ugly machine guns.

"Hold it right there," Porter said very loudly and very clearly, just before they had time to cock their weapons, and his voice, in spite of the apparent calm, froze the men's motion.

They watched Porter carefully.

"What's the deal, Porter?" Carl asked.

"Salagen is not your problem," Porter said. He made a move with his chin, indicating the weapon in Carl's hand. "If you move one more inch you're dead, both of you," he added.

The other soldier, the sniper, took position against the wall, his machine gun covering Carl and his man at cross angle from Porter.

Carl flashed them with an angry look. "The order is for a total clean up here," he said. "Salagen included."

"The orders have changed."

"Says fucking who?"

"I got my orders. I'm taking charge of Salagen."

None of them moved or said anything. They were careful even how they breathed.

And then Carl's hand moved in a flash. Simultaneously he turned left and ducked towards the floor.

He wasn't fast enough. Porter's body didn't move. Only the gun in his hands burst silently and precisely. The sniper man fired simultaneously.

The pack of slugs threw Carl and his man backwards towards the bodies of their victims. Yet their body armor took the slugs and kept them alive. Injured and bleeding, they both rolled on the floor and fired back.

Porter and the sniper moved like ghosts. The stream of bullets fired by Carl and his man hit only empty concrete and steel. Deadly ricochets bounced and flew around the room.

Four guns kept firing simultaneously. And then there was silence.

Slowly, my senses became aware of a new and pure reality that seemed fresh, tangible. As if there had been a threshold of desperation and surreal which, if passed beyond, would empower one with a new sort of knowledge and understanding closer to revelation rather than logic and reason.

And I so clearly observed in accurate detail that the air was full of smoke, the smell of sulfur from the burnt gunpowder mixed with the strong scent of blood. Victor Petrescu lay on the floor. I knew he was dead. Carl and his man were also dead, having joined their victims in whatever afterlife was waiting for them. In my new perception, all dead men in the room had become empty shells just like the spent cartridges filling the floors.

'*There are souls, floating around*', I thought, and almost searched the smoke for their shadows.

Gradually, I became aware of the beeping sound in the background. It came from the black timer box.

I stood up slowly. The acuity of my perception was almost nauseating. I leaned against the wall, exhausted.

Porter held me. The slender sniper grabbed my arm.

"Are you OK?" he asked.

The voice. It was the voice of a woman.

I look closely at the painted face. Under the paint, the features were familiar, and in my newly acquired acuity of perception I recognized the features with clarity.

"Jane," I said. "Jane."

"How're you doing, cowboy?" she asked.

6 2

She held my head and kissed me. A quick brush with her lips. Her skin had a synthetic smell, from the camouflage paint.

Porter threw a curious look at us and went to the beeping black case. He bent over it, studying it without touching anything.

I searched Jane's face for a connection with the woman I knew. I couldn't find any.

"Who are you people?" I asked.

"I'll explain," she said.

"Why didn't you stop them?"

"We didn't know what they had in mind."

"Who's responsible for this?"

"It's complicated, Matt. These men were mercenaries."

"Mercenaries?"

"Paid soldiers, yes."

"And you?"

"We're all professional soldiers. My mission is to get you out of here alive."

"Who sent you?"

"Hal Mason. I'll explain everything, but now we got to leave!"

Hal. How? I gave up even formulating the thought. I pushed the question away. Everything had happened too fast. But there were old questions, freed up and burning in my chest. I made up my mind.

"You and Porter leave wherever you need to leave, Jane," I said. "There is too much unfinished business here, things chained to my life. I need to unlock it all."

"What do you want to do?" she asked.

I didn't answer. I checked the clothes and equipment on the dead bodies of Carl and his man. Carl's aide seemed my size. I removed his boots and tried them on. They fit. I picked one of the submachine guns from the floor and recovered spare ammo clips from the men's packs. Carl's pistol was a compact .40 caliber Smith and Wesson. There were still spare clips for it in his pack.

"What are you doing?" Jane asked again.

I kept silent. I gently rolled Victor's body on his back. I pressed his eye lids closed and laid his hands on his chest. I did the same for the other dead men. Porter and Jane watched, their weapons ready, nervously listening to the beeping sound.

"I need a candle," I said.

They looked at me perplexed.

"What do you need a candle for?" Porter asked calmly.

"It's a tradition. Light for the souls of the dead."

"I have a lighter," he said.

He produced a one dollar green plastic lighter.

"I'm gonna say a prayer," I said. "Keep it lit. Don't let it extinguish, you understand?"

"All right," he said.

I closed my eyes and said a prayer, in Romanian. I opened my eyes. The cheap lighter was still lit in Porter's hand, and he was grimacing, focusing to keep the flame going.

"Thank you," I said.

He nodded and pocketed the lighter.

"Now, Mr. Salagen, we need to leave," he pointed to the black box. "We have less than six minutes left.

I stood up and indicated the door through which Conta had brought me in the first time. "This door leads to an underground tunnel, which in turn leads to the office of the man who's the mastermind behind all this hidden weapon development business. He's got materials in his office I need to see. I need to understand why a lot of people were killed, and why I lived what I lived through. I just have to do it."

Porter and Jane exchanged a look. Neither said anything.

"You two have to understand where I stand," I continued. "I can't just walk out of here without getting some sort of a closure. It's personal. I know the danger, but I need to do it."

Porter scratched his ear. "No matter what you want to do, we need to get the hell out."

"That tunnel you mentioned," Jane said. "Where does it lead?"

"Into a different building."

"What sort of access ways we're talking about?"

"Concrete stairs, four flights down at this end, four flights up at the other end."

"I don't like it," Porter said.

"It allows us to separate from the others," Jane said.

"We can be trapped on the stair cases."

"We did stairs before."

He nodded, with a bad frown on his face.

"One important thing," I said. "There are cryogenic propellant tanks somewhere in here. Those can have a large destruction radius. I don't know their capacity."

Porter's face froze. "Fuck," he said.

"It's four minutes left now," Jane said. "Let's move."

Porter opened the access door carefully. He took the lead, weapon ready. Jane pushed me in between them, her weapon ready as well.

We walked down the stairs checking the angles at every turn. At the foot of the stairs, the tunnel access door was locked. Porter broke it with carefully aimed shots, kicked the door opened and searched the tunnel.

"Stay behind me," he ordered and we followed him into the tunnel. "What's the timing?" he asked Jane.

"Three minutes," she said.

We reached the door at the other end. Jane pointed to the submachine gun I was carrying.

"Have you ever used one of these?" she asked.

"No."

She showed me the safety and selector mechanism. I set the weapon on bursts of three shots.

"I'll blast the door," Porter said. "Assume enemy presence beyond this point."

The ground shook. A wave of pressure blasted though the tunnel. Stronger, a second wave followed, this time bringing intense heat with it. Noises of crushed metal and hard structure crashes reverberated on the concrete walls. I felt like a rat trapped in a whole and about to be burned alive.

Porter fired at the door's lock. The lock broke and the door cracked open.

We exited the tunnel. The staircase was full of smoke and the stairs were covered with chunks of concrete. Daylight came through large holes in the concrete wall up the stairs. The blast had knocked off parts of the structure.

With Porter on the lead we climbed up the stairs through the first two floors. No one seemed to be around.

Suddenly Porter stopped and listened.

An object fell from above. It bounced and rolled on the stairs and then bounced again. A dark, round piece of metal.

"Hand grenades!" Jane warned, but Porter had already sprung out without a noise. He grabbed the object and threw it back fast, up the stairs.

The detonation came sharply, amplified by the reverberation of the concrete walls.

Porter extracted a hand grenade of his own from a pocket of his uniform. Jane produced one as well. Perfectly synchronized, they both removed the pins and released the levers, counting. Simultaneously, they each threw their grenade up the stairs with trained skill, using the walls to bounce the grenades into reaching behind the upper stairs into hidden corners.

The two detonations came in the same time, with similar sharpness.

"Go!" Porter ordered, even before the sound reverberation was out.

He rushed up the stairs at fast speed, followed by Jane, their weapons angled up and firing rapid bursts.

I ran after them.

All the way through the top of the stairs we found no one, dead or alive.

The wall had collapsed at the top of the stairs. The access door towards the passageway had been bent and twisted. Beyond the large holes in the wall, there was darkness.

Porter and Jane crouched and talked in a strange sign language. They prepared new grenades, fragmentation type. Perfectly synchronized again they threw the grenades in opposite directions along the passageway. Yells came from behind the walls, cut off by the blasts. Porter rolled into the passageway trough an opening on the collapsed wall. His weapon fired silently. Jane followed, and covered the opposite direction.

From far along the passage way a weapon responded, loudly. Slugs hit Porter in the chest. He shook and fell on the floor. I fired at corridor section where the muzzle flashes came from. My gun spat silent bursts of bullet triplets. A shadow moved. I jerked the gun towards it, and kept firing. The slugs hit the shadow which became the silhouette of a man bending and collapsing into a dark mound on the floor.

Jane and I stood still, eyes strained to pain level, searching the ill lit corridor, listening. There was no more fire, no more movement.

Porter gasped, rolled slowly on the floor and cursed.

"Porter!" I whispered. "How bad is it?"

"Calm down," he said, and cursed again. "Fucking nine millimeters."

He patted on his chest metal plate.

"You OK?" Jane asked him, in a low whisper.

"Yeah, let's move," he said, and raised his eyebrows at me.

"Salagen, which way?"

The darkness in the passageway was confusing. I closed my eyes and imagined it lit by fluorescent lights. Conta's men had taken me twice from his office through the tunnel. Each time, we had made a right hand turn towards the stairs.

"This way," I said, and led them along the corridor.

Jane produced a small flashlight and put out just enough light to see the floor. After one turn, I recognized the corridor branching towards Conta's office.

"There," I said.

"Clean it up," Porter said.

They used fragmentation type grenades again. The detonations reverberated dryly against the walls, but nothing else happened.

I stepped forward.

Porter stopped me.

"There's some big fish around," he said, "I feel it."

I nodded and walked straight to the door. It was riddled with shrapnel but it wasn't locked. I held the submachine gun ready, opened the door, and walked in.

Raoul Conta stood motionless in the middle of the office, his face frozen, his hand holding a cell phone to his ear.

The couches had been pushed against the walls like sand bags offering a false protection from expected gun fire.

On one of the couches, Carmen Conta sat tensed, half turned, as if interrupted from an attempt to run somewhere, her face whitened with fear. On the other coach, near her, there was a man dressed in a gray suit who sat on the smooth leather with the rigidity of a plastic dummy.

I stood in the door, my weapon ready, waiting for something to happen. Nothing happened, no one moved, just the tension made the air feel like poison gas.

I walked around the couch, carefully, keeping all of them under my gun. I stopped in front of the man dressed in the gray suit whose eyes were bouncing fast from Carmen to Raoul, to me, and back.

"Howya' doing Mr. Feng?" I asked him in English, steadying the gun barrel towards his face. "Xiao Lin sends his greetings from the grave."

63

Feng Zhijian, the man at the Ocean's star restaurant and the shocked Feng Zhijian watching the Heckler and Koch's suppressor muzzle pointing at his eyes seemed two different men. The man in front of me was hypnotized by the weapon, his face muscles tight as if in a cramp.

On the other couch, Carmen looked like a trapped wild animal, but one determined yet to survive the trap. Her nerves appeared under control.

"Did you bring him here?" I asked her, indicating Feng. "I heard you're in charge of the Chinese connection."

She didn't answer. She watched me for a moment and then her eyes lost focus.

Jane and Porter entered the office without a sound. Conta studied them fast, furtively, assessing the threat, his chances.

"We're running short on time, Matt," Jane said.

I moved the submachine gun on its strap to my back and held out the Smith and Wesson pistol. I placed the barrel in between Feng's eyes.

"Let me explain to you how we stand, Feng," I said. "There are questions burning in my mind and I ache to pull this trigger. Just give me the smallest reason and I will kill you."

"First, I want to know how you got the MORPHEM design. I'm talking about the engine that blew up at Base 67 in Xi'an."

Feng remained silent, his face a mask.

I hit him in the face. He took the blow quietly, stiff, without a gasp, only raising his arm to protect himself. I put the gun back to his head.

"Did Xiao Lin have anything to do with it? Is that why you killed him?"

I hit him harder. I grabbed him by his coat and pressed the barrel on his skin. Adrenaline flowed. I felt I could really pull the trigger.

Feng coughed, choking. With a careful move he raised his hand and pushed me back, slowly but steady, silently indicating a change of mind. I released him from my grip but kept holding the gun on his head

"We do not kill people, Dr. Salagen," he spoke with a strained voice. "I do my business by asking for things, and paying for them. We do not kill people. We pay, or wait for people to change minds, we have patience. Please, do not hurt me; it is of no use to anybody."

The gun felt good in my hand. I hated the man. But I lowered the barrel.

"Good," I said. "Then speak. How did you get the designs?"

"We received a full set of computer design files from our Romanian associates."

It took me a second to process his answer. I hadn't expected it. I looked at Carmen. "You?"

"Aren't you going to put that gun to my head too?" she asked.

"How could you possibly get the designs?"

She glanced towards her husband, still standing in the middle of the office, under Porter's watch. I resisted the urge to go smash Conta's face and focused back on sorting the issues with Feng.

"Who killed Xiao Lin? Why did he have to be killed?"

"I have nothing to do with it, Dr. Salagen," Feng said.

"You said that already. Who did it?"

He went silent again, his face recomposed to a rigid mask. I hit him again, but this time he took the blow inertly, as if ready to suffer any consequence of his silence.

I place the barrel on his left thigh. "I'm going to ask again," I said. "If I get no answer, I'll pull the trigger. You understand?"

He stood still, and silent.

"Who killed Xiao Lin?" I asked. "Why?"

He made a desperate sound, and shook his head.

"We didn't do it!" he cried. "Our American partner insisted! They did it!"

Jane came closer, her eyes focused on Feng. "Your American partner?" she asked, her voice steely cold.

Feng raised his eyes. He registered Jane's presence and his face whitened.

There was a sudden movement in the room. A human form emerged silently from a hiding place, sprung and flip-flopped across the room. Too fast to register or to react. It impacted me and Jane simultaneously throwing us on the floor.

I jerked back, one knee on the ground, the Smith and Wesson ready. The attacker was a woman who now stood still in front of Feng, a small gun in her hand. She fired the gun on Feng's head. Porter's weapon fired simultaneously. Feng's head jerked and his body slumped. Porter's slugs threw the woman against the wall, in the corner of the office. She collapsed on the floor.

I went and rolled her on her back, carefully. Even if smeared with blood, Evelyn Chang's lips retained their gracious shape. Her eyes lost light and became opaque.

"You know her?" Jane asked.

"She's one of his agents. I met her back in the States."

"She shut him up. It was important."

She searched the room, as if finally realizing the place was important. "We need the get the hell out," she said, but her mind was on something else.

"I'm not done," I said and went to Raoul Conta who had crouched on the floor during the shooting. The gun hung heavy in my hand, at the level of his eyes.

"I have questions for you, Raoul," I said. "We can do this the easy way, or the hard way. The choice is yours."

He laughed as he rose to his feet, a hysterical burst. His eyes shot gleams of madness.

"You think I'm fucking scared, Salajan? Fuck you! I've seen gun barrels pointed at me many times. Death pointing at you, I like that. Makes you feel alive. You don't scare me, boy!"

I inhaled, deeply, slowly, and shot him in his right leg. As he cried and bent to grab his thigh, I slapped him hard across his face, just careful to keep him conscious. The blow threw him back against the cabinets. I walked next to him and fired the gun one inch away from his head. The slug made a hole into the metal drawer. The shot and the blow jerked some of the madness out of him.

Carmen screamed. She rose from the couch, suddenly, and rushed to her husband. She kneeled next to him and embraced his head, protecting him, throwing a haunted look at the room, at me, the same look of a trapped animal, this time driven by the primordial instinct to protect something dear and close.

I watched her eyes. There were no words. Just eyes locked into each other.

Porter walked towards me and pushed me away. He re-armed his submachine gun.

"Fuck your questions, Salagen," he spoke in a cruel whistle. "Let's kill them motherfuckers and get out. Step away!"

"Hold on," I grabbed his arm. "I need my answers, Porter!"

"There are no fucking answers! We're done here! You want answers? Pull that trigger, that's your answer. Fucking clean up this shit hole!"

Carmen cried. It was no longer a controlled display but a deep desperation into that cry. Conta's madness dissolved completely, for a moment.

"What the fuck do you want to know, Salajan?" he asked, pushing Carmen away, holding his leg.

"Who did you send to LA to kidnap me? Why?"

"I didn't send anyone. It was Petrescu's stupid obsession with you. He talked to the foreigners. They tried to get you."

"Which foreigners?"

"People who paid for the packages. Petrescu told them over and over he needs you here."

"How did you get the MORPHEM designs?"

"I paid for them."

"Who did you pay?"

"I still have my network in place."

"What network? Give me names!"

"Fuck you! What good are they gonna be to you?"

He wasn't going to provide any good information. I motioned towards the row of metal drawers. "I want these cabinets open."

"Can't do that," he said, stubbornly.

I put the pistol barrel on his other leg and cocked the gun.

"Yeah!" Porter yelled. "Fucking kill them!"

Carmen cried, shaking her head. Raoul defied me with his gleaming eyes from behind her arms. She searched his coat in a febrile motion, extracted a set of keys and threw them at me.

I picked up the keys, looking at her. Carmen's eyes refused mine. There was neither hate in her, nor love, everything was down to basic instinct, live or die, hold on to the male individual who fathered your children. Survive.

I unlocked the cabinets, opening every drawer one by one, examining their contents in a rush. I took out folder after folder, thumbing through the papers and throwing them on the floor.

There were no technical documents. Most of the papers were of financial sort. I didn't quite know what to look for. I just felt something important may be hidden in there.

From between two folders, a large photograph print fell on the floor. I picked it up. In great detail, the picture was showing the woman with black hair whom I knew as Evelyn Chan sitting on a chair, naked, giving a blow job to the Asian man with a cruel face.

I threw the photo down towards Conta.

"Why did you place this on the Internet?"

The picture landed near him, face up. He looked at it as if drunk.

"Petrescu's brilliant idea," he said.

"She's laying there, on that corner," I said.

He looked at me, almost human, normal.

"Too bad," he spoke, grimly. "I liked her."

In a lower drawer there was a row of folders with dark red covers. I opened the first one. It was the dossier of one of the stand engineers. I quickly checked the rest of the folders one by one. They weren't simple personnel files but rather intelligence sort of dossiers with detailed information.

The last two dossiers were Victor Petrescu's and one belonging to a man named Cornel Oniga. I opened the dossier to the first page. A photograph of a young man was glued to a printed form filled out in blue ink. The paper had become yellow and the picture discolored with time.

"I'll be damned," I said, looking at the face of the man in the picture.

I went back to Conta.

"You son of a bitch! What is this? What the fuck is this?!"

He didn't answer. His head was bowed down, fallen on his chest, and he seemed in shock.

Porter touched my shoulder. He was focused on his head set. "Intervention teams arrived," he said.

"Time's up Matt!" Jane said, firmly. "We gotta get out now! This very second!"

I looked around the room. I searched Carmen's face, then Raoul's. His leg was bleeding, but the intervention teams on the spot he was going to make it. I had no sense of revenge, no connection left with anyone there. They were just strangers. People I could leave behind and let them become very distant memories. I packed the red dossiers in my back pack and walked towards the door.

Porter moved with expert hands and tied all of them up to a heavy file cabinet's hinges using similar type of plastic ties as the ones used on me less than two hours before. Jane placed a

"Be good, boys and girls!" he grinned at them. "We only need ten minutes, then you can do whatever you want."

We rushed out of the office.

"What the hell was the matter with you, back there?" I asked Porter. "Were you in the mood to kill people, all of a sudden?"

"Just gave you a hand," he said. "You were so fucking soft in there I tough you were gonna start give candies around."

64

Once outside we began running. At steady, fast, and unforgiving pace. I couldn't keep up. Pain ripped through my lungs, and I fell behind.

Porter pushed me into a narrow space between two thick ducts. Jane threw me a small bottle of water. She used a white cream from a tube to remove the camouflage paint job on her face. Porter grabbed the tube and did the same. They undressed, turned their uniforms inside out and dressed back. The uniforms became some sort of outdoor sports clothing. The weapons and body armor got disassembled, packed and hidden into the back-packs. Porter helped me pack my stuff. I studied his face, cleaned of camouflage paint.

"Do I know you from somewhere?" I asked.

He shook his head, "Nah."

Yet my eyes ran along the features of his face. I was sure I'd seen him before.

We began running again towards the west edge of the refinery perimeter. Porter cut a passage through the mesh wire fence. Beyond the fence there was a double railroad track laid on a wide embankment. A freight train passed at full speed making us hunker down and wait in the tall dry weeds by the fence. Once the train passed, we crossed the tracks.

And suddenly we found ourselves on a regular city street. It was early evening. Decrepit apartment buildings ran parallel to the rail tracks. Scents of food came from open windows. It felt strange to be so close to normal life again.

A block away, a small crowd was gathered, watching the smoke billowing towards the sky from inside the refinery. Several late firefighter trucks and cars crossed the crowd blowing their horns and sirens.

Jane led the way up a street running steeply uphill. As we gathered elevation, I could see the ensemble of the refinery grounds. The firefighter trucks and police cars were crowded around the test stand building which was mostly destroyed and still burning. The large petroleum reservoir towards east looked as if a mad giant had stepped on it, with its top lying flat and distorted on top of various debris and torn side walls.

Jane pulled on my arm, "Let's keep moving, Matt."

After two more blocks up the street, Jane checked a map and said to Porter, "The following cross street."

Porter produced a small pair of binoculars and searched along the street.

"You trust these people?" he asked.

"I trust Mason," she answered stubbornly. "He made this arrangement."

"I'm not sure," Porter said.

I borrowed Porter's binoculars and studied the subject of his mistrust. Half a mile away, two men were standing, waiting discretely by a Nissan sport utility. One of them was dressed in a dark suit and looked very fit. The other one was older and heavier, his white hair combed neatly.

Porter searched the buildings around and unpacked his weapons.

"Keep your headsets on," he said to Jane. "You and Salagen go ahead. If things don't go by the plan, I'll raise hell."

He vanished on a side street. Jane handed me a set of miniature ear and mike pieces. We both put the gear on, and waited. I leaned against a tree. Jane leaned against me and I held her. Her eyes kept watching the street.

"*Go ahead. Make contact,*" Porter's voice came in my ear.

We headed up the street and walked straight towards the two men. Their eyes trained on us immediately. The younger man was also wearing an ear piece. The older man whispered something to him and turned towards us. He wasn't wearing any observable communication gear.

"Doctor Salajan," he said calmly. "We've been waiting, I'm glad to see you have been rescued unharmed."

"How do you know who I am?"

"I'm good at memorizing physiognomies, doctor. I studied pictures of you, carefully. Are you in need of any special care?"

"Thank you, I am all right."

"No injuries?"

"No."

"Good. Does your companion speak the language?"

"No."

"How very impolite, then," he said, switching to a heavily accented English. "My task is simple, and we should not face any difficulties. A chartered private jet has landed two hours ago here on the airport. It's waiting on stand by, fueled. I have arranged for a waiver on formalities, so the flight can be routed directly abroad. I was instructed to expect three people. I see we have two, then?"

He spoke in warm and calm tones, yet without smiling.

"That's correct," Jane said, "two people, thank you. As you may be aware, time is of the essence."

"I understand," the man said.

He walked to the Nissan and opened the trunk.

"Please place your back packs in here" he requested.

We did.

"Thank you," he said. "Hand guns too please. I need you to place them in your packs as well"

I felt Jane coiling. The man felt her tension. He raised a hand, slowly, and placed it on my shoulder. He looked at each of us, thinking.

"*Salagen stay clear of him!*" Porter's voice came on my ear piece. "*Move away!*"

The man looked up towards the roofs of the buildings as if hearing my ear piece. His hand kept resting friendly on my shoulder. Somehow, I felt incapable of moving.

"Let me explain something to you people," the older man said, searching for his words. "You don't know who I am, and except for doctor Salajan, I have only a vague idea of who you are. Yet I am here, following a plea from people I trust and respect. You follow me?"

"Go on," Jane said. She stood at an angle where the man's body was masking her from the younger man.

"Good," the old man continued. "You understand that you are here on my turf. This is my country, my city. You have your third man on the roofs here somewhere, and I have my men there as well, for a minimum of insurance. But if this was a trap, I would have several dozen men, all top trained professionals with their sniper rifles trained on you this very second. Do you understand?"

"How do we know it's not so?" Jane asked.

"You don't, young lady. But even if it was a trap and you did realize it, it wouldn't make any difference. The game would be over for you, wouldn't it?"

We all froze. The only motion was breathing. Pairs of eyes were scanning each other for clues of trust or for reasons to pull guns out and squeeze triggers.

"*Get the fuck away from him!*" Porter's voice pressed again. "*What the hell is going on?*"

With a slow move, Jane took her pistol out, opened a side pocket of her back-pack in the Nissan's trunk and placed the gun inside it. I took the Smith and Wesson and did the same.

"Thank you both," the man said, "I appreciate your trust."

He turned towards the young man.

"Start the car, we'll be going now."

He courteously opened the door for Jane.

"Forgive me for asking," he addressed Jane with a vague smile, "shouldn't we get your back-up man with us as well?"

"How do you know it's only one?" Jane snapped.

The man extracted a sealed envelope from his breast pocket. He handed it to Jane.

"Before removing the seal, please examine the handwriting on it. I need to know if you recognize it."

Jane studied the envelope.

"Hal Mason sent this to you?"

"Thank you, that's the correct name. I didn't have the pleasure to meet Mr. Mason. It has been sent to me, indirectly. Now, please look inside."

Jane opened the envelope and extracted three American passports. I looked over her shoulder as she opened each of them one by one. Her picture, mine and Porter's were on the documents. The names, unknown.

"I'm just assuming that this third person, your friend, is somewhere around, backing you up," the old man explained.

Jane exhaled, leaning back on her seat.

"All right, Porter, come down," she spoke in the mike. "Everything is OK."

"*OK my ass,*" Porter's voice said in the ear piece.

"These are yours, then," the old man gestured towards the passports.

We got into the Nissan. The young man drove slowly away from the curb. Porter came straight to the car and the driver stopped the Nissan only long enough for Porter to get in and then floored the gas pedal.

The ride was short. The car followed a narrow street branching of the city's main north-south avenue and reached a check point manned by military personnel.

The driver flashed a badge. The officer at the gate saluted. The car moved forward along a narrow alley up to and isolated building next to an airstrip. It was a small concrete and glass building lit by fluorescent lighting inside. Behind it, on the strip, there was the silhouette of a business jet.

The driver parked the car by the front entrance and we all got out and retrieved the back-packs from the trunk.

The air smelled of burnt kerosene, the familiar smell of an air base. Further south there was the line of parked MIG jet fighters. Towards west, beyond the runaway, there were farm fields all the way to the Magura hills.

"Please follow me," the old man invited. He opened the door to the building, and courteously held it open for us.

The only people inside the small hall were two paratroopers and a customs officer. The old man handed the three passports to the officer.

"Be fast, please, they're behind schedule," he spoke to the officer, amiable but with unmistaken authority.

"Right away, sir," the officer said and walked fast to a desk where he stamped the passports. In less than a minute he handed the three passports back to the old man.

"Thank you," the old man said, with a tone indicating dismissal. The officer saluted and walked away. The military patrol soldiers remained, several feet away, watching us.

The old man held the passports in his hand without offering them back. Instead, he spoke with calm inflexibility.

"I will hand these passports to you and you'll get in the plane waiting for you. But before that, I must set a few things straight."

Porter crossed his arms across his chest. Jane squinted at the man. We all were in his power. We knew it, and he knew it.

"I belong to a small and old fashioned crowd that is not corruptible," he explained in his calm way. "It is a very small crowd, in this country. I also have an old habit I can't really shake off: I like to understand things, to the largest extent possible and permissible."

He locked his eyes on mine. They were greenish brown intelligent eyes. Eyes which could be both friendly and dangerous.

"I ask the lady and the tall gentleman to wait here and not do anything stupid. The two soldiers over there are special forces, very well trained. Doctor Salajan, please follow me."

He led me to a small room furnished with a table a two chairs. He indicated a chair, sat on the other, and placed a recording device on the table, its red eye lit. I sat and studied the old man's face. He wasn't so old, in fact, perhaps late fifties. A man I didn't know one hour before. One more man in the chain of people holding my fate in their hands. He spoke in a flat and formal voice.

"Doctor Salajan, a younger colleague of mine has been shot to death in your presence in Los Angeles. I would like to know what happened."

"Chris Popa," I said.

"Yes."

I gave him the full film of events at the LAX.

"Carmen Conta said she sent Chris Popa to me. After I was rescued, the CIA told me you people denied Chris Popa had any mission assignment in the US."

"Mrs. Conta tried to play a tricky game with our agent. He was on an assignment, yet not one we are willing to admit."

"Why?"

"Political complications, Doctor Salajan. Do you think Raoul Conta's activities were unknown to us?"

"How should I know? Everything seemed well hidden."

"You can't really hide such an enterprise, Doctor Salajan. But Mr. Conta has too much political pull in this country. We got interested when your name surfaced on the intercepted conversations. Agent Popa made the mistake of approaching Mrs. Conta on account on your former relationship with her."

"Did she send Chris Popa to me?"

"She knew about his trip. When we understood the details of the kidnap operation planned we send Chris to avert it and establish a connection with you. Mrs. Conta tried to deviate this task and establish her own contact with you, through our agent.

Unfortunately, things rolled on a different path. Our only choice left was to assist the American operation."

"How did you assist?"

The old man smiled.

"You had a very fruitful meeting in Bucharest, as soon as you arrived, hadn't you, Doctor? Don't you think it was strange for things to line up so nicely?"

I understood. "I led the killer teams right into Conta's nest, didn't I?"

"It had to be done, Doctor Salajan."

Without a word, I reached my back-pack, opened it and extracted the personnel dossiers of the people killed by Carl. I handed the pile to the man.

"Perhaps I am responsible. These people have been executed in cold blood. Their bodies were left in the building that was destroyed. Years ago, I knew most of them."

The man glanced at the folders and left them on the table.

"We have people there, searching," he said. "I'd like to thank you for your recounts and apologize for the ordeal you've been put through. I believe I can offer you something in exchange."

He extracted an envelope from the inside pocket of his coat and handed it to me.

"This is an official clarification. Your file says you have shot a police officer on duty on June 14th, 1990. The man who died was in fact on duty at a different location in Bucharest. The file has been manipulated. Now it has been clarified and corrected. You will be able to come and enjoy your homeland, doctor Salajan. Put all this behind you."

"Thank you," I said.

He rose from the chair and invited me back into the hallway. Without a word he handed the passports to each of us and led us to the door towards the runaway. A Gulfstream V jet was parked with the front access door open and a ladder propped ready.

"Have a safe flight," the man said, and raised his hand in a farewell gesture.

I turned around. We walked towards the aircraft, carrying the back-packs.

Too simple, too good.

Yet, we reached the access ladder and got inside the plane as the engines were already starting.

The door closed powered by a hydraulic mechanism. The cockpit door was open. One of the pilots came out and eyed us briefly.

"Welcome aboard," he said. "Take a seat and buckle up. We'll be taking off ASAP."

He spoke with a brawl. Texas or Arizona. I can never tell the difference.

65

The Gulfstream's engines reduced their roar and settled on a steady rumble. The intercom came alive. "We've reached cruising altitude," it said. "There is a bar in the rear. Feel free to indulge."

I couldn't relax. My body felt coiled like a steel spring. Jane leaned over and studied my face carefully. Like an emergency room nurse evaluating a patient. She brought a large glass of scotch from the bar, forced it in my hand and helped me hold it. My hands seemed crippled.

I drank the scotch. The alcohol, the steady rumble of the engines and the luxurious interior diffused away my instincts of defense, the fabric that had held me together from the moment I'd landed in Bucharest. Emotions I'd completely suppressed since the arrival erupted at full pressure.

I broke down. I needed to cry and yell madly, shed tears and bang my head against a brick wall. I didn't know how to do it. I opened my mouth and made a ludicrous moaning sound. I lacked air, and I inhaled, only to gasp and moan deeper. There was a feeling of rupture, deep inside.

Jane pushed a new glass towards my lips. "Drink it!" she urged me. "C'mon, drink it!"

I drank. The whisky burned my guts.

"He's OK," Jane spoke to Porter. "He's just decompressing."

"If you say so," he said.

Images invaded my head, my eyes. Victor, running for the hydrogen tank. Victor, getting hit by Carl's stray bullets. Carmen's breasts in the night, and her whisper. The smell of her skin. Carmen, protecting Raoul from my cold rage, fearing I could kill the father of her children. Madness.

"Porter, go in the cockpit," Jane said, pulling at his arm. "Tell dirty jokes to the pilots."

He looked at her, at me, and slowly rose from his seat.

"Gonna give him the warrior treatment?" he asked. "Lucky son of a bitch."

"Get the fuck out."

"All right, all right."

I saw him opening the cockpit door and closing it behind him.

Jane worked on my seat, lowering it and extending it into a narrow bed. She undressed me like you undressed a sick child. She threw her own clothes away.

"No," I moaned. "No, not this, not now."

I spoke more words but she didn't care. She kissed me wildly and then bit my chest and arched over me with grace and violent vigor. Her scent of sweat came strong and arousing, her muscles were steel, yet her mouth was smooth and hot on my skin, forcing basic instincts alive, forcing my mind away from the haunting shadows. She moved good and fast, blurring my mind.

I raised my hands and cupped her breasts, resisting the rising climax, trying to give her time.

She felt it. "Don't hold it," she whispered at me. "Finish it!" Her body waved faster over me. She took my hands and bit my fingers.

I exploded, in a quick spasm, and it was over. She slowed down and stopped, caressing my chest slowly, with smooth touches.

Exhaustion and sadness were the only feelings left. Her instinct had been right. Lovemaking had swiftly exorcised my mind. Raw and effective, the orgasm had depleted me. Madness consumes energy. She'd spent it away, for the moment.

***

"I have never witnessed death like back there, at the refinery," I said. "I don't know how to deal with it."

We'd dressed back. We were squeezed together in my seat. She moved her hand on my chest, under the shirt.

"Just take it one hour, one day at a time," she said. "This is how the world is made Matt, heaven and hell, mixed together."

"Who are you Jane?"

She rested her chin on my chest.

"For starters," she said, "I'm Hal Mason's daughter."

"Daughter!?"

"Adopted recently, merely for business reasons. Long family story, we do have a blood relationship as well. I lost my natural parents when I was ten. Let's leave it at that. I am the heir of Hal's estate and his firm, Mason and Associates."

She smiled and let the information sink in.

"Hal never mentioned a daughter, or any relative for that matter," I said. "I always wondered how come he's so totally alone. What about the meeting at the coffee shop? The phone call in the middle of the night, you overdosing on drugs?"

"Hal asked me to get close to you. I was to be your guardian angel. I played it my way."

"How did you know it was gonna work?"

"You were a lonely man, Matt. Hunger for someone was written all over your face. I improvised. Besides, Mason has a full file on you. It has a picture of you and this woman, Carmen, from years ago. Hal noticed we have a similar look, a coincidence. He advised me to use it on you; he knew you were a sentimental man."

"And you did."

"Yeah, I used it. You behaved as predicted. And that was my problem."

"Why?"

"You played the hero, in full honesty. Offered and gave me this goodness you have in you. It's a rare thing, these days."

"Where is the problem?"

"Emotion is the problem. I didn't want it. Loving you is weakness. In my line of work, emotion can get you killed."

"And what is your line of work, Jane?"

She didn't answer but broke away from my embrace, rose and brought two more drinks from the rear, and then sat on her seat.

"I gotta give you some background on Mason first, so you can understand," she said, handing me the glass.

I grasped the glass. "I'm listening."

"He is a contractor for defense and intelligence business. His firm does special and confidential business operations for the government and private clients. Some of these operations are not only confidential, but clandestine as well."

"Like the job at the refinery?"

"The refinery job is a special case."

"Is it legal?"

"That's a useless question."

"I'm asking if one can own and operate such a firm legally."

"It's a firm with a very solid reputation, but only in the restricted circle of people who know about it and use it. Hal started it back in the eighties. The Iran-Contras affair gave him the idea. Are you familiar with that scandal?"

"Only from the news; back during the Reagan administration, the CIA sold weapons to Iran and used the money to help guerillas in South America."

"It was Nicaragua, to be precise. It was a large scale operation, in fact. It required very complex movements of money, weapons and equipment without leaving any trace. Hal got involved mainly in the financial part. He worked with a guy named Secord, retired Air Force general employed by the CIA. He didn't like the way Secord was operating and pulled out. He knew he could do a better job and figured he can open his own private firm specialized in covert operation jobs, do them good and clean, and make money."

She sipped from her drink. "You follow me?" she asked.

"Yes, go on."

"The idea worked. Hal got specialized in moving financial assets and materials, and built his own network of people. In this business reliability is very much valued and he delivered it. The money was good. He branched the firm in several directions. One direction is expertise in weapon counter-proliferation, nuclear or chemical stockpiles, portable missile launchers, that sort. It's a big problem. Especially in the zones of Pakistan, North Korea or China, there are all sorts of operators moving dangerous shit around. Another direction for the firm came from the strong demand for extreme operations necessary in counter-proliferation."

"Extreme operations?"

"Go and blow things up. Eliminate certain key people. Hal understood there was much less political implication for a private operator to go and blow stuff up in Pakistan or Brazil than it would be if the CIA or Special Ops did it."

"That's dirty shit, Jane."

"Maybe. Some parts of this world are made for people with tough stomachs. Certain things need to be done."

"Strange. I've been friends for years with Hal Mason. I never imagined he was hiring private commando killers."

"He never has. Mason's firm only does the logistics and the finance operation. Nevertheless, he's aware of the overall picture,

Hal has a peculiar sense of patriotism. He considers there are things that must be done by people with the guts to do it. He doesn't employ killers, but guys like Porter, who's an ex Navy SEAL."

"What about Carl and his men?"

"Those were not hired by Hal. The people that issued the contract send their own team. Hal only sent me and Porter. He's a good judge of people. Before he got sick the firm had developed an excellent track record, a success rate of over ninety five percent.

"What was he doing in Romania when I met him?"

My voice sounded angry.

She noticed it. "Calm down. Nothing extreme," she said. "He was only collecting data on weapon trafficking. In 1990 the State Department knew the fall of governments in the soviet satellite countries would bring chaos for a while. All those governments falling like domino pieces, it became a free for all everywhere in terms of military equipment and weapons."

"Who was he working for when I met him?"

"The State Department. He had a contract to survey the weapon trafficking in the Balkan countries, Yugoslavia, Bulgaria and Romania. It was difficult to track things in that area. The stockpiles depots had loose accounting. Blue prints for weapons were being sold to anybody ready to pay."

"I met him in Bucharest," I said. "On a back street, by the burnt down archives supposed to store documentation and blue prints for military projects. All the documentation there was ashes."

"Hal was sure that was a cover up."

"Why?"

"Because of the political dynamics in Romania at the time. The country was a problem for the State Department. The new government was engaged in nasty maneuvers. Former secret police and communist apparatchiks morphed overnight into businessmen and began doing murky deals. Nobody knew who was in whose payroll. The KGB was playing games and so were other spooks. Various groups' agendas were overlapping. It was pretty chaotic. Hal talked to me right before his trip. I was twenty at the time, on training and also studying political science. He felt he didn't understand the situation in Bucharest, it was very confuse."

"I don't blame him. I was there the middle of it, and things didn't make much sense either. You said you were training? Training for what?"

She grinned.

"I was to become la femme Nikita of his joint."

I laughed. It felt strange to laugh.

"I guess you've accomplished it." I said.

She smiled and didn't answer. "Anyway, go on," I said.

She settled more comfortable on her seat.

"When Hal returned from Romania, he was very much marked by you saving his life," she continued. "He filed his report with the Defense and State Departments and raised all the red flags possible. He was sure the fire at the archives was a cover and sooner or later some bad stuff was going to emerge on the black market."

"Did he specifically mention my engine?"

"No. Only later on, after you've explained to him the potential of that technology, he understood it could be very dangerous."

"He never spoke to me about that."

"He always thought you should be left alone, live your life. He could've helped you with your Lockwell conflict, but you didn't ask for help. Later, after you divorced and got fired by Lockwell, he also restrained himself from interfering."

I leaned back on my seat. The whisky had worked its way into my brain. I closed my eyes thinking about the beach at Point Dume at night, feeling the smell of the sand still hot from the day and the touch of metal on my hand holding the Beretta.

"He did interfere, finally," I said. "I was on a beach. Almost at the last moment, he did make the right phone call."

"It wasn't by chance that he called you," Jane said.

I opened my eyes.

"What do you mean?"

The cockpit door opened. Porter was laughing at something one of the pilots had said, as he stepped out of the cockpit into the cabin.

"You guys done here?" he asked.

I looked carefully at his face.

"I knew I saw him before!" I said. "He's that damn copper on the beach!"

He grinned widely, showing large strong teeth.

"Funny what some proper treatment does to men," he spoke to Jane in his typical growl. "This feller here seems pretty much well an alive."

"Porter, it was you playing state trooper back there at Point Dume, wasn't it?"

He sat down.

"Take it easy man," he said. "Yeah, it was me. I'd just called Mason and told him you're sitting your butt on the sand playing with a toy gun. He'd figured you may hurt yourself and ordered me to get on your case right away. He called you to stall you. I borrowed the jeep and a uniform from the state beach troopers. They're really bad with locking their cars and beach cabins. I was a bit concerned about you holding that gun. Folks ready to blow their brains have a death wish that can be dangerous. But it turned out OK."

He slapped me hard on the shoulder.

"You're OK, Salagen. I saved your butt twice. Let's consider it a payment for some other shit I did years back. If that wise fellow up there keeps count."

"Matt Salagen the pathetic idiot," I said. I rubbed my face, fighting retroactive frustration on top of exhaustion. "A fucking idiot, all these years."

"Don't take it so hard," Jane said. "We're all maneuvered by the big system. It's a big machinery we're dealing with, Matt. Governments, power, tons of money. You just got caught in the tooth wheels. Let it go."

"I need more clarification. Who set me up for this trip? That whole nightmare at the refinery. Who has set that one up?"

"The set up is bigger that you may suspect," Jane said.

"How big?"

"Big. The game is not over yet."

"Not over? What's left?"

She searched her pockets and found a pack of cigarettes. She lit up, reminding me of the other Jane, the one I carried to an emergency room. She inhaled and blew smoke slowly, as if the process had the ability of streamlining her thoughts.

"It's something this Chinese guy said before he got shot. He said, '*our American partner*'. It's something Mason has been suspecting for a while."

"Let me ask you something," she said, leaning towards me on her seat. "That long meeting at the Lockwell headquarters, didn't it strike you as very strange?"

The question left me perplexed.

"Strange to say the least," I said. "I walked in there and I thought I was going to get out in chains, accused of treason and espionage and whatever else. I got out with a fat contract."

She threw me a sharp look, as if following a chess game.

"There was some shit thrown in that meeting strong enough to shake anyone's common sense," she said. "First, the picture, shocking in its own, a blend of vulgarity and secrecy. Second, the altercation. Hal played perfectly your personal conflict with Lockwell. He wanted a conflict, a crisis and he got it when that Lockwell guy accused you to have sold out. Third, the stick and the carrot maneuvering followed. The stick: the possible legal threat for the Lockwell Corporation as a whole. The carrot: the money offer, a big fat contract with Uncle Sam. Everyone was glad to grab it, and show patriotism in the process."

"I'm not sure I follow, Jane. The government people wanted the MORPHEM project back on track. They basically realized the potential."

"Wake up, Matt. Everything was a big piece of theater organized by Mason."

I shook my head, trying to throw away mind blur of the whisky.

"You're saying the whole Lockwell work we started on MORPHEM is a big scam? But there is money being spent, several million bucks at least, so far, on all that work. There is a contract."

"Nothing is real except the dollars. It's Hal Mason's money."

"What about Bronson?"

"He's with the FBI. Just like Balder is with the CIA. But they act at Mason's orders. The firm Mason and Associates has been contracted for this operation."

"How? Why?"

"Hal was the first man to understand the whole picture. First, that internet picture got intercepted by the NSA. They didn't know what it really meant. Someone at the NSA showed it to Hal. He immediately knew the images must be related to your engine work in Romania."

"How did he know?"

"He's got an extraordinary intuition. He ordered intelligence work on the Romanians and on Lockwell. Lockwell intelligence revealed a link to the Chinese. He put together the information about the explosion at Base 067 in Xi'an and the Lockwell explosion. He was sure it was exactly the same engine design. The source of the web picture was unknown, and only some murky information came from Romania. But the Chinese connection to this project forced him to make up his mind. He didn't know the Romanian connection, and suspected the Chinese have a direct American source to have provided them with the Lockwell design.

"But Feng said they got the design from the Romanians."

"Except that your Lockwell friend, the Chinese researcher, got killed by the *'American partner'*. That's what the Chinese operative at the refinery said before he got silenced. We have a big problem in out hands still."

I had too much alcohol in my system to process all the information.

"One more question," I said. "Back in LA, after I was kidnapped, who rescued me? Was it Porter, still?"

She smiled.

"Hal wanted to let the kidnapping take its course. But he was troubled, he feared for your life, and yet he didn't know how to let the operation evolve. I didn't listen to any of them. Just got a team, burst in there and got you out."

The memory came back, strongly.

"Those fingers feeling my pulse on my neck. It was you."

"It was me. But I couldn't reveal you who I am, I had to let things follow course."

I went to the bar and found some bottled water. I sat back down and drank it all.

"What's the objective of all this operation?" I asked. "What do you people want?"

"We made a stir, at the beginning of this operation, and waited for people to react. This is how you get moles to reveal themselves. Meanwhile, that group, back there at the refinery, Matt, it had to be neutralized. Not the way it happened, but one way or another it had to be done. Now, we got to take care of the American side of the problem. And there is a bonus too. Hal wanted to set your record straight with Lockwell. He forced them to call you back and admit their incompetence. He felt he owed you this."

"That's several million dollars spent."

"It's only money, Matt. He's dying."

"He encouraged me to return to Romania. Why? Made me do more stirring back there?"

"It just developed this way, Matt. It was a heritage of your own past that was linked to the operation at the refinery. You had to go back in person and search for that link. Hal knew you have been carrying that stone on your chest ever since you left Romania the way you did. He considered you his adoptive son, Matt. And he knew your life would be in danger during all this operation. That's why I'm here."

I watched her face for several long moments. I tried to understand everything she said, sort it out.

"Is this why you're here?" I asked.

She leaned forward and kissed me, gently.

"Yes," she said.

Porter growled from his seat, still gulping whisky.

"Lucky son of a bitch," he said.

66

The plane started maneuvering, descending.

The cockpit door opened and the pilot who had welcomed us aboard in Bukow went and leaned over Jane's seat.

"We've received some news over secure transmission," he said. "I'm instructed to talk to you, Ms. Mason."

"I'm listening," Jane said.

"Mr. Harold Mason has died at the Cedars Sinai Hospital in Los Angeles an hour ago."

Her face whitened and she stood still. The pilot waited. There was no other reaction from Jane and he continued.

"Also, the arrangements for this flight may have lost confidentiality. We'll need to change flight plans."

"Who sent the transmission?"

"Ernesto Cuerva. Secure ID confirmed."

"Set up another transmission. Feed back the following to the corporation: we didn't show up for rendezvous in Bukow, you're flying empty."

"Understood. We'll divert flight plans nevertheless."

"Any support in team in LA?"

"Negative. The only secure contact is Mr. Cuerva"

Jane nodded. "Thank you."

***

The Atlantic Ocean was hidden at the bottom of the endless darkness surrounding the jet. The cabin lights were off. I watched the stars, peeking upwards through the small round window.

Porter was snoring louder than the engine background noise. There was vague motion noises from Jane's seat. She was awake. I went and turned her seat light on. She wiped her face. She had been crying.

"He practically was my father," she said, in a whisper. "I knew his death was coming. I had been expecting it, yet, I feel alone, all of a sudden."

I sat next to her.

"I can't remember of any instance when Hal failed," she said, straightening up on her seat. "I'm not sure, this time."

"I think I can help you, this time," I said.

Quietly, she became focused.

"How?"

"I have some information we can use."

"What information?" she asked and her voice felt cold, professional.

"The blueprints they had back in Bukow had some hand written corrections on dimensions that were determined as incorrect only by recent measurements. I am convinced there is a key connection between Lockwell and the Chinese. A person with advanced engineering expertise."

"The key connection man," she said, dreamily. "There is always someone like that. It's one of Hal's theories."

I brought my back-pack and sat on the seat opposite to Jane. I extracted the folder with dark red covers I had found in Raoul Conta's cabinets and laid it on my lap.

"There is an unexpected link I found back there," I told Jane placing my hands on the red covers. "I believe we have our key man."

67

"What's your plan?" Porter asked.

The city of LA was getting baked by a scorching sun. One hour before noon the temperatures were above 100 F.

"I'll get in with Matt," Jane answered. "You and Ernesto keep watch."

Porter's eyes searched the street, squinting.

"The place may be under surveillance."

"We got no other choice," Jane said.

"Why don't just wait? Nab him somewhere else, when he gets out of the house."

"No time, Porter. We gotta act before they react to the refinery clean-up."

He made a grimace, and surveyed the sidewalks. With quick and discrete moves he distributed the communication gear and weapons.

We got out of the car. It was a Grand Am, powerful and boring, an unnoticeable presence. That's what GM does best. You never look twice at some of the cars they make.

A similar four door sedan rolled slowly towards us and flashed his lights, barely visible in the sun light. It came to a stop at the curb across the street form us, while the driver's window opened half way. I recognized Ernesto.

I walked casually along Jane towards the building, both of us carrying the weapons wrapped in t-shirts.

She walked to the entrance door and broke the lock with a small flat head tool. She pulled the door knob and opened it.

"Get in," she whispered.

I stepped in the hallway.

"Third floor" she said. "On foot."

We walked silently up the stairs. Smells of curry and other spices filled the air. A radio tuned to a Santa Monica station was playing bossanova. The city of Bukow was several thousand miles away, its corpses lost in geography.

"Ring the bell," Jane said. "And relax."

I shrugged, feeling dizzy. The domestic smells of the building made me think we're just a crazy bunch, living through an endless hallucination.

I rang the bell.

Nothing happened. There was silence behind the door. Couple of doors away, someone was yelling in Spanish.

I rang the bell again.

There was light movement behind the door. I looked straight at the peephole. The door opened.

"Matei?" Cam exclaimed, holding the door only a few inches open. "I… I wasn't expecting you."

She opened the door and I walked in. Cam pushed the door to close it behind me, but Jane blocked it with her foot and walked in as well.

Cam jerked, surprised. She looked at me and back at Jane, eyes wide.

"This is Jane," I said. "She's with me."

"Oh," Cam said, and then she noticed the headsets on both of us and the objects wrapped in white t-shirts we were carrying. She opened her mouth to speak, but her brain worked faster, and she probably understood. Her face froze. Her features morphed into a mask of stone.

"Where is Stefan?" I asked.

She didn't answer. I looked around the living room. It was empty, except for a pile of cardboard boxes taped and stacked in a corner. Paper plates and foam cups were spread on the kitchen counter next to a cheap coffee maker.

Someone coughed. The bedroom door opened and Mora came out wiping his face with a white towel. He stopped suddenly when he saw me. Cam watched him with a silent scream on her eyes.

There was tensed silence. Mora's eyes searched Jane and then me.

He dropped the towel on the floor and said "I see we have guests."

He suddenly rammed me against the wall. I was prepared and blocked him. Jane hit him in the back of his neck. Mora fell on his knees, all his strength taken away by the precise blow.

Came made a weak move at Jane. She wasn't a fighter. Jane twisted her arm and put her on the floor.

"Stay there!" she ordered Cam, steel in her voice, "I don't need to hurt you. Stay there!"

Cam kneeled and buried her face in her hands. She exhaled in a long sod.

Stefan Mora stood up slowly, sliding against the wall. He watched me with a dark look, the depths of his mind hidden behind hate.

"What the hell do you want?" he asked in Romanian, but somehow appearing to address the question to Jane.

Jane unwrapped the gun from the t-shirt. The ugly barrel of the silencer pointed to Stefan's knees.

"Sit down!" Jane ordered him. "On the floor! Sit down!"

He obeyed, watching the gun. Cam moved next to him and sat on the floor, embracing his arm, crying.

Jane looked at me. I dropped my backpack on the floor and sat down on one of the cardboard boxes. I pointed to the rest of the boxes in the room.

"Are you guys leaving town?" I asked.

There was no answer.

I extracted the file with dark red covers from the back-pack and threw it at Stefan. It landed on the floor, in front of him.

"I found it back in Romania," I told him. "Couple of people got killed in cold blood in front of my eyes, Stefan, and then I found this. A fellow named Raoul Conta kept it in his drawers. Rings any bell?"

He glanced at me when I said the name. His attitude changed. Hate vanished, replaced by prudence. He carefully grabbed the file and browsed through the pages.

"Very instructive reading, you'll see," I told him.

He read the pages fascinated, as if under a spell.

Cam stopped crying, sensing the change in Stefan. She leaned forward, her eyes searching the pages. She read for a minute and then threw her head backwards, leaning back against the wall.

"Oh God," she sobbed, shaking her head as if rejecting the reality of the file's pages. "Our lost souls."

"Since when did you know, Cam?" I asked her. "Was it from the very beginning? Or you found out later?"

She didn't answer. It felt unreal. They were people I cared about, and I wished the whole thing was just nonsense, one huge misunderstanding that could be cleared up and then we could all have coffee together some place nice, on a sidewalk. But the room was filled with the sort of cruel silence which confirms the ugly reality.

"No," Cam said, her eyes closed. "I didn't know for years. I believed with all my heart we had escaped communism for good, I believed we had been rewarded with good luck for our courage to force our way out."

Mora stopped reading for a second and looked at her, without interrupting. He slowly turned his eyes back to the file.

"Once we arrived here, I really believed we can build a new life, that we can build happiness."

She was speaking head down, watching the floor. Jane lowered the gun, slowly. She didn't understand the Romanian gibberish but she sensed Cam was breaking into talking.

"When did you find out about him?"

Stefan jerked his head at my question, but controlled himself. He seemed to feel better if she talked.

"Back when I tried to leave him. When I stayed at your house"

"How did you find out?"

"He told me," she said, leaning her head towards Stefan.

He avoided looking at her, keeping his eyes at the pages.

"There's something I don't understand," I said. "Although I read the file over and over. It says Stefan has been sent out by the KGB, not by the Romanians. Why the KGB? Why not the DIE?[16]"

Cam shook her head, and covered her face again. She started crying.

"Leave her alone," Mora said. "It was my judgment at the time. I thought I could pull it off."

"Pull what off?"

"Back in Romania they approached me several times. The KGB. They had a grand plan in the early 80's when Andropov[17] was in charge. Reagan was starving the USSR economy to death

---

[16] DIE: "Directia Informatii Externe," Romanian spy agency during communist regime of N. Ceausescu.

[17] Yuri Vladimirovich Andropov, Director of the KGB between 1967-1982. Soviet politician and General Secretary of the CPSU from November 12, 1982 until his death just fifteen months later.

forcing the soviets to overspend on military. Then, the soviets made an analysis and realized they would collapse. The communist system was inefficient, crippled. Andropov came up with the idea to drop off communism for a while. Replace it with a wild and ruthless capitalism, a system allowing them to make fast progress."

"Bullshit," I said. "They would have shot him had he proposed such a thing."

"It was no longer the Stalin's USSR era, Salajan. Those men were big thinkers. Who the hell are you and your fucked up brain to judge what I say?"

He flashed a furious look at me. Yet, I sensed he wanted to talk.

"I'm not judging you," I said. "All I want is to understand."

"Then keep your stupid judgments for yourself!" he snapped.

"What the fuck is he saying?" Jane asked.

"Ah, the muscle girl wants to know!" Mora exclaimed in English. He was flushing his panic and stress with sarcasm.

"The KGB came to me, and asked me to defect to the West," he spoke loudly, in English. "They were sending scientist sleepers into the West, as many as they could find, from all communist states. It was part of the grand plan."

"What grand plan?" Jane asked.

"The USSR was to switch to wild capitalism for a while. Simulate the break down of the Eastern European communist governments and integrate those countries into the West. KGB agents were trained to become capitalist moguls, the new tycoons. We were sent here to capture as much technology as possible and send it back."

"Science and technology sleeper cells?"

"Yes! What do you think Putin[18] was doing then? Working hard in East Germany, in Dresden, with their STASI, to send out guys like me. As many as they could recruit."

"You freely accepted," I said. "There is your affidavit, right there in that folder. Your agent code name is Cornel Oniga."

---

[18] Russian President Vladimir Putin (1999-2008) worked as a KGB colonel in East Germany from 1985 to 1990 recruiting spies to be infiltrated into the West.

"I didn't care, my friend. All I wanted was to get out of the fucking old country. I was sick of everything there. I was ready to sell my soul to the devil, just to get out."

Jane watched him coldly.

"And I guess you did," she said.

"Did what?" Mora asked

"Sell your soul."

"Don't you fucking judge me either, muscle girl! You've been born here, free, with ten different sorts of milk and orange juice at the corner shop, and bored by so many choices of cereal for breakfast."

Jane smiled, coldly. She didn't reply.

"Let me tell you this," Mora spoke, pointing a finger at me, "I came here on my own ability. The KGB wanted it done realistically, and all they did was provide me with the schedule of Soviet and Bulgarian patrol boats on the Black Sea. I sailed through, right under their noses and got out. I did my time in the Istanbul camp, and then Treiskirchen, and then made it here. I did it on my own, pal, no help."

"What about her?" I indicated Cam. "How did she get through Yugoslavia and cross the border into Italy without a visa?"

He hesitated.

"It doesn't matter," he said, after a moment.

"It doesn't matter," I said. "I want you to listen carefully, Stefan. Should I call you Stefan or Cornel?"

"Try Tutankhamen. I don't give a shit"

"I do give a shit you son of a bitch! We're in the middle of a mess. People died, and some more may die. Screw your brain convulsions. I need to understand all your involvement into the MORPHEM project. Everything you did and all your connections. We can do it the easy way or the hard way, your pick."

He studied me.

"What's in it for me?" he asked.

Jane locked her black eyes on him.

"I'll explain what's for you in all this," she said, her voice cold as ice. "You'll talk and I'll listen. If I like what you say, you may get out of here alive. I like it more, you may even get out of this country and go wherever you like. I don't like it, I'll put a bullet on your right knee cap. I still don't like it, I'll continue with the left one. And we'll keep going. Is that clear?"

Mora opened his mouth. His eyes moved from Jane's face around the room and back, hesitantly. He mumbled a word.

"I didn't hear," Jane said. "Is it fucking clear, my friend?"

Mora looked away.

"What do you need to know?"

"Start from the beginning," she said. "Give me a timeline."

Stefan removed Cam's arm from around his own and separated from her, rubbing his face, focusing.

"I came here in '87. I wanted to go to the FBI as soon as we arrived. But time passed and nothing happened. We started a new life. Began with low level jobs, and then better ones. Two years after I left, the Berlin wall went down and the whole Eastern Europe fell apart. I knew it was part of the plan, and it was funny to watch how it was all sold to the great public. Gorbachev was playing it in his version with Perestroika and Glasnost[19] shit. Still, nobody looked for me. I was ready to give myself in as soon as someone would show up asking me to do shit for the KGB. One year after Eastern Europe, the whole USSR collapsed. There was no more Soviet Union. The KGB was reformed and renamed FSB. I thought I was home free; their grand plan had back fired. I started working, doing science. She started teaching. I wasn't stealing technology, I was creating it. I have always been a good scientist. I've consulted for Northrop, Raytheon, and Lockheed-Martin. I had a small consulting firm that was doing very well."

"I felt we were OK," he continued. "I didn't tell Cam anything. After a few years I hired at Lockwell as a consultant scientist. When I ran into Salajan here in LA, I recommended him for job there as well. I worked with him on his engine, back when he started the project. He was a poet and didn't see the Lockwell guys were ready to screw him. He didn't see his own wife was ready to screw him. He was floating up there in the skies."

"Spare me the psychoanalysis," I said. "Stick to the fucking facts."

---

[19] USSR leader Mikhail Gorbachev introduced in 1986 the concepts of Glasnost and Perestroika intended to bring open market mechanisms in the Soviet economy and more free expression into the media and arts. Limited in scope, these concepts ultimately failed.

He flashed me with his angry look.

"Here are some facts for you," he said. "Your wife chose her profession instead of you, and Lockwell kicked you out, all patents for the MORPHEM engine belonging to them. After you re-created the physics you had developed in Romania and gave Lockwell the technology. That's how stupid you were."

I didn't answer. He was right, after all.

"I don't know how they found me," Mora continued. "I don't know how they got hold of my KGB file. I had been living here in peace for twelve years."

"Who found you?"

"Raoul Conta."

"You knew him?"

"No. I met him then, the first time, about six years ago. He called me and established a meeting place. I didn't tell Cam. He came to the meeting with another, older guy."

"What was his name?"

"They were using fake names I didn't bother memorizing. I know of Raoul Conta's real name, if that one is real, from the newspapers, he's now a big shot back there, I saw his picture several times. The other one pretended he didn't know me, but I knew him, he used to be the director of the Institute in Bucharest, years back. Military type. Short, fit, funny thick fingers, like tree roots. Gold rimmed glasses. Upset face."

"Bolek," I said.

"What?"

"Nothing. A nickname Petrescu gave him after you defected."

"I met them and they showed me my KGB file. They offered a deal. A one time transaction, only. I give them the MORPHEM plans, all the details, and I was free, off the hook."

"How did they know about MORPHEM?"

"The older guy knew who you were. You had published some stuff about it in a propulsion journal and they tracked you down."

"And what happened?"

"You had just been fired. Lockwell was building the prototype based on Varese's design, the one that later blew up. I made copies of all CAD models and gave the disks to Conta after a couple of months. I haven't heard from him ever since."

"And then what?"

He looked at me and at Jane, as if searching for words.

"Then, I lost it. I didn't have the guts to go to the FBI. All my initiative for business died. I was depressed and I confessed everything to Cam. I couldn't take it."

Cam looked at him, and caressed his face. He held her hand over his face.

"She wanted to leave me. That's when she came and stayed at your house.

He watched me with a dark look. He had neither forgotten nor forgiven.

"You're bad luck, Salajan, and not much of a brain. Had I not crossed paths with you, I would've been fine. I'm a true scientist, I can create technology. You've been chasing your one thing for all these years. And Conta was after you and after your fucked up engine. That big shit of an engine. It blew up here, and killed people, and it blew up for the Chinese too!"

Suddenly there was cold silence, tensed as if filled with high voltage.

"How do you know about the Chinese explosion?" I asked.

He bowed his head, pulling his hair backwards with both hands.

"It was after you showed up again," he said. "After you came at the boat. Two guys came looking for me. They were Americans. And they had a copy of my affidavit here in this file. They made me work for them. They wanted the new MORPHEM, whatever you would make under the new contract"

"How'd they look like?" Jane asked.

Mora shrugged.

"Men in their forties. Clean cut. Tough. No real technical knowledge. They threatened with jail, or worse. I was to cooperate. Someone was to call with instructions."

"What were the instructions?"

"To work with Salagen, whatever initiative he took, go along with it. And report back."

"Only that?"

"No. After Salagen would have produced a design change, they wanted an update of all design geometry."

"Did you give it to them?"

"No. I told them I don't have the complete information. But in fact, I did. Salagen just gave it to me from the start."

"Why didn't you give it to them?"

"Too easy. Besides, I was interested in the topic."

He looked at me with a glimmer of light on his face.

"I can offer you a deal, Salajan. I have something for you. I know you'll be interested because you've spent all this years chasing it. But I want out. You gotta give me this chance, to get out of this."

"What do you have?" I asked.

"Wait a second," Jane interrupted. "There is something else, more important. Who is your contact now?"

Mora looked at her and me one after another, weighing his chances.

"A voice on the phone," he said. "If I had something to give them, they'd indicate the net address for a server and I would upload the files."

"How would you contact them?"

"I have a phone number for a beeper"

Jane looked at him, thinking.

"What do you have for me?" I asked.

"The answer for the explosions," he said. "The answer for the hard thrust."

"What do you want in return?"

"Just let me go. I want to go back home."

A flicker of hope came to Cam's eyes at his words.

Home, I thought, *you sure you know where home is?*

"No deal yet, Mr. Mora." Jane said. "For now, let's get you out of here. Get your papers, only the strictly important stuff. And Mr. Mora, get that beeper number, all the info. You'll need it."

Camelia Mora began crying. She looked at the pile of boxes

"Everything," she cried in a whisper, "everything that we were all these years, good or bad, photographs, videos, letters, it's all in there, in these boxes."

Stefan grabbed her hand. "Forget it," he said, his voice strangled, swallowing desperation. "Let's bury it all."

6 8

The safe house was in Brentwood Heights, an expensive, one level house on a flat hilltop lot. We had spent the previous night there, just Jane, Porter, and me. With all shades pulled down, the house looked like any Southern Californian good residence, baking in the sun and waiting for its middle class owners to return from work.

"Show them to the south room" Jane told Porter. "See what they need, settle them. We'll talk to them later."

Porter nodded.   Jane placed her palm gently on Ernesto's shoulder.

"It's good to see you, Ernie," she said. "Please come and sit down here for a minute"

He accepted the familiar touch with a smile and followed her. He was changed, aged. Hal's departure from the living seemed to have taken away some of his own vigor.

Jane led him towards a corner furnished with leather couches and chairs. She sat on one of the couches and invited him to the chair next to her.

"I want to know about his last moments," she requested.

He understood.

"You know he was really very ill, miss Mason."

"Was he in pain?"

"He kept it under control."

"Did he leave any specific instructions?"

"There was a visit. A man came to talk to him, early in the morning. They talked for about an hour. Tall old guy, white hair, blue eyes. Strong security with him. Guys I didn't know, good, silent, polite."

"Why is this man important?"

Ernesto extracted a business card from his breast pocket with great care.

"Mr. Mason asked me to take his card and give it to you personally. Here it is."

Jane took the card and examined it. I looked over her shoulder. The name the written on the card was Scott Stirling.

"Was Hal able to communicate?"

"He was coughing a lot, but his mind was clear, if that's what you're asking."

"Yes. What happened then?"

"After that man left, I sat with him in the room. And then, he just went. One long breath, and it was over."

They remained silent. There was nothing to be said. Jane looked out through the windows, gazing at the sky outside. Ernesto sat with his head bowed, his eyes on the floor, tired.

Jane stood up.

"All right," she said. "Now we need to wrap up this operation"

She signaled me to follow her. She led me into a large office room and closed the door after us with a blank stare, weighing things in her mind.

"Is this guy, Mora, that good at his science?" she asked.

"Very good."

"Has he enough to offer? This engine design, I mean, technically, is that enough, what he's got?"

"I can't tell. I'll have to see some data."

"How? Where?"

"I have a private office in Eagle Rock, just west of Pasadena. That's where I worked with Mora on the simulations. He may have data stored there."

She sat on a large brown leather couch and grabbed her forehead, pulling her hair behind her back, eyes fixed on the floor, thinking, switching thoughts in her mind. Her muscles seemed coiled, is if ready to spring in some insane motion.

I touched her shoulder, calmly. "What do you need, Jane?"

She raised her head.

"A hook," she said with vigor. "Bait attractive enough and a hook strong enough to get the big fish."

"Let me see Stefan's material and I'll tell you if it's strong enough."

She walked to the door, opened it and called Porter.

"Set me up a DCS secure com," she requested. "I'll give you the contact info when you're ready."

Porter nodded and left. She left the room as well. I remained by the window, watching the hills.

Can I recover from all this? I asked myself. *What's gonna be left, what is it that will still matter after all will be over?*

Somewhere, not too far behind the hills, was the ocean. I thought I could feel its scents in my mind. I thought I could smell the sand.

69

We left Porter with the car at Figueroa and Colorado, keeping watch.

Stefan Mora produced his security badge from a pocket and unlocked the main entrance door. Up at the sixth floor he unlocked and opened the door to our offices. The computer terminals were on, their cooling fans humming the usual monotonous song.

He sat at one of the terminals, logged in and started working. Then he stopped and turned towards me on his swivel chair.

"Before I show you this stuff I want your word, Salajan. You're that kind of an idealist on whose word I can count. Give me your word that I and Cam can go free after this."

Jane glanced at me and sat down on another chair, away from us. She let me deal with him.

"You got a two part deal, Stefan," I said. "My part, it's about the engine. The second part, it's her deal. You'll have to do a few things she's gonna ask you to do."

"And then?"

"You're free."

"Your word?"

"Yes."

He eyed Jane, concerned, cornered. She confirmed with a nod.

Uneasily, Stefan turned back to the terminal and turned the screen so I can watch it with him.

"You have all the data in here," he started explaining.

"Here is an overlay of your new design – the one that's supposed to work, and the engine core that was actually manufactured. They're very similar in size. The crucial difference, it's in these angles here. The way the engine was actually made, the angles lean more, about 5 degrees more."

I followed the screen contours, checking. The angle difference was clear.

"What does this do to the engine's physics?" I asked. "What is it that you found?"

His eyes got brighter. He brought an engine cross-section image in the screen.

"It's a complicated thermodynamic cycle. There are two simultaneous fluid circuits operating, besides the cooling and the turbopump circuits. The main circuit is a combination between a conventional rocket cycle and an MHD power generator. The second circuit is the important one. Hydrogen at high pressure gets super-heated through a spiraling motion within the electromagnetic field of the radio frequency coils. The arrangement works as a confinement volume. But if no fundamental transformation occurs in the gas, you get nothing; you just spend the mechanical and chemical energy of the fluid into some heating.

"Except that energies are generated."

"That's because there is something else happening. I suspected it from the very beginning, because you've borrowed the physics from the plasma confinement fusion experiments. So I've added one extra element in the calculation: a simple model. It's expressed in parts per million."

"Hydrogen fusion into Helium?"

"Precisely. Look at this curve, you recognize it?"

"Yes, it's the temperature at the core when the Lockwell engine exploded."

"Correct. Now look at this."

On the screen, a red smooth curve appeared on top of the noisy measurement data. It had the exponential behavior I had found weeks earlier.

"This is not a curve fit," Mora said. "This is the big calculation with the extra model added. This thing explodes like a small fusion bomb."

I watched the screen again. He had extended the red curve beyond the time of deflagration. It rose sharp to the upper edge of the screen.

"The critical issue was that I needed to establish a criterion: when and where does Hydrogen fuse. The plasma flow in this engine breaks any stability criteria known. With such a mess of physics in it, why would an engine geometry work and other geometry would not? The trick is the swirl in the hot plasma flow. I read some Japanese papers on this, people at the Osaka University have been working on swirl flow magneto hydrodynamics. But they cannot control the instabilities. You have found your own way to control it, somehow, by luck, I'd say, you probably did trial and error testing."

"Yes," I confirmed.

Mora stabbed the air with his finger, pointing at the screen.

"You use a criterion derived from the amount of swirl but empirically so. All you have is a thumb rule, even if a very sophisticated one, what you call the scaling principle. If the geometry obeys your scaling rule, the engine is stable. That's the difference between your design and the Lockwell engine. Your engine finds a narrow range where the process is stable, whereas Lockwell engine is unstable. If it's unstable to the left, so to speak, you get nothing, a dud. If it's unstable to the right, it blows up."

I nodded. "Yes. Now, can you predict all this with just a simple model?"

"I've only begun…" Mora said and stretched his lips in a bitter laugh, a small interior moment of surrender. He accurately had reverse engineered the whole engine. A good mind, Stefan Mora. And a wrong decision he had made too many years back.

His cold smile died.

"If you ever go back to this, Matei," he said, his voice changed by regret, "if you ever go back to this you gotta dig all the way down to fundamental particle physics. People have tried confinement fusion with huge resources without achieving anything close to the fusion rate in MORPHEM. This is huge, do you understand?"

I nodded, watching his eyes. He had lost his bet with his fate and he knew it.

"It's all in there," Mora said, resigned into letting go of it. "You don't need a report, just look at the data."

"Thank you," I said. "This is really good work."

He sat down, silent, turning his attention to Jane, waiting.

Jane extracted a piece of paper from her pocket and unfolded it slowly, her eyes on Stefan.

"Yes," he said. "What is it you want me to do?"

She gave him the piece of paper. There were several numbers and words on it.

"This is a numbered account with the First Caribbean bank in the Cayman Islands," she explained. "You're going to make contact with the people who are running you, and ask them for an urgent deal. You'll offer the new, good engine design, and all the data they want on it. For this, you'll ask for four hundred thousand dollars transferred into this account, and another hundred thousand delivered to you in cash. Give them a day, and extend it to no more than two days if they press you for time. You'll tell them you're leaving the country in two days. Is it clear?"

Slowly, he took the piece of paper from Jane, and stared at the numbers on it.

"How am I supposed to go to the Cayman Island and get this money?" he asked. "I have never been there."

"It doesn't matter," Jane smiled. "It's all an act."

He crumbled the piece of paper in his hand. His fist was shaking.

"Please calm down," Jane spoke with a smooth comforting tone. "We intend no harm to you, Mr. Mora. You're an actor on this, just play your part."

Stefan eyes searched her face, as if searching for help. Her soothing voice had worked on him.

"What about the cash?" he asked.

"You will go and collect it," she explained with the same good voice. "I'm going to be honest with you and tell you that's going to be dangerous. But it's something you need to do. And we'll be there to protect you."

"You just want to squeeze money out of this?" Mora asked, confused.

"I don't care about this money, Mr. Mora. Just to offer you a small incentive, you can keep it, if all goes well."

"But then, what do you really want?" Mora asked, perplexed.

Jane's face lost its tenderness.

"That, Mr. Mora, it's a bit too complicated to explain," she said. "And it would do you no good to know."

Mora watched her intensely. He didn't understand her, but he felt there is a small door truly open for him, and beyond anything, he wanted that chance.

"Tell me again what I have to do," he requested.

Jane smiled, calmly. Taking each detail one by one, she instructed him. Then, she extracted from her pack two sets of wires and two ear pieces. She attached the ear pieces to the main telephone and fixed one of them to her ear and gave me the other one.

"Now," she spoke to Stefan, "let's call your friends, Mr. Mora."

Hesitantly, Stefan pushed his chair and reached for the phone. He lifted the receiver and with careful moves dialed a number, waited and then punched more numbers on the telephone's pad. Then, he placed the receiver back.

"It's a beeper number," he explained again.

There was silence. The sunlight was gone outside. The office lights were off. Little by little, out eyes had adjusted to the dim light produced by the computer screens.

"If goes well, Mr. Mora," Jane said, "I promise you'll have the chance to start your life again."

He scrutinized her in the dim light.

"Salajan gave me his word, and I trust he'll try his best to honor it, because I know him. Can I trust you?"

He wanted to trust her. He needed to trust her.

"Yes, Mr. Mora," Jane said. "You can trust me as much as you trust Matt."

The phone rang.

Stefan reached towards the phone and stopped, his hand hanging in the air, one inch above the receiver. He stood like that for two more rings, as if afraid to touch the phone.

Then, he lifted the receiver to his ear.

"Stefan Mora speaking," he said.

I pressed the miniature receiver piece on my ear, just as Jane did. There was static on the line. Someone was breathing in a receiver, at the other end.

"Hello?" Mora said into the mike.

"What do you have for us?" a voice asked.

7 0

The location was a coffee shop terrace. It was deserted, at two hours before dawn.

I scouted the terrace from the back seat of the large Ford SUV driven by the enigmatic man who had showed up one hour earlier at the safe house. Jane had woken me up and asked me to get ready and then had introduced the man named Fred.

Fred was a quiet man. Not talking seemed to be one of his life's objectives. He drove the Ford around the block and quietly studied the buildings surrounding the shop. From the front seat, Porter swept the darkness with a pair of night vision goggles.

"Drop me here," he suddenly told Fred, and as the car slowed down he vanished from the car without noise, a shadow in the night. Fred resumed his driving, calmly fixing a headset piece to his ear.

I leaned back against my seat. It was a heated seat, warm and comfortable. Fred killed time taking Sunset all the way from San Vicente to the 101 freeway overpass. Two or three hookers looked at us with tired interest, emerging from shaded corners into the sidewalk. At Vine, a woman dressed in a fishnet blouse and a very short skirt tottered barefoot through the middle of the boulevard while three young men took pictures of her from the sidewalks, flashing streaks of light in the night.

Fred made a u-turn at Western and took Sunset again, in the opposite direction. We found the strange woman again, still on the middle of the street, with a police cruiser driving slowly along.

Fred put a finger to his ear piece, as if listening, and stepped on the gas. He drove straight back to the coffee shop. He slowed down the car at a corner, one block away from the shop and Porter materialized back in the front seat with the same stealthy easiness.

"They have no watchers yet." he told Fred. "Let's do it."

Fred nodded.

From a bag on the floor Porter extracted an object like a gun. Fred drove the car to a side street and parked the car at the curb turning off the headlights.

"I need about six or seven of them," he finally spoke, looking at Porter. "Some may just go out, it happens."

He turned on a dim blue light inside of the car. From the bag, Porter gave him a small flat case and the quiet man opened it, examining its content. Fixed on a layer of foam, there was a row of small black darts, each about two inches in length. Fred extracted them one by one and examined them carefully. He fixed a magnifier goggle on the orbit of his right eye, like a jeweler, and using a sharp instrument he pressed on several minuscule switches on each of the darts. Once finished, he arranged the darts back in the case.

"Ready," he told Porter.

Porter took one dart and loaded the gun with it as Fred drove back to the coffee shop. Porter lowered his side window, and as the Ford passed the coffee shop he raised the gun and pressed the trigger. The gun spat its load on the building's wall without any noticeable noise. He shot three more darts and then vanished again in the night, carrying the gun.

"What are those?" I asked Fred.

Fred turned towards me, from his seat, and addressed me with a peaceful smile.

"Miniature wireless cameras, my friend."

He turned his attention back to the road and drove the Ford around another block.

"The body of the dart is the antenna," he explained. "At the tail, there is a micro-lens. It points backwards, in the direction you shoot them from. They broadcast on wireless routers' frequency. Undetectable, buried in the noise of the city."

He swerved the car in a tight u-turn, driving back and slowing down, allowing Porter to slip back into his seat.

"We should be OK," Porter said. He asked me, "You sure you want to be there?"

"I am responsible for Stefan Mora."

"It can get nasty."

"I know. But I gotta be there, see and listen."

***

The terrace was warming up under the late morning sun. It appeared slightly distorted on three small screens installed in the back of the Ford. Fred's electronics were picking up the wireless transmissions of the dart cameras implanted on the walls. A powerful machine, installed at our feet, was performing the signal decryption.

Triangulated by the hidden micro lenses, Stefan Mora sat at a table, pretending to read the LA Times. Fred fiddled with the sound settings, and Mora's breath came strongly into the ear receivers. Fred adjusted the volume.

Somewhere close to Mora, a woman's voice worked hard on a man who was only mumbling short replies. I searched the screens: a dark haired woman past her prime, talking and waving her hands at a young and muscular Latino man wearing sunglasses wrapped around his face as if he was due to break the sound barrier with his mug. A thin girl entered the field of view, masking the pair. She was a presence you couldn't miss: baggy pants, spiky hair colored in a rainbow of strident colors, belly button and face filled with piercing silver pieces. She sat, with a large cup and a stack of magazines, three tables away from Mora.

"Fine species, the human kind is." Porter's voice came on the ear piece.

"Cut the shit traffic," Jane's voice ordered.

More people came, enjoying the late morning sun. All tables got occupied. I relaxed. The place was so busy it felt safe.

We waited and listened to the coffee shop's sound system pouring jazz in the air.

"Our friends are here," Porter's voice said.

Three men.

Two of them very much alike, muscle men, athletic, very fit, not too tall, military hair cuts, both dressed in Dockers slacks and cotton blouses large and baggy enough to fall over the gun holsters they were surely wearing at their belts. One of them carried a sports bag.

The third man was David Chang. He was dressed the same way I remembered him from the meeting at the Ocean View restaurant: an expensive collarless shirt under a light jacket, sporty elegant slacks and fine leather loafers. He placed a briefcase on the table.

Mora raised his head in a jerky move, as if surprised or scared.

"Good morning, Dr. Mora," David Chang's voice greeted. "May we join you?"

"Go ahead," Mora said, narrowing his eyes at them. His breath accelerated fast on my ear receiver. "You're late," he added.

The men pulled the chairs, installing themselves at the table.

"And how are you this morning?" one of the two short men asked loudly, over noise of chairs being pushed around, metal legs scratching the terrace's pavement.

Mora didn't answer.

"Let's get some coffee" the other muscle man said. "What do you guys want?"

"Get me some plain drip," his partner requested.

"A latté," David Chang said.

"Anything for you, Dr. Mora?"

"I'm fine" Mora said. His voice didn't sound good.

Hold it together. Just hold it together.

The man left. His partner and David Chang remained sitting, cold smiles on their faces, watching Mora.

"How do you guys want to do this?" Mora's voice asked.

The muscle man laughed calmly. On the screens he seemed relaxed, leaning back on his chair, one arm over the chair's back rest. He slowly bent forward closer to Mora. His voice came very clearly on my receiver. It was steel.

"Get your material ready," he said. "Whatever you have, we'll review it here on our system."

David Chang opened his briefcase and extracted a thin, silver colored laptop computer. He raised the screen and turned the machine on.

"Where is it?" Chang asked.

Mora extracted a thin disk case from a side pocket of his large fisherman style jacket.

"Do you have the CAD system installed as I instructed?" he asked Chang.

"Yes."

"Good. Everything is in here," Mora said, laying the disk case on the table. "It's encrypted and protected in two layers. As we'll work on it, I'll key in passwords in a sequence I've memorized. They'll give us access to the files on the disk for fifteen minutes at a time. You understand?"

"Why the trouble, Dr. Mora?" David Chang grumbled, with sudden irritation in his voice. "We have an agreement."

"I have to take my precautions," Mora said. "No offense."

The muscle man laughed, coldly.

Chang pushed the computer towards Mora who inserted the disk in the reader and started setting up the files.

The three of them blended well in the crowd on the terrace; people at several other tables were working on portable computers as well.

The second muscle man returned with a small tray. He sat down next to Mora and distributed the coffee cups to Chang and his partner. They all remained silent, waiting. Mora's fingers worked fast, keyboard clicking sounds streaming on my ear receiver.

"This is the engine core," Mora started explaining and David Chang leaned close to him, concentrating on the screen.

It was all there. We had decided to place the real data on the disk, no tricks. It had to be perfect.

Chang pulled the computer towards him and examined the screen, working the keyboard.

"Interesting" he mumbled, "these angles are even less than I thought."

He kept working the computer, focused at the screen, while the others waited, Mora watching him from a side.

All of a sudden Chang clicked nervously on the keyboard.

"Why did it freeze?" he asked, strongly irritated, suspicious.

"Calm down," Mora said. "The fifteen minutes are up."

He pulled the computer towards him and pressed a key combination, then typed a password. He then pushed the computer back towards Chang.

"Here," he said, "fifteen more minutes."

Chang was visibly annoyed.

"This is unnerving," he spoke in a sharp tone.

The two muscle men stared at Mora with dead eyes.

"That's the deal," Mora said. "That's the only insurance I got."

Chang didn't comment. He reluctantly started to work again. He asked details and Mora explained them.

Time passed. Chang kept asking questions about the engine's physics. He was good at picking up the essentials, judging from his questions. Mora keyed in his passwords several more times. This is how we all knew an hour had passed. It was a game of patience.

Chang declared himself satisfied. He leaned back on the chair's rest and made a sign with his head towards the other two men.

One of them grabbed the sports bag he'd brought with him and pushed it towards Mora.

"Here's your stuff," he said.

Hesitantly, Mora opened the bag's zipper half way, and examined its content. I saw him nodding slightly, somehow unsure of himself.

"Is everything all right?" the man asked Mora.

"Yes," Mora said. "What about the other part?"

The man reached for Chang's laptop and pulled it towards him.

"It's all prepared, ready for the transfer," he said.

Mora watched the screen over the man's shoulder.

"It's simple to follow, Dr. Mora," the man explained, while working the laptop's pad. "This is the web-site of the bank we'll issue the transfer from. Please verify one more time the destination account number."

He offered the computer to Mora with exaggerated courtesy. Mora leaned over, his eyes into the screen. On my receiver, his breath was heavy.

"Is the destination account information all right, Dr. Mora?" the man asked.

Mora cleared his throat.

"I guess it's all right," he said.

"Very well, then," the man said, and worked the keyboard. "Please follow me here, on the screen. This is the amount, this is the account, and boom, here it goes."

They remained silent again. Chang and his men were watching Mora carefully. The man operating the computer smiled. Mora kept watching the screen.

"It all looks very good," he said. "But I can write myself a piece of software to do just that, show these nice boxes on the screen with money and accounts and all that."

"What are you implying here, Dr. Mora?" the man asked.

"Nothing," Mora said. "No offense, please, I'm used to check things out."

He pulled his chair back, and scrutinized the three men.

"Here is what I'm going to do," he told them. "You have the disk, it's here in the laptop's drive. I'll verify my account. As soon as the money is there, I'll give you the total access password to the disk and that will complete the deal"

They weren't expecting it.

"How do we know you're not gonna just vanish with the dough?" one of the muscle men asked.

"I won't," Mora said. "Logically, I have no reason to."

"Are you shitting us here?" the other muscle man barked, irritated, thrusting himself towards Mora, aggressively.

David Chang raised his hand, with discretion, glancing around.

"Let's calm down, gentlemen," he said.

He pulled out a cell phone from his pocket and dialed. He talked in Chinese, mostly listening, speaking very little.

He ended his conversation and turned towards Mora.

"We'll take a chance on you, Dr. Mora," he spoke with a flat, cold voice. "You have to understand, however, that if you fault your end of the deal in any way, say this disk doesn't read anything after we leave this table, we'll find you again, wherever you may go. The world has become a very small place. This is how we work, Dr. Mora, we pay, and we wait, with patience, to get what we need. We reward and we punish. We never forget, and never forgive. Is that clear?"

Stefan Mora looked at him without speaking. On the screen he seemed placid, mute, but I could hear his breath, his chest shaking. He had done everything he had been instructed to do.

Leave, I thought, *just leave, man, now!*

"Good bye, gentlemen," Mora said, as if hearing me, and stood up.

The three men at the table watched him in silence as he walked away.

"Careful now," Jane's voice came on the air. "This is critical."

David Chang exchanged a look with the two men. He quickly packed his computer and they all rose and left, separate ways, without a word.

Fred switched the transceiver reception to different cameras, viewing the street from a higher elevation. The one looking towards east had a blind spot, a structure on the wall blocking the view. On the screens, Stefan Mora walked fast and disappeared into the blind spot.

On the corner of the screen, I saw a silhouette moving fast. It moved through the parked cars and when it came into full view, I recognized one of the muscle men. He was walking fast after Stefan Mora.

"Porter!" I shouted in my mike. "One of the guys is moving on Mora!"

I kicked the car door open, and ran after Stefan.

"Porter, you hear me?" I cried again on the mike, desperately. "One of them is going after Stefan!"

There was no answer.

I ran as fast as I could. I realized I had no weapon. But I kept running; there was no time, Stefan had to be warned.

From the run, I saw Stefan turning towards the muscle man, only feet away from him. The latter reached under his shirt at the back of his belt.

"Run, Stefan!" I cried as hard as I could.

Mora turned his head towards me. The muscleman raised his arm straight towards him, holding a gun, steady.

The shot hit Mora in the chest. The slug threw him violently backwards. His body hit a car, and fell to the ground.

The man turned and fired in my direction. I plunged behind a car, and rolled on the pavement. I crawled and spied the gunman through the vehicle's windshield. His head jerked hard, unnaturally. For a second, he seemed dizzy, inert, his head on the side as if he was looking at something behind him. His legs gave way, twisting his body as he fell to the ground. The left side of his head was missing.

"Get the fuck moving, Salagen," Porter said, from behind me. He held a small rife in his hands

"He shot Mora!" I yelled at Porter. "Mora's dead!"

Porter harshly pulled on my arm, "Just get moving, for Christ's sake!"

He pushed me towards Mora, behind one of the cars. Mora was lying on a side, coughing hard. Porter grabbed him by his jacket and pulled him on his feet without much care. He ripped off the baggy jacket and his shirt, searching his chest, revealing a bullet proof vest deformed by the bullet hit.

"You fucking geniuses!" Porter yelled at Mora, "I told you to get the steel plated one. I could've sworn one of them motherfuckers gonna try kill you."

A car came fast roaring its engine and broke hard, inches away from Porter.

"Get him in!" Jane ordered from behind the steering wheel. "He's hurt? Get him in!"

Porter pushed Mora in the car and threw the bag with the money after him. The car left screeching its tires.

"You, get going!" Porter told me. "Get to Fred's car and leave!"

I looked at the dead man. I couldn't decide to move away.

"I said move!" Porter yelled in my face. "Get the fuck outta here!"

I ran back to Ford. People around were shouting.

Fred drove slowly towards me. I got in the car, and shouted at Fred to floor it. My instinct cried for high engine revs and burnt rubber. Instead, Fred slowly drove the ubiquitous Ford along the sunny streets of the city, signaling left, taking a left turn, signaling right, taking a right turn, following the traffic.

Stefan was alive but probably injured. One of the muscle men was dead. Too big of a commotion. It all went fucking wrong. Just so fucking wrong.

***

"It all went perfect," Jane said.

"Perfect?" I asked. "Perfect how? We left one of them dead on the street. Your big fish must be gone by now, Jane, vanished for ever!"

"Please sit down, Matt," she said. "Sit down, and calm down."

I tried toned down my voice.

"What went so perfect? There is one dead body. We probably show up on a dozen store and street surveillance cameras. The cops are gonna roam everywhere. Whoever your big fish is, he's got a big warning to lay low. What the fuck is so perfect?"

She came to me and grabbed my shoulders.

"I needed an identity, remember?" Jane said, her eyes shining. "We forced them to move around, to move money, to panic and make phone calls, make noise. By tomorrow, Matt, we'll have our man."

"How?"

"Everything was tracked, all the noise, all the moves, all the calls."

"What's gonna happen tomorrow?"

Her eyes lost some of their gleam.

"Tomorrow is Hal's funeral," she said.

She forgot me for a moment, her mind caught in a thought. She suddenly turned again towards me, and examined me.

"You need a good suit." she said.

7 1

The closed casket containing Harold Mason's earthly remains lay on the chapel's display platform at the Forest Lawn cemetery, its polished wood spotted with golden patches of light from the discrete recess lamps on the ceiling.

The sight gave me a final confirmation: my life, as I used to know it, was over. Hal had been watching over me, patiently and wisely expecting my past to catch up with both of us. He had understood my life better than I had, yet he'd let me make my decisions, waiting for me to grow up from my tardy immaturity. But now Hal was gone.

Would things have been different had he shared everything with me? Could the massacre in Bukow have been avoided. ?

I wound never find out. For the moment, I was an anonymous presence, a dark suit in the chapel crowded with many other dark suits. I sat on the rearmost row and didn't know anyone around. The air felt tense as if charged with powerful electricity; no one spoke, except for few, rare, whispered exchanges.

Ernesto had dropped me there earlier. During the night before, Jane had become quiet and tensed, and separated from me. For the first time after being rescued from Bukow I was alone. Her voice came in my mind, "*Loving you is a weakness, in my line of work.*"

The chapel doors opened. Dressed in an elegant navy blue suit, Roger Bronson entered the chapel with his typical sober walk. He eyed me for a short moment, and slightly bowed his head in a greeting, his face void of any expression as he headed towards the front rows. Shortly behind him came the red haired voluptuous woman named Yvette Nahman, the one who had played the NSA decryption analyst at the Lockwell meeting. She rushed elegantly to catch up with Bronson, who turned slightly towards her and offered his arm.

I looked outside through the glass doors. In the growing heat of the morning, young men dressed in dark suits and wearing sunglasses were waiting around.

A dark limo came and discharged three more men in suits. One of them was Ben Balder. As the three of them approached the chapel's door, Balder's men were stopped by the bodyguards. Balder turned around and barked some words at the guards, but they firmly and politely shook their heads and invited him in. Balder arranged his suit with nervous moves and entered the chapel alone. His men were escorted to a car.

I leaned back in my seat, and placed my hands on my pockets. Their inner fabric felt dry and good, empty pockets of a new suit.

The doors opened again. Stan Jackobs walked in and headed towards the front rows, fast, preoccupied, his head slightly bowed, a discrete gleam coming from his gold rimmed glasses.

As I followed Jackobs with my eyes, one more man walked in, without any noise from the doors. Scott Stirling greeted me with a slight nod of his head, and after I responded, he stood there and watched me as if weighing the meaning of my presence. Then, he walked towards the front rows. His presence had changed the nature of the electric tension in the air. It had become acute.

As Stirling reached the very first row of the chapel, an elegant woman dressed in black approached him. She was wearing an exquisite dress, with a gossamer dark veil covering her face. Stirling held her hand and talked to her in a whisper. The woman turned her head and I could see her face.

"Jane!" It was her and not her anymore. She had morphed into a presence displaying a strange touch of royalty. There was maturity, elegance and power in the woman standing next to Stirling. The Jane I knew, the charming creature of the wild had vanished. It suddenly felt as if everything that had happened, the search for the shadows, the sweat, the blood, the deaths, the love and the secrets unearthed, it felt as if everything had been suddenly ejected into the past, and now we were in a void space, but separated by a strong divide. And then, I understood. That separating divide was power. Jane's presence emanated power. She belonged to a world different than mine, a world living behind a tall wall of power and influence.

The crowd stood up, as an old man wearing a yarmulke came from behind the sumptuous curtains and approached a large microphone. He introduced himself as Rabbi Kenneth Greene, greeted everyone and spoke at length about a Harold Mason I'd never met. He delivered the eulogy reading from some notes and described a two-dimensional Hal Mason as flat as a newspaper page.

I stopped listening. After a while, there was silence. Rabbi Greene had finished. No one else spoke. Ushers invited everyone to the actual burial place, somewhere further uphill.

Six muscle men in dark suits played pallbearers and carried the casket outside, where they placed it in a silver white hearse. I let the crowd flow out and remained behind. There was nothing left for me to do for Hal, or for Jane.

Mercedes-Benzes, Jaguars, Bentleys and other makes of limos swallowed the men in dark suits and the few women and started the procession uphill.

I waited for everyone to leave and then exited the chapel and walked slowly after the procession. The sun burned hard on the dark fabric of my suit. I eyed a fat and bald guy dressed in work overalls coming from a side alley and sucking at a butt.

"Sorry, man," I stopped him, "can you spare a smoke? This is a new suit, I'm out and I'm dying here."

He eyed my suit, grinned and produced a deformed pack of Camels from the breast pocket of his overalls. I lit from the cheap lighter he held for me.

"Friend of yours?" he asked, pocketing the pack and jerking his head towards the procession uphill.

"Yeah," I said.

He nodded, "God rest his soul."

"Thanks again," I said, and the fat man waved it off and walked away.

The Camel tasted good. I drew from it, and kept walking.

The distance to the crowd was longer than I thought. Everyone was now gathered in one place.

Shouts came from uphill. Men's voices yelled with anger and urgency. A strong commotion crossed the crowd. An engine roared and a large BMW cut its way across the lawn, made a tight turn on the grass and sped downhill, fishtailing in large swings, throwing grass and dirt with its back wheels. Other engines roared and three other cars followed in pursuit of the BMW, splitting ways in an attempt to cut its way towards the exit.

The cars narrowly missed some of the people scattered across the lawns by the resting places; families with kids, women carrying bouquets of flowers. Voices cried with anger and fear.

I followed the cars with my eyes, while still drawing from my smoke.

"Dr. Salagen!"

The voice had called from behind me. A tall and long Rolls Royce had rolled on the asphalt without any noise. The rear door was open, inviting.

I threw away the stub.

"Please get in," Scot Stirling invited me with a sense of urgency.

I got in the Rolls and sat opposite to him, in the manner I used to sit in Hal's limo. Next to Stirling, Jane sat with her veil removed, her face pale as if badly injured. I realized it was only strong emotion.

"Do you have your man?" I asked her.

The Rolls swung hard. I reached for a handle to hold myself straight.

"We do," Jane said.

She didn't make eye contact.

We rode in silence for long minutes.

A discrete chirping sound came and Stirling took the call on a black and rugged mobile phone. He listened without a word.

"We'll be there shortly," he said, and pocketed the phone.

Jane watched me and smiled. "Never saw you in a suit before," she said.

The Rolls followed 134 into 101 and then 405 south. There was little traffic. We took Mullholand up the hills towards the north side of Bel Air.

7 2

The gates were worked in wrought iron, thrown open, two guards in dark suits standing by and a blue sedan blocking the way. The car backed up to make way for the Rolls, which rolled through the gates, accelerated hard and cut fast through several acres of manicured landscape towards the mansion at the southern end of the property. Two other blue cars were stopped in front of the house at crooked angles, thick dark streaks on the pavement indicating the cars had broken hard to a stop and were left there by men in a hurry.

The Rolls maneuvered around the blue vehicles and stopped in front of the mansion's majestic entrance where more dark suited men came and opened the car doors. Jane and Stirling stepped out of the Rolls and were led towards the house. I followed them.

Stirling had obviously taken the lead. He radiated a sense of power similar to Jane's, I felt them equal, but the men's eyes were on him, awaiting his orders.

The mansion was decorated with exquisite taste. An oil painting lit by a thin and discrete golden lamp showed a blue window open into a universe of thick streaks of color, heavy with luscious yellow and orange. In a niche, a marble head of the ancient god Serapis looked at me with his hollow eyes. The sculpture seemed to be an original, one of the ancient marble sculptures discovered at sea in the Mediterranean.

The man leading us opened a large wooden door. I followed the group into what I realized was the mansion's kitchen. It had the square footage of my entire house and looked like a luxurious surgery room, shining steel mixing with fine essences of wood under warm recess lights.

Porter and two other men stood in the middle of the room, waiting. A fourth man sat on a chair, erect, arms resting on the arm rests, legs cleverly lined up with the chair's legs.

Porter turned around towards us, while the other two men stepped aside.

The man on the chair was Stan Jackobs. His arms and legs were tied to the chair with plastic ties, the ubiquitous ties. He was looking straight ahead, ignoring everyone, a mesh of hair falling on his forehead. He wasn't wearing his gold rimmed glasses. I spotted them, carefully placed on a counter.

Stirling stopped next to Porter.

"Everything all right?" he asked.

"No," Porter said. "We have casualties. Three men down, two of his, one of ours. He made it here before us and we had to fight our way in. Some chopper came close, almost landed, but changed its mind and flew away."

Stirling watched Porter, thinking. He turned towards the man who had guided us through the house.

"Follow up on this chopper. Get everyone connected to the flight. No loose ends."

"Yes sir. We're already on it," the man said, and left.

Stirling turned his attention to Jackobs.

"How are you doing, Stan?" he spoke to the tied-up man.

Jackobs flashed him with a dark look. "You're making a big mistake," he snapped. He opened his mouth to add something, but bit his lips and stood quiet.

Stirling extracted a small shiny recorder from the pocket of his coat. He pressed a button on it, and placed it on the kitchen counter.

"*He gave us a disk, some encrypted shit on it,*" a voice said on the tape.

"*Encrypted?*" Jackobs voice asked.

"*All the stuff this guy is selling he's put on a disk, encrypted,*" the first voice explained. "*He says he's gonna give us the password to it when the money's in his bank.*"

"*What about Chang?*" Jackobs voice asked.

"*He's pissed but he says that shit is good and it's worth waiting. He says it ain't nowhere in this world his people can't nab Mora if he bails.*"

There was a moment of silence, filled with static

"*Screw it,*" Jackobs voice said. "*Get rid of Mora.*"

"*Waste him?*"

"*Yeah,*" Jackobs voice confirmed. "*Clean up!*"

Stirling reached the counter and pushed the stop button.

"I guess there is no mistake, Stan," he said.

Stan Jackobs flashed him with another ugly look, and tightened his lips.

The coldness of his voice on the tape had run shivers down my back. I had been there, close to Stefan, when Jackob's man had pulled the trigger, following the cold order.

The tall door opened, and two more men entered. One of them was Roger Bronson, carrying a thin leather case. The man behind him closed the door and stood by it.

"Anything on him we didn't know?" Stirling asked Bronson, with a vague sign towards Jakobs.

"Plenty," Bronson said, placing his case on the counter. "We need some privacy for this."

Stirling threw a quick look at Porter.

"All right, men," Porter said calmly. "We need a moment here."

Porter's two men walked towards the door, while Bronson's man opened it for them. After they exited, he followed them and closed he door behind him.

Bronson opened his briefcase, surveying the small group, Jane, Stirling, Porter and me, ignoring Jackobs. He extracted a neat folder from his briefcase and opened it.

"We have a rare bird here," he said. "There is quite a bit of history on him."

"Take it from the beginning," Stirling said.

Bronson flipped the pages.

"It starts back in 92, when the Chinese pulled a large scale intelligence operation on us." he said. "It was a stunning coup, and it went on until 1996. They used banks in Hong Kong as fronts, and through a connection in Indonesia they've opened banks here in the US and funneled money into political donations and private loans to top politicians. People at the very top. The money bought influence, export licenses for manufacturing and defense equipment they needed, and a position in the Department of Commerce for one of their men by the name of Huang. Naturalized US citizen. Huang worked under the Secretary of Commerce Ron Brown. Our man here worked as Huang's personal assistant. Secretary Brown got Huang a top secret clearance after waving all standard verifications, I've never heard of such thing before. Through that clearance Huang got access to secret briefings by the CIA and documents on US government trade strategies. Huge breach of security. As Huang's private assistant, Mr. Jackobs here has been involved in many of these deals, to the extend we will need to investigate. He did not disclose any of these facts on his interviews with Mason. His association with Huang was made through a small private consulting firm Mr. Jacobs owned at the time. It took some big magnifier glass to obtain this information."

Bronson paused and examined Jackobs with the eyes of a surgeon looking at an ugly tumor. Jackobs ignored him, looking straight ahead, again, without blinking.

Bronson flipped more pages and continued.

"The Commerce operation was terminated around January 1996. Huang left Commerce and played fundraiser for the democrats. He solicited donations from wealthy Chinese, and slipped some extra funds into the donations, money he got via chains of wire transfers from various locations in East Asia. The press smelled it and raised hell. The Congress started investigating. Brown also got under investigation. We suspect a clean-up was ordered at this point. We have indications that Mr. Jackobs here was assigned the job."

In silence, Bronson flipped through his pages.

He read a paragraph from his file, again in deep silence.

"Apparently, Secretary Brown had become a problem. While under investigation by the Justice Department, it appears he had agreed to disclose information deemed as very damaging. The political implications could've been significant, to an extent we'll never know. Brown left for a business trip to the Balkans in April 1996. His plane crashed in Croatia. Very strange crash[20]. Secretary Brown died in the crash, together with the plane crew and twenty-six other government folks, one of them a CIA operative, our man. Mr. Jacobs was scheduled to be aboard that aircraft as well, but had bailed out of the flight in the last moment, together with another associate of Secretary Brown by the name of Mohamed Ferrat. Ferrat died later in the TWA Flight 800 disaster. As you may remember, the Flight 800 explosion had been found to be an

---

[20] On April 3 1996, an Air Force CT-43 airplane crashed under strange circumstances in Croatia, killing all 34 people on board, including Secretary of Commerce Ron Brown. Among the extensive literature examining this event, the most comprehensive source is the 2004 book titled "Body of Ron Brown" by Jack Cashill

accident, a faulty wire triggering an explosion of fuel fumes in an empty tank. We never understood why a transcontinental flight would take off with an empty tank."

Stirling whistled and watched Jacobs with some surprising appreciation. Everyone else remained silent. Bronson read another paragraph from his file.

"The second victim, was a secretary at the Commerce Department, Barbara Alice Wise[21]. She'd been at the department for fourteen years. Found dead in her office."

Stirling started pacing the room, frowning. "Go on," he requested.

Bronson flipped though the pages and continued.

"No remarkable event related to Mr. Jackobs until he joined Mason and Associates in January 99, after a few months at the DARPA. He has become active again after 9/11. We were all focused on terrorism and the Chinese got a break. There is data here on Mr. Jackobs, a list of trips and contacts. One name stands out because it cross-checks with a contact Dr. Salagen made here in the LA area, a man with the name of Feng Zhijiang."

Porter pointed a finger at me.

"The Chinese dude shot by his girl agent back in Bukow?" he asked.

"Yes," I said. "He's the one who offered me money for the engine design."

"We know you rejected it, Dr. Salagen" Stirling said.

Jane looked at him, surprised. "I thought Hal asked for your help only recently, Mr. Stirling," she said.

Stirling smiled. "Ms. Mason, your father, who my very good friend and colleague, had asked Roger to give me complete briefings early on during this operation. Hal was a wise man, Ms. Mason, always looking ahead, always anticipating. I must say, Ms. Mason, he was very much aware of his health condition."

Bronson smiled towards Jane as well. There was cold and tensed courtesy extended by both men towards Jane, with great care.

---

[21] On November 29, 1996 Barbara Wise was found dead and bruised from head to waist in her Commerce Department office.

She accepted it and made a sign towards Bronson, "Please continue, Roger."

Bronson obliged.

"About a year ago, I had the bureau place Mr. Jackobs' bank operations under surveillance," he continued. "Mr. Jackobs had come to our attention because of his close ties with lobby firms employed by foreign governments and corporations with large interests abroad. These specific lobby firms operate with large amounts of cash which sometimes must be covertly moved around. Mr. Jackobs provided this service, retaining a percentage of the sums he covertly moved through Mr. Mason's firm."

The information angered Jane.

"He was using our accounts?" she asked, coldly. "Why wasn't he detected at the firm?"

Bronson smiled, while Stirling watched her with polite patience.

"Clandestine operations can go both ways, Ms. Mason." Bronson explained. "Mr. Mason had established very effective ways, hard to track, unless one is tipped about a specific transaction."

There was silence. Stirling rubbed his chin, watching Jackobs and rolling decisions in his mind. Jane had coiled, reminding me of the woman I had known until the day before. Porter was just waiting. The price of blood was not up for discussion, for any of them.

I broke the silence.

"Why the killings, Mr. Jackobs?" I asked, my voice louder than I wanted, with a touch of despair I didn't intend. But I kept speaking.

"Why all these killings in cold blood? There must've been other, legal ways to stop the Bukow operation."

Jackobs grinned at me with sinister gleam in his eyes, without bothering with the mask of a bureaucrat he used to put on. He fixed his eyes on me for several moments and then suppressed the grin, turning his eyes straight ahead again.

"It was a risk item for him, Dr. Slagen." Bronson spoke. "The clandestine research in Romania was an aberration, an accident produced by historical, political and technical conjectures. It was an activity waiting to be uncovered, revealed, and thoroughly investigated. It was a threat for Mr. Jackobs' network."

I looked in Jane's eyes.

"You knew then?" I asked her. "You let me lead them to Bukow and to Victor. You put that tracking toy in my shoes."

She held eye contact.

"Wake up to the real world Matt. That Bukow shit had to be taken down. We didn't know the location, it was only Hal's instinct to let you go back. He knew it was going to be dangerous so he made sure I'm with you. And he planned for me and Porter to be inserted into the team, stay with you all the way."

Porter shook his hand and waved off my questions. "Take it easy, Mr. Salagen. You were really close, back there. Really close."

A sarcastic laugh came from Jackobs. Everyone turned towards him. He shook his head and laughed again.

"Very good, people, very good!" he said. "Now you can all go to sleep on your pink mattresses, hug your fucking teddy bears and have a good night sleep. Good work!"

He surveyed us from his chair, with a cynical grin, his eyes reflecting demented lights. Stirling watched him calmly.

"Is there something you want to tell us, Stan?" he asked.

Jackobs laughed again.

"Yes, Mr. Stirling, I can tell you a few things."

"I'm listening."

Jackobs shook in his chair, furious.

"You and Bronson belong to the grave, next to Mason. Your generation is out. Out of touch, out of time, driven by an obsolete mentality."

"What mentality is that, Stan?"

"The mentality of old power, Stirling. Uncle Sam's old boys club. The good old times. The CIA making and taking out dictators in the sugar and banana republics. What's good for our corporations it's good for the USA. That mentality."

Stirling lips stretched in a cold smile.

"Perhaps you can educate me into newer mentalities, Stan?"

"Don't fucking patronize me, Stirling! All those fucking clean-up jobs in Bronson's files, you think the Chinese ordered them?"

"Who ordered them, Stan?"

"You don't want to know! The Chinese rarely kill, Stirling. They pay, and they wait. They collect small from a large number of people. They have thousands of front companies, and our universities are filled with thousands of Chinese graduate students. They hold trillions in US debt paper. They hold us by the balls. Why kill? It is our people that ordered the kills. Our greedy folks, gobbling cash in unlimited amounts. Folks for which there is never enough. People playing the money game, the bribery and counter-bribery we call political donations. They're the ones who ordered the clean-up."

"And you're willing tell us a few names, Stan?"

"Perhaps I will! And you'll shit in your pants when I do."

"Good, please do and let us get scared."

"You really don't get it, do you?! You really think I am alone in this? Some isolated operator? Gentlemen, wake up! The US multinationals are globalizing. They know no boundaries, no allegiance to anything other than the bottom line. Billions of dollars are invested annually in China by our corporations which are not 'ours' anymore. It's way more than they invest in the good old USA. There are people with billions at stake. If you try to play patriot games with these people they will wipe you out. They'll wipe everyone out, you, your secret power organizations, your money, your existences, everything!"

There was silence again. Stirling frowned. He turned towards Porter.

"Get your men. Take the prisoner to a safe house. We've spent already too much time here."

"How long do you need him for?" Bronson asked.

Stirling looked him in the eye. "I don't know, Roger. It depends. It may be he should never surface again."

Bronson bowed his head. "You know I'm against extremes, Scott."

"This is different," Stirling said.

Bronson stood silent.

"All right," Stirling spoke louder. "Porter, take care of the place, have your men remove all items. Clean up!"

Jane took may arm and pulled me towards the door. My head was spinning. Stirling had spoken again the words. *"Clean up!"* I hated those words. No man on earth should be given the power to *clean-up*.

Jane was rushing me out of the house. Out in the sun, I held her arm and stopped her. "Hold on a second."

"What is it?"

"What's next?"

"Not now. Let's just get out of here."

"Just have someone take me to my house."

"Your house? It's dangerous, Matt."

"I don't care. Just have someone give me a ride."

She looked at me and smiled.

"All right," she said. "Let's take you home."

73

My house was quietly radiating out the heat built up during the day. The Mustang was there, by the curb, dusty and covered with tree leaves, and I didn't care to know how it had gotten back home. Hal's men, perhaps, after my departure. By the door, I realized I can't get in. My keys had been left somewhere amidst the rubble of the Bukow refinery.

Jane's hand touched my shoulder, holding a key. The one I'd given her when stayed in Julia's room. She placed the key in my hand without a word, embraced me hard, kissed me, and left.

I unlocked the door and entered the living room filled with stale and dusty air, the distillate of emptiness. I opened all doors and windows. Then, I saw the red display of the answering machine showing the machine memory full. I took off my coat and tie and found two inches of scotch left on a dusty bottle. I drained half of it and I pressed the play button.

Several messages in a row came with empty static noise. Then, John Meinhardt voice came, asking me to call him back at Lockwell, ASAP. Several more empty messages, just static from a long distance call. Then, again, John Meinhardt.

"Matt, John Meinhardt here again, I left a message couple a days ago, haven't heard back from you, I hope you're OK. News from here is not so great. The MORPHEM contract has been terminated, and it seems that Lockwell is being sold. When you get a chance, stop over to pick your stuff from the office, we're out of A25 in a rush. Thanks, bye."

A few more empty messages. Someone had been checking.

Lockwell was being sold. I felt nothing about it. Lockwell was no longer important, just a distant place, somewhere.

I walked into the bedroom.

The Beretta was there in the drawer with its smell of oil, steel and sand. It felt proper in my hand. The Smith and Wesson captured in Bukow had felt rough, with the wrong volume.

Bukow. My head spun. When did it all happen? Had it been real?

I dropped in bed, holding the gun, and fell asleep.

***

The phone rang at five in the morning. I wasn't dreaming anything. I opened my eyes and the phone rang. I picked up the extension by the bed.

"Salagen?" a voice asked

"Speaking," I said.

"Heard some rumors you kicked the bucket, my man. I'm kinda glad to find you OK."

"Cruiff?"

"In person."

"Old devil. I thought you cashed in the chips yourself!"

"Why is that?"

I rolled out of bed, holding the receiver. A heavy object fell on the floor. The Beretta.

"Xiao Lin flies of a cliff, then you fucking vanish," I said. "That good enough of a reason?"

"I see," Cruiff said.

We waited for each other to continue, listening to our breaths. There was static on the line.

"Lin was sacked," Cruiff said.

"I know. Where the hell are you? Sounds like North Pole"

"Far enough," he laughed. "It'd gotten unhealthy there in So Cal and I left."

"What was between you and Xiao?"

"You're probably bugged there, my boy, you know that?"

"My phone line, you mean?"

"Yeah,"

"Don't give a shit,"

There was silence. He was thinking.

"Some tough guy did Xiao," he said. "A hit man."

"How did you find out?"

Cruiff sighed. "I worked with some people in Nam, many years back" he said. "Still keep in touch with them. They knew something, not much. Put together with what I knew."

"Like what?"

"McNutt was working to open a branch in Shanghai. They all do it, you know, these big corporations, they open divisions in China. For Lockwell, Lin was in charge of it."

"How can you open a division in China for a US defense corporation?"

"Believe it or not, there are ways. Anyway, some people from there came to Lin and asked him to cooperate and get you together with them. On account of them facilitating the opening of the branch."

"He did get me together with them."

"I know he did. I don't know what happened."

"They made me an offer for MORPHEM and I said no."

"That's very patriotic of you."

"Fuck you."

"Take it easy, bubba. Lin called me that Saturday, wanted to know how to get in touch with the feds. He said he was gonna explain more, on Monday. He didn't live until Monday."

"What else your old Nam friends told you?"

"Some rumor you went back to Europe and got wasted over there."

"Where did they get that from?"

"Rumors. Always rumors, pal."

"Funny, these rumors."

"Somebody bailed you out?"

"It's a long story."

"All right. On the home front, Lockwell is closing down."

"Yeah. Meinhard left a message, said it's being sold"

"Sold? You're kidding. Dismantled is the word. Whatever is left is being moved to Palmdale or Victorville, in the High Desert."

"Dismantled and moved? That's a big place, Bob."

"It sits on very expensive land, my man, I told you. Lot's of folks are salivating to get their hands on it. Instead of rockets, sell pizza, TV's and shoes made in China."

"Do you care, Bob?"

He laughed, slowly.

"I always did, kid." he said. "I buried twenty seven years of my life in there. I'm getting my dough, don't get me wrong, I have a lawyer taking care of it, but I do care."

"I understand. Perhaps I care too."

"You're all right kid. When you feel like traveling, I'll give you the coordinates, on a secure line. Come over, my man, and we'll have a night of beer and talk."

"Will do, Bob. Glad you're OK, you old bastard."

"Same here. Just watch your back."

He hung up. I placed the phone back in his cradle.

The shower water smelled of desert dust again. Mojave dust. One tile was broken and I watched the water flowing over it. The memory of the crude shower in my Bukow improvised prison flashed in front of my eyes. I pushed it away.

After shower, I fixed an espresso and looked for a smoke. Didn't find any. Meinhardt's extension at Lockwell rang five times before the answering service kicked in. I hung up.

I drank the coffee outside, looking at the mountains. It was already hazy and the air was heating up. I sipped the bitter black liquid, empty of thoughts, watching the sky.

***

The Mustang's engine started with vigor. I put the car in gear and took off. 210 westbound was still in the morning crawl. I joined in and moved with the slurry traffic all the way through 134. It thinned out in a while and I made it fast under the bridge on the Forrest Lawn exit, drove along the ramp and entered the cemetery.

The green lawns were almost deserted. Here and there, one silhouette of a man or a woman leaning down by a grave.

I drove uphill, and parked the Mustang at the spot where the crowd of suits and dresses had gathered the day before. It took me a while to find the plaque. It was a bronze plaque and it just said "Harold Mason."

I sat down on the grass. My mind wandered, images flashing at random. Hal, taking me to a Ralph's supermarket to buy steaks, after we had arrived in California. It was the first time I'd ever entered a supermarket. I felt I wanted everything I saw. Hal had bought one steak and one big potato. He'd explained he's got another steak and another potato at home, that's all we needed. Indeed he had those at home, one other steak, one other potato. He'd cooked the potatoes in the microwave and the steaks on a small grill, meticulous and precise, using a timer. We had steaks, potatoes with cream, salad and red wine poured in wide and beautiful glasses. We ate outside on the terrace of his house on Citrus street. All my possessions, then, were the clothes I wore and a back-pack filled with handwritten research and test notes on my engine. I'd felt strangely free, my nostrils filled by the alien smell of the LA city.

The flow of images stopped. Nothing else came to mind. I remembered a Jewish custom and walked around looking for small pieces of stone. I found four small white stones, placed them at the four corners on Hal's bronze plaque, walked to the car and left.

***

134 traffic was easy until it hit 101 and became a stop and go under the baking sun. I let the car flow with the slur until Topanga Canyon where I took the Canyon southwards, towards the Pacific. After twenty minutes of driving, the air temperature gage dropped by 20 degrees Fahrenheit and the hills opened into the ocean. I watched the waves while waiting the interminable red light at the Pacific Coast Highway.

I turned north on the PCH. I rolled down both windows, and let the scent of the ocean fill the car. It took another fifteen minutes to reach Point Dume.

The beach was gorgeous. It had been cleaned, with its sand shining fresh in long stripes imprinted by the machines, the contours still untouched, too early in the day for anybody else besides the surfers.

I walked to what seemed like a good spot and lied down on the sand watching the sky. That was my place. The place where I came and cried in silence when I realized Christine, my wife, was a perfect stranger. The place where I munched on regrets and questions about the way I had left my homeland, about the unknowns I had left behind. The place where I wanted to meet the end of my existence. It just felt good being there. I loved the ocean. The smell of sand. That sand was my frontier. Over the water, beyond it, there was nothing else but the other half of the world, or the realm of the other world.

Steps on the sand approached. I felt the presence, the scent of the ocean water on the wet suit, the sound of water dripping on the sand.

"I was waiting for you," Jane said.

I didn't move, just watched her. Her hair was wet, tangled. Her black eyes were searching my face, asking for me to respond, to define myself for her by defining who she was for me.

I felt the earth, the sand underneath me, felt one with the planet, sensing its rotation while watching the sky behind Jane's shoulders, looking into her eyes. There was no answer to her muted question.

She kneeled, slowly bringing her face close to mine, dripping water over my chest and my face. I raised my head and collected drops of salty water from her chin with my lips. The drops had the taste of the ocean, the taste of her.

"We belong to different worlds, Jane" I said. "Sooner of later, we'll hit the divide."

She kissed me.

"Please don't be stupid," she said. "Divides, boundaries, they can be crossed, removed, ignored, thrown out altogether. It only requires intelligence and imagination."

I felt again the sand underneath me, soft, clean and warm. I let go of thoughts and embraced her wet suit. It seemed like a long time before other steps approached on the sand. They were slow and steady. Jane's body slowly left the embrace, rolled on a side and sat on the sand. I half rose and rested on my elbows.

Scott Stirling was dressed in a large Hawaiian shirt and baggy shorts. He wore worn-out flip flops on his feet.

He sat down on the sand next to me while Jane leaned against me, relaxed.

"Dr. Stirling," I greeted him.

"Please call me Scott," he said. "I'm glad Jane's instinct was right and we found you here, Dr. Salagen," he said.

"Please, call me Matt," I said.

He smiled and nodded. His eyes swept the beach and the ocean.

"It's a wonderful beach," he said. "I used to surf here, years ago, with my sons."

He filled his fists with sand and let it flow back down.

"Many things have changed, since then," he continued. "We live now through very interesting times, Matt. Trying times."

Dark shapes flashed out of the water, beyond the waves, and disappeared back into the deep. Dolphins, scouting the surfers.

"These are times for men who show they can take a hard test from life and get through it," Stirling continued.

"A hard test?" I asked.

Stirling turned his head towards me, making the eye contact between us direct and firm.

"Life is a non-linear journey, Matt," he said. "Yes, it's been a hard test for you. And there may be other hardships coming your way."

In the ocean, a perfect blue wave rose too fast and the surfers missed it. Three dolphins sprang through the wave, playing.

Jane caressed my back and stood up.

"I'll go change" she said. "I'll be back," she added and left, walking fast on the sand, with her boyish grace.

Stirling watched Jane walking away, and focused back on me.

"This country had it good for almost sixty years, Matt," he said. "I'm old enough to remember. After the big war, we were the only ones left standing, and the whole world was paying attention to every fart of ours. We were strong and rich, and it was OK to make mistakes, there was enough margin to correct them. Korea, Vietnam, killing our presidents, we managed."

Out in the water there was a full game between the surfers and the dolphins. The surfers and the mammals were catching the waves, making the best out of the push of the water crests. Yet the animals were careful in their play to keep distance from the humans.

"We've grown fat, dumb and indulgent," Stirling continued. "Our government lives on credit, and the world has become a much smaller place. There are new, tough players in the world, eager to rise, hungry for a larger share of the pie."

"Listen Scott," I interrupted him, "I can appreciate a good pep talk when I hear one. What's the deal?"

He laughed.

"I liked how you made it through your journey, Matt. I need people like you. This country can use any good mind and strong spirit it can find."

"For what? Sell pizza, shoes and big screen TV's made in China?"

He raised his head, frowning, looking far into the ocean, timing his words.

"Some people do that, and they do it well. Nothing wrong with it, Matt. But you're not part of that crowd."

"Which crowd am I part of?"

He watched me carefully without speaking. My anger diffused, which is what he wanted.

"I understand there is a strange effect in the operation of your MORPHEM device" he said.

"What about it?"

"Would you agree that effect has the potential to produce large amounts of energy?"

Fundamental physics of elementary particles, Stefan Mora had said. *If you ever go back to this.*

"Yes," I said.

He leaned towards me, eyeing me closely, firming again our contact.

"We need to push a hard thrust in the immediate future, Matt. Beginning now. There are visionary people ready to invest. Just as there are visionary people who privately invest in space technology. It's the essence of this country."

"What are you proposing Scott? A job, or some patriotic duty?"

"I'm proposing both. I want you to lead a research program."

"I'm done with weapons research."

"Don't be a fool. Someone somewhere across this ocean is already looking into it. The golden rush to the Moon has started already, unknown to the public at large. It's all a tight race, Matt. And for this race, knowledge is power, science is power."

Jane returned, dressed in jeans and a white t-shirt. She reminded me so much of the first time I saw her. A small jolt of joy went through my chest, and I felt an old hunger, a forgotten instinct.

I stood up and took her hand.

"Right now, I need a break, Scott," I said. "I'll think about it, and I'll get back to you."

He smiled and waved a hand towards us.

"Life will not allow you too long of a break, Matt," he said, and leaned back on the sand, as if determined to enjoy his day at the beach. "Nevertheless, enjoy the moment."

I walked towards the Mustang holding Jane's hand, pulling her close to me. Just before getting into the car, I turned towards the water to feel one more time the scent of the ocean, and the smell of sand.